STRONGER

JANET NISSENSON

This one's dedicated to my mother. I miss you every day, Mom, and still expect the phone to ring every afternoon at two o'clock with a call from you. The passing of time will never dull the memories.

1

February – San Francisco

DANTE SABATTINI STARED in disbelief at the woman seated to his right - the woman he'd fallen in love with soon after they had first met, and the same woman he had believed was *the one* for him. The woman he was *this close* to proposing to. In fact, he had casually begun to look at engagement rings for her recently, and had planned to pop the question in just a few more weeks, on the anniversary of their first full year of dating. But it seemed that the woman in question had a very different idea of the direction their relationship was headed.

"You're breaking up with me?" he asked incredulously. "Katie - what the hell is this all about? We've been together for close to a year now. I thought - no, make that *knew* - we had something really, really special. So what gives?"

Katie Carlisle looked distinctly uncomfortable, an expression that rarely if ever appeared on her beautiful, flawless face. She avoided looking directly at Dante, staring down instead at the slim, smooth hands clasped nervously on her lap, and was clearly ill at ease with what she was about to tell him. "I'm moving back to L.A.," she began in that sweet, high-pitched voice that had always aroused Dante, oftentimes with a single word. "Remember that TV pilot I shot last summer - the one I was so sure was going to get picked up by one of the networks?"

He nodded, regarding her warily. "I remember very well. It was a sitcom, and you were devastated when none of the networks were interested. What about it? You told me that had turned out to be a total dead end."

Katie's light blue eyes, enormous in her perfect oval of a face, were shining with excitement. "Well, the producers for the show kept shopping it around to different networks, and one of the up and coming cable channels is picking it up after all! Thirteen episodes, in addition to the pilot. Fortunately the rest of the cast is available, too, so we can start filming right away. In fact, I'm flying down to L.A. day after tomorrow to start looking for a place to live, and we start filming in about ten days. Isn't that the most wonderful news, Danny? My dream of being an actress is finally going to come true after all this time!"

Dante tried, *really* tried, to summon up enough enthusiasm to appear convincing as he pulled Katie into an embrace. 'God, she smells so good,' he thought with a groan. 'And feels even better. No way in hell am I letting her get away!'

Out loud, he told her warmly, "That's fantastic news, baby. I'm really, really happy for you. But what does that have to do with breaking up with me? Did you think I wouldn't be supportive or understanding? I know how much this means to you, Katie, how hard you've worked to get that big break. And, hey, it'll suck for sure to have you in L.A. most of the week, but it's just an hour's flight from here. We can see each other on the weekends, Skype in between. And I have a ton of clients in southern California so it gives me the perfect excuse to make lots of business trips down that way."

Katie's slender, toned body felt unnaturally stiff in his embrace, and she continued to fidget until he reluctantly withdrew his arms. "Danny," she protested weakly, "that's just not going to work. It - it wouldn't be fair to you for starters. I mean, I know how much you look forward to seeing your family every Sunday, and if you were flying down to L.A. to see me all the time you'd have to skip your visits with them."

He shrugged. "So maybe I have to cut down on seeing them quite as often. Or I come down to see you during the week. Besides, didn't you say it was only thirteen episodes? That's barely three months time. Does your agent already have something else lined up for you after the series wraps up?"

She shook her head. "Not yet, anyway. But given that all of this just happened over the last couple of days it's too soon for anything to have come up. Though Doug is convinced that this is going to be my big break - that once the series airs his phone will start ringing off the hook with offers. And of course we're all hoping that the series will get picked up for a second season. So if you're thinking that I'm just going to move back here after we finish filming, that's not going to happen. I'm planning to stay in L.A. permanently, Danny. Which is why we need to end things between us."

Dante fought off the sense of panic that was threatening to overwhelm him, forced himself to remain calm, and resisted the urge to raise his voice and start issuing demands - behaviors that were sometimes second nature to his passionate, hot-tempered Italian personality. Instead, he gently placed his hands on Katie's shoulders, turning her to face him, and tried to ignore the way she resisted him.

"Katie," he began in the suave, persuasive voice that had successfully seduced too many woman to count over the years. "Baby, we do *not* need to end things between us. Lots of couples have long distance relationships and find ways to make them work. Howie and I have talked about opening another branch of the business, possibly in southern California since we do a lot of business there. I could pursue that idea further, get an office opened up within a few months, and arrange things so that I work out of that location at least half the month."

She shook her glossy blonde head stubbornly. "I don't want you to go to that much trouble, Danny. You'd practically be rearranging your entire life for me. And it's not - that is, I don't think - well, you shouldn't do something that drastic."

He leaned over and kissed her, then frowned as she turned her head away. "What the hell, Katie?" he asked in disbelief. "What exactly is going on, anyway? Because I'm more than willing to do whatever I need in order to make things work between us, and all you can do is come up with reasons against it." A sudden, ugly suspicion popped into his head, causing him to drop his hands and lean away from her. "Is there someone else? Is that it, Katie? Is that why you're so dead-set against me moving to L.A. part-time or trying to work out arrangements for us to keep seeing each other?"

"No! No," she assured him, placing a hand on his chest to calm him down. "I swear, Danny. There's no one else. But, well, Doug thinks that - that it would be a lot better for my career if I was known to be single, especially since my character on the show is a real party girl."

Dante gave a snort of derision. "I think your agent is an idiot. There are plenty of successful actresses who are married or in relationships. Why does he think your situation is any different?"

This was clearly a conversation that Katie didn't want to have, given the way her fidgeting increased and she continued to clasp and unclasp her hands in agitation. "He - he just does, that's all," she replied faintly.

"Well, I think he's full of shit," declared Dante bluntly. "You've already got the role in the TV show, and once everyone sees what a great actress you are I'm convinced that not only will the show get renewed but you'll get all sorts of other offers. And I'll do everything I can to support you, baby. It'll suck not to see you as often, but we *will* work this out, Katie. I promise you."

Katie gave another small, stubborn shake of her head. "No, Danny. I'm sorry, but it's got to end between us. I - I don't want the sort of lifestyle you do. I love L.A., all the excitement and nightlife and energy. And I don't think I'd ever want to move back to San Francisco. While you have your business here and your family and all your friends. I'm not going to ask you to give that up for me. I guess we just want different things from life, you know?"

"No, I don't," he retorted, beginning to lose patience with her half-baked excuses. "For the third time, we can figure this out, Katie. I'm not saying it's going to be easy, but, for Christ's sake - I'm crazy in love with you, woman! You're the only woman I've ever felt this way about, I've been with you longer than anyone else, and, well, I was going to wait for a few more weeks until the anniversary of our first date, but I was planning to ask you to marry me, Katie. To be my wife and spend the rest of your life with me. So I'm sure as hell not willing to just end things between us because you think it won't be fair to me. Let me be the judge of that, hmm?"

But rather than look thrilled at his unexpected announcement, the expression on Katie's face more closely resembled horror. Her blue eyes held a panicked look, and she inched away from him even further on the sofa. "Marry you?" she whispered in disbelief. "My God, Danny, I'm nowhere near ready to get married! To you or anyone! Not only is my career just beginning to take off, but I'm way too young to even think of settling down for years and years yet."

Dante flinched visibly at her outburst, shocked by the vehemence of her statement, and was more than a little taken aback by such a reaction from the woman he'd been convinced was his soulmate, his future wife and the mother of his children. "Katie," he reminded gently, "you're almost thirty years old. That's not such an outrageously young age to not be thinking about the future or getting married. I'm thirty-three and practically the last one of my family or friends to get married."

"I am *not* almost thirty!" protested Katie, her high-pitched voice escalating to a near-shriek. "I just turned twenty-nine a few months ago. And I've already told you multiple times that my agent tells everyone I'm only twenty-four. But that's beside the point. I'm sorry, Danny, but getting married just isn't part of my plan right now. Or for a long time to come."

He shook his head in disbelief. "How in the hell could I have read you so wrong for almost a year?" he mused as though to himself. "I mean, I know your career means a lot to you, but when your show didn't get picked up last year you seemed to have resigned yourself to moving on. And while we never actually discussed getting married, we definitely have a connection, Katie. We *love* each other, for Christ's sake! And I can't believe you're just going to walk away from me as though the last year meant nothing to you."

"It's not that," assured Katie quietly, her voice sounding a little choked up. "I already told you, Danny - it just wouldn't be fair to you. I mean, who knows how busy I'll get, how unpredictable my job might become. What if you flew all the way to L.A. and I couldn't spend any time with you during your stay because I was filming all day, and doing promotional stuff at night? And let's face it - you're an awfully macho guy, and I already know you'd get fed up with that sort of unreliability pretty quick. So it's just - better this way."

"Better for who?" he sneered. "Certainly not for me, baby. So you must be referring to yourself. And now that I think about it, having a boyfriend - not to mention a fiancé - would definitely cramp your style if you're trying to project the image of a single, fun-loving party girl. I'm surprised that this sleazeball agent of yours isn't already planning for you to be seen out on the town with a string of hot guys as a way to reinforce that image."

It was the expression on Katie's face that gave her away, and Dante knew that he'd hit the nail on the head with his suspicion. He shook his head in disgust, giving her a scathing look.

"Jesus, Katie," he muttered. "It's all true, isn't it? You're breaking up with me, refusing to even compromise on how we could make a long-distance relationship work, all because your asshole of an agent thinks it would be better for your career to date other guys? You're throwing away everything we've had together for the past year, not to mention our future, on the chance - a slim one at that - it will help your career?"

Katie's blue eyes were shimmering with tears now, and the hand she placed on his chest was trembling. "Don't be mad," she pleaded. "It's nothing to do with you, Danny, honest. You've been wonderful to me, spoiled me rotten, and you're the nicest guy I've ever dated. But I can't be what you want, Danny. Can't give you what you need. I knew from the first time we met that you were an old-fashioned kind of guy, that sooner than later you'd want to get married and have kids. And I thought for a few months that maybe I wanted that, too. That my career was going nowhere, that I was probably being stupid and unrealistic to think I'd ever get my break."

"But now that you have, all of a sudden settling down is the last thing you want," finished Dante sarcastically. "Yeah, baby, you've made that pretty fucking clear. Now that your luck has changed and Hollywood is calling, it's bye-bye Dante, forget about this last year, and have a nice life. Well, I get the message loud and clear, Katie. But here's my message for you, sweetheart - lose my number, okay? Forget you ever knew me. Because I sure as hell plan on following my own advice where you're concerned."

And before Katie could utter a single word of protest, Dante surged to his feet and stormed out of her apartment, slamming the door behind him for good measure and not bothering to spare even a single backwards glance.

2

April

NICK MANNING GLARED in annoyance at the man seated across from him as they waited for their lunch to be served. "Jesus, will you snap the fuck out of it already, Dan? It's been over two months, for Christ's sake! When was the last time you ever mooned over a woman for this long? Correction - when have you *ever* mooned over any woman for even a day?"

Dante sighed, taking a sip from the glass of Pinot Noir he'd ordered to accompany his meal. "Never," he admitted reluctantly. "But then I've never had a relationship that lasted more than a couple of months, much less almost a year. And there's never been anyone who could hold a candle to Katie. She's - special, Nick. And I was so sure she was the one. It's going to take a long time to get over her."

Nick made a sound of disgust, refilling his glass from the bottle of Pellegrino water he'd ordered. "Why? Because she stabbed you in the back and chose her career over you? A career, by the way, that's gone nowhere for ten years until now. I'm willing to bet this sitcom of hers is going to bomb, and that Katie will come running back and beg you to forgive her in that sweet little girl voice. Did I ever tell you how annoying that voice of hers is?"

Despite his bad case of the doldrums, Dante couldn't help grinning at his friend's unabashed candor. "A few times, yeah. You aren't exactly known for holding back, Nick. And you've made it pretty obvious that you didn't like Katie very much."

Nick shrugged. "She was okay. I mean, she seemed to make you happy, and that's really all that matters, right? Except now, of course, when you're starting to embarrass yourself by the way you keep mooning over her. Even Angela told me you need to snap out of it. And this is coming from a woman who was in a funk for over two years after I broke up with her."

Dante took a slice of sourdough bread from the basket, then dunked it into the mixture of olive oil and balsamic vinegar he'd poured into a small dish. "You treated Angela like shit when you were together," he commented matter-of-factly. "I was speechless when I learned she actually agreed to give you another chance. And I hope you say a prayer of thanks every single day that she decided to take your sorry ass back."

A smirk crossed Nick's darkly handsome features. "I'll leave the praying up to you, Catholic school boy. But I make sure to let my woman know how much she means to me on a regular basis, and that I still have a lot to make up for. You don't have to remind me how much of an asshole I was to her. But frankly, Katie didn't always treat you very well either."

Dante's dark eyes narrowed dangerously. "What the hell do you mean by that? Except for the way she broke up with me two months ago, my relationship with Katie was just about perfect."

"If you say so," drawled Nick. "And, hey, you know the old saying - 'no one knows what goes on behind closed doors'. But from what I could see your sweet little Katie knew exactly how to play you, Dan. Did you ever bother to total up how much you spent on her over the last year? Between the four-star restaurants, the exotic vacations, and an entire designer wardrobe, I'm betting it was a pretty penny. Oh, and I forgot about the brand new car you bought her for Christmas.

I'm just assuming she didn't return that to you when she flitted off to Hollywood to quote unquote 'pursue her dream'?"

Dante could feel his cheeks grow warm, and he fidgeted awkwardly in his chair. "No," he acknowledged sullenly. "And why would she? The car was a gift, like all the other things I gave her. Things that any man with the means would give to the woman he loved. And I resent your implication that Katie was just using me for material gain. She wasn't like that, Nick."

"Yeah, whatever," replied Nick dismissively. "The bottom line, my friend, is that you've got to snap out of this funk you've been in since she took off and start living again. You need to start dating, enjoying your life, and moving on. You're too young to start acting like a hermit."

Dante sighed. He'd heard this same lecture from Nick before - as well as from his business partner Howie, his mother, his grandmother, his brother, and half a dozen other friends and family members. And each time the message was more or less the same - Katie wasn't the one for you; she didn't appreciate what a good man she had in you; you'll find the right woman one of these days.

"I know," he agreed quietly. "Problem is I don't want anyone else but Katie. Every time I start thinking about asking someone else out - not to mention going to bed with them - all I can see is her face. And anyone else would just be a poor substitute for the real thing."

Nick scowled. "Does this woman have an enchanted pussy or something? Come on, Dan. I mean, even though Katie wasn't exactly my type, I'll admit she was a real looker. But there's a lot of beautiful women in this city, and you've never had a problem getting as much action as you wanted. So forget about Katie, hit up one of the clubs or bars you always used to hang out at, and find someone to help you forget about your fucking broken heart for awhile. Otherwise, we're going to start conducting our monthly reviews by phone from now on, because you're depressing *me* every time I have to stare at your sad mug."

The retort Dante would have made was halted by the arrival of their lunch. Once a month, the two men would convene in Nick's office at the stock brokerage firm of Morton Sterling to review the extensive investment portfolio he managed for Dante. The meeting was almost always followed by lunch at one of their favorite restaurants.

Tactfully, Nick steered the subject away from Dante's broken heart as they ate. The two men were close friends despite their very different personalities - Dante was easygoing, charming, and friendly, while Nick was, by his own admission, a cold-hearted SOB who was intensely private and disliked most of the people he met. He'd begun to change for the better in small, subtle ways, however, ever since Angela had come back into his life, and Dante liked to joke that there just might be hope for him after all.

But despite their different personalities they had a lot in common, especially their careers in the financial industry - Nick was one of the top stockbrokers in San Francisco, while Dante co-owned one of the most successful venture capital firms on the West coast. Additionally, they had both played collegiate sports - Nick for the Stanford football team, and Dante on the soccer team at UC Berkeley. Their respective universities had a long-standing rivalry, and the two men ribbed each other mercilessly when their alma maters played the other, no matter what the sport was.

And until Nick had met Angela, and Dante had fallen hard for Katie, the two friends had both been rather notorious womanizers. Nick in particular had never been one for long-term relationships, and more often than not the women he'd slept with had been one-night stands, never to be seen or heard from again. Dante on the other hand had always managed to end his relationships on good terms, and had even kept in occasional contact with some of the women, at least until they got too pushy or clingy. This breakup with Katie had been one of the very rare exceptions. He'd forced himself not to email or text or call her, having far too much masculine pride to lower himself to that level. As much as he longed to hear her voice again, there was no way he was going to grovel and beg her to take him back. No matter how crazy he was about Katie, he had too much *machismo* - a trait inherited from multiple generations of strong Italian male relatives - to beg any woman to come back to him.

The close relationship Dante enjoyed with his extensive family had always been something of a sore spot with Katie. And while she'd never actually made him choose between her and them, or outright complained that he spent too much time with them, it had been obvious to Dante that she would have preferred if he'd cut down on his weekly visits to his family. He'd justified her lack of enthusiasm in accompanying him on those visits to her own vastly different upbringing.

Katie was the adopted only child of an older couple who had been so grateful to finally have a baby that they had spoiled and indulged her to excess. Katie's adoptive parents were both highly intellectual individuals - her father a law professor, her mother a biochemist - and more than a little old-fashioned and a bit on the nerdy side. They had adored their pretty, popular daughter, and had willingly given her whatever she'd asked for. They had been disappointed when she'd chosen not to go to college, and instead pursue a career in acting and modeling. Their disappointment in her chosen career, however, hadn't prevented them from paying for acting classes, modeling school, regular sessions with a photographer to keep her portfolio updated, designer clothes, and all manner of other indulgences. And even though they lived less than an hour from San Francisco, Katie had seldom visited her parents during the year she and Dante had been together. She'd claimed that she was just too busy to go see them, or that they had such little in common anymore that talking to them on the phone was pointless.

Unlike Dante, who kept in constant contact with his family, whether it was exchanging texts with his sisters, calling his widowed mother, hanging out with his brother who also lived in San Francisco, and especially going to lunch at his grandmother's house every Sunday afternoon after church, where the place would be bursting at the seams with so many family members present. They were happy, relaxed occasions, filled with good food and wine, conversation, and always lots of laughter. The fact that Katie had never seemed to enjoy herself during those times, and had always seemed aloof when it came to his family, had certainly given Dante cause for concern. But he'd explained his unease away by assuring himself that everything would be different once he and Katie were officially engaged, that she would make more of an effort to get closer to his family, and that they in turn would accept her as one of them.

Instead, he'd had to break the news to them that he and Katie were over with, and that she had moved back to Los Angeles to pursue her career. His grandmother - a tiny but fearsome woman of eighty-four who was the undisputed head of the family - had given a little "hmpff" of disgust upon hearing the news, and as usual hadn't hesitated to speak her mind.

"You're better off without her, Dante," Valentina Sabattini had declared *loudly, not giving an apparent damn who else in the room heard her. "She was not the right woman for you, I always said so. She didn't eat bread, she didn't eat pasta, she didn't eat my delicious braciole. She looked like a good strong wind would blow her over she was so skinny. And always fixing her makeup or checking her phone instead of joining in the conversation. No, my boy, it wasn't meant to be. But trust your Nonna, hmm? The right girl will come along for you one day. I have a feeling that something good is going to happen to you very soon now."*

Wisely, Dante had chosen not to argue the point with his very stubborn, very opinionated Nonna. Even before his grandfather Pietro had passed away some seven years earlier, Valentina had been a force to be reckoned with, and was widely considered to be the head of the family. Since Pietro's passing, she had taken her role as matriarch very seriously, a role that apparently included giving her blessing to the prospective spouses her numerous grandchildren brought before her. And if Valentina Sabattini didn't approve of someone - well, she didn't bother to hide her feelings.

At least his mother had been far more diplomatic in regards to Katie, even though Dante had always sensed that she wasn't entirely pleased with his choice, either. Jeannie Sabattini was a woman of quiet strength, not nearly as outspoken and opinionated as her domineering mother-in-law, but not a woman you wanted to piss off or get on the bad side of regardless. She'd had to prove her mettle at far too young an age, having been widowed when she was in her early thirties with four children to raise. Dante had only been eleven when his beloved father Dominic - a dedicated firefighter - had been killed in the line of duty fighting a three-alarm fire. Overnight, Dante - as the eldest - had become the man of the house, though both sets of grandparents, uncles, aunts, and cousins on both sides of the family, along with neighbors, friends, and co-workers of Dominic's had all gone out of their way to support Jeannie and her four fatherless children. It was just one of the reasons why Dante's loyalty to his family was so steadfast and long lasting. They had all been there for him and his mother and siblings at the time of their greatest need, and he would never forget everything they had done for them.

Since his business had become so successful, the gratitude he felt towards his family had been expressed in financial terms as well. Aside from extensively remodeling his mother's house, and helping his siblings with college expenses, Dante had also financed an addition and renovations to the Italian restaurant that had been owned and operated by his father's family for well over a hundred years. Sabattini's was a veritable landmark in his hometown of Healdsburg, located about seventy miles north of San Francisco in the Sonoma Wine Country, and nearly every employee at the expansive restaurant was a member of the family. Jeannie had been the hostess during the lunch hour for more than two decades, and Valentina stopped by the restaurant nearly every day to make sure everything was running like a well-oiled machine.

There had been other relatives that Dante had helped out as well - loaning one the money he needed to start a small business, helping another out with some medical expenses for her mother, and always buying generous gifts for birthdays, weddings, christenings, and graduations. Family should always look out for each other had been his motto for a long time, and since he had more money than he could possibly spend in twenty lifetimes, Dante figured it was the least he could do to spread some of his wealth around among the people who meant the most to him.

The subject of Katie didn't come up again during his lunch with Nick, the two friends instead discussing recent developments in the financial markets and how they might impact certain investments. Dante was always left a little in awe of what a truly brilliant financial mind Nick had, and how his friend seemed to have the golden touch when it came to investments. While the venture capital firm he co-owned with his old college roommate Howie Erlichman was certainly successful and earned both men an extremely lucrative salary, it was Dante's personal stock portfolio that had really vaulted him into millionaire status. And it was because of Nick's investment advice and suggestions over the past seven years that Dante's net worth had skyrocketed. When Dante had first met Nick at a forum featuring the U.S. Treasury Secretary as the guest speaker, he'd thought the retired NFL player an arrogant ass and had nearly tossed aside the business card Nick had given him. Fortunately, Dante had kept the card, taken Nick up on his offer to meet for lunch one day, and both a friendship and a professional relationship had been firmly cemented. The two men frequently referred clients to the other as well.

Nick waved Dante off when the bill arrived, plunking down his own AMEX Centurion card first. "My treat," he declared. "Even I'm not enough of a bastard to make you pay for lunch when you're this depressed. It'd be like kicking a puppy or something. And I swear to Christ I *will* kick you – *hard* - if you don't snap out of this goddamned funk you're in. You need to get laid, Dan, and quickly. So do both of us a favor, and boink the next woman you meet. Or call up one of your former girlfriends. After all, you've always bragged about how you pride yourself on parting on good terms with your exes. I'm sure any number of them would be all too happy to make you forget about Katie."

Dante opened his mouth to remind his friend yet again that he didn't *want* to forget about Katie, didn't *want* to move on and have meaningless sex with some random woman, but then glimpsed the scowl on Nick's devilishly handsome face. "I'll think about it," he conceded, too dispirited to debate the matter further at the moment.

"And thanks for lunch. My treat next time - when I promise to be in a better mood."

Nick's dark eyes narrowed skeptically. "Let's hope so. And be sure to get those forms I gave you earlier signed and back to me by tomorrow. The IPO releases in less than a week and I don't want you to miss out on it. You're going to make a killing on it."

Dante grinned. "All because of you, *mio amico*. You've got the Midas touch, Nick, always have."

Nick shrugged carelessly as he signed the credit card receipt with his usual bold scrawl. "Give the credit for this one to Angela. She's known the investment banker since they were classmates at Stanford, so they refer a lot of business to each other. And when she brought this one to my attention I knew it would be a good fit for your portfolio."

"I'll send her some flowers to express my gratitude."

Nick waved his hand dismissively. "She's not really the flower loving type."

Dante arched a brow in disbelief. "I find that hard to believe," he protested. "Maybe that's just what she wants you to think because her asshat boyfriend never brings her any. In my vast experience, *all* women love flowers. So try real hard to act just a tiny bit romantic once in awhile and bring her some, hmm?"

Nick scowled. "Okay, Lover Boy. Any other sappy romantic ideas you want to share?"

"The flowers will do for a start," replied Dante cheerfully. "Let's see how that goes and we can progress from there."

"Why don't you concentrate on your own love life - or lack thereof - and let me worry about my relationship with Angela?" suggested Nick sarcastically. "In case you hadn't noticed, *I'm* not the one who looks like he forgot to take his anti-depressants for the last month. Go get laid, okay?"

Despite his otherwise glum state of mind, Dante couldn't help chuckling just a bit during the short walk back to his office. Nick might be the most unsympathetic, cold-hearted bastard on the planet but his blunt, straightforward way of speaking did make a person sit up and take notice. And while Dante knew his friend was right about forgetting Katie and moving on with his life, it was going to take some more time before he could actually follow that advice.

As it turned out, however, that particular timeframe was accelerated in a major way later that evening.

'SOMETIMES IT'S NOT SO bad being single,' thought Dante as he settled himself on the plush black leather sectional sofa, and reached for the TV remote.

On the glass topped table in front of him rested a takeout box of one of his favorite styles of artisan pizza - a Napolitano with fresh tomatoes, anchovies, capers, and olives - and a bottle of craft beer. He was wearing a ratty pair of jeans, an ancient UC Berkeley T-shirt, and was blissfully barefoot. He was getting ready to watch two basketball games back to back, and overall he considered this to be a pretty damned good end to his day.

In between bites of pizza, sips of beer, and closely following the action of the first game, he exchanged texts with his younger brother Rafe and answered an email from his baby sister Gia. Dutifully, he'd called his mother upon arriving home earlier, and expected he'd hear from his other sister Talia before the night was over. They were close that way - he, his siblings, and their mother - bonds that had been strengthened and deepened when they had lost his father so tragically. And despite the fact that his siblings now ranged in age from thirty-year-old Talia to twenty-five-year-old Gia, Rafe being sandwiched in between his sisters, Dante still felt responsible for them, still considered himself their surrogate father. He'd been the one to give Talia away at her wedding two years ago, the one to bail Rafe's sorry ass out of jail after a drunken frat party, the one who'd shed more than a few tears when little Gia had boarded the plane that would take her to the other side of the country so she could attend college at Dartmouth. And it had been his siblings and his mother who had helped him the most these past couple of months to cope with the breakup, even if at times their advice wasn't always welcome.

He was on his second beer, and flipping channels on the enormous flat panel TV that took up most of one wall of the living room when he froze, unable to believe what he was seeing on the screen. Hastily, he set the beer down, then rewound the program several seconds before freeze framing it.

The program was some sort of entertainment news show, one that Katie had always loved to watch because it included lots of gossip about TV and movie stars and other celebrity types. It hadn't really been Dante's sort of thing, and he'd paid the show little heed - until now when Katie herself was being featured on one of the segments. Or, more accurately, the handsome, well known actor who had his arm wrapped tightly around Katie's waist was apparently the focus of the segment and she was simply along for the ride. And the free publicity that she was undoubtedly receiving as the bastard's date.

The pizza that had tasted so delicious a short while ago was now churning acidly in Dante's stomach, and suddenly the beer in front of him was nowhere near strong enough to dull the burning ache he felt at seeing Katie smiling and laughing happily with the man at her side. He stalked over to the built-in wet bar located midway between the living and dining rooms, took out a crystal shot glass, and a very expensive bottle of tequila.

In between shots, he replayed the footage of Katie and her celebrity lover over and over again, until he abruptly turned off the TV, no longer in the mood to watch the other game.

What he *was* in the mood for, he decided with a slowly simmering anger, was to finally forget the traitorous, disloyal blonde he'd been making an ass of himself over. It had taken seeing her in the flesh again, albeit on a television program with her new lover in tow, to snap him out of the gloomy mood he'd been in since she had left two months ago. He was going to follow all of the advice his friends and family had been giving him for weeks now - to get out there, meet some new girls, and have a good time. Rafe's cheerful but rather crude words in particular came to mind at this moment - 'flirt with 'em, fuck 'em, and forget 'em'.

"Well, little brother," declared Dante out loud. "For once the shoe will be on the other foot and I'll be the one following *your* advice. Starting tomorrow, I'm back in the game, and I'm going to ask out the first attractive female I see. And given the mood I'm in right now, I hope she can handle me."

3

Cara Bregante stared glumly at the cheerful bouquet of pink and white daisies, accompanied by a Minnie Mouse balloon that wished her the happiest of birthdays. It wasn't that she didn't appreciate the gift her best friend Mirai had sent, but it was all just a little too – well, *cute* for someone who was turning twenty two today. As it was, most people Cara met thought she was still in high school, and were always startled to realize she wasn't a teenager any longer. Most of that, of course, had to do with the fact that she was barely over five feet tall, while the rest could be blamed on her lack of makeup and the untamed mass of her dark brown curls. No matter what it took, thought Cara fiercely, one of these days she was going to cut half of all this hair off and have the uncontrollable curls straightened. The problem was – as most of her problems were these days – that every penny she earned was so tightly budgeted that there was nothing left over for luxuries like hair cuts, makeup, or new clothes. So any sort of makeover was going to have to wait another year and a half until she finally got her college degree and no longer had to pay tuition.

And Mirai's gift also served as an unwitting reminder that the daisies and the balloon were likely to be the only gift she received today. Her boss Angela was taking her out to lunch, a gesture Cara appreciated, but if she was being completely honest getting flowers from her best friend and going out to a celebratory meal with her female employer wasn't exactly the stuff birthday dreams were made of. Not, for example, like getting red roses and having a romantic candlelight dinner with a really hot guy. Problem was that there hadn't been a hot guy in Cara's life for more than two years, and the last time there'd been one it had ended – well, *badly*.

And it was already a foregone conclusion that she'd be receiving nothing in the way of birthday greetings from her useless father – not even a phone call or one-line email to commemorate the occasion, much less a gift of any sort. When Mark Bregante had moved to Florida four years ago to effectively start a whole new life, Cara had more or less ceased to exist for him – not that he'd ever been a model father by any means.

It would be different, she thought wistfully, if her mom was still alive. Sharon Bregante would have done her utmost to make Cara's birthday special, as she'd done for so many years. Mother and daughter had been closer than most, definitely best friends, and when Sharon had died four years ago from the pancreatic cancer that had destroyed her body with terrifying swiftness, Cara had been devastated. At barely eighteen years old, her entire world had collapsed by losing her beloved mother, and things had only gotten worse from that point on.

But, no – she wasn't going to dwell on the negative today of all days. If Sharon had still been alive, she would have wanted Cara to enjoy her birthday to its fullest, and Cara intended to do just that – even if it wasn't exactly the sort of celebration most twenty-two year old women dreamed of.

Her co-worker Leah stopped briefly by Cara's desk to give the balloon a quick flick. "Cute," she commented in her usual semi-sarcastic tone. "Oh, and Happy Birthday. Doing anything fun to celebrate?"

Cara shook her head. "Just lunch out with Angela. The friend who sent me the flowers is visiting her father in New York right now so we'll celebrate when she gets back. Plus I have class tonight."

Leah grimaced, lending her features a pinched look. "I don't know how you manage working here all day with all the stress, and then sitting through a three-hour lecture on investment strategies or risk management."

Cara grinned. "Tonight's class is actually on derivative securities. I usually have to down a pre-class espresso and then take sips of Red Bull every fifteen minutes to stay awake."

Leah shuddered. "God, I definitely don't miss college! And there was no way I could have stomached going to night school like you do. Too bad you aren't able to attend regular classes, but I guess what you're doing is better than nothing. Oops, gotta go, Tyler's waving me over, which means he's screwed something up again that I'll have to fix. Later."

The high-strung, over-achieving Leah scuttled away before Cara could remind her yet again that the evening classes she attended at UC Berkeley's San Francisco Extension were the exact equivalent of what was offered during the daytime at the main campus. Leah was nice enough, but her snarky side definitely surfaced on a frequent basis, and she didn't always bother to couch her more cutting comments diplomatically. Cara often felt beneath Leah, who was always perfectly put together with her expensive pantsuits, elegant leather pumps, and sleek auburn bob. And Leah had a real knack for putting people down, albeit in a subtle, seemingly innocent manner, and unfortunately for Cara she was more often than not the target of her co-worker's thinly veiled insults.

"It's because she's so damned insecure herself," Angela had assured Cara after overhearing one of Leah's particularly snide comments. "I honestly don't know what Nick was thinking of to hire a husband and wife team to work as his associates, because too much togetherness has definitely not helped that relationship. If Tyler wasn't such a pompous ass himself I'd feel sorry for him having to deal with Leah's bossiness and constant need for attention."

Cara had sniffled, trying desperately not to betray how hurt she felt at Leah's latest barb. "I'm surprised their marriage has lasted three whole years, given how much they bicker during the day."

Angela had nodded in agreement. "They're both ultra-competitive, and it seems to me that the two of them are constantly trying to one-up the other. It doesn't make sense to me, but – hey, it takes all kinds, doesn't it? My family still doesn't get my relationship with Nick, doesn't understand why I don't care if we ever get married or not. Fortunately, I'm way past the point where their opinions matter very much. We may not have the most conventional of relationships, but it works for Nick and me. I wasn't sure how it would pan out when I agreed to go into partnership with him, but it's been great so far. Separate offices help, of course. Leah and Tyler might want to consider that one of these days."

Nick's married associates shared a small office adjacent to his, with two desks crammed into a space really only meant for one person. But neither of them had been willing to lower themselves by agreeing to occupy a cubicle while the other took the office, so they worked literally side by side.

Cara knew that Leah in particular had been visibly miffed when Nick had brought Angela into the group as his partner, probably because she had entertained hopes of doing the very same thing at some point in time. And while Leah had initially treated Angela with polite disdain, it hadn't taken Angela very long to put Nick's associate very firmly in her place. Since resuming her relationship with Nick last year, Angela's confidence and self-assuredness had really begun to bloom, and she'd wasted no time in letting Leah know the score.

At least Nick's PA – Deepak – was nice enough, if a little on the serious side. He and Cara worked well together, though Angela thought he tended to take advantage of Cara's easygoing, helpful nature and pass on too much of his work to her when things got really busy. But it was hard for Cara to say no most of the time, something she knew she really had to work on.

Even now Deepak – wearing another of his nerdy argyle sweater vests over his shirt and tie – approached her desk, a thick sheaf of papers in hand.

"I need to go drop this off to the copy room," he announced in his very precise British accent. He was of East Indian birth, but had been raised and attended school in England. "Can you please listen out for Nick's calls for a few minutes?"

Cara nodded. "Of course."

"Oh, and Dante Sabattini is supposed to be dropping off some signed documents. If he arrives before I return, let Nick know right away. The forms are for some new IPO due out next week so we need to get everything filed as soon as possible."

Cara couldn't suppress the little thrill that shimmied up her spine at the mere mention of Nick's client's name. As a retired professional football player, many of Nick's clients were former athletes themselves, and most were tall, well-built, and good-looking. But none of them were anywhere near as dreamy and sexy and swoonworthy as the dark-haired, olive-skinned Dante.

From the very first time that she'd met Nick's client – who was also one of his closest friends – Cara had found herself tongue-tied and hoping desperately that drool wasn't running down her chin. Not only was Dante incredibly handsome – with his chiseled features, expertly cut black hair, and a panty-melting smile – but he was also extremely personable, charming, and maybe even a little bit naughty. He always had a teasing grin for Cara, always asked how her day was going, and each time she had to struggle to think of something clever to say in response – she who rarely if ever was at a loss for words. She only hoped he had no idea just how massive of a crush she had on him.

Cara was glad she'd worn one of her better outfits to work today, knowing that Angela would be taking her someplace trendy for lunch. Not that she had much of a wardrobe to speak of, but this dress was her favorite – the short-sleeved bodice of black and white stripes attached to a solid black, slightly flared skirt. The dress flattered her petite, curvy figure – the figure that was packing an extra twenty pounds and was *this* close to being considered chubby. The "freshman fifteen" she'd gained during her first year of college had never gone away, and she'd added a few more pounds since then. But working a stressful, demanding job during the day, going to college full time at night, studying, doing laundry, grocery shopping, and keeping her tiny apartment clean didn't leave much time for working out or cooking healthy meals on a regular basis. Thus, losing weight had also been relegated to the "things to do after you get your degree" list, discouraging as that thought was.

But at least the little dress she was wearing hid most of what she considered her figure flaws and made her appear a bit thinner, a fact she was exceedingly grateful for considering that Dante was supposed to be making an appearance here in the office today. Cara had been disappointed to have missed him yesterday when he'd met with Nick since she had been tasked with delivering some paperwork to a client's attorney, and had glumly resigned herself to having to wait another month before seeing him again. Deepak's casual announcement moments ago had considerably brightened her day, and she wondered if she would have time to dash to the ladies room to check her hair and the bit of makeup she'd applied today. Deciding that she didn't want to risk missing Dante again, she took out the small compact that Mirai had given her and quickly fluffed her hair and reapplied the deep rose lipstick, also a gift from her BFF. Mirai was a self-professed shopaholic, and almost always bought things on impulse, only to realize afterwards that what she'd bought was the wrong shade or size or something she already owned. And since she was too lazy to return most of what she bought, it was far easier to just pass things along to Cara. It was too bad, thought Cara regretfully, that her half-Japanese friend was a good four sizes smaller than she was and therefore couldn't share discarded clothes. Otherwise, Cara would have a wardrobe to envy instead of one to pity.

Deepak returned to his desk a few minutes later, unknowingly depriving Cara of the opportunity to interact with Dante whenever he arrived. Sighing dejectedly, Cara turned her attention instead to the considerable pile of work that awaited her. Officially she worked exclusively for Angela Del Carlo, her boss of nearly two years, but lately seemed to be absorbing more and more tasks handed down by

Nick Manning – Angela's business partner and exceedingly intimidating live-in boyfriend. And if Cara had a hard time saying no to the mild-mannered Deepak when he asked for her help, there was no possible way she could refuse anything the demanding, often brusque Nick requested of her. Thus far she had resisted the urge to say anything to Angela about it, not wanting to appear as though she was whining or not willing to be a team player. She knew that Nick had initially opposed her addition to his team, but Angela had insisted that Cara was part of the deal if she was going to agree to the partnership. So it was extra important that Cara made a good impression on Nick now, to make sure he didn't regret his decision, and hopefully score points for the future.

Cara was on a phone call with the customer service department about an issue in a client's account when Dante arrived, but she glanced up just in time to give him a smile and a little wave. His answering grin thrilled her as it always did, and she couldn't help staring after him as he quickly disappeared into Nick's office. She hurried through the rest of her phone call, and had just replaced the receiver when Dante re-emerged. She smiled at him again, and while she sensed he was in a hurry and would have otherwise been on his way, he crossed over instead to her side of the aisle.

He, too, gave the embarrassingly juvenile Minnie Mouse balloon a little flick. "This wasn't here yesterday," he commented, indicating the vase of daisies. "So I'm guessing that means today is the day."

She nodded, hoping that she wouldn't start blushing as she usually did in his presence. Or stammering. Or otherwise acting like an idiot. "Uh, huh. I'm officially twenty-two today."

"That old?" teased Dante, giving her a little wink. "You'd better start checking for gray hairs. I've already sprouted a few, though I'm vain enough to yank them out by the roots."

Cara could only muster up a nervous little giggle in response before shaking her head. "I don't think I have to worry about going gray for a few more years," she joked. "Maybe when I turn thirty."

"So what are your big plans to celebrate?" inquired Dante. "Bar-hopping with your girlfriends? Dinner with the family? Or more likely a hot date with your latest boyfriend."

She had to contain herself from bursting out into semi-hysterical laughter at his seemingly innocent suggestions. Cara had neither a boyfriend or any real family to celebrate with, her only real close girlfriend was out of town, and bar-hopping had never really been her thing – even if she'd been able to afford it. Unwilling to admit any of these equally humiliating facts to Dante, she simply told him the truth.

"Angela is taking me out to lunch today. And since I have a class I need to attend tonight, that's pretty much the extent of any celebrating I'll be doing this year," she acknowledged matter-of-factly.

"Class?" Dante's brow wrinkled inquisitively. "You mean like yoga or spinning? Or what's that Latin dance thing called – Zimba?"

Cara laughed. "I think you mean Zumba. And, no, it's not an exercise class. It's – well, this."

She reached beneath her desk where she kept the ratty old backpack she'd had since her freshman year of high school, pulled out a textbook that weighed at least five pounds in her estimation, and plunked it on her desk.

"Managing Financial Risk – Guide to Derivative Products, Financial Engineering, and Value Maximization" read Dante out loud, just before emitting a long, low whistle. "Wow. Just reading that title is intimidating. You're actually studying this stuff?"

The tone of his voice reflected both his disbelief and admiration, and Cara's heart swelled with pride. "Yep. Working on my degree in finance. Unfortunately that process takes a little longer going to night school, but I hope to finish everything up by next summer."

Dante was regarding her with an expression that she couldn't quite describe – a combination perhaps of surprise, approval, and something else that she wasn't quite able to put her finger on. "Where are you taking night classes?" he asked. "San Francisco State?"

She shook her head. "UC Berkeley Extension. I, um, attended the main campus for two years but, well, circumstances changed and I had to switch to night school after that."

He nodded in understanding. "Yeah, Berkeley's a tough school, that's for sure. I had to study my ass off when I attended, especially since I had to keep my grades up in order to keep playing on the soccer team."

Cara quickly realized that he thought she'd had to settle for night school because she couldn't keep up with regular classes. "It is a tough school," she agreed. "But my grades weren't the reason I had to transfer to the extension. I – I was at the top of all my classes by the end of sophomore year."

Dante frowned. "Then why the hell did you make that sort of change? You'd be graduating next month if you had stayed at the main campus."

"Don't I know it," sighed Cara. "And, well, my financial status changed. I wasn't able to scrape together enough financial aid to stay in school full time, so I work during the day and go to school at night. And FYI – night classes are every bit as tough as day classes."

He chuckled. "I stand corrected, Ms. Top of Her Class. And that's a shame about having to work full time while getting your degree. Your family isn't able to help you out with expenses?"

Cara felt the smile disappear from her face. "No," was all she murmured in reply. "Not any longer. I'm pretty much on my own these days."

Dante studied her quizzically for long seconds, and she had to quell the urge to fidget while she tried desperately to interpret what thoughts might be going through his very handsome head. But she could never in a million years have anticipated what he said to her next.

"Tell you what," he drawled almost lazily. "It's a damned shame that a pretty girl like you isn't doing something fun to celebrate her birthday. Do you have a class tomorrow night, too?"

Cara shook her head. "No classes on Friday, just Monday through Thursday. Why do you ask?"

Dante grinned down at her. "Because I'd like to invite you to have dinner with me tomorrow night. That is, provided you don't already have plans. Or a boyfriend who'd object to my poaching on his territory."

She stared at him, completely at a loss for words, and unable to believe what she'd just heard. "Huh? Are you – I mean, you're actually asking me to – to go out with you? And, no, I don't have a boyfriend or anyone I'm seeing, but I thought you did. I mean," she corrected herself hastily, miserably aware that she was babbling like a moron by this point, "not that *you* had a boyfriend, but a girlfriend. Of course you don't have a boyfriend, why would you, because you're about the least likely person I could think of who - "

Dante placed his index finger over her lips, giving a quick shake of his head. "It's okay," he assured her, the corners of his mouth lifting up into a smile. "I know what you meant. And to answer your question – at least, I think there was a question in there somewhere – I'm not currently seeing anyone either. I, ah, was in a relationship for a long time but that ended a couple of months ago."

"Oh. I'm sorry. I hope I didn't, um, touch on a sore spot," she apologized awkwardly.

"It's okay," replied Dante gently. "I had a rough time of it for awhile, but I'm happy to say that things are finally starting to look up for me. And I'd be even happier if your answer to my invitation is yes."

Cara beamed up at him, nodding enthusiastically. "It is definitely a yes! I'd love to have dinner with you tomorrow."

He glanced around anxiously, as though to make sure no one had overheard their conversation. "That's great news, Cara. Though you should probably keep it to yourself, hmm? I don't know what the company policy is about employees socializing with clients, but no sense in rocking the boat, is there?"

"Oh! Oh, gosh, of course!" she agreed. "I won't say anything to the others, I promise."

Dante looked relieved, then extracted a business card from the inside pocket of his suit jacket before picking up a pen from the holder on her desk. "Why don't you meet me in the lobby of my office building?" he suggested, scribbling something on the back side of the little card. "That way we don't risk running into anyone here. If you don't mind, that is."

"I don't mind at all," Cara answered with enthusiasm. "What time should I meet you?"

"Let's say six o'clock? And I can send a car or a taxi to pick you up."

She shook her head. "Your office is less than three blocks away, and it's not supposed to be raining or anything tomorrow. Besides, I can use the exercise."

He gave her one of those sexy, flirty little winks that he was wont to do whenever he stopped by the office. "I wouldn't say that," he replied, his dark eyes giving her a brief but all-too-assessing onceover. "You look very healthy to me, very fit."

Cara grimaced. "That's because I'm usually sitting down when you see me, and you can't tell how big my ass is from where you're standing."

Dante gave a shout of laughter, causing Deepak to glance over in their direction, frowning at having had his concentration disrupted. Grinning wickedly, Dante lowered his voice.

"You're very outspoken, aren't you?" he asked in amusement. "I like that. And I have a feeling this is going to be a very interesting dinner. Now, I've got to run, but I wrote my personal cell number on the back of that card. Give me a call when you're on your way tomorrow, so I can be waiting for you in the lobby."

"Okay." She picked up the business card and tucked it into her purse for safekeeping. "I'll be looking forward to it."

"Me, too." Dante gave the Minnie Mouse balloon another flick. "And Happy Birthday, Cara. Though consider tomorrow night the real celebration."

He gave her a farewell wink, and she could only stare in slack-jawed admiration at the sight of his broad-shouldered frame in that expertly tailored navy pinstripe suit as he hurried off. She counted to fifty, making sure Dante was well and truly out of sight, before digging her battered cell phone out of her purse. A glance to her right revealed that Deepak was engrossed in whatever he was doing, so she quickly dialed up her best friend, almost bursting at the seams with the news she had to share.

"Mirai? Yeah, I know I already sent you an email and a text thanking you for the flowers and the balloon – by the way, I'm not five years old, you know. And I know I sent you a Hello Kitty balloon for your birthday, but you actually still *like* all that stuff. Now, listen up because you are *so* not going to believe what just happened!"

4

Cara fumbled for the light switch as she stepped over the threshold of the in-law unit that she'd called home for close to two years now. Once the room was illuminated, she wasted no time in dropping her purse and the shopping bag she'd been carrying on the floor, then eased the frayed straps of the staggeringly heavy backpack from her tired shoulders. For a moment or two she slumped against the door jamb, so exhausted that she was having trouble remaining upright. It had been a very long day, beginning before sunrise, and now, after two bus rides home from her night class, it was drawing close to eleven p.m. If she was lucky, she'd get a full six hours of sleep before waking up and starting all over again. At least, she thought sleepily, tomorrow was Friday which meant no class tomorrow night. Instead, she would actually be going on a date for the first time in what felt like years. And not just any date, mind you, but with the gorgeous, hunky guy she'd had a massive, unrequited crush on for the past six months.

Cara was still in disbelief that Dante had actually asked her out to dinner. After all, while he had always been nice to her, had even flirted a little on occasion, he had never before given any indication that he might be interested in dating her. That had, no doubt, been due largely to the fact that he'd been in a serious relationship, at least until the recent breakup he'd alluded to.

And she knew from having overheard Leah's overly loud gossiping that Dante's ex had been some sort of model or actress, and that she was drop dead gorgeous. Cara couldn't recall the ex's name, admittedly because it had bothered her to think too much about Dante being seriously involved with someone, but she had no doubt that the woman must have been a knockout to hold his interest for a whole year.

But now it sure seemed that his relationship with this woman was over and done with, and that maybe - just maybe - Cara might have a chance with the guy she'd been fantasizing about for months. From the very first time Nick had introduced her to Dante - soon after she and Angela had moved over from their previous location in the office - Cara had been spellbound by the man. He was older than she was, of course, by at least ten years, and certainly far more mature than any of the boys she had dated these past few years. He was also sophisticated, obviously wealthy, and pretty much in an entirely different league than herself. But for some reason he was attracted to her, at least enough to ask her out to dinner tomorrow night.

'Now, don't go jumping to conclusions, silly,' she scolded herself as she began to put her things away. 'He probably just asked you out this one time because it's your birthday and he feels sorry for you. And for all you know this isn't even a real date, just a casual thing between friends. Or whatever we are to each other. Most likely it will just be this one time and then he'll find a hot new girlfriend to take the place of the last one, and you'll go back to being nothing more than his friend's admin assistant. So prepare yourself for that, Cara - okay? Don't start getting your hopes up or expect anything more.'

Since it was already past her bedtime, Cara quickly changed into the loose fitting nightshirt that was her normal sleeping attire, then washed up for the night. She fixed her lunch and snacks for the next day, and was about to set out work clothes for the morning when she belatedly remembered the shopping bag she'd brought home.

'You're such an airhead sometimes, Cara,' she scolded herself. 'How long has it been since you bought clothes? You think you'd remember bringing home a new dress and pair of shoes, wouldn't you?'

She extracted the sheath dress of vivid scarlet and hung it up in her cramped, tiny closet before pulling the pair of black strappy sandals from the same bag. She ran a hand lovingly over the dress, thinking again how lucky she'd been to snag such a bargain. It was difficult for her to find pretty things in her size - a petite size ten - that weren't too matronly or, at the opposite end of the scale, too youthful. In addition she had something of a "problem figure" to dress - with big boobs, a surprisingly tiny waist, curvy hips, and a generous booty. It was rare when she found clothes that fit well, and since she couldn't afford expensive alterations Cara was usually resigned to wearing things that were too long or ill-fitting.

But the little red dress had fit her like a glove, and was made of some sort of rayon blend that had a bit of stretch to it. The vibrant color flattered her dark hair and the light olive tone of her skin, and she had felt both sexy and confident while inspecting herself in the dressing room mirror. The high heeled sandals had been on clearance, leaving her just enough left on the gift card Mirai had impulsively emailed over to also pick up a new set of lingerie.

Mirai had been so excited to hear about Cara's upcoming date that she had literally screamed into the phone, loud enough for Deepak to have overheard and given Cara a scathing scowl. Cara had shushed her friend after that, but while Mirai had grudgingly modulated the volume of her voice there was no way she was going to tone down her level of excitement.

"OMG, girl, I cannot believe it!" Mirai screeched. "You're finally going on a date after all this time, and with Mr. Tall, Dark, and Super-Hot to boot!"

Cara had discreetly snapped a photo of Dante once when he'd been chatting with Deepak, and shown it to her BFF. Mirai, who generally preferred men with blond or light brown hair, had nonetheless conceded that Dante was undeniably smokin'.

"And Italian, just like you," she'd pointed out.

In actuality, Cara was only half-Italian on her father's side, but she had definitely inherited his coloring. If only, she'd thought longingly on multiple occasions, she had also taken after him in body type - tall and lean and long-legged - instead of resembling her petite mother whose figure had been slightly on the plump side.

During their conversation earlier today, Mirai had quizzed Cara about what she was planning to wear on her date the next evening, a question that had caused Cara to sigh in regret.

"Honestly, I have no idea," she'd admitted. *"I'm wearing the black dress with the striped top right now so that's out. The only other decent dress I own is the navy shirtwaist."*

Cara could almost see her friend shuddering over the phone line at the mention of that particular dress.

"No way," Mirai had protested vehemently. *"That's the sort of dress you wear to a funeral. Or out to lunch with your grandmother. Definitely not on a dinner date with the hottest guy you know."*

"What about my black skirt?"

"The one you always seem to wear with a white blouse, that makes you look like a waitress? Uh, uh, that's not going to work either."

Cara had heaved a frustrated sigh. "Well, I'm fresh out of ideas. And since you're as familiar with the meager contents of my wardrobe as I am, I'm open for suggestions - so long as buying something new isn't one of them. I'm so short on funds right now that I can't afford to buy milk until next paycheck. I've been eating dry cornflakes for breakfast all week."

"Give me a sec, okay?" Mirai had pleaded.

There had been silence on the other end for nearly two minutes, with Cara keeping her fingers crossed that Angela wouldn't need her for something. Fortunately Mirai had come back on the line then, sounding triumphant.

"There. All set," she'd declared. *"I just sent you an e-gift card to Macy's. Not my favorite store at all but you'll get more for your money there than you would at Barney's or Nordstrom. Check your email, would you?"*

"Mirai," Cara had protested, even as she opened up her email. *"You already sent me a birthday gift. A gift card is way too much, especially one for a hundred and fifty bucks. I can't let you do this. Besides, didn't you tell me your credit cards were all maxed out?"*

"They were," agreed Mirai cheerily. "At least until I sweet talked Daddy into paying them all off for me. He also treated me to a big time shopping spree at Saks and Bergdorf's yesterday, and wired twenty grand into my checking account. Oh, and I charged your flowers to his account, so technically this gift card is the only thing from me."

Cara hadn't been able to contain an exasperated chuckle or two. *"You're kind of a brat, you know that, don't you?"* she'd asked teasingly. *"Such a Daddy's girl. You can schmooze him into just about anything, can't you?"*

Mirai had giggled in reply. *"I know how to get on his good side, that's for sure,"* she'd admitted. *"And since I'm staying on while he recovers from foot surgery to help him out, he's feeling very generous right now. So quit bitching about a little gift card and go buy yourself something pretty for your date. And for God's sake, Cara, use some of the money to get a decent set of undies, will you? Something sexy. That matches. Unlike the stuff you currently own. I think homeless women have nicer bras and panties than you do."*

"They're not that bad," Cara had protested weakly. *"But I'll follow orders, ma'am, and buy something pretty. Though I'm not really sure why it matters."*

"Well, duh, of course it matters, silly!" Mirai had scolded. *"You've only got one chance to make a good first impression on the Italian Stallion, after all. And plain white cotton undies are not what you want to be wearing at the time."*

Cara had been taken aback at this. *"Um, aren't you sort of jumping to conclusions just a bit here? I mean, he asked me out to dinner - probably because he feels sorry for me. I don't recall also hearing an invitation to have sex."*

"Trust me, sweetie, it will happen," Mirai had assured with confidence. *"Your Dante looks like the type who can show a girl a real good time in the sack. Not to mention one who needs to get his rocks off on a regular basis. So listen to your BFF, hmm? Black lace. Make sure the bra shows off those great tits of yours. And either bikinis or hipsters, definitely not boy shorts or briefs. And please promise me you'll get up fifteen minutes early so you can shave all over?"*

Cara had been laughing softly when she'd bid Mirai goodbye, needing to get back to work by then. During her birthday lunch with

Angela - where she had gone out of her way not to even mention Dante, much less the fact that he'd invited her out to dinner the next evening - she had asked permission to leave work an hour early. Angela had agreed without hesitation, knowing full well that Cara frequently worked through her lunch hour, arrived at the office early, and stayed past her assigned quitting time.

She'd been lucky to find the dress and shoes at Macy's fairly quickly, then followed Mirai's orders and bought herself a new set of lingerie - and in black lace as instructed. Cara placed the admittedly sexy bra and panties that were far more provocative than any of her other undies on top of the narrow set of drawers that was set into an alcove of her cramped apartment.

And calling this place an apartment was being overly generous. In reality, it was one small room with a tiny bathroom, a single closet, and an efficiency kitchen. The room was an illegal in-law unit attached to an older house in a so-so neighborhood in San Francisco. The house belonged to the invalid aunt of a client of Angela's, and it had been through that connection that Cara had found this place. It definitely left a lot to be desired, with its decades-old gold shag carpet, faded curtains, and cracked blinds that covered the single window, and its overall lack of space. But since she had practically no furniture or household goods, the limited amount of storage wasn't a problem. In addition to the narrow dresser the small room held a futon, a coffee table, a floor lamp, and a round table with two mismatched chairs. All of the furniture was secondhand, well worn, and functional rather than attractive. There was no TV because she simply couldn't afford cable or satellite dish fees, and precious little leisure time to watch it to boot.

At least there were several paintings, framed photographs, vases, and other decorative pieces that had been passed on from her mother, the few precious things she'd been able to salvage when her father had rather ruthlessly sold nearly the entire contents of their former home before moving to Florida with his new, very young wife.

Cara picked up a framed photo of herself and her mother, one that had been taken when she had been around thirteen, and ran a finger over the beloved face of Sharon Bregante.

"I miss you," she murmured out loud. "I miss you every single day but especially today - on my birthday. I know if you were still here you would have done something special. Even though we never had much money, you always found a way to make things special."

She replaced the frame. "And I really wish I could talk to you tonight in particular, so I could get your advice about my date tomorrow night - the date that might not even be a real date. I think I'd be a little less nervous if I could hear you tell me that everything was going to be fine."

But then Cara began to recall what a disaster her parents' marriage had been, and thought wryly that perhaps her mother might not have been the best person to offer romantic advice after all.

5

Portland, Oregon - Four and a half years ago

"Thanks for the ride home. I'll call you later tonight, okay?"

Cara reached across the passenger seat to plant a quick kiss on the lips of Jack McManus, her boyfriend of the past few months. She and Jack had known each other since their freshman year of high school, but had really just noticed each other at the beginning of their senior year. Jack had matured over the course of a summer from a skinny, somewhat geeky guy to a leanly muscled, more confident young man, ditching both his glasses and braces in the process. Cara, on the other hand, had grown another paltry inch but, more significantly, had finally developed boobs and hips so that people no longer mistook her for a twelve year old.

She and Jack had sat next to each other the first day of AP Calculus, struck up a conversation, and their budding romance had begun that day. Both of them had been virgins, at least up until a few weeks ago when they'd had sex for the first time - a somewhat awkward, fumbling encounter. Fortunately their subsequent times together had been better, and Cara had conceded that sex was definitely a learning process, and one that she hoped would continue to improve in the coming weeks.

She hadn't thought much beyond the end of senior year and possibly this summer in regards to her relationship with Jack. After all, they would be going their separate ways come late August when she headed south to California to attend UC Berkeley, and Jack moved east to start college at Duke. Cara was enough of a realist to know that long-distance romances rarely lasted, especially between two people who hadn't been dating all that long.

But for now, at least, she was having fun with Jack, enjoyed spending time with him, and they had begun to make initial plans for their Senior Prom in April.

Life in general couldn't be much better right now, thought Cara as she let herself inside the small, modest home she shared with her parents. School was going great - she was excelling in all of her classes and was on track to be selected as the valedictorian come late May. She was involved with several clubs and groups as well - Debate Club, school newspaper, Italian Club, and the Junior Kiwanis, who performed various acts of community service. In addition, she also took dance classes at the same studio she'd begun attending as a tiny five year old, and helped teach some of the youngest students in order to help pay for her own tuition. She was popular and well-liked among her wide circle of friends, though she tended to hang out with the brainy, studious kids rather than any so-called "in-crowd". She'd been offered early admission to Berkeley, and would be the third generation of women in her family to attend the prestigious university, following in her mother's and grandmother's footsteps. Life was definitely good, and her future couldn't be much brighter.

But a sudden shiver of premonition crept up her spine as she dumped her backpack and jacket in the entryway. The house was almost eerily silent, even though she knew both of her parents were at home since their cars were in the driveway. Normally at this time of the day her mother would be getting dinner ready, while her father - provided he was actually home and not out drinking with his buddies - would be plopped on the living room sofa watching sports or the news and not lifting a finger to help his wife. But the TV was off, there were no welcoming scents coming from the kitchen, and no sign of either parent.

Cara located them moments later, both seated at the kitchen table, and both with equally somber faces. Sharon in particular appeared pale and upset, the dark circles under her eyes pronounced, and Cara wondered why she hadn't noticed until now that her mother had lost more than a few pounds.

"What's going on?" she asked, her gut instinct telling her that something was very, very wrong. She pulled out a chair and sat down next to her ashen faced mother and glum, silent father.

Sharon reached over and took Cara's hand, squeezing it hard as her eyes filled with tears. "Oh, baby. Your dad and I have something to tell you. It's bad, Cara. Really bad. I wish with all my heart that I could spare you this, but it's not something I'll be able to hide much longer."

Trying hard not to let the panic overwhelm her, Cara glanced worriedly between her parents. "Oh, God. You're getting a divorce, aren't you? You both figured that I'm almost eighteen now and getting ready to graduate so it's time to end things. That's it, isn't it?"

But a divorce, as awful as that would have been, was not the bad news Sharon had been referring to. Instead, it was much, much worse - the absolute worst possible news there could have been. Sharon had been diagnosed with stage four pancreatic cancer and given no more than a handful of months to live. Because this particular form of cancer was so difficult to diagnose on a timely basis, oftentimes the deadly disease had already spread to other parts of the body by the time the person even realized they were sick. Cara recalled now that her mother had been complaining every so often about stomach pains and fatigue, starting around Thanksgiving, but Sharon had simply put it down to stress and overwork. In addition to her full time job teaching high school mathematics, Sharon also taught a night class at community college as well as an SAT prep class on occasional Saturdays. The extra income helped to make ends meet when Mark, Cara's often undependable father, was between jobs.

It hadn't been until a few days ago, right after returning to work from the Christmas break, when Sharon's condition had become apparent. She had fainted at school, and one of her fellow teachers - and lifelong best friend Frannie - had insisted on driving her to the ER. The staff there had conducted a slew of tests, and Sharon had just received the terrible news earlier today. She hadn't said anything to Cara until now, not wanting to worry her unnecessarily if it had all turned out to be nothing.

Cara clutched her mother's hand tightly, fighting off the flood of tears she longed to spill, determined to be strong now for the woman who had always been there for her. "There has to be something they can do," argued Cara stubbornly. "Surgery, chemo, radiation. You're young, strong, in good health. I know you can fight this, Mom."

But Sharon only shook her head sadly. "No, baby. Trust me, I had the exact same reaction when the doctor broke the news, told him I was ready to fight this thing tooth and nail. But it's already spread too extensively - the lymph nodes, stomach lining. And they expect it will go to my liver next. There's no way to halt the progress, Cara, and the doctors can only help with managing the symptoms now, mostly through pain management. I'm so sorry, baby. Sorry that I probably won't be here to see you start college, get you moved into your dorm, and all the other plans we made."

This time Cara couldn't hold back the tears as they began to trickle in hot paths down her cheeks. "What about my graduation?" she whispered brokenly. "You'll make it at least until then, won't you?"

Sharon enfolded her beloved daughter in her arms, giving her a reassuring hug. "I hope so, baby. God knows I'll fight like hell to be there."

And fight Sharon did. Stubbornly, she insisted on finishing out the month of January with her high school students, though she did give up her two other jobs immediately. At first, life went on pretty much like normal, though Cara noticed that her mother looked increasingly exhausted by the end of each day. Cara took on more and more of the household chores and fixed dinner each night, despite Sharon's protests that she didn't want to be babied, that she felt okay. But by the end of the month, Sharon had lost an alarming amount of weight, struggled visibly to get through each day, and began to look every bit as sick as she was.

Once she stopped working, Sharon seemed to grow weaker with each passing day. During the first two or three weeks of February, she forced herself to keep going, to remain positive and cheerful. She insisted on accompanying Cara to shop for a prom dress and accessories, as well as a dress for graduation. She made it to a birthday lunch for Frannie, a baby shower for one of the teachers she had worked with, to see a movie with Cara. She expressed renewed optimism that she would get to see Cara graduate, and certainly be there for both her prom and eighteenth birthday - events that would happen within mere days of each other.

But a new scan towards the end of February revealed that the cancer had indeed spread to her liver, and that her life expectancy had been greatly shortened. Sharon was no longer able to fight the pain, and unwillingly began to take the strong drugs that had been prescribed for that purpose. She began to sleep more and more, and was barely coherent when she was awake. Her appetite waned, then disappeared altogether, and her once plump frame became skeletal. The hospice nurse assigned to the case advised Mark and Cara that Sharon now required round the clock care, and gave them the number of an agency who provided home health care workers. When Mark realized just how much that would cost, he protested loudly, claiming there was no possible way they could afford it. Cara knew that her father was already beginning to panic about how he was going to cope financially without Sharon's income, but was incensed that he would object to paying whatever it cost to make sure his wife was given the care she needed.

Impulsively, Cara declared that she would take care of her mother, and made plans to speak with the vice principal at her school to arrange some sort of home study program. She had already cut way back on her other school activities, dropping out of certain clubs entirely while doing the bare minimum with others. She had told her dance teacher that she most likely wouldn't be able to participate in the studio's big recital in June, and had stopped her student teaching. And she'd had to cancel any number of dates with Jack, who thus far had been understanding and supportive - unlike her own father. But then, given his history of being unreliable and irresponsible, Cara wasn't all that surprised at her father's overall lack of support.

Mark Bregante was an extremely handsome, charming, schmoozer who had swept the shy, studious Sharon off her feet soon after they first met. Sharon had been so crazy about him that she had postponed getting her doctorate - a necessary step towards becoming a college professor like she'd always dreamed of, and following in the footsteps of her own mother - in order to help support Mark while he finished his college degree. By then Sharon had become pregnant with Cara, and the plans to obtain her PhD had been put on hold again. She had always vowed to pursue the advanced degree, but circumstances had continued to interfere with those goals - circumstances that had usually revolved around Mark being unable to hold onto a job for very long.

Over the years, and especially as she'd grown a little older, Cara had frequently overheard her father's multiple excuses for why he'd quit one job or been let go from another. The reasons had run the gamut from his being overqualified for the job or not getting the raise he deserved or the boss having it in for him. Whatever the reason, it had been rare for Mark to stay at a job more than a few months to a year, often with lengthy periods of unemployment in between. And when he did work more often than not it was at some sort of sales position, where the bulk of his salary came from commissions and was usually unreliable. It had become necessary, therefore, for Sharon to take on first one and then two part-time teaching jobs in addition to her day job, and she had also taught summer school for as long as Cara could remember - all to help support her family and compensate for Mark's shortcomings as a breadwinner.

But his unreliability at keeping a job was far from the only way he had always let his wife and daughter down. Being such an attractive, charismatic man, Mark had naturally attracted female attention wherever he went, and he had far too large an ego to turn down all of the offers he received. As a little girl, Cara had often come upon her mother weeping quietly, or overheard her grandmother or Frannie advising Sharon to "leave the good-for-nothing bastard and let him support himself for once". But each time Sharon would admit that she loved Mark too much to ever consider such a thing, that no matter how many times he let her down or hurt her, she would always forgive him. He was her weakness, her obsession, and she would put up with just about anything to keep him with her - even overlook his frequent flirtations and infidelities.

As she'd grown older and more aware of what was going on, Cara, too, had urged her mother to leave Mark and live her own life. It had been perhaps the only time Cara could recall her mother snapping at her, visibly losing her temper, and telling Cara to stay out of things she couldn't begin to understand. Shocked at this very uncharacteristic outburst from her normally placid mother, Cara had never broached the subject again. But it had been very obvious that her father felt free.to do exactly as he pleased, and Cara had quickly learned not to depend on him. Throughout her life, in fact, there had been far too many times when Mark had been late for dinner or found some excuse not to attend a school event or didn't bother showing up for one of her dance recitals.

But Cara had hoped that for once Mark would face up to his responsibilities and be there for his wife in her time of greatest need. Admittedly he was there each evening for dinner and to help when needed, but the bulk of Sharon's care was provided by Cara. Thankfully her plans to do home study hadn't been necessary since Frannie's mother - a recently retired nurse who was like a second mother to Sharon - had insisted on looking after her during the day while Cara was at school. And Sharon's fellow teachers and friends not only offered to take shifts on weekends but brought over meals for Cara and Mark and anyone else who happened to be visiting.

It was early April when the hospice nurse took Mark and Cara aside and gently told them it would likely be a matter of days now until Sharon's death. Cara spent every possible minute at her mother's bedside, barely taking the time to eat or do much else but attend classes and do homework. Jack began to sound less and less understanding when she couldn't make time to go out with him, and was definitely put out when Cara broke the news that going to prom was most likely not going to happen. But there was no possible way she could leave her mother's side at such a critical time, and wouldn't be able to enjoy herself anyway. Cara had shook her head in disbelief after that call with Jack, wondering how the guy she'd been so close to these past few months could now be so insensitive and totally lacking in support.

During one of Sharon's few lucid periods - the frequent doses of morphine keeping her largely out of it - she called weakly for Mark and Cara to sit with her. She took Cara's hand in between her own two frail ones, and spoke in a barely audible voice.

"Promise me, baby," she murmured, "that no matter what you'll do all the things we talked about - go to Italy, have at least two kids someday, and above all get that degree from Berkeley. I'm counting on you to keep the tradition going, hmm? Three generations. Make me and your grandmother proud. Promise?"

Cara nodded, blinking back tears as she kissed her mother's forehead. "I promise, Mom. No matter what it takes."

Sharon had turned to Mark next, making him promise that he would always be there for Cara, would always look out for her, and, most importantly, would vow to use the money that had been left to Sharon by her mother three years earlier to finance Cara's college education. Mark had assured his wife that he would do as she asked, and at that point Sharon nodded, closed her eyes tiredly, and slipped into a coma.

She died two days later, without ever having regained consciousness. Cara, Frannie and her mother, and the hospice nurse were all gathered around Sharon's bedside at the end, while Mark was nowhere to be found. It was also the night of Cara's prom, the prom she would later find out her so-called boyfriend Jack had brought another girl to as his date.

'Like mother, like daughter,' Cara thought tiredly. 'Both of us with rotten taste in men, picking the ones who always let us down.'

Numbly she got through the ordeal of Sharon's funeral, willed herself to get through the last few weeks of school, and even resumed her extracurricular activities, including her dance classes. Jack had offered up a sheepish apology, admitting that he'd acted like a jerk about the whole thing, and wondered if they could start over. Cara had been too grief-stricken to offer up much of a protest, had been desperate for a distraction from her constant sorrow, and had taken back up with Jack despite her better judgment. What did she care about her pride or self-esteem, after all, considering the terrible loss she had just suffered.

And Cara's pain had really just begun, as had her losses. Less than two months after Sharon's death, and barely a week prior to her high school graduation, Cara arrived home to find her father deep in consultation with a realtor. But the news that Mark was putting her beloved childhood home - the only home Cara had ever known - up for sale was only the tip of the iceberg. Mark was also getting remarried - to his twenty-something, cocktail waitress girlfriend, the one who was four months pregnant - and moving to Florida with her. The realtor figured the house would sell fairly quickly, though he promised that Cara could remain in the house until it was time for her to move to California and start college.

Frannie and the rest of Sharon's friends were incensed at Mark's callous, insensitive actions, and Frannie in particular didn't hesitate to express her opinion directly to his face. It was obvious that Mark had been having an affair with this woman while Sharon had been dying from cancer, a fact that had made both Cara and Frannie spitting mad. And when Cara refused to attend the wedding ceremony, Mark got vindictive and promptly instructed the realtor to move up the close of escrow on the house to two weeks before she was due to leave for Berkeley, leaving her without a place to live. But Frannie saved the day yet again, insisting that Cara stay with her during that time, even though she and her husband had three teenagers of their own. Frannie also made arrangements to drive Cara to Berkeley and get her settled into the dorm, stating that Sharon would have done exactly the same if it had been one of her children, and that it was the very least she could do to honor her best friend's memory. Frannie had also offered to store several boxes containing mementoes and other items Cara had managed to salvage from the house, mostly books, photos, and personal items of her mother's. Mark had rather callously taken what he wanted – though his new wife Holly had disdainfully declared most of the furniture too worn out and old fashioned for her taste – then sold the rest at an estate sale.

Cara's first semester at Berkeley had been a miserable one. To save money, Mark had insisted that she occupy a triple dorm room – which was essentially a regular double with an extra person squeezed in. Her two roommates – Kylee and Rylee – not only had names that rhymed in an adorably annoying way, but the girls had been best friends since the age of eight. They had been as close as sisters, and had even resembled each other to an almost startlingly degree – tall, slim, tanned, and blonde. They had been nearly inseparable, each of them pursuing a degree in communications and taking the same classes, and spending practically every waking minute together. The girls had also been very adept at shutting Cara out of their tight-knit little circle, never inviting her to go out with them, or even acknowledging her presence most of the time. They had frequently brought friends – especially boys – to the already cramped room, and Cara had often arrived back after class to find strangers sprawled on her bed or sitting at her desk.

She had missed Sharon terribly, had missed being able to call or email her for advice and guidance or to be consoled, and the grief she had felt at losing her beloved mother had consumed her at times. Mark had offered zero support or guidance, far too wrapped up in settling into his new home and job down in Florida, and starting his new life with Holly. Cara had rarely heard from her father, and usually only when she had been the one to make contact. All of her close friends from high school had been scattered around the country at various colleges, but unlike her they had all seemed to be settling in nicely and having a great time. Not wanting to feel like the biggest loser of all time, Cara hadn't voiced her unhappiness to any of them, not even to Frannie who checked up on her from time to time. Cara had known that Frannie had her hands full with a full-time job, husband, and three teenagers to raise, and that the last thing she would have needed was to listen to Cara's whining about how miserable she was.

So Cara had very unwisely tried to bury her grief and forget her troubles in a number of ill-advised ways – drinking a little too much at the parties she was invited to; eating too much junk food and sugar, which caused her to pack the extra pounds on with almost revolting speed; and allowing herself to get sweet-talked, coerced, or otherwise compelled into having sex with guys who were all wrong for her in one way or another – one who basically used her for free tutoring in math; another who was trying to make his ex-girlfriend jealous; a third who was really interested in Kylee and wound up sleeping with her – a rather unpleasant sight for Cara to walk in on.

But it was after one of the guys she'd unwisely succumbed to – the good looking, smooth talking one she was so sure things would work out with – posted nude and semi-nude photos of her that he'd taken while she was asleep all over his social media pages that Cara swore off guys, booze, and partying. Fortunately, the gossip and lewd comments she had to endure after the photo fiasco died down pretty quickly, though she'd had to temporarily shut down her own social media accounts as a result.

Her resolve to stay away from those vices that had temporarily provided some form of distraction had unfortunately brought all of the pain back into razor sharp focus. She compensated by eating, gaining the dreaded "Freshman Fifteen" by the Christmas break.

And spending Christmas with her father and Holly in Florida certainly hadn't been any help. If anything, she'd been even more unhappy, especially since her father's new wife was anything but warm and welcoming. Cara had been miserable during the time she'd spent there, virtually ignored by Holly and her family members who lived nearby and always seemed to be over at the house. Mark had fussed over his heavily pregnant young wife in a way he'd never, ever done with Sharon. The house in Florida – purchased with the money from the sale of the Portland house that Sharon had inherited from her mother – was much larger, newer, and more luxurious and boasted a swimming pool. It had made Cara's stomach clench with anger, and her heart to ache with sorrow, to witness her father wait on his new wife hand and foot and give her anything her greedy little heart desired – all while her own mother had worked three jobs to support him and gone without so many things in her life.

She had wanted to quit school more than a dozen times during that first awful semester, quietly crying herself to sleep night after night because she was so unhappy and lonely. But every time she was ready to throw in the towel, Cara remembered the promise she'd made her mother just before Sharon had slipped into a coma, and knew that one way or another she would find the determination to stick it out.

The only bright light of her freshman year, in fact, had been meeting Mirai Robinson at the beginning of the spring semester. The petite, perky half-Japanese girl had been in her English class, and had taken an almost instant liking to Cara. It had been readily obvious that Mirai was in over her head at such a tough, competitive school like Berkeley, and she'd admitted that it was largely due to her father's influence that she had even been accepted. Lars Robinson was an extremely wealthy alumni of the university, who made frequent and sizeable donations to the school, enough to have gained admission for his younger daughter who would never have been accepted otherwise.

And while Mirai was almost the polar opposite of the sort of friends Cara normally hung out with – chatty, obsessed with fashion, celebrities, and social media. and more than a little ditzy – she was also kind, generous, and soft-hearted. One thing she was *not* however, was an especially good student, and in fact was in imminent danger of facing academic probation. Cara offered to help her study, and in return for the tutoring Mirai frequently treated her to lunch or dinner or a movie.

As their friendship deepened, Cara began to spend more and more time at the off-campus apartment that Mirai's father had rented for her, and eventually was there far more often than she was in her own dorm room. It was only a one-bedroom place, but Cara vastly preferred sleeping on the sofa than she did in the uncomfortable dormitory bunk.

However, despite Cara's best efforts, Mirai simply couldn't pull her grades up enough to be able to return for her sophomore year. Mirai had been philosophical about the whole thing, admitting that she really didn't like school and had only agreed to attend Berkeley in the first place to please her father. She decided to take the summer and fall off from school until she could decide what she wanted to do, and made plans to travel – first to Japan and Hong Kong with her mother, and then to Europe and the East Coast with her father. There was more than a thirty year age gap between her parents, and Cara had learned that Mirai's mother was her husband's third wife. And while they were still officially married, her parents spent more time apart than together.

Mirai insisted that Cara stay on in the apartment over the summer since the lease didn't expire until the end of August, for which Cara was profoundly grateful. She worked three different part-time jobs over the summer to help with expenses, since Mark was complaining more than ever before about how much her education was costing him. He balked at paying for another year of on-campus housing, so Cara wound up living in a house with a whopping total of seven roommates. Cara's room wasn't even an official bedroom since there was no closet or window, and barely enough room to squeeze a narrow cot and a dresser inside. The house was a constant beehive of activity, with residents coming and going at all hours, and friends visiting daily. It was noisy and crowded and untidy, and Cara found herself doing most of her homework on campus in the library or a study hall.

Still, it was better than sharing a room with her nasty ex-roommates, and Cara was able to really devote herself to her studies. She had taken an extra class this year, in the hopes of getting her degree a little bit sooner and cutting back on expenses. Between attending classes, studying and doing assignments, and working two part-time jobs, she had zero time to socialize or date. But after the fiasco of her freshman year, she considered that a good thing.

It was Christmas when the next blow landed, and she was caught completely off-guard when it came. She had flown to Florida for the holidays – at her own expense since Mark had protested he couldn't afford the airfare – and had steeled herself to endure another week of being alternately ignored or glared at by Holly and her never-ending procession of relatives. And since her little half-brother Hunter was nearly a year old and almost walking, nearly all of Mark's attention was focused on his son. So it came as something of a surprise to Cara when, on the last day of her visit, her father took her out to lunch. But she all too quickly realized his purpose in doing so – to try and soften the blow his devastating news would have on her, as though a Cobb salad and glass of iced tea would somehow make up for it all.

Cara had stared at her father in disbelief. "Excuse me – I don't think I heard you right. What do you mean you can't pay for any more of my college fees? I still have two and a half years left, in case you forgot."

Mark had scowled, clearly uncomfortable with the conversation he was being forced to have. "I didn't forget," he replied sullenly. "But circumstances have changed, Cara. Holly hasn't been able to return to work since having Hunter because she's so exhausted, so we've been relying on one income to get by."

"So what does that have to do with my college expenses?" she'd asked. "I know for a fact that Mom set all of that money aside from what she inherited from Grandma. That money was always intended to pay for my college education, Dad. *Not* to pay for the diamond earrings you gave your wife for Christmas. Or the mani/pedis she told her sisters that she has every single week. Or the roomful of toys that Hunter has. That's *my* money, not theirs."

Mark's face had grown red with anger beneath his tan. "Wrong, sweetie. Your mother and I held everything in joint name, so when she died it all passed to me. So that's technically *my* money now. And I can do whatever I want with it."

Cara's eyes had filled with tears, her heart breaking with just one more betrayal from the father she had idolized as a girl. "Dad," she had whispered brokenly, "you promised Mom on her deathbed that you would always take care of me, that you would make sure you paid for my education. How could you do that to her? To me? The very last thing she asked of you."

He had had the good grace to look guilty at this accusation. "I realize what I promised both of you," he admitted grudgingly. "And I know you'll hate me for this, Cara. But I have a wife and a baby to look after now, and Holly wants to get pregnant again next year. Unfortunately, life doesn't always work out the way we want it to. Circumstances change, people change. I would hope you can understand that, be supportive and charitable."

"Charitable!" she had burst out. "Jesus, Dad. I live in a fucking closet. I work two part-time jobs. I have no money for clothes or to go to a movie or even buy a cup of coffee most days. I live on ramen noodles and peanut butter sandwiches, and I haven't been able to afford a hair cut for almost a year. Meanwhile, your *wife* is in there bragging about how much her Brazilian Blowout cost, and showing her mother the Jimmy Choo stilettos she bought for a bargain at the outlet stores – only four hundred dollars. Do you have any idea how hard I have to work to earn that much money? Or how much that amount would help me with expenses?"

Mark had waved a hand in dismissal. "Don't pay attention to everything Holly says," he'd instructed. "She tends to exaggerate at times."

"Whatever, Dad." Cara had blew out a frustrated breath. "So, tell me. Since you're apparently cutting me off – from the money that was promised to me, no less – how do you suggest I pay for tuition and books and my living expenses?"

"You're a smart girl, Cara. I'm sure you'll be able to get scholarships and grants easily," Mark had replied confidently. "Besides, I've already paid for the spring semester so you have plenty of time to figure this all out before next fall. And you're an adult now, after all. Time you were looking out for yourself and not depending on me to do it."

Cara had been so upset and angry that she hadn't been able to think of a reply, and had pushed the rest of her lunch away, her appetite long gone. She hadn't said a single word to her father for the rest of her visit, and given the smug, satisfied look on Holly's overly made-up face Cara knew that her bitchy stepmother had been behind all of this.

She hadn't wasted even a day upon her return to California in filling out applications for scholarships, loans, and grants, desperate to find enough funding to be able to continue her education the following school year. But no matter how hard she tried to juggle the numbers, she kept coming up short, leaving her no alternative but to work fulltime during the day and attend night school. She'd counted herself lucky to land the job working for Angela, who was not only a considerate boss but a generous one, too, who gave her occasional bonuses.

And while she had Mirai and a few other good friends, Cara had come to the realization more than two years ago that she was otherwise alone in the world. Contact with her father was practically nonexistent, and he'd cut off all support long ago. She worked hard, studied hard, and barely made ends meet most of the time. She couldn't remember the last time she had gone on a date, bought herself anything new prior to today's mini shopping spree courtesy of Mirai, or stopped worrying about how she was going to scrape together enough money for the next semester's tuition. But it would all be worth it one day, she kept telling herself, when she finally got her degree and fulfilled the promise she had made to her dying mother.

And, of course, there was also the extra added bonus of tomorrow night's date with the guy she'd been lusting after for the past six months. Maybe – just maybe – thought Cara, her luck was finally starting to turn.

6

Dante checked his watch for what was likely the tenth time in the past fifteen minutes, and wondered yet again what the hell he'd been thinking about yesterday morning when he'd made such an impulsive dinner date for this evening. When he had arrived at Nick's office to drop off the signed documents, he'd still been in a foul mood from the previous night – and nursing a bitch of a hangover to boot. Seeing Katie in living color on his TV screen, smiling and happy on the arm of another man, had set something off in him, and Dante hadn't recognized – or liked - that cold, angry part of himself. It hadn't helped matters in the least when he had given into temptation and entered Katie's name into a Google search on his computer. The results had yielded a good half dozen recent hits, all showing the beautiful, sexy blonde he had harbored hopes of making his wife out on the town with other men, the headlines of each article causing Dante's blood to boil – "Rand Dennison, star of the upcoming film *The War Room*, on the red carpet with starlet Katie Carlisle". "Alt-Rocker Magnus Kennedy at the Billboard Music Awards with new squeeze, actress Katie Carlisle". "Are Ramon Huerta and Katie Carlisle more than just co-stars? The cast members of the new series *Frenemies* looked awfully cozy at a recent dinner at Verlaine".

He might not know much about the entertainment industry, save for what he'd learned from Katie, but Dante was savvy enough to realize that these so-called dates and potential romances that the media loved to speculate about were most likely just photo ops and publicity stunts. But whether or not Katie had actually gone on a real date with any of these guys didn't matter. No, what made him furious - and caused him to keep reaching for the bottle of tequila – was the realization that the woman he'd thought of as the love of his life had given up everything he'd offered her for a shot at fame. Dante had been prepared to give her his name, his love, his lifelong devotion - his fucking *soul*, for Christ sakes - and she had tossed it all aside so that she could finally see her name and photo in the press. The hard truth had made him feel like a piece of crap, like the biggest loser ever, and, mostly, it had made him feel like a total fool.

It had also pissed him off to no man's end, and that anger had still been with him full force when he had woken yesterday morning, his fury only compounded by one of the nastier hangovers he could recall suffering from in recent years. And that rage only strengthened his resolve to ask out the first attractive female he encountered that day. Unfortunately, that female had turned out to be little Cara – the cute, perky admin assistant who worked for Nick – well, technically Angela. Asking her out to dinner tonight had been an impulse, an unwise one that had been triggered when he'd learned it was her birthday, and that instead of celebrating it by doing something fun she was attending some hair-raising class on derivative securities.

And it had been the revelation that Cara was pursuing a degree in finance, and from his own alma mater UC Berkeley to boot, that had caused Dante to suddenly look at her in a very different light, to realize that there was far more to her than he would have believed possible. He had always thought of her as slightly ditzy and more than a little naïve, and she'd reminded him of someone's semi-annoying little sister. He had been well aware that she had a little crush on him, something that had been rather obvious given the way she tended to stare at him wide-eyed or giggle nervously whenever he teased her. Dante had found her attraction to him oddly flattering, but he had been extremely careful never to take his lighthearted flirting any further. That had largely been due to his relationship with Katie and his commitment to her, but he had also refused to lead Cara – or any other woman – on when he'd been involved with someone else. Not to mention the fact, thought Dante wryly, that Nick would have thoroughly kicked his ass if he even suspected that anything was going on between Cara and his best friend. From offhand comments Nick had made from time to time, Dante knew that he was rather protective of Cara, as was Angela.

And neither of them would be happy to learn that he was taking Cara out to dinner tonight, even if his intentions were good ones. Dante had seriously considered cancelling the ill-advised date at least a handful of times today, going so far as to pick up the phone and start dialing the number for Nick's office. But then he'd recalled how thrilled Cara had looked yesterday morning at his invitation, how her enormous golden brown eyes had sparkled with delight, and how her infectious smile had instantly made him feel better about life in general. So he had reluctantly put the phone down, resolving to show her a good time tonight and coax a few more of those dazzling smiles from her. They'd have an enjoyable dinner – though at a discreet, out of the way place where there would be zero risk of running into Nick and Angela or anyone else he knew – some pleasant conversation, and then he would take her home and be on his way. He would keep things nice and casual during dinner, not giving Cara any false hopes that there would be a repeat of this evening, and then he would resume his search for a woman he could actually fuck and forget – because that woman sure as hell wasn't going to be sweet, perky, and too damned young Cara!

His phone buzzed with an incoming call, and he saw from the caller ID that it was Cara. Dante hesitated for a brief moment, realizing that this was his last chance to back out of a date he should have never made in the first place. But when he heard her happy, animated voice on the other end, he lost his nerve, knowing he couldn't ruin this for her.

"Hi, it's me," she trilled cheerfully. "Cara, that is."

Dante chuckled. "Yeah, I know. Does this mean you're on your way?"

"I'm about two blocks from your office building, so I should be there in less than five minutes. Should I wait for you in the lobby or would you rather I came upstairs to your office?"

He shuddered to imagine the ribbing he would take from his business partner if Howie was to catch a glimpse of Cara. Howie was not only something of a practical joker, but he fancied himself a would-be comedian as well. Dante wouldn't put it past him to ask Cara for her ID to make sure she wasn't jailbait. Or make an even more distasteful comment.

"Nah, that's okay. I'll be downstairs waiting for you, and then we can go to dinner. I hope you like French food."

Cara sighed in bliss, a sound that was oddly arousing. "Love it," she assured him. "Actually, anything that isn't ramen noodles, PBJ, or dry cereal would be amazing, but French food sounds incredible."

Dante shuddered at the thought of having to survive on the sort of diet she'd just described. He was admittedly something of a food snob, having grown up in a family of cooks and restauranteurs, and even during his college years he'd shied away from the usual sort of junk foods most students subsisted on.

"Well, then I think you'll love the place I picked out tonight. I'll see you in a couple of minutes."

He put on his suit jacket and walked out of his spacious, lavishly appointed office. The venture capital firm that he co-owned was on the small side in terms of staffing, but Dante and Howie had both insisted on making sure the office decor shrieked class and money – a detail they had deemed essential in attracting high end clients.

Dante's assistant had already left for the day, and since it was a Friday the office was more or less deserted as he headed for the elevators. During the descent down to the lobby, he steeled himself anew to keep things as casual as possible tonight, to make it very clear to Cara that this was a one time thing, and that their dinner together wasn't even a real date.

But all of his good intentions got shot to hell real quick when he got his first look at her as she waited for him in the lobby. The girl – correction, *woman* – who hovered somewhat nervously near the front doors bore little resemblance to the Cara he'd seen at Nick's office over these past few months. That Cara had looked even younger than her twenty-two years, like a fresh-faced high school student, and he couldn't truthfully recall what she'd been wearing yesterday except perhaps that it had been black and white.

The young woman who waited anxiously for him to arrive now was stunning – there was really no other word for it. And Dante knew he'd remember quite well what she was wearing this evening, perhaps for months to come.

The red dress hugged her lush curves closely without being too tight or revealing. The vivid color was perfect for her skin tone, and the style of the garment gave the illusion that she was a little taller than she actually was. She'd taken some pains with her makeup, so that those twinkling golden brown eyes looked enormous in her small, heart-shaped face, and her full-lipped mouth with its defined cupid's bow was glossed over in vivid scarlet. Her dark brown hair fell in tousled waves over her shoulders and more than halfway down her back, the sheer volume of it nearly overwhelming her petite frame.

For the first time since meeting her six months ago, he thought of her as a full grown woman, and not someone who'd barely left her teenaged years behind. And not just any woman, but a sexy, sultry one who reminded him of a young Sophia Loren, calling to mind the old Italian movies he'd once watched with his grandparents as a child.

Cara glanced up and met his eyes at that particular moment, and the smile on her face froze in place momentarily when she noticed the way he was staring at her. It was only when he smiled at her reassuringly that she seemed to relax, and the familiar sparkle returned to her eyes as he began to walk her way.

He took her hand in his, surprised to realize how small it looked clasped in his much larger one, and also to notice that she was trembling a little. And she gasped out loud when he brought that same hand to his lips and pressed a light kiss to her knuckles.

"Hey, gorgeous," he greeted with a mischievous grin. "I barely recognized you. This isn't your usual office attire, after all."

Cara's cheeks flushed becomingly. "Um, no, that's for sure. And you aren't the only one who noticed. For example, Nick asked me who my hot date was with tonight. I, ah, told him it was with someone I met at school."

Dante nodded in approval. "Good move. Because the last thing I need is for Nick to kick my ass. Which he would threaten to do in a heartbeat if he knew I was taking you out to dinner to night."

Cara pressed her lips together, and pretended to run a zipper across them. "Sealed tight," she declared. "Besides, I really doubt Nick would care that much. He barely says more than a few words to me at a time. And," she added confidently, "you definitely look like you could hold your own with him."

She rested her free hand on his bicep, and for some reason that light touch felt electric. To mask his reaction, he gave a shake of his head. "I wouldn't even want to try," he admitted. "I mean, I work out a lot, but Nick's like an animal in the gym. He's the one wearing his personal trainer out instead of the other way around. And even though he's getting close to forty years old, he's in good enough shape to still be playing pro football today. So, thanks for the vote of confidence, honey, but I'm pretty sure I'd get my ass kicked by lean, mean Nick Manning. Now, enough about your asshat boss. I don't know about you but I'm starving. Let's head down to the garage and get my car, hmm?"

He steered her towards the elevator with a light hand on her back, belatedly realizing that even with heels on the top of her dark head barely reached his shoulder, giving him close to a full foot in height advantage. That knowledge pleased him in an odd sort of way – odd because he nearly always dated women who were of at least medium height or taller. Katie, for example, had only been about three inches shorter than his own height of six foot two, and with the stilettos that she had been so fond of wearing she'd often topped him by an inch or so. Cara's petite stature instinctively made him feel protective of her, and, in some bizarre, unexplainable way, also made him feel more – well, *manly*.

Dante unlocked the passenger door to the car he was driving today, one of an even dozen vehicles he owned, and held it open for Cara. She was staring at the dark silver gray car, touching her hand almost reverently to the hood.

"You drive an – an Aston Martin?" she asked in disbelief. "Wow. I didn't think anyone but James Bond actually owned a car like this."

He chuckled as he assisted her inside. "Well, this is a newer model than the one 007 typically drives in movies – the Vanquish. It's the most recent addition to my car collection."

As he drove halfway across the city to their destination, Dante told her about his longtime fascination with cars – a fascination that had started during his boyhood when he'd hung out at his maternal grandfather's automotive repair shop. He confessed to having something of an obsession with cars, to the point where he had actually had a special garage custom built on his mother's property to house the bulk of his collection.

"I have three parking spaces allotted to me at my condo building," he told her. "I keep the rest of the cars up in Healdsburg. And since I try to visit my family every weekend I rotate vehicles each time I'm up there."

"Wow." Cara looked a bit dazed at this information. "Are all of your cars this awesome?"

He shrugged. "Depends on your definition of awesome, I suppose. Most of them are considered high end, but I also own a few classic cars. Including my Dad's Camaro, one of the most popular of the old muscle cars. Though if I had to pick a favorite out of all of them, I'd have to go with my 1963 Corvette Stingray. That was the only year they made it with a split-back window. It took me about five years to track one down and then another three to restore it. But it was well worth it. That car's my pride and joy, though I don't drive it very often."

As the drive continued, Cara seemed to hang on his every word, though he was willing to bet she knew next to nothing about cars. Still, it was flattering as hell to have her undivided attention, something he wasn't always used to getting from his dates over the years. In his experience with women – which was both extensive and varied – Dante had often found that the majority of them tried to keep the conversation focused solely on themselves. They expected him to be totally interested in every aspect of their lives, to want to know everything about them, but seldom reciprocated by asking him about himself. Unlike Cara, who gave the impression of being more than content to let him control the conversation.

She looked around curiously when they arrived at their destination - a cozy French bistro named Chou Chou, located in a largely residential neighborhood. "Where are we exactly?" she asked as he assisted her out of the car. "I mean, I know we're still in San Francisco but I have no idea what part."

Dante locked the door and made sure the alarm system was set. "It's called Forest Hill," he told her. "A little out of the way, and I'm not surprised you aren't familiar with this area since it's not exactly trendy. But I think you'll like this place. The food is out of this world, and it's very charming inside. You'll see."

What he didn't add, of course, was the fact that the bistro was so far out of the way that none of his acquaintances would be likely to see him here. And once inside the admittedly appealingly decorated restaurant, Cara's face lit up with pleasure.

"Oh, it's so pretty!" she exclaimed, her small hand drifting up to clutch his upper arm. "Just like what I'd imagine a little Parisian bistro to look like."

The interior of the place was small and intimate, with brightly painted walls, patterned carpet, and wooden tables covered in pale pink linens. Dante had only dined here once before, to have a quick lunch with a client who lived in the neighborhood, but he'd been sure that Cara would like it. He was pleased to see that his instincts had been right.

"I'm afraid they don't have a full liquor license here, just wine and beer," Dante advised after they had been shown to their table. "I hope that's okay."

Cara nodded. "It's fine. I probably shouldn't be drinking much anyway."

He grinned teasingly. "Why? Are you the sort who has one glass of wine and starts dancing on tabletops?"

She laughed in response. "It would take most of a bottle before I was that far gone! Not that I haven't experienced a few ugly hangovers, of course, but not since freshman year. I figured out pretty early that partying wasn't really my thing. No, the reason I shouldn't have too much to drink is because of the calories. Empty ones at that. If I'm going to splurge a little tonight I'd rather it be on food."

Dante waved a hand in dismissal. "Hey, it's your birthday, don't forget. You can have a few glasses of wine plus a delicious dinner *and* dessert. Why do you think you need to be counting calories anyway?"

Cara rolled her eyes before patting herself on her shapely ass. "You're joking, right? Or just being nice because it's my birthday. I'm a good twenty pounds overweight, maybe more since I've been terrified to get on a scale for months."

"Who says you're overweight?" he challenged. "I guarantee that no one in my family would think something like that. In fact, my grandmother would probably say you were too skinny and insist you ate an entire plate of her homemade linguine with pesto sauce - for starters."

"Pasta with pesto. God, that sounds amazing!" she groaned, licking those full, scarlet glossed lips as though she could actually taste the food. "I hardly ever eat pasta anymore because it's so fattening, but linguine with pesto is one of my favorites."

Astonishingly, Dante felt his cock harden just from the sight of her licking her lips. He guessed that Cara was totally unaware of how naturally sensual she was, or how expressive her eyes and mouth could be. And he was pretty damned sure she had no idea that her nipples were hard, or that the fabric of that sexy red dress was molding itself to the lush curves of her full breasts. Hastily, he took a long gulp of his water, and wondered what was taking the waiter so damned long to bring the bottle of champagne he'd ordered.

"If I'd known you loved pasta so much I would have chosen an Italian restaurant instead," he lamented, willing himself not to stare at her cleavage.

She shook her head, causing her glossy dark brown curls to tumble over her shoulders. "Oh, no. This place is perfect, really. And I can make Italian food for myself anytime I want to. Well, within limits, of course, given that I don't have an actual stove in my apartment. Just a cooktop. But you'd be surprised at what you can make using just a skillet or a pot."

He frowned in concern. "Why don't you have a stove? A dishwasher I could maybe understand, considering how old some of the buildings in this city are, but a stove is a fairly basic appliance."

Cara looked distinctly uncomfortable at his question. "It's, well, just a really small apartment. An in-law unit, actually. An *illegal* unit," she confessed in a whisper, looking around her anxiously to make sure no one overheard.

Dante laughed, his good humor restored. "Your secret is safe with me. And I know exactly how many different dishes you can make on a stovetop. My family owns one of the oldest and best known Italian restaurants in northern California, and I've spent an awful lot of time there, both in the kitchen and out."

The waiter arrived just then with the champagne - the most expensive bottle the bistro offered. He filled two flutes before handing them dinner menus, and reciting the two specials of the evening.

Dante had noticed Cara eyeing the bread basket discreetly more than once, and as soon as their waiter left he held it up to her.

"Come on. Take a piece. And don't even think about the calories. Or those so-called twenty pounds you absolutely *don't* have to lose. You can't truthfully call yourself an Italian if you don't eat bread and pasta. That's what my grandmother always tells anyone who'll listen to her."

Cara laughed and carefully took the smallest slice of bread from the basket. "I'm actually only half-Italian," she admitted. "On my father's side. My mom was of Irish and Scottish descent mostly."

"Was?" inquired Dante as he spread butter over his bread, giving her a mock scowl when she refused the butter.

Cara took a small nibble of her bread and nodded. "She's been gone four years now. She died just a few days before my eighteenth birthday, on the night of my senior prom. Pancreatic cancer. By the time the doctors diagnosed her it was already too late."

"I'm so sorry." He reached across the table and took her hand in his, giving it a comforting squeeze. "I know what it's like to lose a parent. My father died when I was only eleven. He was a firefighter, lost his life in the line of duty."

She gasped, and squeezed his hand back. "Oh, God, how awful! You were just a kid when it happened! At least I had a few more years with my mother. Is your mom still living?"

"Yes. Along with my younger brother and two sisters. I'm the oldest. Plus we have too many aunts and uncles and cousins to count any longer, and my grandmother, who's more than likely going to live until she's a hundred or even older. What about you - do you have a big family?"

It was almost as if the light in her expressive eyes had been snuffed out at this question, and an expression of such utter sadness crossed her face that it made his heart ache a little.

"No," was all she said in response. "Just my dad, and he's not one to keep in touch very often."

Dante was oddly incensed to learn that her father had remarried within mere months after losing his wife, and that his new bride had been pregnant at the time. The newly married couple had moved clear across the country to Florida, and now had two very young children. He could easily read between the lines, and determined that Cara's father had more or less pushed her out of his life so that he could focus on the new life he'd made for himself, and on the new family he now had.

But he could also sense that it was a very upsetting topic for Cara to talk about, so he quickly changed the subject. The waiter arrived to take their order, and before she could protest he ordered several courses for them - appetizer, salad, soup, entrée - and merely grinned at her when she protested that it was way too much food.

"As I recall, they serve small portions here," he assured her. "At least compared to what we dish out at my family's restaurant. Besides,

I'll remind you once again that it's your birthday, so indulge yourself for once, hmm?"

Cara sighed in resignation, reaching for a second slice of bread. "Okay. I guess for one night it won't hurt. I'll starve myself for the next week to make up for it."

"Hey, knock it off, okay?" Dante scolded her. "You do *not* need to starve yourself. Or lose anywhere near twenty pounds. I think you look great just the way you are. Especially in that dress. It, ah, shows off all your best assets."

She blushed profusely at his very pointed comment, especially when his eyes dropped to her breasts. Her tits really were spectacular, he thought as he took a slow sip of champagne - full and high and temptingly round. He wondered if her skin was that same pale olive tone all over, and if her breasts and belly and ass felt as soft as her hand had done when clasped in his a few minutes ago.

It was the arrival of the appetizer course - beef tartare for him and smoked salmon for her - that put an abrupt halt to Dante's lecherous imaginings. And reminded him that he was absolutely *not* supposed to have such thoughts about the young woman seated across from him. This was strictly a friendly, casual dinner, and not to be construed in any way, shape, or form as an official date. They would enjoy a nice meal, finish off the bottle of champagne, and then he would bring her home and that would be the end of it. After tonight Cara would simply be one of the assistants who worked for his friend Nick and his girlfriend/business partner Angela. He would see her once or twice a month when he stopped by the office to see Nick, they would exchange pleasantries, and there would be no more dates that weren't really dates. He'd start hitting up the clubs and bars and other hangouts where single, beautiful, and willing women were plentiful, and he would *not* have inappropriately lecherous thoughts about the female he'd always thought of as a young, innocent girl until this evening.

He kept the conversation light and somewhat impersonal after that, asking about her classes and the sort of career path she had in mind after getting her degree. He was both surprised and delighted to discover she was incredibly bright, highly intelligent, and had a keen financial mind. Most of the women he'd dated in the past had little to no idea about what it was he did for a living, and even less desire to discuss the stock market or financial futures over dinner.

And when the champagne loosened her tongue a little, he discovered that the reason she'd had to stop attending school full time and take night classes instead was because her asshole of a father had reneged on the promise he'd made to his late wife – on her deathbed no less. Dante, who came from the sort of family who always looked out for each other, was silently appalled that a father could treat his own daughter so callously, all to please his new and no doubt trampy young wife.

But, once more, he could tell that the subject matter was making Cara sad, so he quickly ordered coffee and dessert before she could offer up a protest about how many more calories she was going to have to work off to compensate.

"Mmm. Oh, God, this is *sooo* good!" moaned Cara in near-bliss as she swallowed a bite of the apple tart she'd selected for dessert. She licked her fork slowly, savoring each crumb, and Dante was instantly aroused yet again. The women he'd dated in the past had typically pushed their food around in their plate, taking a few slow, reluctant bites. None of them had ever made the simple act of eating quite so – well, erotic.

To distract himself from the uncomfortable budge at his crotch, Dante poured what remained of the champagne into Cara's flute. He'd actually had very little to drink this evening, mindful that he was driving, and she had consumed more than half of the bottle. She was a bit tipsy as a result, giggling frequently and chattering away even more than she usually did, but he found her talkativeness oddly endearing. Cara was spontaneous, honest, and amusing, and her down-to-earth manner was a refreshing change of pace.

The extra alcohol, however, also made her slightly unsteady as they walked out to his car, and he was obliged to slide an arm around her waist to keep her from wobbling. He forced himself not to stiffen in reaction - in any part of his anatomy - when Cara wrapped her own arms around him, resting her head on his shoulder with an almost easy air of intimacy. He cursed himself now for re-filling her glass so frequently, and gingerly eased her onto the passenger seat of the Vanquish.

After giving him her address, she closed her eyes and appeared to doze lightly during the drive. Dante was grateful for the sophisticated navigation system built into the Aston Martin, since the neighborhoods it directed him through were largely unfamiliar to him. He frowned as the houses began to look a bit more rundown, the residents appeared a little rougher, the sidewalks more littered with trash.

Fortunately, the house he pulled up to looked in reasonably good condition, even if there were metal bars on the windows and no visible landscaping. The in-law unit where Cara lived was accessed via a side entrance, one that didn't have any sort of outdoor lighting.

"Watch your head," she cautioned as she unlocked the door and flicked on a light switch inside the unit. "The doorway's a little low."

That, thought Dante as he stepped across the threshold, was far from the only downside of the apartment that was technically just a room. It had a faint but still discernible musty odor, carpeting that had to be close to fifty years old, and was so small that he couldn't believe anyone actually lived here. He noticed that she didn't have much furniture, and that the few pieces she did own were well worn and mismatched. The paint was peeling off the walls in several places, and even in the dim light he could see the water spots on the ceiling.

Cara seemed well aware of how small and shabby the place was, but tried to make light of the situation, her arm making a sweeping motion to encompass the room.

"Well, this is it," she declared in a falsely bright voice. "Home sweet home. It's not much, I'll admit, but the rent is affordable and the bus stop is only two blocks away. Would you like a cup of coffee? Or tea?"

Dante glanced at the rickety chairs that flanked a small, round table, and wondered if they would be able to support his solidly muscled hundred and eighty pound frame.

"I'll pass, thanks. And I should head out, let you get some rest. You did mention having to do homework this weekend."

Cara groaned. "God, don't remind me! This has been the toughest semester ever. If I can just get through the next two months, I think anything after that will seem easy."

"You're going to do fine," he assured her. "I swear you know way more about finance and investing than I did at this point in my life. Angela had better be careful that I don't try and hire you away from her."

She giggled, swaying a little on her three-inch heels as she did so, and placed a hand against his chest to steady herself. His own hands drifted to her waist to hold her in place.

"Easy there, honey," he cautioned. "Maybe you should make yourself that coffee you just offered me."

Cara shook her head. "I'm not drunk. Just a little tipsy. But only because it's my birthday."

He chucked her playfully on the chin. "Well, you deserved to enjoy your birthday. At least, I hope you enjoyed it."

"Oh, yes!" she exclaimed happily, her hands now sliding to his shoulders. "I had a wonderful time! Thank you for dinner, it was delicious. Even if I gain another pound or two as a result."

And then she took him by complete surprise by leaning in and placing a soft, sweet kiss on his cheek. Her breasts brushed against his chest, and he had to bite down on the inside of his cheek to stifle a groan as he felt the hard points of her nipples graze the fabric of his shirt. Somehow or other her arms were now clasped around his neck, and she was gazing up at him with a sultry promise in those big eyes, her full lips parted as she breathed a bit unevenly.

"Cara," he began to protest, the warning bells in his head cautioning him to move away – *now* - before things got carried away.

But as she touched her mouth to his - tentatively, almost shyly - Dante growled deep in his throat and yanked her close. And as the kiss deepened, and quickly, very quickly, became something else entirely, he forgot all of the good intentions he'd begun this evening with, and instead wondered wildly how quickly he could peel her out of the sexy red dress.

7

Cara whimpered beneath the fierce pressure of Dante's hot, firm mouth upon hers, his tongue parting her lips smoothly and invading the inside of her mouth. He pressed her up against the narrow wall that separated the bathroom and the closet, his tall, muscular body trapping her in place. Not, of course, that she had any intention of trying to escape his arms – especially since this was exactly where she'd dreamed of being for months now.

She had wanted this, craved this, since the very first time she'd seen the gorgeous, dark-haired man stroll casually past her desk on his way to visit Nick. She'd daydreamed about him taking her out on a date much like tonight's, had fantasized about him kissing and caressing her just like he was doing now, had tried to imagine what it would feel like to be naked in bed with him, their limbs closely entwined, and his cock buried inside of her all-too-willing body. Her arms were wrapped tightly around his neck, pulling him in closer, and she felt surrounded by him – his big, hard body pressing her against the wall, his hands roaming freely over her body. His skin was hot to the touch, and his scent – a combination of soap, a light cologne, and his own unique essence – was the most deliciously arousing fragrance she'd ever smelled.

"Ah, God," she gasped as one of his hands cupped her swollen, achy breast, his thumb brushing over the ultra-sensitive nipple. "Yes, please, please!"

The sound that escaped Dante's throat sounded a lot like a growl, and he responded to her breathless pleas by squeezing her breast more aggressively. He captured her lips in another hungry kiss, even as he began to rock his hips against the notch of her thighs, letting her feel the hard, huge bulge of his erection. Cara was lightheaded, dizzy even, from his demanding kisses, and she realized faintly that this was the first time in her life that she'd been kissed by a *man*. The high school and college boys whom she had kissed had all been rank amateurs when compared to Dante's finesse, which had undoubtedly been honed from years and years of experience.

"Let me see you," he rasped in her ear, his hands deftly lowering the zipper of her dress.

The top half of the dress spilled from her shoulders and was caught up just below the hips, baring her upper body to his hot gaze. Cara gasped as he deliberately trailed a finger along the exposed curves of her breast, and she offered up a silent prayer of thanks that she'd followed Mirai's advice and bought new undies.

"God, your tits are gorgeous," whispered Dante, just before bending his dark head to press a kiss to the top of her cleavage. "And I love a woman in black lace. Though not quite as much as I enjoy taking it off of her."

He made quick work of the sexy black lace bra, unhooking it before tossing it aside, and then cupping both of her full, round breasts in his big hands. Cara's head fell back limply against the wall, and her breathing grew even more erratic as his tongue flicked over one of her nipples. As if of their own volition, her hands slid into his hair, holding his head to her breasts as he sucked first one and then the other nipple between his lips. With one hand he pushed her dress down past her hips to pool at her feet, revealing the lower half of her body now as well.

She was too aroused, too dazed by his kisses and caresses, to be self-conscious about her less than flat belly, or slightly chubby thighs, or all of the other figure flaws she normally fretted about. It was obvious that he was really, really good at this, that he knew exactly how and where to touch her, and how to bring her right to the edge without much effort on his part. But when his hand slid down to cup her vulva through her panties, he seemed startled.

"Jesus, you're so wet, honey," he murmured in her ear, sliding his hand inside the black lace undies that matched the already discarded bra. "So sweet. I'll bet you're nice and tight, too, aren't you?"

"Ohhh." Cara's pelvis bucked up against his body as he slid his index and middle fingers inside of her drenched slit. She couldn't remember ever being this aroused, this wet, and she grasped his muscular forearms for support as he began to thrust his fingers in and out of her vagina.

"Tight as a fist," Dante purred. "Just like I thought. I can't wait to see how this snug little pussy is going to feel clamped around my cock. But since it's your birthday, let me make you feel good first, hmm?"

It was on the tip of her tongue to confess that he'd been already been making her feel very, *very* good. But when his thumb brushed knowingly over the hard nub of her clitoris, the only sound that escaped her lips was a long, low moan, followed by a startled gasp as the orgasm took over her body. He wrapped an arm around her waist, holding her up as her legs shook in reaction, and then pressed a kiss to her flushed cheek.

"Easy, honey," he soothed, shaking his head as if in disbelief. "Man, you're a hot little thing, aren't you? I barely touched you and you just went off. Wait until I have you in bed. Where is it, by the way?"

"Huh?" Cara wondered dazedly if she looked as out of it as she felt. It had been a really long time since she'd had any sort of orgasm – much less a really, really good one like she'd just experienced. "Where's what?"

Dante chuckled. "Your bed, honey. This wall isn't exactly wide enough – or strong enough – for the way I'm planning to fuck you. We need to get horizontal – and quickly. It's been awhile since I've been with anyone, and, well, you can feel for yourself how much I need to be inside of you."

He grabbed her hand and brought it to his crotch, where his erection was visibly straining against the fabric of his suit pants. Awestruck by the sheer size of him, Cara ran her palm up and down the thick length of his cock, pleased to hear the indrawn hiss of his breath as she gave him a little squeeze.

"Temptress," he growled, clamping his fingers around her wrist and stilling the motion. "Enough of that or I'll take you right here against the wall. So I strongly suggest we head to your bedroom pronto."

"Um, about that." She glanced to her left uncertainly. "There – there isn't a bedroom. Or a bed. At least, not a real bed. I mean, it's a bed, but more like a futon."

"A futon." Dante closed his eyes a moment and shook his head. "For God's sake. Seriously?"

"I'm sorry," replied Cara meekly. "But it's actually really comfy. And it will just take me a minute or two to open it up."

Before he could protest, she hurried over to the aforementioned futon, so intent on her task that she completely forgot she was more or less naked save for the lacy panties and her high heeled sandals. She converted the futon from sofa to bed in record time before stretching out on top of the fabric covered mattress and patting the space beside her.

"There. All done," she announced cheerfully. "Told you it would only take a minute."

But Dante didn't reply, merely raked his hot gaze over her prone body, seeming to linger on the heavy swell of her breasts. She gulped when their eyes met, almost recoiling at the lustful expression on his sinfully handsome face. He continued to hold her gaze captive as he undressed, his movements swift but unhurried at the same time, and Cara's mouth watered as more and more of his bare flesh was revealed.

His male body was beautiful – a true work of art, she thought dazedly as he peeled off his suit jacket, tie, and shirt in quick succession. His chest, shoulders, and arms were heavily muscled and well defined, visible evidence that he worked out frequently. His abs were rock hard, and looked like they'd been chiseled from a slab of marble. His skin was the same dark olive tone as his face, his body hair as black as that on top of his head.

He made quick work of the rest of his clothing, until he was clad only in a pair of gray cotton briefs. As he picked up his suit jacket to retrieve something from the inside pocket, Cara's eyes were glued to the massive swell of his penis where it strained to be free of the tight, confining underwear. She couldn't suppress the little whimper that escaped her lips when he discarded his final article of clothing, baring his magnificent body entirely to her hungry gaze, and especially that rather intimidating cock.

Dante eased himself onto the mattress gingerly, as though to test the sturdiness of the futon, before pulling her into his embrace and re-claiming her lips. She instantly forgot any uncertainty she might otherwise have felt at her relative inexperience with sex, and for once didn't think to feel embarrassed about her less than ideal body. Especially not when the hot, hunky guy beside her on the mattress didn't seem to give a hoot that her butt was on the generous side, or that she had a definite Buddha belly.

Dante's hands were roaming all over her body – cupping her breasts, squeezing her ass, tunneling into her hair to hold her head still for his kiss. Their legs were entwined, her boobs all but crushed against his chest, as she somewhat timidly began to touch him in return. His skin was so hot that she nearly jerked her hand away in reaction, but Cara found it impossible to resist caressing the broad expanse of his upper back, those beautifully defined biceps, or those sculpted abs that could have belonged to a Greek god – or, in his case, a Roman one.

He eased her onto her back, rising above her almost intimidatingly as he spread her thighs apart. The veins in his fully erect penis were visibly throbbing by now, his need for her more than obvious. Cara licked her lips, wondering briefly how he would feel in her mouth, or just how deep she could take him. Her skills at performing oral sex weren't exactly top notch, at least according to one of the guys she'd unwisely hooked up with after a drunken college party, but she sensed that Dante wouldn't give a damn about how experienced she was. Once again she was reminded that he was a man, not a boy, and not just any man. He was handsome, well built, charming, sexy, considerate, and a really, really amazing kisser. And as he rolled a condom with practiced ease onto his cock, Cara shivered in anticipation of what a fantastic lover he was sure to be.

Dante continued to rest on his haunches as he gazed down at her, then slowly trailed a single fingertip down between her breasts. "You are so fucking sexy," he told her, his voice husky with lust. "Except that you're still wearing too many clothes. These will definitely get in the way."

She sucked in a breath as he worked the lacy black panties down over her legs until they landed on the floor. He made quick work of unbuckling her high heeled sandals, then took an extra moment or two to give her right foot a little squeeze.

"You have such tiny little feet," he mused. "You know what they say about a man's shoe size being equal to the size of his dick? I always wondered if the same was true for a woman. Let's find out, hmm?"

He took hold of his straining cock and placed the tip at the opening of her body, then eased himself inside a little at a time. Cara gasped with each gradual thrust, wondering dizzily how much more she could possibly take, glancing down to where their bodies were joined worriedly.

"Easy, honey," he soothed, his hand rubbing her hip reassuringly. "Has it been awhile for you?"

She nodded, closing her eyes in embarrassment that he could tell how inexperienced she was. "Uh, huh. Al-almost two years."

"Shh." Dante leaned over her, his bare chest pressed flush against her breasts as he kissed her cheek tenderly. "Then I'll go easy this first time, okay? Even though what I really want is to fuck you until you're screaming my name at the top of your lungs." He cupped her breast, brushing his thumb over the nipple. "But considering how tight you feel, and how long it's been for you, that will have to wait for the next time. Easy now, hmm?"

"Ahhh!"

Cara dug her fingernails into the futon mattress, her hips lifting off the bed as he thrust deeper this time, until he was buried snugly inside her tight, wet pussy. It had, in fact, been such a long time since she'd had sex that it seemed her body had all but forgotten what it felt like. And she'd never, ever, had a partner as well endowed as Dante, never had sex with someone who obviously knew *exactly* what he was doing.

She willingly let him take charge, let him lift one then the other leg to wrap around his hips, a movement that only intensified the sensations he was coaxing from her body. For a short while he levered himself up over her prone form, his hands braced on either side of her as he fucked her with slow, deep thrusts, staring down at her the entire time and compelling her to maintain eye contact. And then he lowered himself until their bare skin connected, the coarseness of his chest hair abrading her sensitive nipples, as the force and rapidity of his thrusts increased. The last coherent thought Cara could summon up before he took her over the edge was that if this was what he considered "going easy" on her, she wasn't at all sure she'd be able to handle anything more intense.

And then any sort of thinking was off the table as she felt the unfamiliar approach of her climax – unfamiliar because she'd never been able to orgasm vaginally before, only through the stimulation of a hand and/or tongue. It was far, far more intense this way, touching every nerve ending in her body, and causing her toes to curl up in reaction at the same moment his name escaped her lips. It wasn't the scream he'd wanted, barely more than a whisper, but Dante seemed more than satisfied with her response.

"Cara *bella*," he murmured hoarsely in her ear, his big body still thrusting into hers as he prolonged his own release. "Cara *mia*. So sweet, so responsive. So lovely."

She clutched his shoulders as the spasms continued to reverberate through her body, pressing a kiss to the side of his neck as she did so.

That small, innocent gesture, however, proved to be all Dante needed to climax himself, and he was nowhere near as quiet as she'd been. The somewhat rickety futon frame shook with the power of his release, his big body shuddering almost violently as he came, his dark head thrown back as he shouted out incoherent words. Cara peeked up at him and couldn't suppress a gasp at how magnificent he looked this way, how primitive and male – the muscles in his arms and abs contracting, the fine layer of sweat that covered his chest and face, his dark hair curling damply around his beautiful face. Instinctively, she cupped his cheek, silently offering him solace, and he emitted a long, low groan as he claimed her swollen lips yet again in a deep, almost savage kiss.

He collapsed onto the mattress next to her, breathing heavily, one sinewy arm draped over her torso as if to hold her in place.

'Like I'd want to actually move anytime soon,' she thought dreamily. 'Or ever, for that matter.'

She rested her head on his shoulder, not quite able to believe that it was actually *Dante* beside her – the guy she'd been crushing on and fantasizing about for more than six months. Cara had an admitted weakness for hot guys, had been gullible and naïve in the past when it came to her choice in men, but she knew somehow that Dante was different from any other guy she'd ever met. And it wasn't just because he was older, more sophisticated, more experienced. No, it was simply because he was a genuinely nice guy, someone who treated women with respect and consideration, and who cared about the feelings of others. And even if he'd only taken her out to dinner tonight – and to bed afterwards – because he felt sorry for her spending her birthday alone – well, Cara didn't really care very much. Because if she was only to have this one night with him, what a night it had turned out to be! This night had far surpassed any expectations she might have harbored, never having anticipated that Dante might actually be physically attracted to her. It was, she thought dreamily, the best birthday present *ever*!

Dante lifted his head from the mattress with a groan before pressing a kiss to her shoulder and smoothing the long, tumbled mass of her hair off her neck. "Hey," he murmured, smiling at her gently. "You doing okay there, honey?"

Cara smiled back at him. "Oh, yeah. Way more than okay. That was – beyond words, you know? Which considering how much I can babble at times is pretty rare for me."

He laughed. "I don't mind your babbling, as you call it," he assured her. "I told you before I like the fact that you're so open and honest. Don't ever stop doing that, okay? You have no idea how refreshing it is to know someone who doesn't play dumb emotional games or pretends to be something they aren't."

She nodded. "I promise. Mostly because I've never been very good at playing any sort of games – emotional or otherwise. My dad was disappointed when I proved to be a total klutz at soccer and too short to play basketball and decided to take ballet and tap classes instead."

Dante scowled. "The more I hear about this father of yours the less I like him. So we should probably stop talking about him. Be right back, okay?"

He dropped a kiss on her forehead before easing himself off the futon and heading in the direction of the bathroom. Cara could hear sounds of running water, and shivered a little without either bedcovers or Dante's body heat. Belatedly she became aware of the fact that she was stark naked, with all of her "jiggly bits" on full display, and was thankful for the dim lighting of the room. She sat up, pulling her knees to her chest, and then wrapping her arms around her shins. This position wouldn't hide everything, but it helped.

Dante strode out of the bathroom, having disposed of the condom, and walked over to the futon proudly naked. Cara's mouth watered at the sight he made – all hard, rippling muscle, smooth olive skin, and chiseled features. She still couldn't quite believe that someone as gorgeous and hunky and hot as he was had just made love to her so thoroughly and with such passion. She knew without being told that Dante could have most any woman he set his sights on, that women would flock to him without the slightest bit of encouragement. And out of the countless number of women in this city he could have had sex with tonight, for some baffling reason he'd chosen *her* – naïve, geeky, and insecure Cara with her ever increasing list of body flaws and other shortcomings. It was only the unfamiliar soreness of her private parts that served as confirmation that it had, in fact, been *her* that Dante had chosen as his lover this evening.

He sat down on the mattress beside her, this time tucking a long strand of hair behind her ear.

"I should be going," he told her gently. "It's late, and I'm pretty sure I wore you out a little while ago."

She unsuccessfully stifled a yawn. "Um, maybe a little," she admitted. "But I don't mind in the least. It's, well, a good tired, you know?"

Dante grinned wickedly. "Yeah, I do know. In fact, it was so good that I think we ought to do it again. Not," he added, holding up a hand, "tonight, however. I could tell it's been awhile for you, honey, and even though I went easy you're probably going to be a little sore. Besides, I didn't exactly plan on this happening, and only had the one condom. But I would like to see you again. Tomorrow night, in fact, if you're free."

Cara gaped at him in astonishment. "T-tomorrow? Really? I didn't think you'd want to – I mean, yes, yes, of course I'm free! I'd love to see you again tomorrow night."

He tapped her playfully on the bridge of her nose. "There's that honesty I like so much again. The more time I spend around you the more I'm convinced that you wouldn't know how to be anything but completely open and spontaneous. So tell me – how does pizza and a movie sound?"

She wondered if her features looked as awestruck as she felt. "They sound great."

Dante stood and began to pull his clothes on. "Any particular movie you've been wanting to see?"

She shrugged, not wanting to admit how long it had been since she'd gone out to see a movie given that her meagre budget wouldn't stretch that far. "Not really. At least, I haven't looked to see what's out in the theaters right now. Was there something you had in mind?"

He looked a bit sheepish as he finished buttoning his shirt. "Uh, I don't suppose you like action flicks, do you? There's a new *Fast and the Furious* movie out that I've been wanting to see."

Cara clapped her hands in delight. "Oh, I love those movies! The car chase scenes are the best ever! I'd love to see that with you."

"Really?" he asked in disbelief. "You aren't just saying that, are you?"

She shook her head vehemently. "Nope. If I didn't like the idea I wouldn't say so."

Dante looked both relieved and pleased. "I'm not sure anyone I've ever dated before actually liked those sort of movies. As for the pizza, I know of a little family run place in North Beach that's the best I've ever had. It's something of a hole in the wall, so don't expect much."

"It sounds great," enthused Cara. "And I'm not fussy about where we go."

She didn't add that she would go anywhere with him, no matter how casual or inexpensive the place was, because being with him was the real motivation and not the sort of meal they would have.

He was fully dressed now, making her even more aware of her own nudity, but Dante seemed not to mind in the least.

"I'll see you tomorrow evening then," he told her. "I hope you had a good time tonight. I know I did. But do me one favor, hmm?"

Cara nodded. "Sure. What is it?"

He winked at her. "Make sure this thing is already opened up when I pick you up, okay?" He nudged the wooden futon frame with his foot, and she laughed as she nodded in understanding.

He bent and gave her a hard, swift kiss before letting himself out the door. Less than a minute later she heard his car engine start up as he drove away.

Any disappointment she might have felt that he hadn't stayed longer, or asked if he could stay the night, was allayed by the reminder that she would be seeing him again tomorrow evening. And that what had happened tonight was much more than just the best birthday ever – it was a dream come true.

8

Dante took a sip of the robust Chianti that he'd ordered to accompany their pizza - not that he'd had a lot to pick from since Pasquale's had a very limited wine list. He hadn't been exaggerating the previous evening when he'd told Cara that this place was a real hole in the wall. If anything, he might have been overly generous in describing it.

But judging from the animated expression on her face, Cara didn't seem to mind in the least. She'd gone along willingly with his suggestion about ordering red wine instead of a beer, and confessed somewhat sheepishly that she had more or less sworn off of beer after a few nasty hangovers during her first two years of college.

And his already favorable opinion of her had only soared when he discovered she liked the exact same pizza toppings he did - mushrooms, salami, and black olives. It seemed, in fact, that they had quite a lot in common, and liked many of the same things. And while it was possible that Cara was just pretending to share the same likes and interests as he did to please him, he truly didn't think so. She seemed too honest to fake it that way, too inexperienced, and simply too damned nice.

He frowned a little as he observed her across the small, well-worn wooden table as she munched on a slice of pizza. Dressed in jeans, a cotton sweater, and sneakers, her face mostly free of makeup, and her long hair pulled back into a thick ponytail, she looked a lot younger than she had the previous evening. And without heels on she was even more petite, the top of her head not quite reaching his shoulder.

Last night, with Cara all dressed up and looking far more sophisticated than usual, the age difference between them, as well as her fresh-faced innocence, hadn't bothered him so much. And her surprisingly passionate, uninhibited response to him physically had given him cause to think that perhaps she wasn't quite as naive and inexperienced as he had always assumed.

But this evening she was back to looking like the college student that she was - hell, maybe even a high school girl, he thought in revolt. Which gave him serious cause to start re-thinking the plans he'd begun to format earlier in the day.

He had never intended, of course, for things to go as far as they had last night. After driving her home after dinner, he had only meant to bid her good night and be on his way. But then Cara had kissed him on the cheek - a sweet, innocent gesture, not so different from something one of his sisters might have done. But his body had sure as hell recognized that this was *not* his sister but instead a beautiful, sexy, and willing woman. And since he'd rarely been one to refuse such a woman, he had taken full advantage of everything she had offered, especially since he hadn't had sex in over two months.

Cara's unexpectedly passionate response to him had been such a pleasant surprise, in fact, that he'd impulsively asked her out again this evening. And during his workout this morning, and while running errands this afternoon, Dante had mulled over the possibility of seeing Cara on a regular basis. It would, of course, have to be a no-strings-attached sort of relationship, with zero promises made, and any talk of the future would have to be off the table. There was no way he wanted to become seriously involved with anyone so soon after the stinging betrayal he'd suffered at Katie's hands, and certainly not with someone as young and inexperienced as Cara. In fact, he should be having his head examined for even considering the idea.

But despite her relative innocence, Cara was also mature and sensible, and it was obvious that she'd been forced to look out for herself for a long time now. Dante couldn't think of even one other female of his acquaintance – save perhaps for his mother and grandmother – who would have demonstrated the sort of strength and resolve Cara had these past few years. She was determined to get her degree, to honor her mother's dying wish, and fully prepared to make whatever sacrifices necessary in order to see her goals through.

And what sacrifices she'd made. To call the room she lived in an apartment was being overly generous, he thought sardonically. There wasn't even a full kitchen, he'd noticed, just a few cabinets, a cooktop, and dorm room sized refrigerator. The bathroom had old, barely functioning fixtures, and was so tiny he'd barely been able to squeeze himself inside to dispose of the condom and wash up. The lighting was dim, the carpet well worn, and there had been a discernible mildewed odor clinging to the place that had been apparent, even with Cara's attempts to mask it using bowls of scented potpourri. The few pieces of furniture she'd possessed had looked ready to fall apart, and while he'd had sex before in some rather questionable places - the back *and* front seats of a car, an elevator, the supply room of his family's restaurant - fucking on a futon had been a first for him.

Dante had been more than a little appalled that she didn't even have a proper bed, and had wondered again how a man - a *real* man - could willingly allow his own daughter to live in such conditions. But from what he'd been able to glean from Cara, it seemed that her worthless father had more or less forgotten that she even existed.

He felt an odd sense of protectiveness towards her as a result - odd because he was really just getting to know her and had no obligations of any sort towards her. But that desire of wanting to help her, to maybe make her life a little bit better, had played into this idea of having some sort of relationship with her - definitely a friends with benefits type of arrangement, and where it would be clearly understood that when it was over they would each walk away with no regrets or recriminations.

Dante refilled their wine glasses. "Two slices left. One for each of us."

Cara shook her head and groaned, patting her belly. "No way could I eat another bite. I mean, it was delicious, but I'm really full. And before you ask - no, I am *not* just saying that!"

He grinned, then snagged one of the two remaining slices of pizza. "I wasn't going to argue with you. I'd forgotten how good the pizza was at this place. It's been awhile since I last ate here."

She took a sip of her wine. "It doesn't seem like the kind of place a guy who drives an Aston Martin would eat at."

Dante shrugged. "Maybe not so much in recent years, but I didn't always have money. And I can appreciate good food no matter the surroundings. I know it's not as fancy as last night's meal, but I hope it was okay with you."

Cara's eyes widened in alarm. "Oh, gosh, of course it was! I didn't mean to imply that, honestly! It doesn't matter in the least to me where we eat. And you're right - the food was fantastic. Plus, this place has, well – *character* - I guess you'd call it."

He snorted. "I guess you could say that. I'm just not sure what kind of character it is. My grandmother would have some choice words to describe this joint, none of which I'd be able to translate correctly from Italian."

"It's fine," she assured him gently, then gave his hand a little squeeze. "The food, the wine, and especially the company. I - well, I just like being with you, no matter where it is."

Dante's heart gave a little lurch, touched by her sweet admission. He picked her small hand up in his and brought it to his lips. "I like being with you, too, Cara *mia*," he told her earnestly. "You make me smile just by being in the same room. And if it's okay with you, I'd like to keep on being with you."

"Huh?"

Her big eyes were enormous in her small face, her jaw hanging open in astonishment at his casually uttered words. He smiled at her obvious shock, and merely tightened his hold on her hand.

"I'd like to keep seeing you," he clarified. "Go out to dinner like we are tonight, see a movie or maybe a concert, hang out. Just once or twice a week, especially since you have classes during the week and I try to visit my family on Sundays. And, ah, I'd very much like to continue seeing you in other ways as well - if you catch my meaning."

Cara blushed furiously and took a quick gulp of her wine. "You - you mean sleeping together, right?" she asked in a hushed voice, glancing around worriedly to make sure no one could overhear them.

Dante winked at her. "Well, sleep doesn't really figure into my plans," he drawled wickedly. "Just lots of hot sex like we had last night. Frankly, I doubt I could sleep a wink on that futon of yours. And I have no idea how you manage to do so."

Her eyes had widened even further at the mention of "hot sex". "You get used to it," she acknowledged. "At least it's better than the bunks in my old dorm room. Or the cot I slept on sophomore year. And before you ask, I slept on a cot because the so-called bedroom in the house I rented with a bunch of other roommates was technically a storage room. Or a closet. I was never really sure which. So at least the futon is a full size and fairly comfortable."

"I didn't mean to sound so critical," he apologized. "Or like a snob. I admire you like hell for following your dreams, Cara, for doing whatever it takes to get your degree like you promised your mother you would. I just wish things weren't so hard for you."

She shrugged. "It's not for much longer. Less than eighteen months. I figure I can put up with almost anything for that length of time."

"Speaking of time - that reminds me. There's a few things I want to make sure you understand if we're going to continue seeing each other," he cautioned. "First, I'm not looking to have a serious relationship with anyone in the foreseeable future. My last relationship didn't end very well, and because of that I'm steering clear of any sort of commitments or expectations. So if you're thinking this is going to be something different, some traditional boyfriend/girlfriend situation, then you need to know the truth."

"I don't have any expectations whatsoever," she murmured quietly, her eyes downcast. "Frankly, I was shocked when you said you wanted to see me again tonight. As far as relationships go, I'm not exactly at a place in my life where I can make that sort of commitment, either.

Between work and school and studying, I hardly have an hour to myself most days. So I'm fine with just hanging out with you once or twice a week."

"You're sure about that?" he pressed. "I want there to always be complete honesty here, Cara. This just isn't going to be the type of relationship where I bring you home to meet the family, or offer you any sort of promises about how long things might last between us. And when one of us decides it's time to move on, I don't want there to be accusations or regrets."

"I'm sure." Cara squeezed his hand. "I promise that if you tell me it's over that I won't call you a rotten bastard or throw something at you or - or spread false rumors on social media that you're lousy in bed."

Dante threw back his head and roared with laughter, not caring if his actions caused several patrons to glance his way quizzically. "I think that last part would be the worst of the things you could do," he joked. "But I am serious about wanting to be honest with you, honey. I'm not in the market for another long term relationship right now, and have no idea when I will be again. And I can already tell you're the kind of girl who's going to want it all one of these days - a husband, kids, a big house in the suburbs. Just don't start thinking that you're going to have all that with me, okay?"

"Okay. Besides, as you're well aware, I'm only twenty-two," she pointed out. "And while maybe I want that sort of happily ever after one of these days, it's not going to be for a long time yet. I need to finish my degree, get a kick-ass six-figure job, travel to at least fifty different places, and break a few hearts along the way. You're not the only one who isn't interested in a long term relationship right now."

He reached across the table to cup her cheek in his palm, regarding her in amusement. "Why do I have the feeling that one of those hearts you're planning to break is going to be mine?" he teased. "So, now that we've got that settled, let's toast, shall we?"

She clinked her wine glass against his. "To having fun together, not to mention really good sex, but nothing else," she offered. "And I promise when it's over to say only good things about your performance in the sack."

Dante guffawed as he took a swig of his wine. "I'll hold you to that promise, Cara *mia*," he vowed.

Cara's expression turned solemn all of a sudden as she placed a hand on his forearm. "She really did a number on you, didn't she?" she asked sadly. "Your last girlfriend, I mean. She must have hurt you very badly when she broke things off."

He stiffened beneath her touch, but resisted the urge to yank his arm away. "I never said that she was the one to end things," he replied coolly.

"But she was, wasn't she?" persisted Cara. "And that's why you're so gun shy about getting too close to anyone again."

"Maybe. But I'd really rather not discuss it." Dante polished off his wine, then checked his watch. "We'd better head out if we want to make the eight-thirty show. You ready?"

Cara looked dismayed at his rather brusque brush-off, but merely nodded and stood, picking up her purse and jacket.

He felt instantly guilty for having snapped at her, and quickly slid an arm around her shoulders, hugging her against his side. He dropped a kiss to the top of her head, and when she beamed up at him, it felt like the last bit of anger and ugliness that he'd been harboring since Katie's betrayal disappeared in an instant.

Dante vowed to himself at that moment to forget he'd ever been so stupidly, blindly in love with the beautiful blonde, that he had ever permitted himself to be so vulnerable. He had a warm, willing, and passionate woman by his side, one who was all too eager to help him forget and move on.

"WELL, not only did you follow instructions, you even put sheets and blankets on it this time."

Cara laughed nervously as Dante pointed at the futon, which she had indeed made sure was folded out into a bed as he'd requested last night. As for the addition of the bedding, she wished she could say she'd used her best set of sheets, but considering it was her *only* set that wasn't exactly the truth.

"It, um, can get a little drafty in this place, especially at night," she mumbled. "I thought we'd be, um, warmer this way."

He pressed his chest against her back, sliding his arms around her waist as he hugged her close. "Honey, you were practically burning up in my arms last night," he purred in that deep, sexy voice that made her shiver in response. "If things got any *warmer* in here, we might have to use the fire extinguisher."

"I, uh, don't have one of those," she offered up weakly.

Dante chuckled. "Why am I not surprised?" he murmured, his lips caressing the side of her neck and traveling slowly down to her collarbone. At the same time, his hand slid up the side of her ribcage to squeeze her breast, causing her to gasp in surprise.

"Oh, yes," she whimpered, her head falling back in surrender against his shoulder as his thumb rubbed over her nipple.

"Mmm." He continued to nuzzle her neck as he plucked at the nipple with his index finger and thumb. "You've got great tits, honey - big and firm but soft at the same time. Let me see them now."

Before she could protest, he was lifting the hem of her sweater up and over her head, and Cara only hoped he didn't notice that the lace of her pale blue bra was slightly torn or that the straps were starting to fray. Mirai had been all too accurate in describing the condition of her meagre supply of lingerie - most of which wouldn't be worthy of a thrift shop.

She gasped again, louder this time, when he unhooked her bra and tossed it aside - practically in one motion - before cupping her bare breasts in his hands.

"Beautiful," he rasped, his breath tickling her ear. "You're all woman, Cara *mia*, all natural. And all I've been able to think about today is having you again, touching these beautiful breasts, and fucking this sweet little pussy of yours."

She squirmed against him impatiently, his seductive words and caresses arousing her unbearably. He, too, was already fully aroused, judging by the size and hardness of his erection as he rubbed against the cleft of her buttocks. Deftly, he unzipped her jeans and slid his hand inside her panties - panties that were a darker shade of blue than the bra and had a little rip in the side seam. But the minute his fingers brushed against her clit, Cara forgot all about her mismatched, shabby underthings. And when Dante plunged two fingers as far inside her wetness as they could reach, she forgot just about everything, including her own name.

"Jesus," murmured Dante in astonishment as she began to grind herself against his hand, seeking the blissful release he was so capable of giving her. "You're such a hot little thing, Cara *mia*, so sensual, so easy to arouse."

"Please." She was already panting, her hips moving in sync with the pump of his fingers inside her body. "Oh, God! I - I need..."

"Shh." His lips brushed against her flushed cheek. "I know just what you need, honey. And I'm going to give it to you right now. And then keep on giving it to you over and over again, as many times as you can handle."

Cara cried out in reaction as his thumb whisked over her clit, back and forth, while his fingers kept up a steady rhythm as they plunged in and out of her vagina, bringing her closer and closer to the edge. This time the orgasm made her shake so hard that her legs would have surely given out from under her without Dante's arm hooked around her waist to hold her steady.

"Easy, honey," he crooned, lowering her down gently onto the futon before kneeling at the edge of the mattress. "Damn, you're so responsive, so beautiful. But once again you have way too many clothes on."

She was still quivering in reaction, her eyes tightly shut as she struggled to calm her racing pulse, and therefore didn't think to be embarrassed as he tenderly removed her sneakers and socks before working the jeans that were a little too snug down her legs, quickly followed by her panties.

Cara gave a little sigh of bliss as he ran his hands up and down her legs, then reached back to squeeze her buttocks. He continued his lazy exploration of her body, cupping her swollen breasts again, pinching the nipples, pressing a kiss to her navel that made her giggle in response.

But it was Dante's next move that caused her eyes to fly open in shock, her upper body vaulting halfway off the mattress. He spread her inner thighs apart slowly, as though she was a present he was unwrapping and trying to prolong the anticipation, and then ran his tongue leisurely over and around her vaginal opening.

"Oh!" she practically squealed in alarm, not having anticipated this particular action. She was also not very experienced in *receiving* oral sex, and the very few times her previous partners had attempted this very intimate act, it had been sloppy and awkward and, well, kind of *gross*.

Dante placed a hand between her breasts, gently but firmly easing her back onto the mattress. "Let me," was all he said, but she didn't dare argue with him, especially when it took mere seconds for her to realize that he was very, *very* good at this.

"*Ohhh.*"

With each slow thrust of his tongue in and out of her pussy, and each time he sucked the swollen little nub of her clit between his lips, her moans of pleasure grew increasingly more vocal. Her pelvis lifted off the mattress in reaction to each lick of his tongue, until his hands bracketed her hips to hold her firmly in place. But he wasn't able to prevent her upper body from arching up, or her head to cease its thrashing to and fro, or to stifle the long, low cry that she emitted as she came again, and then again as he continued to eat her out with his clever, oh so skillful lips and tongue.

Cara's legs felt like wet noodles by the time Dante stood and began to undress, and she had the oddest sensation of drifting aimlessly on a big fluffy cloud somewhere. She had never come close to experiencing the sort of sensations he had coaxed from her body these past two days, had never thought of herself as a particularly sexual person, and had figured that she was destined to be one of those women she'd read about in magazines like *Cosmopolitan* who had all sorts of issues achieving orgasm. Now she knew that it wasn't her fault she had never felt this sort of bliss with her previous partners - it had been totally, one hundred percent *their* fault. Dante was a masterful lover, one who was obviously experienced and highly skilled, and it had taken him mere minutes to reduce her to a puddle of mindless goo.

"Hey, is anyone at home in there?" asked a teasing male voice, as two fingers tapped her forehead.

She laughed, her voice husky as she forced her eyes open. A resplendently naked Dante was reclining on his side facing her, propped up on one elbow as he gazed down at her with a definite twinkle in his dark eyes.

"Just barely," she confessed. "I think maybe I was out drifting on some clouds for a few minutes. That was - *intense*, for lack of a better term."

He grinned, brushing a damp strand of hair behind her ears. "Intense will do. And I hope it was enjoyable as well."

"God, couldn't you tell?" she exclaimed, pushing herself up to a sitting position. "That was like - wow! I'm just glad my landlady is mostly deaf, because I seem to recall I was screaming pretty loudly there."

Dante guffawed, clearly amused by her candor. "It wasn't quite *that* loud," he assured her. "And even though the rest of this place is on the verge of disrepair, at least the walls seem pretty well insulated. Besides, even if your landlady heard you, she probably got a thrill out of it."

Cara shrieked with laughter. "Omigod, you are so *bad*! Actually, you're really, really *good*. Spectacular, even. I've never, ever come close to - well, *coming* that way. So, thanks, I guess."

He caressed her cheek tenderly. "No need to thank me, *bella*. Especially since the pleasure was very, very mutual. Seeing how responsive you are, how much I can arouse you, makes me feel - *manly* I guess is the word. My ego took something of a battering after that breakup I mentioned, but being with you these past twenty four hours or so has more or less healed it all up."

Impulsively, she wrapped her arms around his muscular torso, then pressed a kiss to the base of his throat. "How could any woman be so stupid as to think she could ever find a better man than you?" she asked guilelessly. "You're gorgeous and hunky and such a fantastic lover that my legs are still shaking. Not to mention funny and kind and a real gentleman. And you like the same kind of pizza I do, and drive a hot car, and - oh!"

Dante had swiftly rolled her beneath his body as he loomed over her, his gaze lingering on the swell of her breasts. "Now why," he growled, running a finger down her cleavage, "would you ever imagine I'd want to bring up the subject of another woman when I already have a very beautiful, very passionate, and very naked one right beside me?"

Cara gulped at the ferocity of his expression. "Um, because I'm still kind of brain dead from three orgasms in a row and can't think straight?"

He threw back his head and laughed, her reply evidently the right one. "Well, then," he teased, "maybe I should forget about the other three I was planning to give you tonight. Especially since you still have to do homework tomorrow, and will definitely need to have all of your brain cells fully functioning."

She pretended to scowl as she playfully socked him in the shoulder, wincing a bit as she realized just how hard his muscles were. "I'm very good at multi-tasking, though," she joked back. "At work I can be talking to a client on the phone, printing research reports for Angela, sending an email, and eating my lunch all at the same time."

Dante shook his head. "Uh, uh. No multi-tasking allowed when we're both naked, and especially when it's my turn to have an orgasm or two. I want your full, undivided attention when you're in bed with me. Or whatever this thing is we're on top of right now. Got it?"

She could only nod helplessly, then moan softly as he captured her lips in a blistering kiss, his tongue plunging inside her mouth relentlessly. Once again his hands were seemingly everywhere on her body - cupping, squeezing, caressing, arousing - and Cara felt surrounded by his big, hard body, imprisoned within his strong arms. But it was the very sweetest of prisons, and rather than feel frightened or trapped, she had never felt so protected and cared for in her life.

"I want you from behind this time," he whispered in a rough voice, already pulling her to her knees and positioning her exactly as he wanted. "And you're more than ready for this, honey, I made sure of that. This sweet, tight little pussy is all primed for me, all wet and juicy."

Cara knew he was right, knew now that he'd intentionally used his fingers, mouth, and tongue to get her good and aroused and yes - very, very wet - in preparation for this. But she still couldn't help the sharp, indrawn hiss she made as he inserted just the tip of his rock hard cock - already sheathed in a condom - inside of her. Just like she couldn't control the cry of surprise that escaped her throat when he suddenly thrust all the way in, burying himself to the balls, and pressing his chest against her back.

"Easy, honey," he crooned, one hand stroking her hip reassuringly as he remained otherwise still, letting her get used to the feel of him filling her up. "Christ, you feel so damned good this way, Cara, so incredibly tight. I want to make this last, but I'm not sure I can this first time. Or hold back for much longer."

"Then don't," she urged, bending forward until her breasts were crushed against the mattress, a position that made her ass stick up in the air. "Don't hold back, Dante. Take what you need, as hard as you need to."

He made a raw sound, almost savage, pulling out of her pussy until just the head of his penis was still inside of her. He paused for a moment or two, then shocked her speechless as he rammed his cock so hard and so deep inside of her that she had to shove a fist in her mouth to stifle her screams. She clutched handfuls of the bedcovers, holding on as if for dear life as he continued to plunder her body. She'd never been fucked this hard before, none of her former so-called lovers having anywhere near Dante's skill or endurance or strength, and Cara began to see stars swim in front of her eyes with each powerful thrust of his cock. She wasn't sure if what she was feeling was pleasure or pain or maybe a little bit of both, and from some vague, foggy corner of her brain found herself hoping that he didn't somehow manage to tear her in half.

He was bracing himself with one hand, using the other to continue caressing her body - her ass, hip, thigh. His palm slid down over her belly and past her softly curling pubic hair until his clever fingers once again found her clit, causing Cara to gasp in surprise.

"Come with me now, Cara *mia*," he grunted. "I'm so fucking close, not gonna last much longer, so let yourself go with it."

And with his fingers pinching her super-sensitized clit, his cock fucking her almost ruthlessly, and his lips pressed against her throat, she did as he commanded - coming harder and longer than she could have ever imagined doing, all while Dante was finding his own release. Her vagina convulsed around his cock, squeezing him even tighter, and the words he shouted out in a guttural voice were nothing near recognizable.

But as he held her close within his arms for long minutes afterwards, stroking her hair and rubbing her back comfortingly, he spoke to her in Italian - words and phrases meant to soothe and calm and praise - and she recognized every single word, even if she didn't fully understand them all.

9

May

DANTE BREATHED a sigh of relief as he pulled up to a parking space just one door down from Cara's place. Parking spots in this tired looking residential neighborhood had been at a premium each of the previous times he'd picked her up or dropped her off here, and he had worried a bit about the safety of his car each time. Of course, every one of his vehicles was equipped with both a state of the art alarm, and also a sophisticated tracking system in case the car was stolen. But given how obsessive and protective he was about his collection of automobiles, he didn't like taking any chances.

When he had been visiting his family last Sunday, in fact, he'd half-seriously considered temporarily trading one of his cars for his cousin Eddie's somewhat battered pickup truck. But not only would such a move have entailed an admission that he was dating again - something that he just wasn't ready to share with any of his family or friends - but he had shuddered at the thought of actually driving such a vehicle. The truck, which wasn't even very old, had several dents and scratches, was covered with splotches of dried mud, and the interior was littered with papers, food containers, and a pair of Eddie's work boots. Dante prided himself on taking excellent care of his cars - all twelve of them - inside and out, and was admittedly too much of a snob to slum it in a ride like his cousin's.

He made sure to securely lock the BMW sedan he was driving tonight and engage the alarm system before walking the short distance to Cara's. His arms were loaded with a bottle of a very expensive Cabernet, a bouquet of assorted spring flowers, and a bakery box containing a variety of lavishly decorated cupcakes. This was his contribution to the dinner Cara had insisted on cooking for him.

She'd made the offer last night after they had dined at an English pub on greasy but delicious fish and chips, declaring that since he had treated her to dinner several times already this was the very least she could do to return the favor. He had resisted the idea at first, insisting that she didn't need to feel obligated, and that he was well aware of how hard she worked between her job, school, and homework. He hadn't dared to admit that the real reasons for his reluctance were twofold - one, he knew how little money she had, even if she had never once complained about her financial situation, and he didn't want her to tax her already lean budget by cooking him dinner; and second, despite her claims of being a good cook, he remained skeptical on the matter. Dante honestly couldn't think of one other woman he'd ever dated who had offered to cook for him, figuring there was a reason why – they were simply incapable of doing so.

But there was no way he was going to hurt Cara's feelings, either by acknowledging her lack of funds or by expressing doubt about her culinary skills.

'At least you know the dessert is edible,' he joked to himself as he knocked on her door. 'Cupcakes and wine could probably hold you over until you get home.'

Cara's cheeks were flushed becomingly as she opened the door, her hair pulled back into an untidy braid, and her face bare of makeup. But the smile that lit up her face was really all she needed to make her look beautiful, and he couldn't resist leaning down to place a soft kiss on her lush lips.

"Hi," she greeted breathlessly. "Sorry, I'm a little scattered right now. I miscalculated how long it would take for the sauce to finish cooking, so I'm a few minutes behind."

He shook his head, following her inside and firmly locking the door behind them. "I'm actually five minutes early. I wanted to make sure I got a decent parking space. Anything I can help with?"

"No, no. Honestly, it's almost done, I just need to let it simmer a few more minutes. Here, let me take those from you. What beautiful flowers, Dante! I think I have a vase stashed away somewhere, something that belonged to my grandmother. Ah, here it is!"

Dante had realized early on that Cara tended to babble when she was either nervous, excited, or uncertain about something, and apparently this was one of those times. She was on her hands and knees, the upper half of her body practically hidden inside a kitchen cabinet as she searched for the elusive vase. She emerged with it clutched triumphantly in her hands a moment later, then quickly filled it with water before arranging the bouquet inside it. She dashed over to the cooktop where two pots were bubbling, one with what he assumed was some sort of pasta while the other emitted an incredibly delicious aroma of tomatoes, garlic, and spices.

"I know it's practically passé to cook pasta for an Italian boy, especially one whose family owns a restaurant, but I think you'll like the sauce," she told him anxiously, stirring the contents of first one and then the other pot. "It's just a basic tomato sauce with sausage and peppers but it's got a little kick to it. When you told me you like things on the spicy side, I figured you might enjoy this."

He placed his hands on her shoulders, suddenly realizing she was barefoot and thus even shorter than usual. "I'm sure I'm going to love it," he assured her, taking a deep, appreciative sniff. "Can I have a taste?"

"Sure."

Cara held the wooden spoon up to his lips as he swallowed the surprisingly tasty pasta sauce.

"Mmm. *Delizioso*," he pronounced, smacking his lips. "As good as anything I've ever tasted from my grandmother's kitchen. Though I'd never dare to tell her so."

She laughed, returning the spoon to the pot and giving it a few more stirs. "It should be ready in five more minutes. I just need to toss the salad and slice the bread, and.."

"And relax and take a deep breath and have a glass of this cabernet first," declared Dante. "Not to mention give me a real hello kiss, not just that little peck."

"Oh. Oh, gosh, sorry." Cara hastily wiped her hands on a dish towel before sliding her hands up his chest. She had to rise up on her toes in order to reach his neck. "Um, hello."

The laughter rumbled up in his chest even as she pressed her lips against his, but then faded just as swiftly as she deepened the kiss. He groaned, his hands sliding to her denim covered ass and lifting her a couple of inches off the ground. He wondered vaguely if he would ever stop being surprised at her passionate responses to him, at how spontaneous and affectionate she was. Or how quickly he could become aroused by this young, guileless girl.

Dante set her on her feet, then took a step or two back. "Much better," he teased, pinching her playfully on the chin. "But if we keep that up much longer, all of your hard work making dinner will be for nothing. Pasta tends to get mushy pretty fast if you let it simmer too long."

"Uh, huh." She stared up at him, a dreamy expression on her face, her full lips looking more bee-stung than usual. "I, um, guess I'd better drain it then."

He gave her a pat on the butt as she turned her attention back to their dinner, and began searching for wine glasses. He found a couple tucked in the back of a cabinet, and assumed these were the only ones she owned. A quick rummage through one of the two drawers unearthed a somewhat suspect cork puller, but he managed to open the cabernet after a few attempts. Dante made a mental note to bring her a better corkscrew the next time he was over, given that he probably owned half a dozen of them. A few extra wine glasses wouldn't be a bad idea, either.

"Here you go. You told me that cabernet was your favorite, so I think you'll like this. It won some sort of wine competition last year."

Cara took a slow sip of the wine, as though savoring its taste on her tongue, then moaned in pleasure. "Oh, God! This is without a doubt the best wine I've ever had! Though considering I usually drink stuff with a twist off top, or Two-Buck Chuck - which now costs three dollars, by the way - most anything would be an improvement."

He nearly choked on the sip of wine he'd begun to swallow. "I would hope so," he replied with a hoarse cough. "This cost a hell of a lot more than three bucks. It's Silver Oak, honey, one of the top Napa Valley cabs around. Instead of a single digit price tag it's more like three."

She gaped at him in disbelief. "Please tell me you did not drop a hundred dollars on a single bottle of wine! Omigod, Dante, I'm trying to pay you back a little by cooking you dinner, and here you are bringing me flowers and a ridiculously expensive bottle of wine, and - oh, no! Please tell me those aren't cupcakes in that box. Because I've peeked in the window of that bakery and kept right on walking since each cupcake costs something ridiculous like.."

Dante placed a hand firmly over her mouth. "Shh. You're talking too much. And I already told you, Cara - you do *not* have to pay me back for anything, all right? I happen to enjoy your company very much, and it's been nothing but my pleasure to take you out to dinner these past few weeks. So rather than argue with me about the wine and flowers and a few little cupcakes, just smile and say thank you. Okay?"

She nodded and took another sip of her wine. "Okay. Thank you. Very, very much. And even though a hundred dollars is an insane amount to spend on a bottle of wine, it's worth it. This is - *orgasmic*."

"Ah, none of that!" he scolded playfully. He bent and gave her earlobe the tiniest of nips. "I'm the only one allowed to give you orgasms, no matter how good the wine might be."

She laughed along with him, though he didn't miss the hungry look in her big eyes at the mention of the "O" word. She was, he thought with a deep sense of carnal satisfaction, really turning out to be a very, very pleasant surprise with her depth of sensuality, and how eagerly she responded to him. What she lacked in experience she more than made up for in enthusiasm and unabashed passion.

And the surprises continued as they ate dinner at the scuffed, rickety little table. Rather than be barely edible as he'd feared, the food was delicious, one of the best home-cooked meals he could ever recall having. In addition to the perfectly cooked penne pasta with its spicy sausage and pepper sauce, Cara had made a simple green salad with a dressing of olive oil and balsamic vinegar, and set out a loaf of crunchy sourdough bread. It was exactly the sort of meal he had enjoyed at his mother's or grandmother's house hundreds of times over the years, and every bit as delicious as one they might have cooked.

"How'd you get to be such a good cook?" he asked after finishing off a second helping of everything. "Most girls your age can barely figure out how to fix a Cup of Noodles."

Cara gave him a scolding look. "*Women* who have reached the ripe old age of twenty-two should no longer be referred to as *girls*," she corrected. "As for the cooking, my mom enrolled me in a couple of summer classes at our local Park and Rec when I was in middle school. I always teased her that she had ulterior motives in doing that, though, because she hated to cook and secretly hoped I'd take over that chore."

He slathered butter on his third piece of the bread. "And did you?"

She shrugged. "More or less, though it was a joint effort most nights. My father, of course, was completely useless in the kitchen, as he was in just about everything else."

"What about when your mother got sick? I would hope he was supportive during such a difficult time."

Cara shook her head. "You'd like to think so, wouldn't you? I mean, he did some stuff, mostly ran errands to pick up prescriptions or groceries, but nowhere near as much as he should have done. My mom's friends pitched in, though, and gave me a lot of help."

Dante frowned. "So you were your mother's primary caregiver? Weren't you still in school back then?"

"When the hospice nurses told us that Mom needed pretty much round the clock care, I had initially planned to do a home study program so that I take care of her. The cost of hiring home health care wasn't something my father thought we could afford. Fortunately, a friend of the family who was a retired nurse volunteered to stay with her during the day so I was able to keep going to classes."

He read between the lines and figured out that Cara must have looked after her mother the rest of the time - after school, nights, weekends - a hell of a lot to ask of a high school senior. His poor opinion of her father sank even deeper at this revelation, and he muttered a few choice curse words in Italian beneath his breath.

"More pasta? Or salad? There's some of each left."

Dante groaned, shaking his head and patting his stomach. "Thanks, but I couldn't manage another bite right now. Those cupcakes will need to wait awhile. Here, I'll help you clear the table and then we can finish off the wine. And don't argue," he added sternly as she began to protest. "I might own a dozen cars and live in a penthouse now, but my first job in high school was being a busboy in the family restaurant. Believe me, I cleared more dirty dishes off the table than you'd ever want to imagine."

"Okay," agreed Cara reluctantly. "Though this isn't turning out to be much of a thank you dinner, you know. First you bring wine and flowers and dessert, and now you're helping to clear the table."

He leaned over the table and dropped an affectionate kiss on her forehead. "And I already told you that there's no need to thank me, honey. The pleasure of your company is all the thanks I need."

She beamed at him. "That's one of the sweetest things anyone has ever said to me."

Dante furrowed his brow at her in a mock-ferocious scowl. "Word of advice, okay? Do *not* tell a guy that he's sweet. It totally ruins the big, tough macho man image we all work so hard to keep up."

Cara walked the short distance to his side of the table and wrapped her arms around his neck, giving him a loud smooch on the cheek. "It was still a really, really sweet thing to say," she murmured. "Even coming from a big, tough macho man like you."

She squealed in surprise as he pulled her onto his lap, and then held onto his neck for dear life. At the feel of her soft buttocks rubbing against his crotch, he was instantly hard.

"Does that feel *sweet* to you?" he growled, intentionally grinding his erection against the cleft of her ass.

Cara shook her head, wiggling around until she was straddling him. "I, ah, wouldn't use that particular word to describe that part of your anatomy, no."

His hands ran up and down her denim covered thighs before starting on the buttons of her white cotton shirt. "Yeah? What words would you use then?"

She whimpered as he dispensed of first the blouse then her bra in mere seconds before cupping her opulent breasts in his palms. "Oh, *ohh*. Um, I - I guess I would describe it as - oh, God - hard and - and huge and, well, how about *talented*?"

Dante snickered, even as he bent his head to lick each of her nipples in turn. "I'll take talented over sweet any day. And speaking of sweet, let's get these clothes off of you so I can have my first dessert of the evening."

He surged to his feet, the unexpected movement causing Cara to quickly wrap her legs around his waist as he carried her the short distance to the futon - which had thankfully been folded out into a bed. He deposited her rather clumsily onto the mattress while he made short work of his own clothes, watching her all the while as she tugged her jeans and underwear off.

But as he began to spread her thighs apart, intent on his stated goal, she surprised him by placing a hand on his bare chest and shaking her head.

"My turn," was all she said, but it was more than enough to get his pulse racing double time.

In the few weeks that they'd been seeing each other, Dante had been more than content to take charge of their sexual relationship. He preferred it that way most of the time, if he was being completely honest, though every so often he didn't mind at all if the woman decided to take charge. Since losing his virginity more than twenty years ago to a girl several years his senior, there wasn't a whole lot he hadn't done sexually - within limits, of course. He'd done a little experimenting with some light bondage, a bit of spanking, and the occasional use of sex toys, but hard on kink was definitely not his style. He'd had two women at the same time, but drew the line at sharing his lovers with another man.

And when it had been very obvious that Cara was both inexperienced and unsure of herself between the sheets, he'd happily assumed the role of teacher, showing her different positions, encouraging her to let her emotions run wild, and taking pleasure from *her* pleasure.

But he had also taken care with her, had been exceptionally gentle and patient, even during those times when he was crazy with lust and all he could think about was fucking her into oblivion. Thus far she hadn't attempted to give him head, but from the looks of things his petite temptress was intent on remedying that situation right here and now.

She wriggled around until she was straddling his thighs, her small hand reaching out to clasp his throbbing cock. His breath hissed out between tightly clenched teeth as he struggled for control at the touch of her warm, soft hand on his hot, hard flesh. He always insisted on using condoms, no matter how reliable a woman's birth control might be, and therefore relished this rare opportunity to have his bare cock stroked. Even when she'd touched him like this Cara had been a little awkward and uncertain, causing him to guide her hand over his erection, showing her the exact way he liked to be touched. It had been one of the most sensual and exciting sexual experiences of his life.

She kissed her way from his throat down his chest and past his navel, her hand continuing to pump his penis with the long, slow strokes he liked best. Once she reached his crotch, however, she paused, lifting her head to gaze up at him worriedly.

"I'm, uh, not very - well, good at this, I'm afraid," she confessed.

"Blow jobs, I mean. At least that's what I've been told. I mean, obviously I have no idea of what it feels like, or if the guy who said it was just too stoned to know what he was talking about, but I thought I should warn you in case you..."

He clamped a hand over her mouth. "You're doing it again," he warned her. "And babbling right before you take a guy's dick in your mouth is a really, really bad idea. Now, come here for a minute or two, hmm?"

Dante pulled her against his side, stroking her long hair soothingly. "Now. What drunken, dimwitted moron told you that - no pun intended here - you sucked at giving blow jobs?"

Cara shrieked with laughter. "Omigod, I don't care if it's a really, really bad pun but that's hilarious!"

He grinned. "It's not bad, huh? But seriously, honey. Sucking a guy's cock isn't brain surgery, you know? And even if it had been the very first time you tried doing it, I can't imagine that it still didn't feel good to the asshole who had the balls - again, no pun intended - to complain about your so-called technique." He threaded a hand in her hair, holding it still so he could kiss her. "You don't have to do this, you know."

"I know. But I want to, honestly," she assured him. "You're always such a generous lover, always making sure you take care of me. And I can't help feeling that I'm not doing my fair share here, that I'm not returning..."

"The favor?" he finished, shaking his head. "That's not what this is about, Cara. I've told you before - your pleasure is my pleasure. I happen to like eating pussy, especially when it's as sweet and juicy as yours. So believe me when I say that when I go down on you it's as much for me as it is for you."

Her cheeks grew pink at his very frank words. "That - that's good to know," she stammered shyly. "But maybe I feel the same way. About giving you pleasure, that is. Will you, well, tell me if I'm doing it right?"

He cupped her flushed cheek in his hand. "Like I said," he replied huskily, "it ain't brain surgery, honey. And I'm not exactly fussy when a beautiful woman has my cock in her mouth. So you aren't going to hear any complaints from me, okay?"

She nodded. "Okay."

Cara slithered down his body again, her breasts brushing against his bare skin, causing him to grit his teeth in reaction as he struggled to maintain control. But doing so was damned near impossible when she took his cock in her hand, resuming the slow, sensual strokes that she knew he enjoyed, before running her tongue along its length, from tip to root, and then back again.

"Jesus! Fuck!" he yelped, his lower body bucking off the futon in reaction. He dug his heels deeper into the mattress for leverage as her tentative but incredibly arousing licks continued.

She drew him inside her mouth then - that lush, full-lipped mouth he'd fantasized about fucking countless times - and it was so much better than any of his dirty daydreams that he nearly shot his load off on the spot. The fact that she was both inexperienced and uncertain about what she was doing only made her actions that much more arousing. It pleased him that she hadn't done this dozens or even hundreds of times before, that she wasn't blowing him like she was a semi-pro at oral sex, and that she cared enough about his needs to ask what he liked best.

Cara was gazing up at him with a rather glazed look in her eyes as she murmured that last question, and he could tell this was turning her on as much as it was him.

"Just about anything," he croaked. "That mouth of yours is dynamite, honey - so sweet and hot. Try this, hmm? Put just the head between your lips and suck hard - yeah, just like that! Fucking hell, that's so good!"

Dante had no idea how he was able to exert so much control over his body as he continued to rasp out instructions to her, especially when she followed his directives to the letter - fluttering her tongue up and down the length of his cock, reaching her hand back to lightly squeeze the heavy swell of his testicles, learning to relax her throat a bit at a time so that she could gradually take more of his thick, heavy length inside her mouth. Instructing her in the "fine art" of administering a blow job was easily the most erotic thing he'd ever done, as was propping himself up on his elbows to watch her head bob up and down, those plush lips swallowing up his dick inch by inch until he was almost fully sheathed inside her eager mouth.

Dante prided himself on his stamina in the bedroom, and on the amount of control he could exert in order to prolong the pleasure for both himself and his lovers. But hearing the little moans Cara made deep in her throat as she sucked him off, and watching her through half-lidded eyes as she continued to lavish attention on him, brought him to the breaking point all too quickly.

"Christ, honey, you're going to make me come any second now if you keep that up," he muttered roughly. "Let me put a condom on so I can come inside you."

But she shook her head stubbornly, refusing to budge, and only sucked him harder and deeper, her hand sliding back to cup his balls one more time.

That was all he needed to find his release, the pleasure pouring through his body from head to toe and every nerve and muscle in between. As he came, the thick, hot bursts of semen filling Cara's mouth faster than she could swallow, his arms and legs thrashed wildly, his hips pistoning at a furious pace. The noise that came out of his mouth was part bellow, part scream, and maybe even a little part unmanly whimper.

He was dazed and drained afterwards, his limbs splaying out limply, as though he'd just run an ultramarathon or played soccer nonstop for twenty four hours. He was barely aware of Cara cuddling up against him, the long, damp strands of her hair trailing across his chest. Several minutes passed before he could summon up the strength to drop a kiss on the top of her head, his hand sliding down her bare back to squeeze her ass.

"Hey," he told her half-jokingly, his voice threatening to crack, "I'm guessing whoever that dim-witted college punk was who said you weren't any good at giving head also flunked out of his classes. Because only a real idiot would ever think something like that, much less say it out loud. That was - *spectacular*, for lack of a better word."

Her hand was making slow, caressing motions over his abs and chest, and astonishingly Dante could feel himself growing hard again.

"I give you most of the credit," joked Cara. "I'm just good at following directions is all."

He laughed, and this time his voice did crack. "Yeah, that might be part of it. But you're a very, very sexy young woman, Cara *mia*, and most of it was your natural instincts taking over. And I enjoyed those *instincts* very, very much." He cupped one of her breasts, pleased to find the nipple fully erect, then slid his palm down between her thighs, hissing when he realized how wet she was.

"And it sure feels that *you* enjoyed it nearly as much as I did," he whispered, his fingers slipping inside the slick opening to her body.

Cara gasped as he bent his head to draw one of her nipples into his mouth, his fingers continuing to pleasure her at the same time. "I - oh, God! I did, yes," she panted. "Your - your pleasure is my pleasure."

He laughed softly. "That's my line," he teased, his thumb rubbing over her clit. "But," he added huskily, sliding down her body so that he could replace his fingers with his tongue, "I don't mind in the least if you borrow it."

10

Mirai re-capped the bottle of pale lilac polish she'd been using to paint Cara's toenails, a frown on her pretty face. "Excuse me. He took you *where* for dinner two nights ago?"

Cara sighed, having anticipated that her BFF would have this sort of reaction. "A sports bar. You know the kind of place I mean - big screen TV's, cold beer, greasy burgers. Oh, and some pool tables in the back room."

Mirai looked as though she'd just squashed a really nasty insect. "Actually, I have no idea what you're talking about, girlfriend. Because that's not the sort of place *I've* ever set foot in. Or ever will. Or date someone who would have the balls to even suggest that I should."

Cara shrugged, trying to make it seem like no big deal. "You're a snob," she declared teasingly. "The place was a lot better than some of the dumps we went to over in Berkeley."

Mirai sniffed in distaste. "Correction, Cara - the dumps that *you* went to. I do remember one occasion when you dragged me out with some classmates and tried to make me have dinner at some third-rate sushi restaurant. I refused to set foot in the place, took a cab home, and ordered takeout from a *real* restaurant. You, on the other hand, had food poisoning for three days straight from whatever garbage you ate there. I've told you more than once - do not *ever* go to a place that advertises an all you can eat buffet. Especially when the buffet serves raw fish."

Cara shuddered a bit in recollection of the really, really bad case of food poisoning she had indeed contracted. "Well, we didn't eat anything raw on Friday night, just these tri-tip sandwiches that were delicious. And I'm happy to report that I felt just fine yesterday morning."

Mirai still didn't look convinced. She took a healthy swig of the glass of Pinot Grigio she'd poured for herself before starting on Cara's impromptu pedicure. "Hmm. Thought you told me that you were starting a new diet - one that sure as hell doesn't include tri-tip sandwiches. Or the fries I'm guessing accompanied it."

"Well, they didn't exactly have salads or grilled fish at this place," replied Cara defensively. "If it helps, I only ate about two thirds of the sandwich and hardly any of the fries."

Mirai shook her head. "It doesn't help. Not if you're serious about dropping some weight. And why does this guy keep bringing you to these borderline dives anyway? Sweetie, if he owns a dozen cars - including an Aston Martin, a Beamer, and a Maserati, just to name a few - and wears a Patek Philippe watch, he sure as hell can afford to take you someplace a whole lot nicer for dinner than - than Tony's Sports Bar!"

"Tommy's," corrected Cara in a meek tone. "The place he took me on Friday is called Tommy's."

Mirai glared at her. "It could be called The Waldorf Astoria Sports Bar for all I care, girlfriend, but guess what? It's *still* a sports bar. Where they serve cheap American beer and chicken wings. Uggh!"

Cara made a face as the other girl pretended to gag. "I already told you, Mir. It doesn't matter to me what sort of restaurant Dante takes me to. I just like being with him, you know? We have fun together, he makes me happy, and you know better than anyone how hard it's been for me to feel that way these last few years."

"Hey, it's great that he makes you happy. Great that he's a stud in the sack and gives you some really great sex. That doesn't mean he can't take you someplace a little trendier for dinner once in awhile. Someplace where you can actually dress up and that has valet parking. And where they wouldn't even dream of serving something so bourgeois as French fries or nachos. Have you ever asked yourself," added Mirai pointedly, "*why* he only brings you to places in out of the way neighborhoods? Until you showed me on Google maps, I would have sworn that half of those areas weren't even in San Francisco."

Cara wiggled her bare feet, then touched a fingertip lightly to one toenail to see if the polish was dry. "Of course I've asked myself that," she admitted in a small voice. "And I could only come up with two logical explanations, neither of which are exactly flattering. One, he thinks I'd be uncomfortable or feel out of place at a really fancy restaurant, either because I'm too young or naïve or just not sophisticated enough. That reason actually bothers me less than the second possibility."

"Which is?" prodded Mirai.

Cara exhaled sharply, reluctant to admit the truth, both to her BFF and to herself. "That he's afraid of running into any of his friends or family members if he took me someplace trendy. Because he'd be embarrassed to be seen with me. You know, because I'm more than ten years younger than he is, and I have exactly two nice dresses, both of which I've already worn several times in his presence. Oh, and because I've got a big butt and look *nothing* like his ex-girlfriend who's drop dead gorgeous. I told you that I figured out who she was after Leah mentioned her name one day, didn't I? And, omigod, Mir, I have *zero* idea why Dante would want someone like me after her because.."

Mirai held up her index finger, her longstanding way of letting Cara know that she was talking *waaay* too much. "Enough with the Cara-bashing, okay? God, you know how crazy it makes me when you keep putting yourself down! But let me ask you this, hmm? If you're so sure that the reason Dante's taking you to out of the way places is because he'd be embarrassed to run into some friends, then why the hell are you still seeing the asshole? Not to mention fucking him twice a week?"

Cara had asked herself the same question at least a dozen times over the past few weeks, and hadn't been able to come up with a reasonable answer. "Because I'm pretty sure that I'm in love with him," she replied miserably. "And I'd put up with a lot just to keep being with him."

Mirai gave her a scornful look, then did a complete about face and hugged her instead. "What am I going to do with you, Cara?" she asked in an exasperated voice. "I thought you outgrew mooning over hot guys after the naked pictures incident. Why do you keep letting them just walk all over you? Believe it or not, you are worth a whole lot more than that!"

"Dante's not like that," Cara replied defensively. "He's not a jerk like every other guy I've dated was. And maybe he doesn't take me to the hottest restaurant in town, or out dancing to the new club everyone's talking about, but so what? I told you before - I just like being with him. And he's plenty generous, you know, always bringing over wine and dessert and stuff. *And* he helps with the dishes. I'll bet you can't say the same about any of the guys you've dated!"

Mirai smirked. "That's because I don't cook for them."

Cara shook her head. "And after you spent almost six months at culinary school. Do you even remember anything you learned there?"

"I'm still pretty good at chopping stuff. I figured since Daddy paid a small fortune for that set of professional grade knives I ought to use them once in awhile. Overall, though, I don't remember much. What in the world was I thinking of when I enrolled in that course, anyway? Can you just see me slaving over a hot stove?" asked Mirai in disbelief.

"Not even for a minute," declared Cara. "And I seem to remember telling you exactly that while you were filling out the application. Just like I told you that you probably weren't going to like fashion design school, either."

Mirai sighed. "Yeah, I admit it - I've got commitment issues. Both to men *and* to school. Though at least I've stuck with school for longer stretches than I have with men!"

Cara knew that wasn't saying a whole lot, though. Mirai, who at twenty-three was a year older than Cara, had already spent a year at community college before transferring to Berkeley. Even with her mega-rich father's influence and monetary donations, the university still hadn't been willing to offer her admission as a freshman, and the admissions officer had strongly suggested she take some core classes at community college first.

Mirai had drifted for a few months after her ill-fated year at Berkeley, before declaring that what she really wanted to do with her life was become a chef and open her own restaurant someday. Cara, who knew her friend could barely boil water, had suspected that Mirai's sudden enthusiasm for cooking had been the result of watching way too much *Food Network*, and had tried to talk her out of enrolling. Mirai had lasted less than six months at culinary school, which was twice as long as Cara had quietly predicted.

After another period of time spent visiting her father in New York, traveling between Japan, Florida, and Paris with her mother, and generally goofing off, Mirai had declared herself ready to get serious about school again. Attending design school had seemed a natural for a fashionista like herself. Mirai loved clothes and accessories, had stacks of fashion magazines piled high around the apartment, and had an uncanny knack for being able to identify what sort of designer label someone was wearing with just a glance. What she did *not* posses, however, was any sort of artistic ability whatsoever, and could barely draw a stick figure.

She'd quickly switched her focus over to fashion merchandising from design, and had actually come within a semester of earning her Associate of Arts degree. But then, as was typical of the flighty, easily bored Mirai, she had dropped out again, declaring that she'd lost her passion and needed to re-think her career goals.

That had been almost a year ago, and she'd been drifting ever since - spending time with both of her parents, working for a few months at an art gallery owned by family friends (even though she'd confessed to Cara that she didn't know the slightest thing about art), and wasting a lot of time watching TV, shopping, going to the gym and the spa, and dating a string of guys that she seemed to get bored with after the first date. Cara had more or less given up on trying to counsel her friend, or suggest a possible career path, having realized months ago that this was something Mirai was going to have to figure out for herself one of these days.

But it was hard not to worry about her BFF, or to try and offer her advice now and then. After all, Mirai had done so much for Cara, and would have done a great deal more if she'd been able to swallow her pride and accept the many favors that had been offered to her. Mirai would have literally given Cara the clothes off her back if they had actually worn the same size. Unfortunately for Cara, her ultra-slim friend with the killer wardrobe was at least four sizes smaller than she was. Otherwise, Cara's closet would have been bulging at the seams with castoffs, since Mirai had a serious shopping addiction.

At least Mirai had been able to pass along some accessories, like a couple of really fabulous handbags, scarves, costume jewelry, and belts. She also bought large quantities of cosmetics on a frequent basis - if she liked a particular brand of lip gloss, for example, she typically bought it in eight different shades, only to find that at least two of the colors didn't suit her at all. Which meant Cara had a fairly good sized stash of her friend's discards, even though she didn't wear much makeup most of the time.

Mirai gave Cara's freshly painted toenails the touch test. "Okay, these are dry enough. But leave your shoes off for a little while longer. And - oh, good. Dinner's here. I'm starving."

Cara glared at Mirai as she dashed off to open the door for the delivery driver who'd brought their dinner. As wand slim as Mirai always was, she had the appetite of a football player and could put away an astonishing amount of food at times. She claimed it was either due to good genes on her Japanese mother's side of the family, or just a speedy metabolism. Either way, Cara thought it grossly unfair that she had to watch every calorie she consumed for fear of packing on another pound, while her ultra thin BFF could eat whatever she pleased and never gain an ounce.

Cara only took modest amounts of the pad Thai, chicken satay, rice, and butterfly prawns, even though she hadn't eaten since breakfast. The thought of the admittedly greasy tri-tip sandwich she'd eaten two nights ago made her shudder a bit when she mentally calculated how many calories it had contained. And she'd been too busy studying and doing chores this weekend to fit in any sort of workout. Summer classes were far more demanding than the rest of the year, since the same curriculum had to be squeezed into a much shorter amount of time, and thus the level of homework and studying was heavier than normal.

She was also conscious that - once again - Mirai had insisted on paying for dinner. Cara tried her best to reciprocate, but Mirai was as fussy and particular about the restaurants she ate at as she was about the clothes she wore. And Cara simply couldn't afford the sort of trendy, upscale places Mirai favored, so she would cook for the two of them occasionally to return the favor.

Mirai ignored Cara's protests about not wanting more wine and refilled both of their glasses. "Oh, just drink it, for God's sake! You can go back to counting calories tomorrow. Otherwise, I'll be tempted to finish the bottle and I still have to drive you home later. And I'm not the greatest driver even when I'm sober."

"I'll just take the bus, Mir. I hate to bother you all the time."

Mirai snorted. "Seriously, Cara? Like I have to get up early in the morning or something? And how are you bothering me if I'm the one who makes the offer?"

Cara sighed in resignation and took a sip of the excellent Pinot Grigio. Mirai also had expensive tastes in wine - just like Dante did - and wouldn't have dreamed of drinking Two Buck Chuck, or even using it to cook with.

"What time should Rene be home?" asked Cara.

Mirai rolled her eyes. "Who knows? Between her classes and rounds at the hospital she's hardly ever here. I haven't actually seen her for about three days."

Rene was Mirai's older sister, her roommate, and a third year medical student at the University of California in San Francisco. Rene was everything her younger sister wasn't - serious, studious, and dedicated - and had known since middle school that she wanted to be a doctor. Their father frequently pointed out Rene as an example to Mirai, asking why she couldn't be more like her sister, or at least stick with something for more than a few months at a time. It had caused some friction between the sisters at times, resulting in screaming matches followed by days-long uncomfortable silences. The occasional tension between them was one of several reasons Cara had never taken Mirai up on her offer to move in with them here.

The other reasons were varied, some valid, others not so much. For one, she would have had to sleep in the living room on a plush leather chair that converted to a single bed. Admittedly, the sleeper chair was far more expensive and comfortable than her own futon, but the lack of privacy she would have endured by not having a room of her own hadn't been appealing.

Neither had the fact that both Mirai and Rene were unrepentant slobs. Cara couldn't remember a single time when she'd visited their posh apartment when it had actually been tidy, even though their father paid for weekly maid service. There were always used dishes and empty takeout containers piled high in the kitchen, dirty and discarded clothing strewn about the bedrooms and the single bathroom, and an assortment of mail, magazines, and Rene's textbooks piled on the tables in the living and dining rooms.

After sharing first a dorm room and then a house with multiple roommates during her two years at Berkeley, Cara had cherished having her own place, tiny and old as it was. She liked the quiet, liked having her few possessions neatly in their place, and even though it had been oh so tempting to take Mirai up on her multiple offers to move into this upscale apartment in one of the city's best neighborhoods, Cara valued her privacy more.

And, of course, it always came back to her reluctance to accept yet another favor from Mirai. Cara knew that her friend's heart was in the right place, but there was no way she could allow Mirai to keep on doing these things for her. It didn't matter that Mirai had a rich father who spoiled her rotten, and that she could easily afford to treat Cara to dinner or buy her little gifts or even invite her to move in with her. Cara was both proud and stubborn, and felt strongly that it was her father's responsibility - and not someone else's parent's - to provide for her. And since Mark had stopped supporting her a long time ago, she wasn't going to depend on someone else to take up the reins.

It was later that evening, after she'd reluctantly let Mirai drive her home, when Cara thought back to the conversation they'd had about Dante - more specifically, when she had assured her friend that it didn't matter to her in the least where he took her on their dates, that she was happy just to spend time with him no matter where it happened to be.

The truth of the matter was that it *did* bother her - a lot - to acknowledge the fact that Dante probably took her to all of those small, neighborhood places for dinner because he didn't want to run into anyone he knew. When Cara had learned the name of his ex-girlfriend, she'd looked up Katie Carlisle online, and known immediately that there was no possible way Dante would have dreamed of taking the gorgeous blonde actress to eat pizza at Pasquale's. Or fish and chips at the Black Horse Pub. And most assuredly not tri-tip sandwiches at Tommy's. No, someone like Katie Carlisle would have insisted on dining at only the most popular, upscale places in town - somewhere where she could order miniscule portions so that she could maintain her slender, perfect figure.

But it was all too obvious that Cara wasn't Katie - not even close. She wasn't Dante's actual girlfriend, someone he had deemed worthy of bringing home to meet the beloved family he talked about from time to time. Or to double date with one of his friends whom he'd mentioned on occasion. Cara was merely someone for him to pass the time with until another woman like Katie caught his attention. Or, worse, she was just his fuck buddy, an easy, convenient, and uncomplicated lay who made no demands on him, never asked for anything, and acted like she was perfectly content with their current arrangement.

Except that she wasn't. She wanted more - a whole lot more. She wanted him to spend the night with her, wanted to be invited over to see *his* place. She longed for the freedom to call or text or email him whenever she liked, rather than contact him only when it was absolutely necessary so that he didn't think she was needy or a pest.

She wanted a commitment of some sort from him, a promise that this relationship was important enough to him to put some serious work into. She desperately wanted to meet his family, to hopefully be welcomed into their fold with open arms, and to finally feel that she belonged somewhere for the first time since her mother's passing. She thought how much fun it would be to double date with Angela and Nick, or any of Dante's other friends.

Most of all, though, she wished with all her might that he might one day return her feelings, might whisper that he loved her as much as she loved him, that she was the one he'd been waiting for all his life. And while she might have told Mirai a little white lie that she didn't care where Dante took her out to dinner, Cara had definitely been telling the truth when she'd confessed to being in love with him - as well as being willing to do most anything to keep him with her. And if that required keeping her real feelings for him hidden away, she figured it would be well worth the effort to keep her relationship with Dante going.

11

"Hey, Dante! I'm not used to seeing you here at this time of the day. Don't tell me the Italian Stallion is losing his touch with the ladies and doesn't have a hot date tonight, 'cause I won't believe it."

Dante grinned at the approach of Finn Cassidy, one of the regulars here at the gym he'd belonged to for several years now. Finn was a friendly, talkative guy, and had always been eager to hear details about Dante's latest conquest. Though during the months he'd dated Katie, it had been rare for him to share any specifics. Their relationship had been private, *special*. At least, *he'd* thought of it that way even if Katie apparently hadn't.

"Hey, Finn. How's it going?" greeted Dante, setting aside the dumbbell he'd been using to do bicep curls. He vastly preferred using free weights and barbells to the wide array of machines that the gym offered. "And believe it, man, because the only date I have tonight is with the leftover manicotti I brought home from my grandmother's last night."

Finn, who was on the short side, with dark auburn hair and the build of a marathon runner, shook his head. "Nah. I don't believe you for a minute. You must have some gorgeous babe waiting back at your place to share that manicotti with you."

"Nope. No one waiting for me, I swear. I don't have a date until Friday night, actually."

Finn arched a brow in disbelief. "Four whole nights without a date? Is that some sort of record for you?"

Dante chuckled. "Not even close. After Katie and I - well, split up - I didn't see anyone for over two months, took the breakup pretty hard."

"Yeah, she was something special, that's for sure. I can understand how it would be tough to get over a woman like Katie," commiserated Finn.

"The one that got away," mused Dante, as though talking to himself.

Finn, who was perpetually cheerful, clapped Dante on the shoulder. "Well, sounds like you found yourself someone new. And I'd be willing to bet that she's gorgeous, just like every other woman you've ever dated was. Is she another hot blonde like Katie?"

"No." Dante's denial was emphatic. "She's nothing like Katie in any way. And it's completely casual, nothing serious at all. Just hanging out, having some fun together, that sort of thing. I'm not ready to have an actual relationship right now, maybe not for a long time yet."

"I don't blame you, man. Hey, if I had the sort of luck with the ladies that you seem to have, I don't think I'd ever want to settle down. You've got the right attitude, Dante - have fun, keep it casual, and don't get emotionally attached. That's probably the sort of arrangement most single guys dream of, you know?"

Finn chattered on for a few more minutes, until Dante began a set of military presses and could only grunt in response to his questions. Finn took the hint after that and headed off, leaving Dante in peace to finish his workout.

But their conversation caused Dante to reflect on what his daily routine was like these days, and he realized with something of a surprise that he liked his life right now - liked it a lot, in fact. Not having to be accountable to a steady girlfriend on a regular basis meant that he could pretty much do whatever he wanted. He could work as late as he needed to without having to worry about dashing off to meet a date; he could hit the gym for an hour or two, much like he was doing now, and not have to explain himself; if a friend or client called at the last minute saying they had tickets to that evening's baseball game or a concert, he was free to accompany them. And if he had no plans at all, no place to be, he could look forward to an evening of blissful solitude at his condo where he could eat whatever he wanted for dinner, watch his choice of sporting event, movie, or other program on the TV, or simply read a book or listen to music.

When Friday night rolled around, he would meet up with Cara, usually in the lobby of his office building, and take her out to dinner. She was always good company, always cheerful and upbeat, and never, ever complained about how her day had gone, or whether or not she liked her food, or whined that he hadn't called her all week. She was easy to be around, never made demands, and it was definitely the most uncomplicated relationship he'd ever had.

And the sex, of course, had proven to be something really spectacular with her, a fact that continued to surprise him. Cara was both eager and passionate, a quick learner and an avid pupil. She was affectionate, tender, and responsive, and Dante couldn't recall a time when a lover had ever made him feel quite so much like a man.

Cara had also fully complied with his initial directives about what he wanted from whatever sort of relationship this had evolved into. She made no demands of him, never threw out hints that she wanted more than he was willing to give, and didn't play silly emotional games with him. What you saw with Cara was definitely what you got, he thought with a smile. She was so honest and natural and maybe even a little bit goofy that he didn't think she had it in her to engage in the sort of coy little games that most women of his acquaintance were so fond of playing.

She rarely contacted him, unless it was to send him a quick text apologizing for running five minutes late, or an email to ask if there was anything special he wanted for dinner on Saturday. That in itself was a rarity for Dante, for he was used to the women he'd dated in the past wanting to be in daily contact with him, either via text, phone call, email, or sometimes all three. He appreciated the fact that Cara respected the boundaries they had set, that she was neither needy nor clingy, and seemed - at least outwardly - to be content with what to him was a very satisfactory arrangement.

And despite his protests to the contrary, she still insisted on cooking him dinner on Saturday nights. He continued to be amazed at what a good cook she was, and the variety of dishes she was able to concoct using just a cooktop, electric frying pan, and a microwave. He found that he liked the way she fussed over him, that she didn't take it for granted that he should always be the one to provide dinner.

But what *did* bother him, very much so, was how hard she pushed herself, as well as the rather obvious near-poverty she lived in. By Friday evening, after a full week of working long hours, attending summer school classes four nights a week, and studying, Cara's exhaustion was visible. He found himself hating the fact that she had to work so hard to support herself, and continued to curse out her piece of shit father for basically abandoning her.

Dante wanted more than anything to help her out, to make her life easier, but he had learned early on that she was very stubbornly opposed to accepting what in her mind was charity or a handout. He had tentatively offered to loan her money once, and she had been so adamant in her refusal that he hadn't dared to broach the subject again. It had probably been the only time, in fact, since he'd known Cara that she had exhibited a flare of temper.

And he couldn't help but be aware that she had a very limited wardrobe, particularly since she seemed to wear the same few dresses each time he took her out to dinner. The Saturdays he spent at her place were casual, laidback affairs, where neither of them dressed up, but he was pretty sure that she only owned one pair of jeans that she paired with a scant handful of different tops.

The thought had occurred to him more than once that if she wouldn't outright accept money from him then maybe she would at least let him buy her some clothes. After all, Katie had regularly dragged him along on her shopping sprees, and had looked at him expectantly when it had been time to pay the cashier. And he had certainly bought gifts for other women he'd dated over the years, usually a piece of jewelry but occasionally an expensive purse or couture lingerie.

But thus far he hadn't made an attempt to buy Cara anything, mostly because he was certain she'd refuse any sort of gift, but also due to the fact that he didn't want to hurt her feelings or insult her by implying that her wardrobe left a lot to be desired. Still, it was becoming increasingly more difficult to resist the urge to take her out shopping for clothes or to surprise her with a new dress and pair of shoes on occasion.

She did accept - somewhat grudgingly - the things he contributed to their weekly dinners at her place - a good bottle of wine, a loaf of artisan bread, some sort of delectable dessert. He figured, though, that she gave in gracefully more for his sake than for hers, knowing that he had expensive tastes, and that she wouldn't be able to afford the sort of wine he preferred to drink. And it troubled him each time she cooked that she was spending her meagre funds to buy food for him. But the only way around that issue would have involved bringing a takeout or a pre-prepared meal to her place - something she would have balked at - or inviting her over to his condo, where he could make sure he had all the ingredients she would need to fix a meal.

But that, of course, would cross the boundaries he had erected when he'd first starting seeing Cara. Bringing her to his condo - something that he had really only done with Katie - would signal a level of intimacy and commitment that he just wasn't ready to buy into. And that, he thought with a grimace, was something of a damned shame because he really, really hated that tiny, musty little hovel that Cara called home. And if it was up to him he would have carted that crappy futon off to the dumps and bought her a real bed - one that he knew would hold up to the intensity of their twice-weekly sexual encounters. As it stood right now, Dante kept expecting the rather decrepit futon to shatter into pieces whenever they got a little too enthusiastic with their fucking. So far, so good, he thought darkly, but it was surely a matter of time before that thing collapsed beneath them.

He finished his workout, took a quick shower, then made the five block drive to his condo. He'd been craving a good steak as of late, so he ordered one along with several side dishes from the best steakhouse in the city - a place that typically didn't deliver, but made exceptions for customers like Dante, ones who frequently entertained clients and dropped big bucks at the restaurant.

While he waited for his food to be delivered, he exchanged his usual nightly texts, emails, and phone calls with his mother, brother, and sisters, even though he'd just seen most of them yesterday up in Healdsburg. Rafe wasn't quite as diligent about visiting the family as Dante was, but managed to make it up there at least once a month. Talia and her husband Tony, who were expecting their first child this fall, lived in Santa Rosa, less than a half hour's drive from Healdsburg. Only Gia, the youngest, had spread her wings and flown the coop, choosing to accept a job in Denver after graduating from college, much to their grandmother's chagrin.

Gia had a stubborn, independent streak a mile long, thought Dante in amusement. In that regard his baby sister reminded him of Cara. The major difference between the two women, of course, was that Gia had never had to struggle to come up with money for college tuition or the rent, had never known what it was to go without much of anything, including the love and support of her family. Whereas Cara was basically all alone in the world, since she couldn't count on her dipshit father for anything.

His family would adore her, he mused as he fixed himself a drink. She would fit in as though she'd been born to the Sabattini name, would adore the weekly family dinners, or the never-ending round of baptisms, weddings, and graduations, would love the wonderful holiday celebrations. It would be so easy, so natural, to bring someone like Cara home to meet his mother and grandmother, and he would never have to worry about her enjoying herself because he already knew that she would.

But he couldn't - *wouldn't* - do that to her. Not when he didn't know how much longer this arrangement between them would last, and definitely not when he didn't care about her in the same way he had loved Katie. He liked Cara a lot, admired and respected her, enjoyed her company, especially in bed. But he knew he wasn't in love with her, wasn't sure if he could ever love a woman again the same way he had done with Katie. There had just been something special there with his ex - an indefinable spark, a connection, an overwhelming attraction - that he'd never come close to feeling for anyone else.

He sipped his drink - a refreshing gin and tonic this evening since it had been on the hot side today - as he scrolled through Google News on his computer. Dante mostly focused on political and financial stories, plus a few sports updates, and generally avoided the entertainment news like the plague. But a headline caught his eye and he couldn't help himself from clicking on the story - *"Widely Hyped Mid-Season Replacement Frenemies Cancelled After One Season"*.

The article wasn't very long, and basically cited low ratings and less than stellar reviews as the main reason behind the show's cancellation. There was no mention made of any of the show's cast members or what their future plans were, and Dante restrained himself from entering Katie's name into a web search. He had to assume that this was just a minor blip in her career path, and that she had other projects lined up. She was stunningly beautiful, far more so than other actresses and models, and if her agent wasn't using that to her advantage to get her lots of work then Katie needed a new agent.

Angrily, Dante closed out his browser and finished off his drink, wondering if he had time for a second before his dinner arrived. He had to stop this, he told himself firmly, stop the pattern of drinking too much and feeling sorry for himself and moping around. He'd done too damned much of that in the weeks and months after Katie had left him, and he wasn't about to sink to those depths again. Besides, he had Cara now, and being with her made him happy, had provided him with a very pleasant distraction from his woes.

'But it's not the same, is it?' nagged a pesky little voice inside his head. 'Not really. You were in love with Katie, planned on making her your wife, but you don't feel that way about Cara. You like her, admire her, and she makes you laugh, but what you feel for her isn't love. And admit it - Cara could never compete with Katie, could she? Not even a little.'

The arrival of his dinner diverted him from that troubling internal voice, and the thoughts that were outright mean and unfair. Cara couldn't help it if she wasn't movie star gorgeous like Katie, he told himself firmly. Truth be told, very few women were. That didn't mean Cara wasn't attractive in her own way. She might be a little on the plump side, but was nowhere near as overweight as she made herself out to be. And the fact that she was so petite - just over five feet tall - made every extra ounce she carried that much more noticeable.

But Dante liked the fact that she had curves, especially those amazing breasts. He also found it refreshing that Cara had a healthy appetite, and relished every bite of her food. If he was being completely honest with himself, he would have to admit that one of the very few things that had irritated him about Katie was the way she'd always watched her diet like a hawk. Before she would let him make reservations at a particular restaurant, she'd insisted on viewing the menu online to make sure there was something low calorie. There was no way she would have ever consented to eating at most of the places he'd taken Cara to these past weeks - hell, she probably would have refused to cross the threshold. Katie had made no bones about the fact that she liked nice things, had expensive tastes, and enjoyed a certain standard of living.

As he dug into his steak - which had been perfectly seasoned and was so tender he barely needed a knife to cut it - Dante wondered idly how Katie would have coped had she ever found herself in the sort of dire straits Cara had found herself in. But he already knew the answer to that question, and it made him more than a little uneasy to admit that Katie wouldn't have chosen the hard path - the one Cara had taken. Instead, Katie would have most likely found herself a rich guy, preferably a good looking one, and been content to let him support her. But Katie wouldn't have known any other way, since her parents had spoiled and coddled her all of her life, and she'd never had to take care of herself or do without luxuries, much less basic necessities.

It wasn't really fair, then, to compare the two women, and hardly

Katie's fault that she'd had a happy childhood and two parents who doted on her. It was just too damned bad that the same couldn't be said for Cara. He wished that she wasn't so stubborn, so proud, and that she would accept his offer to help her out. Dante wasn't sure why he felt responsible for her, except for the fact that someone needed to be. But Cara was bound and determined to make her own way through life, a trait that was both admirable and frustrating at the same time.

He'd forced himself not to watch any episodes of Katie's TV show, knowing full well that it would have been sheer torture to do so. But he wanted to prove to himself that he was well and truly over her, that the sound of her voice or the image of her face would have little to no impact on him. So after dinner he scrolled through the list of shows available from On Demand until he found *Frenemies*.

Dante didn't watch a lot of TV, with the exception of sports and news, and therefore didn't have much to compare *Frenemies* to. But he'd only watched about ten minutes of the sitcom to realize that a) the writing and dialog weren't very good, b) for a sitcom the show wasn't the least bit funny, and c) the acting was cringe worthy at times - especially Katie's scenes.

He supposed that most young men watching the show wouldn't have cared in the least that Katie simply couldn't act, because what she lacked in acting talent she more than made up for in the looks and sex appeal departments. Her role on the show was that of a ditzy blonde bimbo who lived in the same apartment building as the male and female leads, and the producers had evidently decided to dress her accordingly. She wore skimpy, flashy outfits that she normally wouldn't have been caught dead wearing in real life, ones that bared a lot of leg, midriff, and cleavage.

She was too thin, he thought critically, but knew that she'd likely been pressured to lose the weight, especially since television cameras tended to pack the pounds on a person. But even now - nearly ten pounds lighter than the last time he'd seen her, dressed in that tawdry ensemble, her silky blonde hair teased and sprayed, and her beautiful face caked with makeup - Katie was still breathtaking, still the most stunning woman he'd ever seen.

And as he continued to watch one episode, then another, of the admittedly awful sitcom, memories of his time with Katie continued to taunt him, to tempt him. He'd been dazzled by her, enraptured, in a way he'd never come close to being with another woman. She'd had him wrapped around her little finger, but he had never minded admitting that to himself, because she was a prize worth keeping, no matter the cost - or so he had always told himself. Sex with Katie had been both exciting and passionate, and he'd been more or less obsessed with her perfect body - all long, lean lines, gentle curves, satiny white skin. He had loved showing her off to all of his friends, taking her to whatever club or restaurant she wanted, and had marveled at times that such a glorious woman was actually his.

Except, in the end, Katie hadn't wanted to belong to him or to any man - unless he had the power to advance the career that meant more to her than anything or anyone. Dante scowled as she appeared on the TV screen now, wearing a barely there mini-dress and sky high heels as she fawned over one of her male co-stars. She had sacrificed all they had meant to each other so that she could appear half-naked on a poorly written sitcom that had been panned by the critics and cancelled even before the final episodes had aired. Her rejection had damaged something inside of him, especially since she had abruptly cut off all ties with him, not attempting even once to get in touch with him.

Dante had always prided himself on ending his relationships with women in a considerate if not friendly manner. And any number of the women he'd dated in the past had made it a point to keep in touch with him - calling, texting, emailing, commenting on his social media posts, or even contriving to "run into him" at his gym or office building or a restaurant he was known to frequent. There had been several such incidences when he'd had to gently but firmly cut off contact at some point when the woman refused to get the message that they were over.

But from Katie there hadn't been a single, solitary word. No communication whatsoever. And *that* had stung nearly as much as the actual breakup.

He wondered idly if Katie would possibly have the nerve to come running back to him now, especially if she had no other acting jobs lined up. He didn't think so, given the way she'd broken his heart, but then again Katie did have expensive tastes. If she no longer had the income to support herself, it was logical to assume that she'd try to attach herself to a rich man, at least temporarily.

Dante bolted down the rest of the expensive brandy he'd been sipping for the past hour or so, grimacing as another scene with Katie filled the screen. "Well, let me tell you right now, sweetheart," he snarled. "You'd have to do a hell of an acting job to ever get me back. And based on what I've seen tonight, the odds of that happening are about ten thousand to one."

Los Angeles

KATIE STARED in mingled dismay and disbelief at the man seated behind the desk. "You're what?"

Doug Ralston sighed, having already anticipated that this particular conversation was not going to be an easy one. But then, giving clients bad news was never a pleasant undertaking.

"We won't be renewing your contract when it expires at the end of the month, Katie," he told her in a gentle but firm voice. "The other partners and I have decided that we're no longer a good fit for you. I can refer you to a couple of other agencies, some smaller ones that might be interested in taking you on. But as of June 30 you'll no longer be represented by RMD Management."

Katie's mouth suddenly felt like she'd swallowed a clump of dry sand, and she had the oddest sensation of her heart plummeting down to her stomach. "But - but we have a contract," she burst out. "You can't just - just dump me this way! I could sue you for breach of contract."

Doug sighed again, louder this time as he patiently pointed to a section of the document on his desk. "We *did* have a contract, Katie. For the period of one year. And that year is up at the end of this month. And as it states right here, at the end of that year, either party has the automatic option not to renew the contract. Our party - RMD - has elected not to renew."

"But - but why?" she exclaimed, trying to stave off a panic attack. "For God's sake, Doug, I'm one of your top clients, one of your most in-demand actresses."

Her agent was unsmiling as he told her bluntly, "No, Katie. No. Actually you are neither of those things. In fact, the main reason why we decided not to renew your contract is because you're our *least* in-demand client. I'm sorry to have to tell you these things, but you need to know the truth. And to face reality. It's my expert opinion that you should forget about pursuing an acting career at this point in your life. Maybe think about going back to school and getting a degree. After all, you aren't getting any younger, are you?"

Katie's initial shock at the very unexpected news that she was being unceremoniously dumped by her talent agency quickly turned into indignant anger at Doug's last remark. "How dare you!" she hissed, her long, perfectly manicured fingernails scoring her flesh as she clenched her fists. "I am very, very far from being too old to even think of giving up my acting career. I don't know why Hollywood is so obsessed with a woman's age, anyway. Male actors don't get subjected to that sort of scrutiny. It's so unfair!"

"I agree," replied Doug evenly. "Unfortunately, that's the way things operate in this town, Katie. It seems that there are always good roles for men no matter what their age. For women, unfortunately, youth rules. And while you're certainly not old, Katie, let's be perfectly honest here, hmm? You're over thirty years old now, despite what your bio claims, and there are dozens - if not hundreds - of aspiring actresses five to ten years younger than you are. And I'm afraid that situation will only get worse for you with each passing year."

She shook her glossy blonde head stubbornly. "But I'm already an established actress, Doug," she insisted stubbornly. "I just finished filming a role in a sitcom."

"A sitcom that had such low ratings it was cancelled before the final three episodes aired," reminded Doug. "And it got panned so badly by the critics it was a wonder it lasted that long."

"It was just the wrong time slot for it," argued Katie. "I swear the network wanted the show to fail before it ever aired. If they had tried even a little to promote it our ratings would have been fantastic."

"Maybe so," agreed Doug diplomatically. "But I'm not sure that would have done anything to help the quality of the acting - in particular *your* acting, Katie. Aside from the critics commenting that you were the sexiest thing on TV nowadays, I can't recall one other positive thing they had to say about your performance on the show. In fact, most every review I read was pretty scathing."

Katie's spine stiffened in anger. "So you're firing me as a client based on what a few uninformed TV critics had to say?"

Doug shook his head. "Actually, I'm basing it on my own opinions of your acting ability - you don't have any. Look, Katie. I swear I don't want to hurt your feelings or crush your spirit. But I've been doing this job for more than thirty years now. I've represented some pretty amazing talent. And, well, I'm very sorry to say that you just don't have it. You're exceptionally beautiful, and maybe we could pull some strings, call in a few favors, and snag you a modeling job or even a commercial now and then. But acting? I'm afraid that's not going to happen for you any longer, Katie. I'm sorry to have to be so brutally honest with you, but you're not a teenager any longer and you deserve to hear the real truth."

The rage that had been slowly building inside of her for the last few minutes grew to the boiling over point. It was only the acknowledgment that she needed to keep Doug on her side, and couldn't risk angering him with a temper tantrum, that kept Katie from lashing out. To control the overwhelming anger pouring through her, she dug her nails so deeply into her palms that she winced in pain.

"Please, Doug," she begged in the high-pitched, little girl-like voice that had been getting her whatever she wanted since she'd been - well, a little girl. It had never failed to work on the men in her life - her father, male teachers, boyfriends. "Please don't abandon me this way. You know how hard I've worked for this, how many years I've waited for my big break. And both of us were convinced that things were finally going to happen for me, that this sitcom would be just the start of bigger and better things to come. Don't crush my dreams now, Doug. I'm begging you not to be that cruel."

Doug merely rolled his eyes in response. "Come on, Katie. That innocent, helpless little girl act might work on whatever gullible guy you're trying to entice into buying you dinner. But I'm old, fat, and balding, a grandfather three times over, and believe me when I say I've seen and heard just about every plea, excuse, threat, and promise from my clients over the years. So whatever tricks you might have up your sleeve are not going to work with me, young lady. Our professional relationship is over, Katie. But I do hope you'll take my advice and find a different career for yourself. Acting is not for you, my dear."

Katie's spirits began to sink as she realized her usual feminine wiles wouldn't work for her this time around. "You - you said something about commercials. Or modeling jobs. I'd be willing to settle for that," she offered. "At least for awhile, until something else came along. I'll do just about anything to remain in the business, Doug - guest spots on other shows, print advertising, whatever it takes."

"That's something you can discuss with your new agent," replied Doug. "Hopefully they'll have better luck or different contacts than we do. Unfortunately, we just haven't had any interest in you, Katie, no matter how hard we've tried to get you work."

Katie's temper flared anew. "Well, whose fault is that, Doug?" she snarled. "You're supposed to be the pros here, the experts. It's why I wanted RMD to represent me, since you're reputed to be one of the best agencies in the business. Maybe you're getting too old and too set in your ways for this job, Doug. Maybe assigning a younger agent to me would get some real results."

Doug, who was normally cool, calm, and collected - three traits absolutely essential for someone who dealt with egocentrics on a daily basis - scowled in response. "Young lady, I'd strongly advise you to get an attitude adjustment - and fast. I can assure you that the reason the job offers aren't coming in have nothing to do with how hard I hustle or my age. I'm afraid you've only got yourself to blame for your lack of success, Katie."

She frowned. "And exactly what is that supposed to mean?"

"It means," retorted Doug, "that it's not just your less than stellar acting skills that have contributed to the lack of offers. You've acquired something of a bad reputation among casting agents, Katie, and that's the main reason you aren't getting hired."

Katie gasped in outrage. "Oh, my God! That's preposterous, Doug! I do *not* have a bad reputation! Why, I've barely dated anyone since moving back here in February, and I certainly have never slept around. That just isn't my thing."

Doug shook his head. "No, no. That's not the sort of bad reputation I was referring to. Hell, maybe if you actually *had* slept around you'd have had more offers. Not," he added hastily, "that I've ever once encouraged a client to do something like that. The bad reputation I was referring to is your professional one, Katie. Evidently you've managed to piss off quite a few people these past months."

"I have no idea what you're talking about," muttered Katie sullenly. "I've always behaved like a true professional when I'm on a job."

Doug snorted in derision. "More like a professional diva from what I hear. According to the reports I received you've consistently showed up late to sets, been unprepared and didn't have your lines memorized, argued with the director, the cameraman, and most of your co-stars, and made all sorts of demands that even big stars rarely get away with. So given all that it's little wonder we've had such a tough time getting you any work at all. And why we've chosen not to re-sign you. Now, as I said earlier, I can give you the names of a few other agents who might be willing to take you on. I'll print their information out for you right now, in fact."

"A few" wound up being exactly three, and two of those were not accepting new clients, no matter how much Katie begged, cajoled, and name-dropped. And the one agent she did manage to snag a meeting with gave her the creeps, staring at her with a lascivious leer and practically drooling as he inspected her face and body. She made a hasty retreat, knowing that even if it meant the end to her acting career there was no way she could ever work with such a slimy, disgusting man.

And it was certainly beginning to look more and more that this was in fact the end. She had no agent, no job offers, no prospects for the immediate future, and, most significantly, no money with which to pay her mounting pile of bills. She had the rent to pay on her trendy but pricey Santa Monica beach bungalow, utilities, car insurance and gas, food, and health insurance. And those were just her basic living expenses. In addition, she had all of the various costs associated with being an aspiring actress - acting classes (which Doug had half-jokingly advised her to demand a refund for); a membership at one of L.A.'s most popular gyms, plus private sessions with both a trainer and a Pilates instructor; keeping her wardrobe constantly updated so that she didn't run the risk of - horrors! - being photographed wearing the same outfit twice; and all of the numerous beauty treatments required to keep herself looking beautiful and youthful - hair color and cuts, mani-pedis, teeth whitening, spray tans, facials.

All of that cost a pretty penny, and pennies were awfully scarce these days. She was behind in several of her bills, and had been forced to cancel a recent appointment at the skin care salon because her credit cards were maxed out. She had just enough in her checking account to cover next month's rent, and no income expected in whatsoever. She was broke and desperate and had no idea how to get herself out of this situation.

So Katie did what she had always done when she needed something or couldn't handle a situation by herself - she called home.

Her mother sounded understandably surprised when she picked up the phone, given that it had been nearly two months since Katie had last been in touch. "Hi, honey. What's going on?"

Louise Carlisle's greeting sounded unusually guarded to Katie, who was used to her mother's normally enthusiastic response whenever she happened to call - which was normally infrequent. Katie guessed her mother was pissed off because it had been so long between phone calls, and knew she was going to have to lay the bullshit on extra thick this time.

"Oh, Mom," sniffled Katie in that little girl voice that had always gotten her whatever her heart desired. "I'm just going through a bad patch is all. And I really needed to hear your voice. After all, if you can't depend on your best friend when you're down, who can you?"

Always before Louise had been thrilled when her beautiful, popular daughter had referred to her as a "best friend". Katie had pulled that particular little trick out of her hat on many occasions over the years when she'd needed something from her mother - most often her help in convincing Katie's father to fork over money for something.

But this time Louise seemed oddly unmoved by Katie's tearful pleas. She listened without comment as Katie spun her tale of woe, giving Katie a distinct feeling of unease. She had always been able to count on her parents, had always known the security of both their financial and emotional support. Now, though, she sensed that something was different.

Louise's voice was flat, rather emotionless, and disapproving in response to her daughter's tearful pleas. "I don't know if we'll be able to help you out this time, Katie. Your father and I are retired now, you know, and our budget is tighter these days."

Katie was shocked at this sort of response from the woman who had never hesitated to give her whatever she wanted. "But, Mom. What am I supposed to do?" she pleaded tearfully. "I'm trying every single day to get jobs, and I've cut way back on my expenses. I didn't even have money to buy groceries this week. I've been living on saltine crackers and chicken noodle soup all week."

In truth, she'd ordered in sushi this evening that had set her back almost fifty dollars, but she had rationalized the expense away since there was enough food for tomorrow's lunch as well.

Louise paused for a moment, and Katie felt sure her mother would cave in. But all she said was, "You'd better discuss this with your father, Katie. He's the one who handles our finances. Hang on a minute or so."

Rather than be dismayed by this development, Katie felt a sense of triumph. Her father had always tended to spoil her even more than her mother, and she was positive he would agree to bail her out one more time.

But she was startled anew when John Carlisle announced in an unfamiliarly stern voice that he was finished bailing her out of these situations. And shocked speechless when he told her in no uncertain terms that she needed to forget these "foolish notions" of becoming an actress and move on with her life.

"Do you have any idea how much money your mother and I have wasted over the years on your acting career?" asked John wearily. "Far more than enough to have put you through an Ivy League college, bought you a house of your own, and set up a trust fund for any children you might have someday. That's a whole lot of money, Katherine Louise. And your mother and I worked far too hard for that money to keep frittering it away on acting lessons and designer clothes and whatever else you insist is necessary for this nonexistent career of yours."

Katie realized with a sinking heart that her father just wasn't going to cave into her tears and pleas this time. When John started calling her by her full name, it was a definite sign that he meant business.

"But, Daddy," she whined. "What am I supposed to do? Can't you just send me enough for a couple of months? I promise I'll find some acting jobs by then."

Even, she thought in despair, if it meant crawling back to that sleazy agent and agreeing to whatever he suggested - up to and including sleeping with the disgusting bastard.

"No." John's response was succinct and unmoving. "No more bailouts. No more loans that never get paid back. This is what's going to happen next, Katherine Louise. You're going to give notice on your apartment. Immediately. I'll arrange to have your things moved up here and put in storage until you can afford a place of your own. Meanwhile, you can stay with us - on the condition that you either get a meaningful, full-time job, or go back to school. And not acting school, understand?"

"Yes, Daddy," she mumbled.

"All right then. Start packing up your things, and I'll contact a moving company. No sense staying down there any longer than necessary. The sooner you're back home the sooner you can start making plans for your future." He paused, and when he resumed speaking his tone was kinder, gentler. "I know how much your acting career meant to you, honey, how you dreamed of little else ever since you were a child. But it's time for you to grow up and face facts and put those dreams aside. Very, very few people actually succeed in show business, and you gave it a good try. Now you get to try something new."

"Like what?" Katie grumbled.

"We'll work on that, hmmm? You're a bright girl, honey, and I know you can be successful. We just have to figure out what you're best suited to. Not to mention," he chided, "you aren't getting any younger. Maybe you should consider settling down and starting a family soon. Your mother and I were brokenhearted when you split up with Dante. We thought for sure he was going to be our son-in-law, be the one to give us grandchildren. He was a great guy, Katie, one in a million. You'll have a tough time finding a better man than he was."

After Katie bid her father good-bye, after grudgingly promising to email him as soon as she gave official notice to her landlord, she thought long and hard about his comments concerning Dante. She had always regretted having to hurt him the way she did, for he had in fact been a great guy, unquestionably the nicest guy she'd ever dated. He was also the hottest, best looking of her former boyfriends, and a fabulous lover - though at times he'd been a little too eager between the sheets, had wanted sex a little too often for her liking.

And he was also stinking rich, owned a fleet of luxury cars and a posh penthouse condo. He'd always taken her to the very best restaurants and clubs, and had been incredibly generous with buying her things. Being the wife of such a man wouldn't be such a bad thing, mused Katie, even if it meant giving up her lifelong dream of being an actress. Being Mrs. Dante Sabattini would be vastly preferable, for example, than working in some boring office or selling designer clothing to some snotty rich bitch or going back to any sort of school.

It wouldn't be easy, of course, mused Katie. She'd hurt him badly, and he had been furious when he'd walked out on her that night. She would have to carefully consider the best way and time to approach him, and, more importantly, would have to deliver the acting performance of her life to convince him of her regret in ending their relationship.

A sudden recollection propelled Katie to begin sifting through a growing pile of mail that she hadn't bothered to do anything with as yet. She pulled out the thick cream colored envelope she'd been searching for, then withdrew the engraved invitation and response card. She was relieved to note that three more days remained until RSVPs were due - not that such a trivial detail would have bothered Katie,

The invitation was to the wedding of a close friend of Katie's, whose intended groom just happened to be one of Dante's numerous cousins. It had been at the couples' engagement party about eighteen months ago, in fact, where Katie had first met Dante. And it went without saying that someone as close to his family as Dante was wouldn't dream of missing his cousin's wedding.

Katie had planned to send her regrets, having little to no interest in attending something as boring as a little country wedding. But now, under the circumstances she found herself in, she had a definite interest in attending.

As she marked the response card with a yes, she just hoped Dante wasn't planning on bringing a date to the wedding. A date would be a complication she definitely didn't need - considering that she already had her work cut out for her.

13

"Time for you to be heading home, isn't it?"

Cara glanced up at the sound of her boss' voice, smiling up at Angela as she stood on the other side of her desk. "Just about, yes. I have a couple of quick things to finish up and then I'll be on my way. You look like you're all ready to leave."

Angela nodded, adjusting the strap of her laptop bag more securely on her shoulder. "Just waiting for Nick to finish up a call, and then we're going out to dinner. My race starts at six-thirty in the morning down near San Jose, so we need to make an early night of it."

Cara grinned up at her tall, ultra-slender boss. Even though Angela had put a good amount of weight back on her previously skinny frame, she was still a little too much on the lean side - even with Cara doing her utmost to shove snacks in front of her face and Nick outright nagging her to eat more. Cara suspected the long miles Angela still insisted on running every week burned off more calories than she could consume.

"How long is this race - like, fifty miles or something?" teased Cara.

Angela smiled, something she'd done a lot more of since moving in with Nick almost a year ago. "No," she sighed. "Just a half-marathon is all. After that accident I had during a trail race last year, Nick made me promise to keep the mileage to something more reasonable. Though I'm planning to run a full marathon this fall up in the Sierras." She held up a finger to her lips and winked. "Shh. That's our little secret, okay?"

Cara gave Angela a thumbs-up. "Of course. Even though I can't pretend to understand this obsession you have with running. Though judging how slim you are and how chubby I am, maybe I ought to consider taking it up myself."

Angela's smile was swiftly replaced with a scowl. "Hey, knock it off, Cara. You are *not* chubby. I tell you that every time you try and diss the way you look. And between your job here and going to night school and studying, I have no idea how you'd find the time to begin a running program anyway."

"Well, I need to do something," groused Cara. "And soon. I've never felt this out of shape in my life. I really miss my old dance classes. Doing tap or jazz dance for an hour or so was great exercise. But it's hard to find adult classes, especially ones that sync with my schedule."

"You could try yoga," offered Angela helpfully. "I mean, it's definitely not my thing, but my friend Julia goes to class almost every day of the week. She goes to a studio on Divisadero Street, and I know one of her teachers. Sasha supposedly has some real kick-ass class on the weekends. I can ask Julia more about it if you'd like."

Cara hesitated before replying, not wanting to admit that she simply couldn't afford yoga classes, or a gym membership, or even a new pair of running shoes. She always hated bringing up the subject of money to Angela, not wanting her boss to think for a minute that she was hinting for a raise or a bonus. As it was, Angela and Nick were both very good to her that way, very generous with quarterly bonuses and such, and Cara didn't want to sound greedy or ungrateful. So instead of admitting the truth, she simply replied, "Maybe after summer school is done. Right now the course load and homework is more than I can handle. But thanks for the offer."

Angela looked at her a bit oddly, as though she suspected her excuse was as flimsy as it had sounded, but tactfully changed the subject. "Any big plans for the weekend? I hope you don't have to study the whole time."

Cara shook her head. "Oh, no. At least not the whole time. I've got a date tonight. And tomorrow night as well. Um, same guy, of course. "

Angela grinned. "Is this the same guy you've been seeing these past couple of months?"

It had actually been more than three months since her first date with Dante, but Cara tactfully didn't correct her boss. Nor did she blurt out that the guy she'd been seeing was Nick's closest friend as well as one of his best clients. She and Dante had agreed from the beginning of whatever sort of relationship this could be defined as that they would keep it a closely guarded secret from both sets of co-workers. Cara felt more than a little guilty at telling Angela half-truths on a regular basis, but she also didn't want to put either her job or her relationship with Dante in potential jeopardy.

"Yep, same one. Still keeping it low-key," replied Cara breezily. "Just hanging out when we can make the time. God knows the last thing I have time for right now is a long-term relationship!"

In truth, if Dante had ever once given her cause to believe that he wanted to take their relationship to a more serious level, she wouldn't have cared how much time she would have had to devote to it. She would happily forego sleep, eating meals, whatever it took to spend time with him. She would even, if need be, postpone finishing her degree or taking fewer classes at a time.

But he seemed perfectly content to keep things just the way they were now, and she was so crazy in love with him there was no way she was going to rock the boat and possibly screw things up. So she continued to be grateful for whatever time they spent together, and to never, ever ask for more.

"Hmm." Angela looked dubious. "What did you say this guy's name was again?"

Cara gulped. "Danny. His name is Danny."

That at least wasn't precisely a lie. Dante had told her once that most of his friends called him either Dan or Danny, rather than use his full name.

"Except for my grandmother, of course," he'd chuckled. "She insists on calling all of her family members by their full name. I think she's the only one who can get away with calling my brother Raffaello. Rafe would go nuts if anyone else tried."

And since Cara had frequently heard Nick refer to his friend as Dan, she didn't want Angela questioning such a coincidence and had chosen to use Danny when discussing him.

"And he's a good guy?" queried Angela. "Treats you right, doesn't try to take advantage of you or anything?"

"He's a wonderful guy," assured Cara. "A real gentleman. The sort of guy you'd never worry about bringing home to meet your parents. That is, if one actually had parents and a home to bring him to."

She'd said the words lightly, almost like a joke, but the underlying hurt she felt uttering them must have been obvious. Angela reached across the desk to give her shoulder a comforting little squeeze.

"I'm sorry," Angela told her gently. "I mean, God knows I haven't had the best relationship with my parents over the years, especially my mother, but I was never alone like you are now."

Cara was quick to steer the subject in a slightly different direction. "I thought you told me that things had gotten a lot better with your family ever since you brought Nick home to meet them."

Angela scowled. "Yeah, he's definitely the man of the hour, that's for sure. In fact, sometimes I suspect the only reason my mother invites us down to their place in Carmel so often is so she can show Nick off to the rest of the family. My sisters certainly never dated a former NFL star."

"Angel, your sisters are lucky they got any dates at all," drawled Nick as he strode out of his office, leather laptop case in hand. "One thing's for sure - you definitely got the good looks in your family."

Cara stifled a chuckle, knowing it wasn't nice to laugh at Nick's scathing critique of Angela's two older sisters. Angela glared at him as he flung an arm around her shoulders and planted a kiss on her cheek.

They really did make a stunning couple, thought Cara dreamily.

Both far taller than average - Nick an imposing hulk of a man at six foot six, while Angela herself stood just over six feet in her modest heels. Each had jet black hair, Nick's cut close to his head while Angela had gradually begun to ditch her former sleek ponytails and tight knots for long, loose waves that fell past her shoulders. They each wore an expensive, impeccably cut suit - Nick's a navy pinstriped today, while Angela's sleekly tailored pencil skirt and jacket were of pale gray gabardine. They fit together well, mused Cara, as though they had always meant to be together. And even though Angela had told her on more than one occasion that Nick didn't believe in marriage, to Cara they seemed happier and more devoted to each other than most married couples she'd had the chance to observe - including her own unhappily wed parents.

"Don't your sisters look like you?" inquired Cara.

Nick answered for Angela, and very emphatically, too. "Hell, no. The two of them are short, out of shape, and going gray fast. They're also way older than Angela, like fifteen years or so, and if you want my opinion they aren't aging well. Unlike my Angel here. Once she gains ten more pounds she'll be perfect."

His dark eyes were twinkling with amusement, but even though he was obviously teasing it didn't prevent Angela from punching him on the arm. However, considering how powerfully built Nick was, it was highly unlikely he felt even a twinge of pain.

"Well, I guess we ought to head out to dinner then so you can try and fatten me up," replied Angela sardonically. "Cara, you have a good weekend and don't spend all of your time studying, okay? And enjoy your date."

"Date?" inquired Nick curiously. "You have a new boyfriend, Cara?"

Cara was quick to deny it. Thankfully, it didn't appear that Angela had told him anything about "Danny", because as shrewd as Nick was he just might have figured it out for himself that Danny and Dante were one in the same.

"Not exactly," she demurred, striving to keep her tone casual. "Just a guy I go out with from time to time. We're just good friends is all."

Nick gave her a wink. "If you say so, kiddo. But if this so-called friend of yours ever does anything to hurt you, or breaks your heart, you just tell me and I won't hesitate to kick his ass. Nobody messes with one of my team, got it?"

"Got it."

Cara was oddly touched by Nick's offer - however crudely made - to defend her honor should it become necessary. But she wondered if his offer would still stand if he learned her date was his closest friend.

"How are the scampi? I didn't use too much garlic, did I?"

Dante brought his fingers to his lips, kissing the air. "They're *delicioso*, Cara," he assured her. "And with just the right amount of garlic. I can't remember when I've had better. But," he added sternly, "you shouldn't have spent this much money. I know how much jumbo shrimp cost, and that you're on a tight budget."

Cara shrugged. "I'm guessing this bottle of merlot, plus the pastries you brought for dessert, cost a whole lot more than the shrimp."

He gave her a reproachful look. "The difference being that I can afford it while you can't. I should never have mentioned that I'd been craving scampi with linguine. Next time I'll make sure I mention meatloaf or beef stew, something more budget friendly."

She grinned. "Well, meatloaf might be a little tricky considering I don't have an stove to bake it in, but I can fix beef stew in a Dutch oven. I'll make it next week."

"Oh. That reminds me." Dante took a sip of his wine before setting the glass down. The glass was one of a set of six that he'd brought over last month, insisting that he had way too many at his condo and that she'd be doing him a favor by taking these off his hands. Cara had seen right through his excuse, knew that the glasses were likely brand new and certainly expensive, but hadn't argued with him and accepted them graciously instead.

"Um, about next weekend," he began hesitantly. "I won't be able to come over on Saturday. Or see you on Friday, for that matter. I'll be out of town for a few days."

"Oh. Okay. Thanks for - for letting me know," she replied, trying with all her might to sound cheerful rather than disappointed. "Are you going on vacation or something?"

He shook his head, and Cara sensed his reticence in responding. "No. It's a family thing. A wedding, to be exact. My cousin Brandon is getting married on Saturday, but I'm invited to the bachelor party on Thursday night plus another family dinner on Friday. So it will just be easier to stay at my mom's for a few nights."

"Of course," she agreed readily, determined that he not realize how dismayed she felt at not being invited to join him. "It sounds like a lot of fun. Where's the wedding being held at?"

"Laine - she's the bride - has an uncle who owns a vineyard in Healdsburg, one of the bigger ones in the area. The ceremony and reception are both being held outdoors. Fortunately there's a lot of shade trees on the property because it's supposed to be in the nineties this weekend."

"Well, I hope everything turns out perfectly for them," she declared, then quickly changed the subject, asking Dante his opinion about a paper she had to write for one of her finance classes.

He seemed greatly relieved to be off the topic of the wedding, and she wondered if it had bothered him even a little that he hadn't seen fit to bring her along as his guest. Spending the weekend attending a family wedding in the Wine Country with Dante sounded like a dream come true to Cara, better even than a week's vacation in Hawaii or the Caribbean. She would finally have the chance to meet his family and friends, attend a beautiful outdoor wedding as his date, and...

As they continued to eat their dinner quietly, a sudden, unpleasant thought filled her with dread. Was it a possibility that Dante was bringing someone else along as his date this weekend? She had never asked if they were exclusive, if he was seeing other women on the days they weren't together. She honestly didn't believe that, not really, particularly since he was always such a gentleman, always considerate of her feelings. He wasn't an immature, selfish jerk like her college hook-ups had been, or even Jack, who'd taken another girl to the prom while Cara had kept watch at her mother's deathbed.

But that didn't mean Dante didn't know other women - ex-girlfriends, business associates, friends of the family - who would be suitable to bring along as his guest to the wedding. Someone who wasn't as young and gauche as Cara, who had the right sort of clothes and a better body, and who would be a much better fit all around for a man like Dante. It was almost a given that everyone at the wedding would be there with a guest, and it would look odd if he showed up solo.

She grew so lost in her thoughts for a few moments that the touch of Dante's hand on her forearm nearly made her jump out of her chair.

"Oh, sorry!" she mumbled hastily. "Were you saying something just now?"

He was regarding her quizzically, a look of concern on his handsome face. "Just asking if you wanted more wine. Are you okay? You looked like you were a million miles away just now."

She nodded. "Fine, just fine. I was only daydreaming for a few seconds is all."

He grinned teasingly. "Sorry if I was boring you. Maybe you shouldn't have more wine if you're going to keep drifting off that way."

Cara wrinkled her nose at him and held out her glass. "I promise to give you my undivided attention for the rest of the evening. So may I please have some more wine?"

"Well, since you asked so nicely, I suppose so," he joked, topping off her glass before pouring the rest of the bottle into his. "And you always give me your undivided attention, honey. It's one of the things I like most about you - the way you make me feel like I'm the most interesting guy in the world."

She gave his hand a squeeze. "That's because you are," she replied easily. "At least, you're the most interesting guy *I've* ever known."

Dante grimaced. "Based on what you've told me about some of the losers you dated in the past, I'm not exactly sure if that's a compliment or not,"

Cara laughed. "It is. Trust me on that. You are nothing like any of the other guys I've ever dated. You're much smarter for one, more mature, and definitely more sophisticated. You drive a hot car - lots of them, actually - and drink wine that comes with a real cork. And of course there's your most attractive quality of all."

He snickered. "Don't tell me, let me guess. Hmm, it's got to be my knack for giving you multiple orgasms in a one hour time frame."

She felt her cheeks grow hot, and her panties dampen at the vividly erotic images his seductive words conjured up. "Um, well, that, too. That sort of goes without saying. But your most attractive quality is that you help with the dishes."

Cara couldn't help herself from laughing with glee at the expression of first disbelief, then dismay, and finally amusement that crossed his face. Dante surged to his feet, emptying his wine glass as he did so, and then unexpectedly hauled her off the chair and into his arms. Her pulse rate ratcheted up a few notches the moment she glimpsed the almost stormy look in his dark eyes, and she gulped audibly as he pulled her flush against his muscular body.

"Honey," he rasped, "if you think my skills with scrubbing pots and pans and drying dishes are my most attractive qualities, then I must be doing something really wrong. Allow me to change your opinion."

He captured her lips in a blistering kiss, his tongue ravishing the inside of her mouth until she was breathless, and maybe even a little dizzy. She'd had one more glass of wine tonight than was usual for her, and was starting to feel the effects. She clamped her hands around his biceps, holding on tight as he continued to kiss her senseless. A little sound that was half-whimper, half-moan escaped her throat as his hands slid to her hips, holding her still as he ground his fully engorged cock against her mound. She was already wet because - well, because he was so gorgeous and hot and sexy that he could arouse her just by being in the same room. And when he set out to deliberately seduce her, she was near-helpless in his arms.

Dante pushed her up against the wall between the bathroom and the closet, in the exact spot he'd kissed her for the first time. Except this time the front of her body was being crushed against the wall, his much larger, more muscular frame trapping her in place as he continued to rub his dick between her ass cheeks. His lips traced a slow, erotic path from her temple to her cheek, then down to her jaw and finally to the side of her neck. At the same time his hands were roaming all over her body - caressing her back, squeezing her ass, skimming up and down the sides of her ribcage. Her boobs were squished up against the wall, at least until Dante slid one hand under her T-shirt, deftly unhooking her bra and taking possession of the swollen globes.

"These are Grade-A tits, honey," he breathed against her ear, his palms fondling her breasts roughly. "Tight, perfect little nipples." He caught the taut peaks between his thumbs and forefingers, pulling them until they were throbbing in part pain, part pleasure. "Remember when you let me tittie fuck you a few weeks ago?"

She could only offer up a quick nod and a muffled whimper as he continued to squeeze her boobs and stimulate her nipples. She was so aroused by now, so wet, that she could feel the vaginal fluids dampening her inner thighs. And she knew from past experiences that it would only take the slightest touch of her clitoris to get her off. Cara began to roll her hips and grind her ass against the massive swell of his cock, growing desperate for release.

But Dante appeared in no real rush to finish this, despite how hard and huge he felt. "I remember it, too, Cara *mia*," he whispered seductively. "That was one of the best orgasms of my life - coming all over these big, beautiful tits, then watching this sweet little tongue lick my cock clean."

He slipped two fingers inside of her mouth, hissing loudly when she sucked them sensuously. "I'm going to do that again tonight, honey," he growled. "Slide my cock up between these beauties until I come. Would you like that?"

She cried out as his hand slid down her softly rounded belly until he was cupping her vulva through her jeans. She was so needy for him, so desperate to come, that she would have agreed to just about anything he asked of her right now.

"Yes," she panted, trying desperately to ride his hand to orgasm. "Yes, I like anything you do to me. Everything you do to me."

"That's because you're so fucking hot, Cara *mia*," he purred. "So responsive. I'll bet if I just keep rubbing you like this that you'll come. Isn't that right?"

She pressed her palms flat against the wall, holding herself upright as her legs began to shake. "Yes. God, yes! Please, please let me come. I need to come so bad."

"Shh." He stroked her hip soothingly. "I'm going to take care of you, honey. I promise. Let's see how ready you are, hmmm?"

He unzipped her jeans before shoving them along with her panties down past her hips, then, without warning, pushed two fingers inside of her drenched slit.

Dante swore softly beneath his breath, the words indecipherable but unmistakably carnal. "And you've got a Grade-A pussy to go along with these amazing tits," he crooned, his fingers swiftly finding a rhythm that was threatening to send her spiraling over the edge with each thrust. "Sweet and tight and hot as hell. I love fucking this pretty pussy, with my fingers and my tongue and especially with my cock. I'm going to use all three of them on you tonight, honey, going to make you come so many times that you'll have trouble walking tomorrow. But you won't mind, will you?"

"N-nnoo!" she cried plaintively, so desperate to come that tears began to track down her cheeks. "I won't mind. I never mind. Please."

"So fucking wet," he rasped. "So damned hot for it. And always, always so responsive. Come for me now, honey. Yes, just like that!"

She screamed as the climax took her over, too far gone with the pleasure that swept through her to even think of muffling her cries. But instead of urging her to keep it quiet, Dante encouraged her to just let go.

And she kept letting go for the rest of the evening, eagerly following his lead as he took her to bed - where he followed through on all of the tantalizing promises he'd made her. He put her on her back first, instructing her to squeeze her breasts together as he began to slide his penis through the deep valley between them. He kept his eyes downcast, as though enthralled at the sight of his cock slipping between her breasts. But unlike the last time he'd done this, he didn't come, instead rearing back on his haunches before patting her on the ass.

"Turn over."

When she complied, he covered her with his body, drawing a gasp of surprise from her lips as he thrust inside of her with one swift movement. His powerful thighs straddled her hips, pinning her in place as he took her from behind. Cara bit down on her pillow each time he slammed his cock deep within her body, each near-savage thrust causing her to shudder in response. The futon squeaked and shook with the force of their fucking, and just before he made her come again she hoped faintly that the rickety frame would hold up under the pressure.

Dante was seemingly insatiable tonight, keeping at her for hours. Even after he'd come long and hard, his cock was still semi-erect, and it would only take a short while for him to be at full arousal again. And in between he went down on her, using his lips and tongue and those clever, talented fingers to bring her over the edge again and again. And then those very actions would make him hard again, and he'd have just enough time to roll on a new condom before sliding back inside of her sore but all too eager body.

At some point, though, he must have exhausted her because she woke groggily when he gently touched her bare shoulder. She peeked up at him through one eye, unsuccessfully stifling a yawn as she realized he was dressed.

'I need to go," he murmured, brushing damp strands of hair off her forehead. "But I cleaned up the dishes, put away the leftovers."

She smiled up at him sleepily, catching hold of his hand. "See?" she murmured teasingly. "Told you that was your most attractive quality."

Dante laughed, bending to press a soft kiss to her lips. "Brat," he chided. "I'd keep trying to change your opinion but you've worn me out, Cara *mia*. And you look pretty wrung out, too. Get some sleep, okay? I'll give you a call during the week."

It was on the tip of her tongue to ask him to stay with her for once, to slide back under the covers and hold her close as they fell asleep. But as she tried to work up the courage to ask for this one thing, he gave her one final good night kiss before leaving - the way he always did.

And as she succumbed to exhaustion, both her body and emotions wrung out from this night in Dante's arms, she wondered how much longer she could hold herself back from asking him for more. Or, worse, one of these nights letting it slip out that she was crazy in love with him.

14

"How many more of these godawful weddings are we going to be expected to attend before we die?" groaned Rafe Sabattini in a low voice. "This damned tie is cutting off my circulation."

Dante grinned at his younger brother, who was clearly ill at ease whenever he had to wear a suit and tie like today. Unlike Dante, who considered such attire a requirement of his chosen profession, Rafe was a general contractor - the owner of a company with nearly forty full-time employees - who was used to wearing jeans, T-shirts, and boots to work every day.

"Well," drawled Dante teasingly, "when you consider the number of cousins we have on both sides of the family, and then figure out how many of them are still single, you'll have your answer. Though, of course, by the time the youngest ones are all married off, it will be time for the kids of the older ones to have weddings of their own. It's called the Circle of Life, little brother."

Rafe scowled, tugging irritably at his collar. "I can think of a different term for what it really is - *dolore nel culo.*"

Dante snickered in response to his brother's colorful language. "Better not let Mom hear you describe attending her godson's wedding as a pain in the ass. He's also her favorite nephew."

Rafe shrugged. "He's also a wuss. What self-respecting dude refuses to have a stripper at his bachelor party because he promised his fiancé he'd be a good little boy. Brandon better be careful or he's going to spend his entire marriage being pussy whipped."

Dante held a finger up to his lips and shook his head. "And you'd really better not let Mom hear you say something like that. Otherwise, *you're* going to be the one with a pain in your ass."

The brothers shared a good-natured chuckle as they continued to mill around the flagstone courtyard where the wedding ceremony was due to start in just about fifteen minutes time. Roughly half of the guests had already taken a seat in one of the rows of precisely arranged white wooden folding chairs. But since the chairs were sitting out in direct sunlight, and it was still over ninety degrees at nearly four o'clock in the afternoon, the other half of the attendees had chosen to stand in the shaded courtyard for a little while longer.

The winery made a nice setting for an outdoor wedding, mused Dante, though this particular place was a bit too commercial for his tastes. The winery was one of the newer, trendier ones in the area, less than fifteen years old, and lacked the character of many of the more established venues. Dante thought fondly of the small, family-owned vineyard adjacent to the restaurant where so many parties and holiday celebrations had been held over the years. Wines were only produced in small amounts, just enough to serve at the restaurant or distribute to family members. The winery boasted a century old stone farmhouse, a grove of shady oak trees, and a pond where swans and ducks cohabitated in peace. It would, he realized, make a much cozier, more intimate setting for a wedding than this ultra-modern facility he was presently at.

Cara would love the place, he thought, then just as quickly wondered why in hell he was thinking about her at this particular moment.

'Maybe,' he scolded himself, 'because you can be something of a dick to her at times. You always used to tell Nick that he treated Angela like shit the first time they were together. Are you really behaving all that differently now with Cara - discouraging her from calling you, taking her places where you won't run into anyone you know, not introducing her to the family when you know how damned happy that would make her?'

Dante reminded himself that he'd made it all too clear to Cara from the beginning what their relationship would be like, and that he had no intention of getting serious with anyone for the foreseeable future. But the rationale that had formerly helped to assuage his guilty conscience had, as of late, been failing to do the trick. It had been especially difficult not to feel guilty after seeing the hopeful look in her big eyes when he'd mentioned the wedding. And though she had tried hard to paste a cheerful smile on her face and maintain a casual tone to her voice, she hadn't been able to entirely hide the hurt she so obviously felt at not being invited along this weekend.

He blew out a sigh of frustration, realizing with a sinking sensation that he was going to have to do something about this situation with Cara very soon. Things had become way more intense between them than he had ever envisioned, and he was starting to develop real feelings for her. It was the very last thing he had imagined happening the night of their first date, but it had been damned near impossible to resist someone as sweet and funny and kindhearted as she was for very long.

The problem, he reflected, was that Cara was too nice a girl to string along for very long. She needed - no, *deserved* - someone who would take care of her, make a real commitment to her, bring her into his family. And what he needed was to decide - soon - if he could possibly be that someone. And if it ended up that he wasn't, then he was going to have to figure out a way to break things off with her gently.

"There you are! I've been trying to hunt the two of you down for the last half hour. Rafe, quit pulling at your shirt collar, will you? Once the ceremony is over you can get away with taking off the tie and jacket. But leave it alone for a little while longer, okay? Christ, you aren't five fucking years old, you know!"

Dante chuckled at the sudden, whirlwind appearance of his baby sister Gia. Though he supposed at twenty-five, with a college degree, and a job in the environmental studies field, he couldn't really think of her as a little girl any longer - especially since she could frequently curse like a sailor.

"Hey, hey," chided Dante, deliberately rumpling Gia's raven curls because he knew it pissed her off. "Let's watch the language, shall we? You're lucky Nonna isn't here to overhear you. You remember what she did the last time she heard you swear."

Valentina was not one of the invited guests today since Brandon was from Jeannie's side of the family - the youngest son of her oldest brother.

Gia shuddered in recollection. "Yeah, unfortunately. I think my ears are still ringing from that time she boxed them. But, hey, forget about that. Dan, you are not fucking going to believe who's here today! I just saw her talking to Laine's mother inside the tasting room. Can't believe she's got the goddamned nerve to show up this way, and the bitch had better not even look my way after what she did to you 'cause I won't think twice about taking her down. Fucking traitorous.."

Dante placed a palm over his sister's mouth. "Cool it with the swearing or this time *I'll* be the one to box your ears. Now, who exactly are you threatening to take down here, tiger?"

Gia's stormy eyes flashed dangerously. She had always been something of a tomboy, battling fiercely to tag along with her older brothers. She'd practically idolized Dante, the only real father figure she had known, given how young she'd been when their father died. Gia had grown up into something of a badass, and Rafe liked to tease that if she didn't stop scaring off men the way she did she would never find one brave enough to marry her. Gia more often than not simply flipped her brother off when he said something like that, and took great pride in projecting a tough girl image.

And even though she was the youngest, Gia was fiercely protective of her siblings. When Katie had ended things between her and Dante this past winter, Gia had volunteered - a little too eagerly for his liking - to "kick that skinny bitch's ass if she ever comes near you again". She had been furious at Katie's betrayal, while the rest of his family - except perhaps for his grandmother, whom Gia took after far too much for his liking - had only been supportive and understanding.

Gia's normally loud voice lowered to a pitch barely above a whisper as she revealed her news to her brothers. "It's your ex - Katie. Can't believe the evil bitch had the nerve to show her face here today. She's just lucky Nonna isn't here, because *she'd* be the one getting her ears boxed this time!"

Dante stared at his sister in shock, unable to wrap his brain around what he'd just heard. "You must be mistaken, Gia," he mumbled. "Why would Katie be here today? Brandon would have told me if she had RSVPd."

Rafe snorted. "Seriously, Dan? Our cousin has his head in the clouds half the time. Even if Laine had bothered to tell him she was coming, how long do you think he would have remembered that fact? Or thought that it might be cool to give you a heads up."

Gia nodded in agreement. "Brandon's an airhead. And he does whatever Laine tells him to do. So it's a surefire bet that if she made him promise not to say anything to you about Katie he kept his mouth shut."

Dante shook his head. "I don't doubt that she's here. After all, she and Laine have known each other since they were kids, and their parents are close friends. It's just - well, surprising, I guess, that she'd attend knowing I'd be here."

Gia looked as though she'd love nothing better than to spit in disgust. "Nothing would surprise me about that witch," she hissed. "She probably just wants to show off to everyone, brag about how she's some famous actress."

Dante hesitated before asking his next question. "Was she - is she here alone? Or did she have a date with her?"

Gia rolled her eyes in disgust. "Seriously, Dan? Please do not tell me you still have it bad for that woman. Please? Because I remember like it was yesterday how depressed you were after she took off for L.A. Every time I talked to you on the phone I wished I could give you a good slap and snap you out of it. So if you're even thinking of hooking up with that skank again, I'll..."

"Just answer the question, Gia," barked Dante. "And knock it off with the insults, okay? Don't forget you're talking about a woman I was seriously considering marrying."

"I actually had forgotten that disturbing fact until you just reminded us," replied Gia sullenly. "But to answer your question - she was alone when I saw her chatting with Laine's mother. Doesn't mean she didn't bring a date, but I didn't see anyone hovering nearby. Now, can we stop talking about that - I mean, your ex and take our seats? Mom saved a row of chairs for us."

Dante acquiesced to his sister's demands, and followed her and Rafe silently to take their seats beside Jeannie, Talia, and her husband Tony. But it was nowhere near as easy to forget the startling revelation Gia had just shared with him - that the woman he'd been crazy in love with for almost a year, who might even now be wearing his engagement ring if she hadn't broken his heart instead was here, possibly just a few yards away.

Discreetly he glanced up every time another guest walked past their row to take their seat, but none of them were Katie. He guessed that she was sitting in a row behind him, but knew that if he dared to turn around Gia would pinch him. Or kick him. Or grind the deadly looking heel of her stiletto sandal into his instep. He sorely regretted all the years he had spent teaching his baby sister how to defend herself, because she was now an expert at fighting dirty.

It was only when he stood along with all the other guests as the bride began to walk up the aisle on her father's arm that he spotted her. Katie was seated on the other side of the aisle from where he sat, and two rows back, and she looked so beautiful that his heart gave a little lurch despite his resolve to remain detached.

She glanced his way then and their gazes met and held. Katie offered up a tentative smile, her blue eyes looking both sad and hopeful. She looked younger, more innocent, and even a little fragile, and he wondered somewhat scathingly if that had been intentional on her part. She was too thin for his liking, a fact that added to the image of fragility, but otherwise looked almost ethereally lovely. Her silky blonde hair was a little shorter than he remembered, tumbling in loose curls about her shoulders. Her makeup looked minimal from this viewpoint, her lips glossed over in a pale, pearly pink. Katie's dress was nearly the same shade as her lip gloss, a slim fitting sheath of blush pink silk, and she wore pearls around her slender throat. It was a very sophisticated and undoubtedly expensive garment, but a far cry from many of the sexier, dramatic outfits she usually favored.

Dante continued to gaze at her for long seconds, until Gia poked him in the ribs with her elbow, calling his attention back to where the wedding ceremony was about to begin.

He resisted the urge to glance back at Katie again, half-afraid that Gia would notice where his attention was being directed and jab him again. Not to mention the fact that there was no way he was going to fall under Katie's siren spell again, or allow himself to become so dazzled by her beauty and charm that he'd do whatever she asked of him. Her betrayal had cut deep, and it had really only been these past couple of months that he'd considered himself well and truly over her. Dante didn't know what her purpose in being here today was, but he doubted it was strictly the desire to see an old friend get married.

Once the ceremony was over, it was time for cocktail hour. Dante mostly ignored the silver trays of canapes bring passed around by the wait staff, being able to tell at a glance that the food wouldn't come close to what was served at the family restaurant. But he definitely availed himself of the open bar, downing two Tanqueray and tonics in quick succession. He needed the alcohol right now as a way to fortify himself against the shock of seeing Katie again so unexpectedly, and, more importantly, to give himself the resolve to continue avoiding her.

Two hours later the wait staff was beginning to clear dinner dishes from the individual tables that had been set for eight guests each. Joining Dante and his family at their table was Laine's widowed uncle and his elderly mother. The uncle - a distinguished, gray-haired man named Keith - was in his early sixties, and had taken an instant liking to Jeannie, even switching seats with his mother so they could sit next to each other. Jeannie, who had dated only sporadically since becoming a widow all those years ago, seemed to return Keith's interest. There was a twinkle in her dark brown eyes that Dante couldn't recall seeing there very often, and she was certainly laughing and smiling more than usual. And he didn't know if seeing his mother openly flirt with another man made him happy for her, or cause his protective instincts to flare up big time.

Rafe nudged him, none too gently, leaving Dante to wonder why in hell two of his siblings seemed intent on causing him bodily harm today. "Mom sure looks like she's enjoying herself there. Think this means we'll be getting a new stepfather for Christmas?"

Dante scowled at his brother. "Do you go out of your way to sound like an asshole, or is that just second nature for you these days?" he groused. "They just met like two hours ago, hardly know anything about each other, and you're already hearing wedding bells. Relax, kid. Mom's been a widow for over twenty years and seems pretty content with her life the way it is."

Rafe shrugged, topping off both his and Dante's wine glasses with the admittedly excellent Zinfandel that was produced here at the winery. "I'm just saying, Dan, that Mom must get pretty lonely these days with all of us grown up and living on our own. Granted, she still has her job at the restaurant to keep her busy, and when Talia finally pops that kid - Jesus, is she positive she isn't having twins 'cause she is fucking enormous - Mom will no doubt be doing a lot of babysitting. Other than that, she doesn't have much of a social life. Can you blame her for craving some action once in awhile?"

Dante made a sound of disgust. "Christ, do you really want to think about our mother having sex with this guy? Or any guy? I mean, she's a good looking woman, kept herself in great shape for her age, but - ewww. She's our mom, Rafe."

Rafe wrinkled his nose in distaste. "I see your point. Okay, let's try this. Can't you see Mom wanting to have a nice dinner and some pleasant conversation with a gentleman close to her age from time to time?"

Dante laughed, picking up his wine glass. "That's more like it!"

The two brothers sipped their wine in silence for a few minutes, content to savor this time together. The evening was far from over, with the dancing still to come, and Dante was glad he didn't have to worry about driving back to San Francisco tonight, given the amount of alcohol he'd already imbibed.

Rafe's voice broke the silence first. "So you've done a helluva job avoiding your ex so far, but do you honestly think you can keep that up for a few more hours?"

Dante paused with his wineglass halfway to his mouth. "I have no intention of approaching Katie for this entire evening," he replied icily.

Rafe shrugged. "Okay. Whatever. Though you have to admit she looks great, probably the best looking woman here tonight. A little on the skinny side but still with those amazing legs. And in case you didn't notice, she's here alone, no date. And she keeps looking over here at you every few minutes. I'd say that's the sign of a woman who wants to get her man back."

"Too bad for her," answered Dante sarcastically. "She should have thought about that before prancing off to L.A. and telling me to have a nice fucking life."

Rafe ran a finger around the rim of his wine glass. "All I'm saying is that you could at least say hello to her. How many times did you tell me that she was the one for you, the love of your life. And then, after she broke it off, you called her the one that got away. She's here tonight, though, isn't she? Why don't you swallow all that macho male pride and talk to her for a few minutes? How could that possibly hurt anything?"

Dante hesitated, unwilling to admit to his brother - and to himself - that he simply didn't trust himself to be around Katie for even a few minutes. He was afraid that being close to her again, hearing her voice, smelling her perfume, would bring back all the memories of their time together. And that those memories would threaten to chip away at the protective wall he'd erected around himself ever since she'd left for L.A.

"I think under the circumstances that Katie should be the one to approach me, don't you think?" he challenged.

Rafe threw his hands up in the air. "Hey, do whatever you think best, Dan. But there's no way Katie's going to approach you with your little guard dog by your side. Especially since Gia's been giving her dirty looks all evening."

Dante finished his glass of wine, then reached for the bottle only to find it empty. "I'm going to get a real drink. Want anything from the bar?"

Rafe shook his head, holding up his mostly full glass of wine. "I'm good for now, thanks."

Dante made his way to the bar that had been set up at the opposite side of the courtyard from where he'd been sitting. He ordered a brandy, and had just stuffed some bills in the bartender's tip jar when he heard a high-pitched, achingly familiar voice just behind him.

"Hello, Danny. Could - could we maybe talk for a few minutes? Please? I've been waiting for the chance to say hello all evening."

He froze in place , the brandy snifter halfway to his lips, as he struggled with the right way to respond. If Gia had been around, she would have demanded he give Katie a scathing look before striding away without a word. His mother, on the other hand, would have insisted he do the polite thing and exchange pleasantries with her for a few minutes.

In the end, his mother's teachings won out, and he found himself turning around slowly to face the woman who had alternately been the love of his love, and the one who broke his heart. And though he was waging an internal battle with himself to remain emotionally detached and present a cool, distant image, the moment he gazed into Katie's blue eyes and smelled the tantalizing scent of her perfume, Dante felt his resolve instantly begin to weaken.

She was smiling at him softly, almost sadly, as she extended a hand towards him somewhat timidly. "It's - it's good to see you, Danny.

Really good," she offered in that sexy, breathy little voice. "How have you been?"

He hesitated briefly before clasping her smooth, cool hand in his lightly. "I've been great, thanks," he told her somberly. "And you look as though living in L.A. is definitely agreeing with you."

Katie squeezed his hand, as though she sensed he'd been about to withdraw it. "Actually," she admitted softly, "I left L.A. a couple of weeks ago. For good this time. I'm staying with my parents for awhile until I get myself settled, figure out my future. It - well, I'm finally done with show business. It hasn't treated me very well, I'm afraid."

Her announcement wasn't all that surprising, given that he'd already known about her show being canceled. "I'm sorry that it didn't work out for you," he replied somewhat stiffly. "But I'm sure things will get better soon. Look, I'd better get back to my family. Enjoy the rest of your evening."

"Wait. Please."

Katie clutched his arm as though holding on for dear life, and her voice sounded desperate, almost tearful. Her blue eyes were, in fact, moist with unshed tears.

"Look, I know how angry you must be with me," she ventured. "How hurt and upset. And I know I have no right at all to ask this but - well, I was really hoping you could spare me a few minutes to talk, maybe have a quick drink. I - I'd like the chance to apologize to you, explain a few things, and beg you to somehow forgive me for the horrible, selfish way I behaved in February. Please, Danny. I'll beg if that's what you want."

He regarded her skeptically for long seconds, trying to determine from her vocal tone, facial expression, and body language if she was truly being sincere or merely trying to play him. But then he recalled what a poor acting job she'd done in those sitcom episodes he had watched, and quickly decided she simply wasn't capable of deceiving him.

"Fine," he agreed tersely. "One drink, that's it. What would you like?"

He ordered her a mojito, then followed her silently to a small, secluded table inside the winery's tasting room. He wondered if she had scouted out this particular location ahead of time, then dismissed the thought as inconsequential as they sat down.

Katie took a tentative sip of her drink, seeming uncharacteristically ill at ease. That particular behavior, more than anything else, gave Dante reason to believe that she was being sincere – because Katie had always been brimming over with confidence, the most self-assured woman he'd ever known.

"You look good, Danny," she told him quietly. "Happy. Are you – I mean, I know that I don't have any right to ask, but I was just curious if you're seeing someone right now."

His mouth tightened, not wanting to think about Cara at the moment, not wanting to wonder if even sitting across a table from Katie would be considered a betrayal of sorts of the woman he'd been dating. "I've been seeing someone, yes," he muttered. "But I have no intention of discussing her with you, Katie. Now, what exactly did you need to say to me?"

Katie looked stricken at his coolness towards her. "I wasn't going to ask you for details, Danny," she replied somberly. "And I'm glad you have someone who obviously makes you happy. She's a very, very lucky woman, whoever she is. And probably a whole lot smarter than I was. Breaking up with you was the stupidest thing I've ever done, the worst decision I've ever made. And I've regretted it every single day since I left last February. You were the most wonderful man I ever met, and I was a complete idiot to let my so-called acting career get in the way of our relationship. I – I just wanted you to know that. And to maybe, possibly, see if you could one day find a way to forgive me for what I did."

Tears were tracking down her cheeks as she spoke, but Katie was one of those rare women who looked beautiful even when she was crying. Dante swore softly beneath his breath, telling himself he was a fool for even listening to her, and handed her a paper cocktail napkin.

She dabbed at her tears daintily before taking a tiny sip of her drink. "Thank you," she sniffled. "I'm sorry to be such a basket case, but these last few months have been so awful, Danny. I'd forgotten how horrible Los Angeles can be since the last time I lived there. Oh, not just the traffic and the smog and the crowds. But how shallow and spiteful and mean people can be, especially in show business. I've missed my family and friends so much, been so lonely. It's hard to make friends in a place like that, you know? You don't know who you can trust, if someone who swears they're your friend is going to wind up stabbing you in the back the next week. It's good to be home, and I'm home for good this time. I'll never, ever, even think of returning to L.A. again. Or trying to make a go of it as an actress."

"Hmm." He tried like hell to sound disinterested. "I read that your TV show got cancelled, but I'm surprised you weren't able to find other work."

Katie shook her head. "It's a tough business," she admitted. "There are literally thousands of young women wanting to be an actress, and we're all competing for the same roles. And, as my agent so kindly pointed out," she added sarcastically, "I'm not exactly getting any younger. He also told me that I'm a terrible actress, and that I should demand a refund from the acting classes I took. I was hurt at first to hear that, but after doing some real soul searching I realized he was probably right."

"He was an ass to say something like that to you," offered Dante. "I'm sure you're far more talented than he told you."

She beamed at him. "You're sweet to say so. But unfortunately, Doug was right. I've been trying for more than a decade to succeed as an actress, and it's time to finally grow up and move on."

He sipped his brandy thoughtfully. "So this is really it, huh? You're really and truly retiring from acting?"

Katie nodded emphatically. "Absolutely. I've been talking to my parents about the future a lot since I moved back in with them, and they think I should go back to college and get my degree, pursue a whole new career. Trouble is, I don't think I'm smart enough to do that, not cut out to be a student at this point in my life. And even if I was I have no idea what I'd want to do."

"You're plenty smart enough, Katie," he assured her. "Don't sell yourself short like that. What you need to figure out is what you might be interested in, do some research on careers in those fields, and then get some professional advice. There's a firm in my building, in fact, that does career counseling and coaching. You should schedule an appointment with them – or someplace similar – and see what your options are."

For the next few minutes, they discussed what sort of career she might be interested in, what she was best suited for. Dante texted her the website of the counseling firm he'd mentioned, and she told him she would check it out the next day and hopefully set up an appointment within the next week or so.

The conversation somewhat naturally transitioned into a discussion about their families, mutual friends, today's wedding. After a time, Dante found himself forgetting that he was supposed to be furious with this woman, or that he'd promised himself to remain coolly detached and treat her impersonally. It just felt, well – *natural* to be chatting with her like this, like they had dozens of times before. And he could almost – *almost* – forget that several months had passed since they had seen each other, that she had chosen her career over a future with him, or that he was currently dating the sweetest, most kindhearted girl he'd ever known, even though he still insisted that there was nothing serious between them.

He checked his watch, surprised to find that more than half an hour had passed. "I should be getting back to my family," he announced, pushing back his chair and getting to his feet. "It was good to catch up with you, Katie. And I wish you all the best with whatever you decide to do. Don't underestimate yourself, okay?"

She nodded, rising from her chair slowly. "Thanks, Danny. I appreciate all of your advice. I always thought of you as the smartest guy I knew, as well as the nicest. And the best looking, of course!"

He smiled faintly. "Thanks. Look, take care of yourself, hmm? And enjoy the rest of the evening."

"Wait."

Katie placed a hand on his forearm as he turned to leave. Dante looked at her quizzically as she seemed to struggle with what she wanted to say next.

"I was just wondering," she began. "Hoping, actually, that maybe we could keep in touch once in awhile? Oh, I know you're dating someone, and I don't want to interfere with that. But, well, maybe we could have coffee sometime? Or lunch? Or just talk on the phone occasionally. I'd love to get your advice about school and careers, since you know so much about business and such."

He hesitated. "Katie, I'm not sure that's going to work out."

"Please." Once again her blue eyes were moist with unshed tears, and her voice cracked a little. "Not a day goes by that I don't regret what I did, Danny. That I don't remember how good things were between us. And I know I've spoiled that, ruined things for good. But I'd really like the chance to make some of that up to you, to be your friend if nothing else. Please?"

Dante called himself ten different kinds of a fool for falling for what he sure as hell hoped wasn't some sort of elaborate act. But then, he'd always had a weakness for sad, helpless women, had always felt the urge to protect them and look out for them. It went back, he supposed, to the time when his father had died, and overnight he'd become the man of his family. Over the years, he had appointed himself the protector of his mother and sisters, and most of his longer term relationships had seemed to be with women who were more than content to let him take charge. And for all of her other faults and past transgressions, Katie was incredibly vulnerable and sad right now, and he would have felt like a real jerk for kicking her to the curb.

"Why don't you give me a call after you contact the career counselor?" he offered. "You can tell me what they had to say. And if you decide to set up an appointment with them, maybe we can grab coffee or a quick lunch if I'm free that day?"

Katie beamed, her lovely face aglow with pleasure. "That would be wonderful, Danny," she enthused. "I can't think of anything I'd love more. I'll make sure to call the counselor right away, and let you know what they say. Take care until then, okay?

She pressed a soft, sweet kiss to his cheek, her breast brushing up against his arm, before giving him a little wave good-by as she walked away.

The spot on his cheek where her lips had touched burned like a brand, and he rubbed at it angrily, as though to erase her touch.

And as he returned to his own table – certain to be grilled about his whereabouts by both Rafe and Gia – Dante told himself that just because he'd offered to have a casual cup of coffee with Katie didn't mean that he was in any danger whatsoever of once again falling under her spell.

15

"Is everything okay? You've, um, seemed a little out of it all evening."

Dante glanced up from the plate of food he'd been staring at for long seconds, a forkful of chile relleno halfway to his mouth. Tonight he'd brought Cara to a little taqueria deep in the heart of the city's Mission district, a place rarely frequented by anyone but the neighborhood residents who knew the prices were cheap, the beers ice cold, and the food both authentic and delicious.

"Yeah, everything's fine," he was quick to assure her. "Sorry I've been so spacey tonight. It's just been kind of a crazy week is all, really busy at work."

"I'm sorry." She reached across the table to squeeze his hand. "We could have cancelled tonight if you weren't in the mood to go out. Honestly, I would have understood."

Dante smiled at her, and linked his fingers with hers. "I know you would have, honey," he told her. "You're probably the most understanding, supportive person I've ever met. But I'm okay, I promise. And it probably does me good to get out, get my mind off of - things."

Cara returned his smile tentatively. "Okay. By the way, these are hands down the best carne asada tacos I've ever had. Thanks for bringing me here tonight."

Her obvious appreciation for every small thing he did for her - including bringing her to the sort of semi-greasy spoon joint that most women of his acquaintance would have balked at setting foot in - only made Dante feel guiltier, like more of a heel, for what he was even considering doing to her.

"I'm glad you like it. Granted, it's far from the fanciest place in town, or even in the Mission, but you can't beat the food."

Cara nodded, washing down a bite of taco with a sip of her margarita. "It's great," she enthused. "And who cares about how fancy it is? Besides, it's way too hot to even think of getting dressed up tonight."

The rare ninety degree temperatures in San Francisco earlier today had been one of the reasons he'd insisted on taking her out to dinner this Saturday evening rather than eating at her tiny apartment as usual. With only one small, inadequate window, her place was stifling hot inside, and the thought of eating inside that dark, stuffy room had been more than Dante could handle. Cara had protested, of course, reminding him that he'd taken her out to dinner last night and that it was her turn to return the favor. In response, he'd merely grabbed her hand and tugged her out the door to his car, ignoring her protests that she wasn't dressed to eat out - garbed in denim cutoffs, a white tank top that clung spectacularly to her eye-popping tits, and rubber flip flops that had seen better days. He'd assured her during the short drive to the taqueria that she would actually be the best dressed patron the place had seen in awhile.

And Cara being the good sport that she was had raved about the food, the authentic atmosphere of the place, and even tapped her foot along to the salsa music being piped out of the wall mounted speakers. For someone who had so little, she was always gracious, always appreciative, and always enthusiastic about the places he brought her to or the things he gave her.

Not, of course, that she let him give her much more than a bottle of wine or a box of fancy bakery cookies when he ate dinner at her place. She had more than her fair share of stubborn pride, and seemed bound and determined to make it through life on her own without depending on anyone to support her.

Just this evening, in fact, when he'd popped inside her stifling hot apartment, he had noticed an unfamiliar laptop sitting on top of the table that doubled as her desk and commented on it.

"Finally got yourself a new computer, I see," he had remarked, noting that the laptop was a vast improvement from her previous one. "About time. Your old one looked like it was ready to give up the ghost five years ago."

Cara had shook her head. "That's not mine. It belongs to Mirai, actually, and I'm just borrowing it for a couple of weeks while mine's being repaired. Hopefully being repaired, I should say. The guy I brought it to couldn't promise anything, but he thinks it just needs a new battery."

He knew that Mirai was her best friend, someone she'd met during her first year at Berkeley, and that she had actually slept on the couch in the other girl's apartment for the entire spring semester. A couple of times Cara had rather timidly suggested going on some sort of double date with Mirai and whoever she was currently dating, but when he hadn't seemed too enthused with the idea she had quickly dropped the subject.

Dante had frowned after hearing this news. "I wish you'd stop being so stubborn and just let me buy you a new laptop. It doesn't have to be anything expensive, there are some good quality ones that only cost a few hundred bucks. That's probably less than I spend on my dry cleaning for a month. Let me do this for you, honey."

Predictably, though, she had given a firm shake of her head. "No, thank you. I appreciate the offer, Dante, as usual, but I really don't want you buying me expensive things. Now, are you positive I'm dressed okay to go out to dinner? I feel like the biggest slob in Slobbovia right now."

He'd chuckled in response. "You do know that isn't an actual place, don't you? And yes, you look fine. Even if you are the most maddeningly stubborn person I've ever met."

He sipped his Negra Modela beer slowly, watching Cara as she savored each bite of her dinner. He wasn't sure he'd ever met anyone who made eating look so sensual, so enjoyable. With each forkful of food that passed her full, lush lips, she made a little sound of pleasure, and he had to smile as he observed her unabashed delight. There was still so much of the young, innocent girl in her, despite the fact that she was also mature beyond her years. And it was the former, rather than the latter, that had been weighing heavily on his mind these past couple of weeks. Cara had always been too young for him, too sweet and guileless and inexperienced, but he'd continued to be with her anyway because she made him laugh, made him feel good about himself, and he'd been too selfish to break things off and allow her to find someone who could offer her the sort of long-term relationship she deserved.

And now there was the added and unsettling complication of Katie being back in town, and the very, very mixed feelings he continued to have for his ex. She hadn't wasted any time in contacting the career counseling firm in his building, and had called him the Monday after the wedding to let him know she'd made an appointment later that week. Against his better judgment, he'd agreed to meet her for coffee afterwards, and it had been a struggle for him the entire time not to simply fall back under her spell.

And Katie wasn't making it easy for him. She was texting and calling and emailing him on a regular basis, always under the pretext of asking his advice about careers and college and even investments. In the two weeks since the wedding, they'd met for coffee one additional time and lunch just yesterday. Katie had casually asked about his plans for the weekend, and hadn't bothered to disguise the crestfallen look on her face when he'd acknowledged that he had a date. But thus far she hadn't said a word about the possibility of getting back together, had been careful to keep things lighthearted and casual, and to tell him on a frequent basis how grateful she was for his friendship. She had also expressed her regrets several times now about the way she'd ended things between them in February, calling herself a fool for letting someone like him go, and wistfully envying the woman he was currently dating.

The suspicion continued to nag at him that Katie was simply putting on an act – for what purpose he wasn't exactly sure. But then he'd recall how awful her performance had been in that sitcom, and thought that she couldn't possibly be acting now because she seemed so genuine and sincere.

Having lunch with her yesterday had felt so much like old times that he'd had to remind himself several times that they were no longer together. He and Katie had always fit together well, had been a perfect match in nearly every way, and she had blended into his social and personal life almost seamlessly. His friends, co-workers, clients, and at least the male members of his family had all been a little in awe of Katie, telling Dante over and over again what a lucky bastard he was to have landed someone as gorgeous, sexy, and charming as she was.

And when Katie had first agreed to go out with him soon after they'd met at Laine and Brandon's engagement party, he had felt like he was back in high school, and dating the prettiest and most popular girl in his class. Katie, in fact, had reminded him of Heather Chase, the only girl in his high school who hadn't fallen all over him. Heather had been incredibly pretty - tall, shapely, and blonde - but had also been an elitist snob. Her father had been a multi-millionaire, and Heather had considered Dante - whose family worked mostly in the restaurant, law enforcement, and construction businesses - to be several rungs beneath her on the social scale. Her rejection had stung more than he had ever admitted, and had served as a motivating factor in making his venture capital firm as successful as it currently was.

Snagging a prize like Katie had more than made up for a long-ago snub by some privileged high school homecoming queen. In fact, Dante had taken great pride in bringing Katie along as his date last year to an event at a local winery in Healdsburg that he knew Heather would be attending. After marriage and two children, Heather hadn't looked quite as good as she had in high school, and there had been little doubt that the woman on Dante's arm had far outshone her.

And, of course, his physical relationship with Katie had been nothing short of dynamite. She'd been experienced, confident, and sensual, and not the least bit hesitant to let him know what she liked in terms of sex. There had been certain times, however, when he'd suspected that she was using sex to get something from him - whether that something was a shopping spree, an expensive dinner out at a new restaurant she'd read about, or simply to coerce him into doing things her way. He'd been too besotted by her, however, to ever confront her with his suspicions.

She had also been a bit difficult at times when it came to seeing his family, teasingly calling him a mama's boy for visiting his mother so often, or acting sullen and withdrawn when he wouldn't forego attending his aunt and uncle's anniversary party so that he could take her to the theater instead. But after he had made it clear to Katie that spending time with his family was very important to him, she'd backed off and acted mostly supportive - even if she hadn't always enjoyed herself during those visits.

Dante had been confident, though, that he and Katie would have worked all of that out, and that once they were officially engaged her attitude towards his family would have changed for the better. At this point in time, however, he couldn't vouch for the sort of reception she might receive from certain members of his family, given the circumstances behind their break-up earlier this year. It would definitely take some time and care before he'd realistically be able to bring Katie to a family event again.

He shook his head in annoyance as he returned his attention to his food. Why in hell was he even thinking about bringing Katie to see his family when they weren't even dating any longer? Just because they were actually speaking to each other again, and she was being especially contrite and sweet, didn't mean a damned thing. Oh, he knew that she would jump at the opportunity to resume their relationship. That much was obvious, and no one could be *that* good of an actor. But he was nowhere near ready to trust her again, was unwilling to simply pick up where they'd left off last winter. And then, of course, there was Cara to consider.

At present, she was busy licking a glob of guacamole from her fingers, moaning in appreciation as she did so, and Dante couldn't suppress a chuckle. God, she was really adorable, and a hell of a lot of fun to be around! But sometimes - like tonight - he became uncomfortably aware of the difference not just in their ages but also in their experiences, level of sophistication, and where they each were in their lives right now. He was more than ten years her senior, had finished his college degree over a decade ago, and owned a successful, established business. He'd traveled extensively, dated dozens of different women, and was at a point where settling down and starting a family sounded more and more appealing.

Cara, on the other hand, still had another year or more before she'd be finished with college. And after working so hard for that degree, there was little doubt that she'd want to have a career for several years before getting married and becoming a mother. Plus, she deserved the chance to travel, date other men, and enjoy herself. Asking her to make a commitment to him at this stage of her life would be grossly unfair.

Discreetly, Dante took in Cara's makeup-free face; her wild, unruly mane of curls that she'd hastily pulled into a messy ponytail; her short, unpolished nails. If she owned any jewelry she had never bothered to wear it in his presence. Her white tank top was probably a size too small, and he winced to notice the salsa stain just over her right breast. The frayed denim cut-offs were also on the snug side, and while she had painted her toenails a bright crimson, the polish was badly chipped. Admittedly, he'd all but dragged her out of her apartment before she had an opportunity to tidy herself up a bit, but there was no escaping the fact that she looked anything but sleek and sophisticated tonight.

Unlike Katie's perfectly put together appearance at their lunch yesterday. Her makeup had been applied with an expert hand, and her blonde hair had looked so sleek and shiny he'd wondered if she had had it professionally blown out that morning. Both her manicure and pedicure had been flawless, and the summery sheath dress she'd worn of a pale saffron yellow had fit her to perfection. A gold bangle bracelet and dainty hoop earrings had completed her classy but sexy outfit.

The contrast between the two women was worlds apart - Cara being the quintessential girl next door while Katie was the girl men dreamed about. One was the girl you brought home to meet your mother, while the other was the woman you paraded arrogantly in front of your friends. And ever since he'd met the latter again two weeks ago, Dante had been tormenting himself about what to do about his current situation.

Cara downed the last of her margarita - the second one she'd had tonight - and regarded him with a concerned expression on her face. "Are you positive you're okay?" she asked worriedly. "Because you've barely eaten half your dinner, and have hardly said a word all night. Are you upset with me about something? Or don't you feel well?"

He felt like the biggest, most insensitive asshole ever born at her obvious concern for him. Especially when he'd just been comparing her appearance to another woman's and finding hers lacking. Dante had never thought of himself as either shallow or unkind, but he had been both of those things - and worse - just a few minutes earlier. Cara couldn't help it, for God's sake, that she couldn't afford to get her hair and nails done on a regular basis, or that her wardrobe left a lot to be desired. And though her refusal to accept gifts from him - like the laptop he'd offered to buy her earlier today - was a source of constant frustration, he also admired her all the more for it.

"I could never be upset with you, honey," he told her earnestly. "I've just got some stuff I'm working through at the moment, that's all. As for the food, I think the hot weather today has me feeling a little off. Plus, I met my brother for a late brunch after the gym so I'm not all that hungry."

Cara reached for her glass of ice water. "Does your brother live in the city, too, or was he just visiting?"

Dante realized just how little he'd shared with her about his family, and felt another pang of guilt assail him. "Rafe lives in San Francisco, too, though fortunately far enough away from my place that he can't just drop in whenever he feels like it. He has a house on Potrero Hill that he renovated by himself. He did a great job on the place, especially considering what a dump it was when he bought it. Rafe's in construction, owns the business, and has done really well for himself."

She gave a hollow sounding little laugh. "You know, it just occurred to me that I don't even know where *you* live! I mean, aside from your place being in San Francisco, that is."

Once more he felt like a total douchebag, all too aware that he'd kept certain facts about his life hidden from her. But he had stopped giving out his home address to the women he'd dated - with the exception of Katie - after one of his former girlfriends had basically stalked him outside of his condo building, and he'd had to file for a restraining order against her.

It went without saying, though, that Cara would never dream of doing something so extreme. He could barely recall the last time she'd even sent him a text. Unlike Katie, he thought guiltily, who had texted him *and* left a voicemail just this morning.

"I live on Russian Hill," he replied. "Not far from North Beach, so that I can get my fix of good Italian food whenever I want."

Cara nodded. "I know the area. One of Angela's clients lives around there, and since she's elderly I've brought papers over to her house from time to time for her to sign. You must have an incredible view."

"Yeah, it's pretty spectacular, especially since I live on the top floor."

"The penthouse, huh? No wonder you get to have three parking spaces in the building," she joked.

Dante smiled faintly in response as he placed his credit card on the plastic guest check holder by his plate. "It does have it's privileges, that's for sure."

Cara didn't push him for any additional details, though he knew she had to be curious to learn more about his personal life. And while he appreciated her respect for his privacy, it didn't make him feel like any less of a jerk for keeping her at arms length.

The drive back to her place - in his father's classic Camaro this time - was made in relative silence. For once, Cara curbed her chattiness, obviously well aware that he wasn't in the mood to do much talking.

Once inside that dimly lit, stifling hot hovel she called an apartment, Dante couldn't repress a shudder as his gaze fell on the folded out futon. As airless as the room was right now, he didn't think there was any way he'd be able to fuck Cara on that scratchy, uncomfortable mattress tonight. But from the hopeful look in her eyes as she pressed herself up against him, she evidently didn't feel the same way.

He ran his palms up and down her bare arms. "Honey, as hot as this place feels, I'm not sure sex is going to happen tonight. I'm already sweating and I haven't even kissed you."

She slid her arms around his waist, gazing up at him mischievously. "We could just take a shower afterwards," she suggested helpfully. "Too bad the stall is so small, or we could take a shower *during* sex."

Dante thought longingly of the enormous granite shower in his master bathroom, more than big enough for two people to have all sorts of fun in. He'd never been as tempted as he was at this moment to whisk Cara back to the car and drive to his condo, where they could happily fuck all night long in air conditioned bliss - not to mention on a huge, comfy king sized bed.

But to do so now would be to take a serious step in their relationship that he just wasn't ready to do - and might never be ready to do, he realized with a pang.

He shook his head. "I've seen your shower, Cara *mia*, and frankly I'm not sure how *you* even squeeze into it, petite as you are. Maybe we should just give it a rest tonight, honey. God knows I've been lousy company these past few hours. I wouldn't blame you in the least for not being in the mood for sex under the circumstances."

In reply, she slid her arms up and around his neck, pulling his head down to meet her very eager kiss. Her small tongue slipped between his lips, and Dante groaned as he began to kiss her back. Her boobs were crushed up against his chest, and his cock immediately hardened at the feel of her hard little nipples poking into his hot skin. And when her hand began to stroke his dick persuasively through his rapidly tightening jeans, he gave up any previous thoughts he might have had of resisting her.

"Let me," she whispered against his ear, rising up on tiptoe to do so. "Let me take care of you tonight, Dante."

"Honey, no. You don't have to do that - ah, fuck!"

The protest he'd been about to make was quickly abandoned as Cara dropped to her knees in front of him, deftly unzipping his pants and drawing his throbbing dick into her hands. Her former inexperience with oral sex was definitely a thing of the past now, and she was all too eager to demonstrate her newfound expertise.

"So fucking good," he hissed, his hands grasping thick strands of her hair as she licked up and down the length of his cock. That sweet little tongue of hers lapped up the thick, pearly beads of pre-cum that had gathered around the tip, just before sucking the broad head between her lips.

She pleasured him unselfishly, sensing his need for her. Her hand slid up and down his cock, stroking him in the slow, arousing way that he'd taught her. At the same time, her mouth continued to work its magic, sucking as much of him down her throat as she could accommodate. Dante shoved his fingers into her hair, holding her head still as he fucked that sweet, hot mouth of hers, the little moans she made as he did so only making him harder and more desperate for release. She loved doing this to him as much as he enjoyed being on the receiving end, adored being able to give him this much pleasure.

She gave his swollen balls a gentle squeeze, but that light touch was all he needed to come long and hard, spilling himself into her mouth gluttonously. And because it felt so damned good, because the pleasure she gave him was like nothing he'd ever felt before, he kept thrusting his still-erect cock between her lips for long seconds after he was empty.

Cara was nearly gasping for breath as she finally let his penis slip out of her mouth, her eyes dark with passion as she stared up at him. Tenderly, he ran a finger over her lush, trembling lips, his thumb whisking away a drop of his semen that still clung to the corner of her mouth.

Without a word, he pulled her to her feet, then just as quickly tumbled them onto the detested futon. He had her naked in less than thirty seconds, her breasts tumbling free from her bra into his waiting hands. He licked her nipples, cupped her breasts, caressed her belly and thighs and ass, arousing her until she was bucking up off the mattress like a wild thing, begging him to please, please let her come. And when he finally gave her what she wanted - slipping two fingers deep inside of her core where she was so wet and hot that all he could think about was sinking his cock inside of that delicious little pussy and staying put for a good long while - Cara sobbed in pleasure, calling out his name over and over again, her legs thrashing uncontrollably as she found her sweet release.

She was dazed and dreamy eyed afterwards, watching as he undressed - a feat he hadn't quite been able to accomplish earlier. Cara's fingers brushed a stray lock of hair from his damp forehead as his body covered hers a moment later, and she smiled up at him teasingly.

"Hate to break the news," she whispered a little unsteadily, "but you're really, really sweaty now."

Dante threw back his admittedly drenched head and laughed. "It was worth it," he murmured, his hands spreading her thighs apart. "Though I'm definitely buying you an electric fan for this place. And *that* is not up for debate. Got it?"

She nodded obediently, then gasped as he entered her body with one deep, hard thrust.

16

"I can't explain it, Mir. Not exactly. All I know is that I've got a really bad feeling the end is in sight. No, it's nothing he's said or done. It's just that he's been really moody lately, quiet. Yes, I've asked him what's wrong, and he just says it's work related, that he's been really busy, yada yada yada. And last weekend he came *this* close to refusing sex. No, we wound up screwing like rabbits, but only after I opened with a BJ. No, he's never not wanted sex before. Oh, God, he's getting ready to break up with me, isn't he?" wailed Cara.

Mirai heaved a sigh of mingled irritation and frustration. "Are you finished with the babbling for a minute or two?" she asked on the other end of the line. "Because if you don't get a grip on yourself, I'm going to come over there and do it for you. Calm down, okay?"

But following her BFF's advice was easier said than done, especially since Cara had been worrying and imagining the worst ever since last Saturday night. It was Thursday now, and she'd just walked in the door of her apartment less than ten minutes ago after her evening class. And even though she was exhausted as usual by the end of the day, she badly needed to hear her friend's reassuring voice.

Since Dante had left her apartment on Saturday, she hadn't heard a word from him. That in itself was hardly unusual, given his general lack of communication in between their Friday night dates. And ever since one of her short-lived college boyfriends had called her an insecure, needy pest for texting and calling him too often, Cara had been scrupulously careful not to repeat her actions - even though in *her* opinion she really hadn't contacted the jerk as frequently as he'd claimed. With Dante in particular, she'd sensed he wouldn't appreciate receiving messages from her on a regular basis, so she only got in touch with him when it was absolutely necessary.

But she'd been sorely tempted every single day this past week to call him or send him a quick text just to see if everything was okay. It wasn't like him at all to be as quiet and moody as he'd been last weekend, and Cara was skeptical that work related issues were really to blame. And maybe it was just her various insecurities - God knew she had too many of those to count! - or her tendency to overreact at times, but she had this horrible, sinking feeling that Dante was growing bored with her, and was ready to move on. He'd warned her, after all, from the very beginning of their relationship, that he couldn't make her any promises or guarantees about how long this would last between them.

"I've been trying to stay calm for the last five days," she told Mirai now. "But nothing's working. You know, come to think of it, Dante's been a little off ever since he went to that wedding a few weeks ago - moody, uncommunicative, like he's got something big on his mind."

"How's the sex life been?" inquired Mirai, never one to shy away from asking personal questions.

"Well, this is Dante we're talking about, after all, so of course any sort of sex is fantastic," replied Cara. "I mean, he could just sort of lay there and let me do all the work and I'd still get off every single time. But one thing I *have* noticed the last few times he's been over - now, this is going to sound really greedy or like I'm some sort of nympho or something - but we only do it one time."

"Uh, and how many times do you usually - as you so succinctly put it - *do* it?" asked Mirai, her voice heavy with sarcasm.

"At least twice. Usually three. And there were a few times when he was really horny and I think I counted four. And that doesn't count the extra times he gets me off - you know, with his hand or his mouth. Did I ever mention that he's really, really good at oral?" sighed Cara, a little mortified to realize she was getting wet just thinking about Dante going down on her.

Mirai made a sound that resembled a snarl. "Yes, damn you, you have definitely mentioned it! Usually right after I had another dud of a date who could barely keep it up long enough to finish the job. Do you know how difficult it is to find a guy who really knows his way around a girl's vajayjay? So stop rubbing it in, okay? And you were right the first time - you do sound like a greedy, selfish twat for expecting more than one fantastic orgasm at a time. Some of us have gone without one of those elusive O's for longer than they care to admit."

Cara chuckled in spite of herself, and was glad she'd taken a few extra minutes to call up the best friend who could always make her smile and feel better no matter what the circumstances.

"Look, stop overthinking everything for once in your life, okay?" said Mirai soothingly. "And for God's sake, be grateful that you've at least *got* a sex life! Now get some sleep. Don't you have to wake up at some ungodly hour of the morning?"

But despite the lateness of the hour, Cara wasn't able to fall asleep easily that night. And in spite of Mirai's so-called pep talk, she didn't feel a whole lot better about the current state of her relationship with Dante. If one could actually call what they had a relationship, that is. For more than four months now, nothing had really changed, and it certainly hadn't moved forward. She would wait for him in the lobby of his office building each Friday after work, despite her repeated offers to meet him up in his office. Cara just assumed he didn't want his co-workers, especially his business partner Howie, to see the two of them together. Just like she had yet to meet any of his friends or family members.

They would have dinner out, always at a place in an outlying neighborhood or even slightly out of the city limits. Last Friday, for example, he'd taken her to a seafood restaurant in Half Moon Bay, a small coastal town about thirty miles south of San Francisco. The fact that the food had been delicious, and the ocean view breathtaking hadn't helped to diminish her growing dismay that he seemed to be going out of his way to keep their relationship a closely guarded secret.

After dinner, they'd return to her tiny hole of an apartment and have sex before Dante would kiss her good-bye and head back to his place. He'd return on Saturday evening when she would cook him dinner before they would wind up in bed again.

That pretty much summed up their relationship, thought Cara with a sigh. Dante had never once suggested seeing her during the week, whether it was for coffee or lunch, and rarely contacted her. Mirai had decreed that Cara was pretty much just his fuck buddy, willing and available whenever he needed to get his rocks off, with a free dinner thrown in once a week for good measure. Cara would just laugh it off when her friend made those sort of observations, insisting time after time that being fuck buddies with a guy was all she had time for these days, and that given her crazy schedule she would make the very worst sort of girlfriend right now. But no matter how many times she kept telling that to Mirai - and to herself - she never really believed it.

If she wasn't careful, she scolded herself, she was going to turn into her mother - a willing doormat for the handsome, charming man she was crazy in love with, who made all manner of excuses for his behavior, and clung to him desperately for fear that he would leave her one day.

Though Dante, of course, was nothing at all like her useless father. He was kind and considerate and generous, always offering to buy her things. Unlike Mark, who'd been too busy to talk the last several times she had called him, or who hadn't returned her emails or texts in almost two months. His new wife and two young children were his family now, with Cara always an afterthought, a nuisance that he probably wished would just go away.

She wondered sadly if perhaps Dante thought of her that way, too - if he'd be relieved if she suggested they go their separate ways so that he could find someone he deemed worthy of meeting his family and friends. And if she was the one to end things, it could be on her terms, and save her pride in the process. And if it broke her heart to do so - well, that was going to happen sooner than later anyway, wasn't it?

But as she tossed and turned, still unable to fall asleep despite her exhaustion, Cara knew that she would never voluntarily walk away from Dante, no matter how much it was going to hurt when he inevitably did the same to her.

SEPTEMBER – LABOR DAY WEEKEND

CARA COULDN'T REMEMBER when she'd felt quite this miserable - stuffy nose, sore throat, queasy tummy, and overall fatigue. Summer colds were officially the worst, she thought, even though there were only three weeks of the season officially remaining. And the foggy, drizzly, and windy weather in San Francisco this afternoon was anything but summery. It would have been an ideal day to curl up under the covers, drink a cup of hot tea, and binge watch as many movies as possible before falling asleep from the cold medicine she'd been taking religiously every few hours.

The problems with that delightful scenario were plentiful. For one, she didn't actually own a DVD player or any current movies. She could have easily borrowed the latter from Mirai, who probably owned a few thousand movies and TV series on DVD. But while Cara's laptop had more or less been fixed, it was still temperamental, and she could almost guarantee that any DVD would freeze up halfway through the movie, and possibly cause something else to go awry with the ancient computer. The laptop had been a hand-me-down from Sharon, given to Cara when she'd started high school. The new laptop that Sharon had bought for herself after scrimping and saving for more than a year had been one of the things Mark had taken for himself when the house had been sold. And when he'd replaced that particular device with a brand new one a year later,

Holly had taken it upon herself to give Sharon's computer to her younger sister instead of returning it to Cara.

But aside from the issue with watching a movie, today was officially laundry day, and no matter how crappy she felt Cara had been obliged to make the tedious trek to the laundromat. Fortunately, she'd just tossed everything into the dryer, so she could get out of here in less than an hour and head home to get some much needed sleep. Tomorrow was Labor Day, so the office was closed, and she could use the time to study and hopefully get over her cold.

To make matters worse, she hadn't seen Dante at all this weekend. He had driven up to Healdsburg on Friday morning, with plans to spend the holiday weekend with his family. He'd mentioned a co-ed baby shower for his sister, who was due to deliver around the end of the month, as well as some sort of informal reunion with several of his old high school buddies.

But it was just as well, thought Cara as she blew her nose, that Dante wasn't around right now to see her like this. Without glancing into a mirror, she knew how awful she must look - puffy eyes, reddened nose, pale skin, ratty hair. She'd dressed for warmth and comfort rather than style today - not that going to the laundromat was any sort of reason to get dressed up. Her navy sweatpants had holes in both knees, while her UC Berkeley sweatshirt had been washed so many times that several of the letters had been worn off. The fake Ugg boots she wore were warm but otherwise - well, they looked exactly like what they were - a cheap imitation of the real thing. Mirai would have shrieked in horror if she could see her BFF right now, thought Cara, so it was just as well that her parents were both in town and keeping her occupied with shopping excursions, brunches and dinners out, and concert tickets.

Everyone she knew, in fact, seemed to have plans for this holiday weekend, thought Cara glumly. In addition to Dante and Mirai, her co-workers were all off somewhere fun and relaxing and *warm* - Angela and Nick were on a ten day vacation to Fiji; Leah and Tyler were visiting her parents in Newport Beach; and even Deepak, the avowed workaholic, had been convinced to go away for the long weekend to Las Vegas with some college friends. Her father was most likely enjoying himself with his new family at their beachfront home in Florida, and wouldn't be able to find the time to reply to her latest email for at least a week, if at all.

Forcing herself to put an abrupt halt to this private pity party, Cara checked how many minutes remained on the dryer cycle, then tried to figure out when she was due to take more cold medicine. Realizing she was almost a half hour overdue for the next dose, she was fumbling through her backpack for the packet of gel capsules when her phone buzzed with an incoming call. Figuring it had to be Mirai calling to check up on her, she was startled to see Dante's name on the caller ID instead.

"Hey, I thought you were supposed to be watching your sister opening up all of the baby gifts," she joked. "Or is it already time for cake?"

Dante's voice sounded somber in reply. "The shower was yesterday. I'm actually back in San Francisco right now. And - are you sick or something? You don't sound very good."

"Just a cold is all, nothing serious," she assured him, then proved herself to be a liar when she began to cough hoarsely.

"That sounds pretty serious to me," he replied. "Have you seen a doctor?"

She didn't dare tell him that due to the thousand dollar deductible on her health insurance she couldn't afford to see a doctor, especially for something as relatively minor as a cold. Knowing Dante, he'd drag her to the nearest urgent care clinic and insist on paying the bill.

"Honestly, it's just a garden variety cold. And I've only had it a few days so it needs to run its course. I don't need to see a doctor at this point."

"Hmm." He sounded anything but convinced, but didn't press her further on the matter. "And where are you exactly? It sounds pretty noisy in the background, like machinery or something."

"Laundromat. Sunday is wash day."

"Why are you doing laundry at a laundromat?" he asked incredulously. "Not," he added hastily, "that you'd be doing anything else at a laundromat. What I meant to ask was why aren't you using the washer and dryer where you live?"

"The rental agreement doesn't include laundry privileges," she explained. "Something about a previous tenant breaking the dryer after overloading it. And another one who literally did two or three loads every single day and ran the utility bills sky high. So by the time I came along, my landlord decided not to take that sort of risk again."

"I guess I never realized that," mused Dante. "Look, I know this is short notice, but I was hoping to see you this afternoon for a little while. How much longer do you expect to be there?"

"Let me check." She walked over to the dryer. "My stuff will be dry in less than fifteen minutes. And the next bus will come by about ten minutes after that. Which would get me to my place in approximately forty five minutes."

"Forget about taking the bus. I'll pick you up. What address is the laundromat at?"

She told him and waited while he plugged the information into the navigational system of whatever car he was driving today. "Dante, you don't need to come all the way out here to get me," she protested. "I take the bus all the time, it's no big deal."

There was a brief pause before he replied. "Cara, for once please don't argue with me, okay? According to the GPS I should be there in fifteen minutes. Is it easy to find parking in the area?"

"Not really. I'll just wait for you outside, that'll be easier. See you in a few."

As she ended the call, Cara frantically began to rummage through her pack, though not for the cold medicine this time. She realized with a sense of doom that there was very little she could do at this point about her bedraggled appearance, but she had to do something. A glance in her little pocket mirror made her shudder in revulsion, and she wished that she'd followed Mirai's oft-given advice about packing a makeup kit with her. She managed to rake a brush through her tangled, semi-greasy hair - having been too lethargic this morning to wash the overlong tresses - before hastily scrabbling it into a thick braid. From the depths of her well worn backpack she unearthed a nearly empty tube of nude lip gloss, and managed to scrounge enough to coat her dry, chapped lips. Without any other makeup on hand, she resorted to the old fashioned tactic of pinching her cheeks to get some color in them.

Unfortunately, there weren't any tactics she was familiar with that would make her holey sweatpants and baggy sweatshirt look any more appealing. If she had a sewing kit on her - another must-have, according to Mirai - then she could quickly repair the visible holes over each knee. But there was nothing she could do at this late notice to get rid of the marinara sauce stains splattered across the front of her sweatshirt. She would just have to keep her fingers crossed that Dante wouldn't notice.

As she stuffed her dry clothes into a duffle bag, Cara was faced with a new worry and tried really, really hard not to jump to conclusions about why Dante wanted to see her so unexpectedly. They never saw each other on Sundays, since those were the times he typically spent with his family. But, she reasoned as she walked out to the curb to wait for him, he had seen his family the last couple of days.

Did he want sex? A home cooked meal? For once, she wasn't in the mood for either, given how lousy she felt. And she was wearing her oldest, rattiest set of underwear right now, a pair of panties and a bra that she would positively cringe at having him see her in. No, as much as she'd missed him, as much as she wanted to be with him, she was going to have to find a way to curb his passions, because hell would freeze over before she'd willingly allow him to see her wearing such tattered undies.

Or did he want to see her unannounced on a Sunday afternoon for some other reason - a reason that she dreaded to even think about. Cara shook her head fiercely, scolding herself for once again overthinking everything. Dante probably just felt bad that he'd been a little out of it lately, or felt guilty that she had been alone all weekend while he'd been having fun with his family. He was kind and considerate in that way, after all, and she felt better instantly at that realization.

He pulled up in the loading zone just outside of the laundromat, driving his BMW this afternoon. He emerged from the car before she could protest, and her heart made that funny little jump it always seemed to do when he was nearby. He looked tanned and buff and extremely fit, dressed in his usual weekend garb of jeans and a fitted T-shirt, this one in a light gray. And while the sight of him in one of his designer suits, crisp white dress shirts, and silk ties always made her go weak at the knees, she actually preferred him dressed like he was right now. The casual look seemed more natural for a big, tough guy like Dante, and it made *her* less self conscious about her own rather pathetic wardrobe.

"Here. Let me toss that in the back seat," he offered, taking the duffle bag from her, then frowned as he realized how heavy it was. "Don't tell me you were going to lug this thing home on the bus? And your backpack as well."

Cara shrugged, not wanting to make a big deal over what for her was simply part of her weekly routine. "I'm stronger than I look," she joked. "Instead of lifting weights I lift laundry bags."

But Dante didn't seem to find her attempt at humor the least bit amusing as he helped her inside the car. Nor, apparently, did he appear to be thrilled with the neighborhood they were presently driving through.

"Is this seriously the closest laundromat to your place?" he asked, shaking his head in disgust as he took in the numerous corner bars, liquor stores, boarded up buildings, and mostly unsavory looking pedestrians. "This area isn't someplace you ought to be hanging out in, even if it's just to do your laundry."

She nodded. "There was one closer but it went out of business last year. And this place isn't all that bad, not really. The neighborhood is quieter on Sunday afternoons than it is say on Friday evenings."

Dante shook his head in disbelief. "Please do not tell me that you used to take the bus to and from this area on a Friday night."

"Just a few times," she assured him hastily. "I switched my laundry day to Sundays after that."

He muttered something beneath his breath that she couldn't quite catch, but she knew without having to ask that it wasn't anything she wanted him to repeat.

"How was the baby shower?" she inquired brightly, anxious to change the subject.

Dante grimaced. "Well, I've got nothing to compare it to, but let's just say watching my sister open up boxes of baby clothes and diaper bags and stuffed toys wasn't the most fun I've ever had. But Talia certainly enjoyed it, so I guess that's one of the sacrifices you make for your family."

Cara patted him on the arm. "You're a good brother. I'm sure your sisters think so, too."

"Yeah, I guess so."

She continued to keep up a cheerful patter of conversation during the short drive to her apartment, forcing herself to remain calm and upbeat when his replies were mostly monosyllabic and seemed forced. But when her constant chatter provoked a coughing spell, and earned her a reproving look from Dante, she fished a cough drop from her backpack and kept silent for the duration of the drive.

He insisted on carrying both the laundry bag and her backpack inside, and she cringed anew as she unlocked the door, recalling now that she'd been too tired and sick this morning to do much tidying up. The bedcovers were rumpled, the dishes unwashed, and she'd forgotten to take the trash out. But Dante didn't seem to care, or even notice, that her usually neat little apartment looked as unkempt as she did today.

"Can I get you anything?" she offered. "Coffee, water, I think I have some beer around. Oh, and there's half a bottle of wine left from the last time you were here. Do you think it's still any good? I didn't want to throw it away since it was so expensive but if…"

Dante placed a finger over her lips. "Hush. You always tell me to warn you if you start to babble too much. Consider this your warning. And no, I don't want anything to drink. We - I need to talk to you about something, Cara. Let's sit over here, okay?"

"O-okay."

Reluctantly, almost fearfully, she allowed him to guide her over to the futon where she hastily attempted to straighten out the bedcovers until he placed a gentle hand on her arm.

"Leave it," he urged. "I don't give a damn if the bed is made, especially not when it's obvious you feel like shit."

Cara nodded and plopped down beside him. His hands were clasped on his lap, and his gaze was directed on the opposite wall as he visibly struggled with what he wanted to tell her. And for once in her life she had never felt less like talking, wanted to beg him not to say anything, but to simply hold her instead. Hold her in his arms and never, ever let her go.

Instead, he spoke the words she had dreaded he would say, the words she had foolishly hoped she would never hear from his lips.

"Cara. This - this isn't easy for me to tell you," he began carefully, almost woodenly. "These past few months spending time with you, going out with you, have been wonderful. *You've* been wonderful. But I told you from the very beginning that I couldn't make you any promises, that I wasn't offering you any sort of commitment. And we also promised each other that when the time came for us to move on, that it would be without regrets. I hope that you still feel that way, because - "

She shut her eyes tightly, already feeling the tears welling up. "Because you're breaking up with me," she finished hollowly. "Because we won't be seeing each other anymore."

He took her hand in his, squeezing it comfortingly. "Yes," he replied quietly. "We had a lot of good times together, Cara, and you made me laugh, made me happy. But it's time for us both to move on now, to go back to just being friends. At least, I hope you'll still want to be my friend."

"Friends." She repeated the word. "Just friends."

"Yes. I care about you, Cara, about your wellbeing. It isn't right that you're on your own this way, that your father isn't doing more to help you. So I want you to know that you can always count on me to be there if you need something. I want to continue being a good friend to you. If that's what you want, of course."

Cara kept her eyes closed, having little to no faith in her ability to stop from bursting into tears otherwise. "I - I guess so, yeah. I mean, you're still Nick's client so we'll have to see each other in the office once in awhile. I just - well, I know we agreed that things between us were casual and all, but, well, what went wrong? Like you said, we had a good time together. Did I say something, do something, to make you mad? I've tried so hard not to be clingy or needy or ask you for stuff and.."

Her voice cracked a little then, whether it was from the unshed tears she was battling to hold back or her cold. Dante slid his hand over her knee, giving it a reassuring squeeze.

"No, honey," he told her tenderly. "God, I'm not sure you have it in you to make anyone angry or upset. And you're the least clingy female I've ever met, not to mention stubborn as hell about accepting gifts. You're kind and sweet and generous, and one of these days you'll meet a guy who can appreciate all of those qualities, and hopefully be deserving of a girl like you."

She sniffled, a loud, decidedly unfeminine sound, but at this point she was beyond caring. "Why can't you be that guy?" she whispered brokenly, feeling what small bit of control she still possessed swiftly starting to disintegrate. "You and I get along really well, we have a lot in common. Why can't we just keep seeing each other the way we've been doing? I've never asked you for anything, Dante, especially a commitment. So if you aren't upset with me about something, and you still like being with me, then why end it this way?"

Dante hesitated, and as she glanced over in his direction she noticed that he was visibly uncomfortable with the way this conversation was going. "Because - well, it isn't fair to you," he answered haltingly. "You deserve someone who *can* make that sort of commitment to you, who *can* be the man you need. You and I are just at different points in our life right now, Cara. I've already finished college and started a business and traveled all over, whereas you haven't done any of that. What if you get a great job offer in another part of the country and have to move away?"

She shrugged. "So what? I'll be through with school in another year, and will see what my job options are at that point. Why can't we just keep seeing each other until then? I'm in no hurry at all to settle down and get married and stuff, and it honestly doesn't matter to me if things stay the way they've been between us. Unless - oh. Oh, God. There's someone else, isn't there? You've met someone new and you think it could be serious with her and that's why - oh, geez, what an idiot I've been!"

The shocked expression on his face gave her all the answers she needed. The real reason he was breaking things off with her - and likely why he'd been so distant as of late - was because there was another woman in the picture now. Dante had met someone new, no doubt someone beautiful and poised and sophisticated, someone worthy of him and of being introduced to his family and friends. It should have been so obvious, so clear, and yet the thought hadn't even occurred to her until just now.

"It's not what you think," Dante insisted. "And it's not someone new. Not exactly. I - well, at my cousin's wedding back in July I ran into my ex-girlfriend there. Katie. And we talked for a little while, mostly to clear the air between us, and.."

"And you realized you still had feelings for her," Cara commented numbly. "Have you been seeing her all this time, then?"

"No!" He was adamant in his denial, shaking his head emphatically. "Not in the way you think, anyway. I've never been a cheater, Cara, or a two-timer. When I'm with a woman I'm only with her, one hundred percent of the way. I haven't been sleeping with Katie, haven't even kissed her. But we have met a few times for coffee or lunch. She's living back in the area again, gave up her acting career for good this time, and wants to go back to school or find a new profession. So I've been giving her some advice, discussing ideas, that sort of thing. And in the process - well, you hit the nail on the head. I realized I still had feelings for her, that I wanted to give our relationship another try."

Cara scoffed. "This is the same woman who chose her career over you, isn't it? The one who turned you down cold so she could become an actress. And now that things haven't worked out so well for her, she's come running back. I thought you were smarter than that, Dante. I guess I was wrong."

"It's not like that," he protested. "And believe me, I know exactly what I'm getting into. Things will be different this time around."

She shrugged, pulling her legs up to her chest and resting her suddenly weary head on bent knees. "Whatever. It's got nothing to do with me, does it? And if Katie is the one who makes you happy, then you should be with her. Thanks for being honest with me, and at least telling me in person."

Dante reached out to stroke her bent head soothingly. "What? You think I would have told you something like this over the phone?" he asked in disbelief.

Cara jerked away from his touch, not caring when he looked dismayed at this rejection. "It wouldn't be the first time that's happened to me," she muttered. "Or via a text message. Anyway, there really isn't a whole lot more to say, is there? I'd suggest you get your stuff and leave, but since you never left any of your things here - since you never once spent the night - that's sort of a moot point."

"I don't blame you for being angry with me," he commiserated. "I haven't exactly been the ideal boyfriend these past few months. But I meant what I said earlier, Cara - I really enjoyed our time together, enjoyed being with you. You made me feel good about myself again, helped me through a rough patch."

She shook her head in disbelief. "A rough patch caused by the same woman you're going back to now. Jesus."

"I know it sounds stupid. And I don't expect you to understand or approve. But Katie and I have a history together, Cara. I was going to ask her to marry me earlier this year. And seeing her again made me realize that I still had feelings for her. Feelings that didn't entirely go away just because I was angry with her. And, yes, we have some issues to work through, some things we need to resolve, but I know I at least need to try."

Hearing him admit that he still cared for the woman who'd broken his heart made her own heart crumble into tiny pieces. And unleashed the floodgate of tears she'd been struggling so hard to keep at bay. The tears ran unchecked down her cheeks, and she brushed them away impatiently, only to find more of them streaming uncontrollably from her eyes. She reached for a wad of tissues that she'd left on the small table next to the futon, and tried without success to stem the tide of her weeping.

"Cara." Dante's voice was reproving. He wrapped an arm around her shoulders and tugged her against him despite her protests. He brushed a kiss tenderly against her temple, and smoothed back several untamed curls that had long ago escaped from her messy braid. And because it felt so good to be held against his big, strong body, even though he'd just broken her heart, she clung to him, burrowing her face against his neck as she sobbed uncontrollably.

"Hey," he chided gently. "What happened to our agreement, hmm? No regrets, no accusations. And you promised not to tell all your friends that I'm lousy in bed."

In reply, she just cried harder, realizing that it was really and truly over, that there would be no more dinners out together, or evenings spent talking over a home cooked meal and a great bottle of wine. And there would definitely not be any more hours-long, mind-blowing, amazing lovemaking sessions. *That* particular privilege, among numerous others, would now belong to his no-longer ex-girlfriend Katie.

"Shh. Shh." He tried almost desperately now to soothe her, to get her to stop crying and calm down. "Come on, Cara. You promised me that you could handle a relationship between us. That you were mature enough to deal with it. And that you wouldn't fall apart when one of us decided it was time to end things."

Cara lifted her head from his shoulder, keeping her eyes downcast as she realized how truly, truly hideous she must look by now. As if having one of the worst colds in her lifetime hadn't been enough, now she'd been crying her eyes out for several minutes. Snippily, she bet that *Katie* looked beautiful even when she cried. And that someone as perfect as she probably was never got colds or the flu.

"I'm not falling apart," she protested weakly. "Even after sitting by my mother's bedside for forty eight hours straight and watching her die, I didn't fall apart. And I know I promised you I wouldn't make a fuss if things didn't work out between us. But - well, I'm *sad*, Dante.

Sad because I loved being with you. Loved being your lover. You made me happier than I've felt in a really long time, and now I'm sad that I won't get to see you again. Oh, I know you said we could be friends, but it won't be the same. Not even close. And I'm going to miss you so much. So I'm sorry if my tears upset you, but I tend to cry when I'm sad. Or am I not permitted to be sad?"

He cursed softly beneath his breath, tilting her chin up to meet his gaze. His eyes held a bleak look, almost as though he wanted to cry himself. Using his thumb to brush away the tears from her eyes, he kissed her forehead this time.

"Of course you're permitted to be sad," he assured her. "Believe it or not, I'm sad, too. This wasn't an easy decision for me, Cara. Not by a long shot. I know the risk I'm taking by letting Katie back into my life. And I also know what I'm giving up by letting you go. I'm going to miss you, too. More than you know."

She got to her feet, badly needing to put some distance between them, and to get control of herself before she did something really disgusting like throw up. Or pass out. Her throat felt raw and scratchy from the cold and from crying so much, so she silently filled a mug with water and stuck it in the microwave before scrounging around for a tea bag.

"You can go now," she told him in an oddly detached voice. "I'm going to have some tea, put my laundry away, and take a nap. Maybe not in that order."

Dante walked over to where she stood in her tiny kitchenette. "I don't want to leave you like this, Cara. Not when you're still so upset. Not to mention being sick. Are you positive you won't let me take you to see a doctor?"

She unearthed a tea bag from a box in the back of a cabinet. "I just have a cold, Dante. Nothing some Nyquil and a few hours of sleep won't cure. As for being upset - well, I'll get over it. Just like I got over my mom dying and my dad remarrying and selling the house and then announcing he wasn't going to pay for the rest of my college tuition. I might be young, but I'm tougher than I look. So, please. You should really go."

"All right." He blew out a breath of frustration. "But before I do there's something I want to give you, Cara. Something that I want you to accept and not fight me on. Okay?"

Cara frowned as he dug something out of his pocket. "What exactly are you giving me - the keys to one of your cars?"

Dante shook his head. "Trust me. If I thought for one minute that you'd actually accept something like that, I would have gladly given you one months ago. Though I suppose you could use part of this - or all of it - to buy your own car. Here. This is for you."

He was holding out a check, and she took it from him warily, reluctantly, only to nearly drop it when she saw the amount.

"Holy crap!" she exclaimed. "This can't possibly be right. You - you want to give me a check for - for twenty-five *thousand* dollars? Are you crazy? Because that's the only reasonable explanation I can think of for why you'd imagine for even a second that I'd accept any money at all from you, much less a fortune like this."

"I want you to take the money and use it on yourself," he explained calmly. "For whatever you want or need. It kills me to know how hard you work during the day, and then have to drag yourself to classes four nights a week. I've seen how exhausted you are on Friday nights. And I know the fall semester has already started, but maybe for the spring you could take a leave of absence from your job and go to school full time during the day. Back at the Berkeley campus, where you should have been all along. That check should be more than enough money to pay for your tuition and help support you for a semester or two."

Cara shook her head emphatically. "I am not taking a leave of absence, Dante. Angela has been good to me, and I won't do that to her. And I'm also not taking this check, under any circumstances. What is this anyway - payment for services rendered or something? Gee, I'm not sure whether to be flattered or grossly insulted!"

Dante looked shocked at her accusation. "Jesus, no! It's nothing like that, Cara. Nothing at all. Frankly, *I'm* the one who's insulted that you'd even accuse me of something so crass. You're the very furthest thing from a whore, and the check isn't payment for having sex with me."

"I'm sorry. I know you didn't mean it that way," she admitted grudgingly. "And while I appreciate the gesture, I am not taking money from you, Dante. I don't care if it's twenty-five thousand or twenty-five cents. Thank you, but no."

But he adamantly refused to take back the check she held out to him. "I knew you'd be stubborn about this," he grumbled. "Knew you'd make it difficult for me to try and do something nice for you. Look, don't use it for school then. Use it for something else altogether. Move to a bigger apartment, a *nicer* apartment. Preferably one with on-site laundry facilities so that you don't have to lug that huge duffle bag on the bus and use a laundromat in a questionable part of the city. Or get a car. Go on a nice vacation. Buy yourself a whole new wardrobe. Or just save it for the future. One way or the other, I want you to take that money, Cara."

"Why?" she challenged. "Because you feel responsible for me? Because you feel sorry for me, or think I'm some sort of charity case? Or maybe it's because giving me this check will help *you* feel better about yourself, make you feel less guilty about dumping me for another woman."

Dante's cheeks reddened, and his dark eyes flashed angrily. "My feelings don't matter," he muttered. "I'll need to deal with those on my own somehow, and even if I gave you half of my net worth it wouldn't make me feel less guilty about how this has unfolded. Look at this way, Cara. Since I became successful, I've helped a lot of people out. I loaned money to different family members for their businesses. Remodeled my mom's house inside and out. Put both of my sisters through college. So why won't you let me help you out the same way I helped them?"

"Because I'm not your sister. Or your mother. Or another member of your family," retorted Cara. "I'm none of those things. I'm nobody to you, Dante. Just some silly, naïve girl you used to bang twice a week."

"Cara," he said reprovingly, shaking his head in denial. "God, honey, you have to know that isn't the truth! Have to know that I never, ever thought of you that way."

"Do I?" she challenged. "And exactly how am I supposed to know that, huh? You thought so highly of me that you kept bringing me to all of these out-of-the-way restaurants where we wouldn't run the risk of seeing anyone you knew. You never once thought I was good enough to meet your precious family, good enough to bring home to your mother. I mean, I know I'm not the best looking girl in the world, that I'm overweight and don't have nice clothes and probably next to your gorgeous actress girlfriend I'd just fade into the woodwork. But I have feelings, Dante. Feelings that were hurt every single time you went out of your way to make sure no one saw us together."

This time the color on his cheeks did the opposite and paled alarmingly. He closed his eyes for a few seconds, shaking his head as he ran a hand over his face. When he opened his eyes, there was such a bleak, desperate look in them that she very nearly rushed over to comfort him.

"Cara. Christ, I don't even know what to say," he replied tiredly. "Why haven't you said something about this before? It's obviously been bothering you for some time."

She dunked the tea bag in the hot water, unwilling to meet his eyes. "I guess because I didn't want to seem ungrateful for starters. And I told you before, Dante. I was just so happy to be with you, enjoyed spending time with you, that it didn't matter to me where we went or what we did. You could have taken me to the closest 7-11 for Slurpees and day-old hot dogs and I would have been over the moon. And I guess I was afraid that if I complained or asked you for something you weren't ready to give me that you'd stop seeing me. And I would have done just about anything to prevent that from happening."

He came to her then, cupping her cheeks between his palms, his voice breaking. "Cara. I can see now that I never deserved you, not even for a day. I can't even think straight right now. But you need to know this. Yes, I brought you places where we wouldn't be likely to run into people I knew. But it wasn't because I was ashamed of you, for Christ's sake. It was just - well, my family is wonderful, the best family in the world. But they're also nosy as hell, want to know everything that goes on in my life. And if word had reached them that I was dating someone new, they would have demanded all the details, insisted on meeting you, hinted that I should settle down. And I just wanted something for myself, wanted to keep my private life private for once. I'm sorry if it seemed that I was hiding you away, even though I sort of was. But not for the reasons you thought."

She nodded. "I get it now. Thanks for clearing all that up. But I'm still not accepting this check."

She tore it into dozens of little pieces, scattering them over her tiny kitchen sink.

Dante sighed, then gave her a frustrated smile. "Of course you aren't. I didn't think it would be that easy. But if you ever change your mind, ever need anything, I want you to call me. All right?"

Cara could feel the tears beginning to well up again, and was anxious to have him leave before her humiliation deepened. "Yes. Though I wouldn't hold my breath if I were you."

"Stubborn till the end." He dropped a kiss on the bridge of her nose, an affectionate little gesture that one might give to a child. "And just so you know, my mother would have adored you. Take care of yourself, honey."

He left then, closing the door quietly behind him. Cara took two sips of her tea before pouring the rest down the drain, recalling now that she hated tea and must have kept the bags here for the times Mirai visited. Thinking of her BFF made her reach for her phone so that she could call the one remaining person in the world she could count on to be there for her.

"Mir?" she sniffled as her friend answered the call. "He broke up with me, Mir. Just a few minutes ago."

Mirai cursed vividly on the other end of the line when she heard how distressed Cara sounded. "Give me half an hour to gather supplies and I'll be right over."

"You're sure?" croaked Cara. "Aren't you supposed to be visiting with your parents?"

"Not tonight. They're attending some fancy party and Rene has a date. So you just need to tell me what to bring over - pizza, chocolate, or booze? On second thought, forget it. As bad as you sound, we're going to need all three."

17

Late September

"AND HERE I was starting to revise my opinion that you were the biggest fucking moron I'd ever known. You just had to go and screw that all up again, didn't you?"

Dante winced in reaction from Nick's scathing retort to the news he'd just shared with him. "Sorry to have disappointed you - *Dad*. But in case you hadn't realized it, I am old enough to make my own decisions. Whether you agree with them or not isn't really the point."

Nick shook his head, not bothering to hide his disgust. "I can agree that this one in particular is a *bad* decision. Seriously, Dan - what the *fuck*! I wish I had taken a video of at least one of the dozen or more times you sat across from me just like you are now moping and whining because that chick had flounced out of your life so she could become a big movie star. Wait a sec. Maybe I actually *did* take a video one of those times."

As Nick scrolled through his phone, Dante scowled darkly at his best friend. He had deliberately put off telling Nick about Katie for close to three weeks now, knowing that the announcement would not be well received. Discretion, tact, and keeping his very strong opinions to himself would never be traits one would associate with Nick Manning, and he was certainly proving those facts to be true this afternoon.

"Knock it off, Nick," growled Dante, who wasn't in the greatest of moods today himself. "Like it or not, Katie and I are back together and giving things another try. And nothing you say is going to change that. Hey, Angela gave you another chance and you were *way* more of a jerk towards her than Katie was to him."

"Hmmpf. Matter of opinion, I suppose," grumbled Nick. "And at least she made me work for it when I tried to get her back. Is Blondie even the tiniest bit contrite? I mean, if a chick had pulled that sort of shit on me - well, moot point, because there's no way in hell I'd have ever considered taking her back after that. But say in some alternate universe I might have thought about it, I'd damn sure have made her grovel and beg. A lot."

"That's because you're an asshole while I'm a nice guy," retorted Dante. "And if Angela had ever bothered to ask my advice before she took you back, I would have told her to get some serious counseling for even entertaining a stupid idea like that."

Nick flipped him off before taking a sip of his Pinot Noir. "Angela's too smart to take advice from a moron like you. Now, I think you and I have traded enough insults for one afternoon. And you're right, Dan. You are a grown man, and God knows with my crappy record with women I'm probably the last person who should be telling you how to run your life."

Dante nodded. "All right. Agreed. No more insulting each other. At least for today. And while I know you don't approve of my decision, or support it, I hope you won't take it out on Katie when you see her this weekend."

Nick's dark eyes narrowed menacingly. "You mean, not threaten her with dire consequences if she fucks you up again? Or ask her how she's planning on making it all up to you?"

Dante rolled his eyes, realizing that nothing and no one was ever going to change Nick. "Yeah, that's exactly what I mean."

Nick shrugged, as though bored with the subject. "Fine. I'll be on my best behavior. Though I can't promise Angela won't try to rip your ex – er, your girlfriend a new one. She's her own woman, after all, and doesn't take it very well when I try to tell her what to do."

"Big surprise there," replied Dante sarcastically. "Especially since you try to control everything she does and says."

A wicked grin split Nick's handsome features. "Not everything. Once in awhile I let her get on top."

"Jesus." Dante shook his head in disgust. "Sometime I forget what a pig you are. Then you open your mouth and it all comes back to me."

"Angela and I are good right now," replied Nick in a far more serious tone. "We get each other, recognize each other's triggers, and know when to back off. Not everyone pretends to understand our relationship, but that's tough for them. So long as we're both happy, then everyone else can go fuck themselves for all I care. Including her family."

Dante picked up his own wine glass. "Are you positive that Angela is happy with the way things are between you? Did you ever bother to ask her if she's satisfied with your relationship? Just because you don't believe in wedding chapels and babies and white picket fences doesn't mean she doesn't."

Nick gave him a glare that would have been terrifying for anyone who didn't know him as well as Dante did. "Butt out, Lover Boy. Angela and I are in a good place right now, so don't start putting ideas in her head. She knows how I stand on marriage and kids and all that shit. So concentrate on your own relationship and stay the hell out of mine."

Dante couldn't resist grinning, realizing he'd hit a nerve there somewhere. "Fine. So long as you stop harping on Katie. Give her a chance, Nick. Give *us* a chance."

Nick looked disgusted, but merely shrugged. "Whatever. All I know is that you've actually been happy these last few months. You never discussed the subject but I just assumed you were getting laid on a regular basis. Was it just one woman or a whole parade of them?"

Dante felt his face redden at his friend's very direct question, and resisted the urge to squirm in his chair. He knew there was no way that Nick or Angela would have suspected he'd been dating - more accurately, *fucking* - their cute, innocent little admin assistant for several months. And he was positive that Cara had never spilled the beans to either of her bosses, because if she had Nick would have broken at least a few of his bones by now.

He'd felt obliged to finally clue Nick in about his reconciliation with Katie since all four of them - Dante, Katie, Nick, and Angela - would be attending a party given by a mutual friend this weekend. And there was no way he would have risked Nick saying something rude and inappropriate, or allowed Angela to look down her nose at Katie as though she smelled bad. So even though he knew he'd be in for an hour of grief from Nick while they ate lunch, Dante had sucked it up and broken the news.

News that he had yet to share with his family, though. 'One step at a time,' he had told himself. The same way he'd imagined his reignited relationship with Katie unfolding.

Katie, however, had initially envisioned a rather different path to their reconciliation. She'd first been shocked when Dante had flat out refused to let her move in with him, a topic she had brought up within a day or two of their getting back together.

"But I can't afford a place of my own in San Francisco yet," she had pointed out. *"I've been job hunting like crazy but haven't been able to find anything yet, and my bank account is more or less empty. So when you told me you'd like to give things another try between us, I was thrilled because not only would we be back together the way we were always meant to be, but I'd have a place to stay in the city while I looked for a job."*

Dante hadn't allowed her to manipulate him into something he wasn't ready for, however, no matter how big and blue her eyes were, or how tempting those lush pink lips looked. "Sorry, but it's way too soon to start talking about moving in together. I told you, Katie, that things need to be different this time around - a lot different and in a lot of different ways. I realize now that I was probably too pushy, wanted too much too soon from you, instead of just having fun together and letting things develop naturally. So that's the way it's going to happen this time around."

She had pouted prettily at his gentle refusal, not used to being said no to, and especially by him. "But, Danny, how do you expect me to keep living at my parents' house while I look for a job?"

He'd shrugged. "Your parents have a beautiful home - gated community, huge house, a pool. Most people would think a place like that was paradise. And I've seen your room there, Katie. Rooms to be exact. It's a lot more space than you had when you lived in San Francisco the last time around."

Katie had given an impatient little huff. "Yes, it's a nice house. But for God's sake, Danny, I'm thirty years old and living with my parents! Do you have any idea how humiliating that is? They expect me to eat dinner with them every night, like I'm still in high school or something."

Unwittingly, Dante had thought of Cara then, envisioning the tiny, rundown room she lived in - a room that was probably the size of the walk-in closet in Katie's bedroom. Cara would have been overjoyed to live in a place as big and beautifully furnished as the Carlisle residence across the bay in Orinda. And would have loved the opportunity to have dinner with her parents on a regular basis - if she actually had parents, that was.

But he couldn't - wouldn't - discuss Cara with Katie. That particular chapter in his life was closed now, but he would always cherish the months he'd spent with her, and keep those memories to himself.

Dante hadn't budged, no matter how sweetly Katie had begged and pleaded to let her move in with him, even temporarily. "If it's that bad at your parents' place - which I know it isn't - then that should be extra motivation for you to get a job and save up some money. I know your parents would never think of charging you rent or asking you to pay for expenses, so you'd be able to save practically your entire paycheck. You'd have what you needed for rent in three months or so."

Katie had not been happy at the prospect of continuing to live in suburbia for three more months, but she'd tactfully changed the subject after realizing he wasn't going to give in to her.

There had been quite a few things, in fact, that he had stood his ground on, and had refused to automatically go along with whatever she decreed. During their time apart, he had really come to like having time to himself during the week, and was reluctant to give that up just yet. He knew that once Katie moved back to San Francisco she would push for them to see each other more often than once or twice a week as they were doing now, but in the interim he didn't plan to change that routine.

And he still hadn't brought her with him on Sundays when he visited his family, mostly because he was trying to find a way of breaking the news that they were back together. Dante knew that his mother would support whatever decision he made, as would Talia - especially since she was due to give birth any day now and had much bigger priorities to deal with. Rafe, who'd always had something of a crush on Katie, would wholeheartedly approve of the reconciliation, while Gia and their grandmother would first curse him out thoroughly in Italian, and then predict that things wouldn't end any better for him this time than they had before. Gia, he'd thought dourly, had spent far too much time with Valentina as a child and young girl, and as a result had inherited both her good and bad traits - mostly the bad ones.

Though he had relented and agreed to bring Katie with him on a business trip next month to a finance conference in New York City. She had been at his office one afternoon, popping in for an unannounced visit after a job interview, and spotted the itinerary on his desk. She had more or less invited herself along at that point, rather coyly suggesting that it would be a great opportunity for them to spend some quality time together and re-start their relationship. Dante's PA had made the additional flight reservation for Katie, and called the hotel to let them know there would be another occupant in the room.

Katie had been so thrilled with the prospect of a week long trip to one of her favorite cities that she'd eased up temporarily with her continued pleas to move in with him. And once he'd grown used to the idea, he'd admitted that getting away for a week in different surroundings would be a positive step forward in their reconciliation.

Dante had turned off the ringer on his phone during lunch with Nick, something both men always did so they could discuss his investments without constant interruptions. But the moment he switched it back on, it was to find a combination of missed calls, texts, and voice mails waiting for him, nearly all of them from Katie. He sighed, for this had very quickly become a habit with her, and not necessarily a good one. He sent her a brief text, promising to call her as soon as he was back in his office. And to figure out in the interim, he thought dryly, how to get the message across - in the nicest possible way - that she needed to dial the constant communications back a notch or two and give him some space.

Of course, this was something he'd had to deal with frequently when it came to past and present girlfriends, including the stalker who'd warranted a restraining order. Katie was nowhere near that bad, and her current behavior was actually rather unusual for her. Before, when Dante had been so crazy about her, she had rarely been the one to initiate contact, content to let him be the pursuer. Now that the tables had been turned somewhat, her frequent calls, texts, and emails at times seemed almost desperate.

But there was one ex-girlfriend who had yet to contact him, despite his parting words encouraging her to do exactly that. Since he'd broken things off with Cara nearly a month ago, there hadn't been a peep out of her - not a single email, voicemail, text, or social media comment. Dante had been too much of a coward to face her as yet, and so had invented some excuse why he couldn't meet Nick in his office today as he usually did. Instead, they had simply had a longer lunch so they could discuss Dante's investment portfolio, though Nick had grumbled mightily about having to bring along all of the reports and graphs. Then again, Nick grumbled about any number of trivial matters he considered to be beneath him, and Dante had learned to ignore him over the years.

As he entered his office building, he couldn't help but recall his first date with Cara - when she'd stood here in the middle of the lobby in that red dress that did such amazing things for her voluptuous little body. He'd been very pleasantly surprised with her that night, both in and out of bed, and she had continued to please and surprise him over the next months. She'd been fun to be around, easy to be with. He'd never had to worry about what to say to her, especially since she was quite a talker. And she had always been so damned grateful for every little thing he had done for her, whether it was bringing over a loaf of sourdough bread from his favorite bakery in North Beach, or taking her to one of those action adventure movies they both liked, or eating dinner at some little out of the way restaurant.

It continued to trouble him, however, how Cara had more or less accused him of keeping her hidden away from his family and friends, and how he'd intentionally brought her to small, neighborhood restaurants instead of the trendier places he normally patronized so that they wouldn't run into anyone he knew. He should have known, he chastised himself now, that someone as intelligent as Cara would have picked up on those tendencies sooner than later. But what he'd told her had been the truth. He hadn't been ashamed of her, or embarrassed by the way she dressed. His sole motivation in keeping their relationship private had been the need for just that – privacy. But it didn't make him feel any less guilty about having hurt Cara's feelings.

He missed her. The thought popped into his head unexpectedly as he got off the elevator at his floor. He missed hanging out with her, missed listening to the sound of her infectious laughter, or discussing the latest lecture from one of her finance classes. And while he would never, ever miss having sex on that crappy old futon of hers, he definitely missed the uninhibited passion she'd always shown in bed.

Impatiently, Dante pushed aside these errant thoughts about Cara, thoughts that he had no business indulging in since he'd broken things off with her – and apparently broken her tender heart as well. Unbidden, the image of how she'd looked that last day – sobbing uncontrollably, her eyes red and swollen, her voice hoarse – taunted him, tugged at his conscience, made him feel like shit all over again. She had looked so small, so vulnerable, and, in her own words, so damned *sad*. And when she had tried so hard to be brave, to assure him that she'd be okay, and had endured far worse things in her life – well, that had only made him feel worse. Because the truth of the matter was that at age twenty-two Cara had suffered more loss, more heartbreak, and more hardships that people three times her age. Even as tough as it had been for Dante to lose his beloved father at the age of eleven, at least he'd had a huge support team around him, had never once felt alone or neglected or that he was entirely on his own. And faced with the same sort of problems that Cara endured on a daily basis, he knew he wouldn't have dealt with them anywhere near as well as she seemed to do.

As he reached his office, his phone rang with an incoming call, and he sighed impatiently as he saw it was from Katie.

"Hey. I just walked inside my office. Literally. I was going to call you in a minute," he told her as he shrugged off his suit jacket.

"I know I'm being a huge pest," she admitted with a high-pitched little giggle. "But I'm so excited about this trip to New York that it's all I can think about! Listen, the reason I've been trying to get in touch with you is because I want to make some dinner reservations. Oh, and get theater tickets. From what I've been reading online it's nearly impossible to get into some of these places, or tickets to certain shows, so I want to take care of all that right away."

Dante sank down into his desk chair, trying not to think about the dozen or more urgent things he had to deal with this afternoon. Worrying about dinner reservations and theater tickets for a trip that was still three weeks away wasn't one of them.

"Whatever you want," he told her, trying not to sound as impatient as he felt. "You know what I like to eat, so feel free to make the dinner reservations. And since I'm not much of a theater buff, I'll leave that up to you as well. Though I can't promise to stay awake during the show."

"Oh, come on! Be a good sport," she cajoled. "You know how much I love going to plays and musicals. And the touring companies out here just aren't of the same quality as the original Broadway productions. I'll bet if it was one of those awful action movies you love so much that you'd be wide awake."

"They're called action movies for a reason," he replied drily. "And I'll do my best to enjoy the plays. Just try to pick something a little lively, okay?"

"Okay. And I can't wait to drag you along with me to all of my favorite stores. The timing of this trip couldn't be better, since all of the fall and winter clothes will be out. I haven't really needed any warmer things living in Los Angeles for the past few months, so I'll need to do some serious shopping."

It went without saying, of course, that he would be footing the bill for this "serious shopping" spree. Katie still didn't have any realistic job prospects, and therefore no source of income. She'd done a couple of very minor local modeling jobs, but according to her the pay had been negligible, and she had been relying on her parents and Dante to more or less support her since she had moved back from L.A.

"I won't have a ton of free time," he cautioned. "Don't forget that the main reason for this trip is the conference I'm attending."

Katie laughed. "No worries. You can just hand over your credit card before you start listening to some boring lecture, and I'll take it from there!"

He had few doubts that she would do exactly that. After all, he'd not only seen the contents of her clothes closet but had taken her shopping on a number of occasions. The bills she could rack up in an astonishingly short amount of time would come close to equaling the gross national product of some small developing countries.

"Look, I'm swamped here, so I'll have to call you tonight, okay?" he told her, already opening up his email account to scan through the messages.

Katie sighed, a little dramatically in his opinion. "Fine. Don't call until after eight, though. I'm going to a yoga class that I found recently. Of course the teacher or the studio aren't nearly as good as the place in San Francisco I used to go to, but it's better than nothing."

"I'll plan on calling you around nine. And enjoy your class."

"Oh, just one more thing, I swear!" she insisted. "What time are you picking me up on Saturday for the party?"

"Five o'clock. I know it's a little early, but we have to drive back into the city after I get you, and traffic is bound to be ridiculous by then."

"If I moved in with you," Katie replied slyly, "then we wouldn't have to worry about traffic or silly things like that."

"No. We've talked about this, Katie. Several times already, and my answer hasn't changed. It's way too soon for that."

Dante could almost hear her pouting over the phone line. "I

remember a time when you were begging me to move in with you," she pointed out. "And now you won't even discuss the idea."

"That was before you decided being a big star was more important than being my fiancé," he reminded her. "So this time around we do things my way. Now, I've really got to go. I'll call you tonight."

He disconnected the call before she could protest further, or think of some other urgent question she had. He knew she was probably bored without a job to do, or friends living nearby, but he had a business to run and couldn't spare the time to entertain her during the day.

Dante turned his attention then to the growing pile of work on his desk, and was making considerable progress when his phone pinged with an incoming text. He scowled in exasperation when he saw that it was from Katie again, though his annoyance quickly changed to interest when he studied the picture she'd texted him. It was of a silky black nightgown lavishly trimmed in lace, and she'd typed in "Can't you just imagine me wearing this during our trip to NY? Good news it's on sale!"

She'd included the purchase link to a luxury department store, but even the sale price of five hundred dollars was ridiculously high in his opinion for one flimsy garment that Katie would probably only wear a few times before she tired of it.

'I could buy Cara a decent laptop for that amount,' he thought regretfully, then mentally scolded himself for once again letting his thoughts wander back to the girl he'd dated only casually.

'You made your choice, Dante,' he told himself sternly. 'And if the price you have to pay for that choice is a guilty conscience – well, you're going to have to man up and deal with that. It's no less than you deserve, after all.'

18

October

"You know, I never thought I'd live to say this, but I think your apartment is officially messier than mine right now. And considering that my place looks like an obstacle course, that's really saying something."

Cara lowered the blanket she'd pulled up over her head just enough to glare at her best friend. "It's not that bad," she protested.

"Oh, I beg to differ, *amiga*," trilled Mirai. "At least at my place the trash has been emptied out on a regular basis, which is more than I can say for this dump. Which, by the way, is starting to smell like an actual dump."

Cara stuck out her tongue. "Maybe that's because you have a maid who does that stuff for you," she replied testily. "Unlike some of us who can barely afford to buy peanut butter and store brand corn flakes."

"Hmmpf. You could have bought yourself *twenty five thousand dollars* worth of peanut butter and corn flakes if you hadn't been dumb and torn up that check," reminded Mirai in a haughty voice. "As well as a new laptop, a new wardrobe, and a visit to the hair salon. I'm not sure which of those things is in worse shape right now. Your laptop is being held together with safety pins and duct tape, your clothes - well, don't even get me started on those. And your hair - Jesus, Cara, do you even brush it anymore?"

Cara made a horrible face. "Of course I brush it!" she replied indignantly. "Just – well, just not today. Yet. But the day's far from over."

"Seriously? It's almost five o'clock. Have you even moved your ass out of this bed all day? Except apparently to get that half-eaten bowl of cereal you left on the end table. And – omigod – tell me you are not still in your pajamas! Though now that I think of it, I'm guessing you haven't showered either."

Mirai wrinkled her pert little nose in distaste, causing Cara to scowl darkly at her BFF. The fact that she hadn't actually showered or changed out of her comfiest jammies as yet was irrelevant.

"Fine." Cara shoved the bedcovers aside with a huff and stood, hastily brushing off the crumbs from something she'd munched on earlier off of her pajamas. "Since the sight and smell of me obviously offends you, I'll go take a shower now. Does that make you happy?"

Mirai sniffed. "It's a start. But what would really make me happy is if you cleaned this place up, ate a real meal, and returned to the land of the living. It's been over a month since that bastard broke up with you, Cara. You need to start finding a way to get over it."

On bare feet Cara padded over to the dresser and started rummaging through it for clean clothes, only to frown in bewilderment when she had trouble finding any. "You've probably got a point there," she agreed with a sigh. "Because I apparently also forgot to do laundry last weekend. The only clean underwear I have is an old sports bra that's a size too small, and these."

She held up a pair of once-white cotton briefs that shrieked "granny panties" and also sported a frayed waistband. Mirai shuddered daintily, as though the very sight offended her.

"I thought I told you to throw those out the last time we did a closet cleaning," reprimanded Mirai. "Or use them to scrub your bathroom floor."

"Well, good thing I didn't," replied Cara caustically, "or I'd be going commando right now. I'll have to make sure I get to the laundromat tomorrow, since these are literally the only clean clothes I have left."

Mirai gave the oversized T-shirt and baggy sweatpants a disdainful look. "They don't look too clean to me. And while you're at it, throw these gross pajamas in the wash, too. What sort of stain is that anyway?"

Cara glanced down at her Minion pajamas – the ones Mirai had given her for Christmas last year – and frowned as she noticed the stain on the top. "I'm not exactly sure," she admitted. "It could be mac and cheese. Or yogurt. Or both."

"Jesus." Mirai shook her head in disbelief. "Okay, listen to me. You're going to take a shower – immediately – and put these things on, disgusting as they are. In the meanwhile I will actually get my dainty little hands dirty for once and take out your trash and make your bed. Though if I break a nail in the process I'm going to be really pissed. Then when you're nice and clean, we're going to load up all of your dirty laundry into my car – including your sheets – and go to my place. You can do your laundry there while I order in some real food. And then after dinner, while I do *your* nails – which are beyond appalling, by the way – it's going to be time for some tough love."

Cara opened her mouth to protest, until she saw the fierce expression on Mirai's face, the one that always meant "you do not want to fuck with me right now". Instead, she meekly gathered up her last remaining set of clean clothes, and headed off to shower.

When she emerged several minutes later, with her hair freshly washed and combed and smelling of soap and shampoo rather than B.O., she admittedly felt better. And seeing how much Mirai had managed to tidy up the apartment in such a short amount of time also helped to boost her mood – which lately had probably been at its lowest point since her mother had passed away more than four years ago. The trash had been hauled away, the sheets stripped from the futon, the dirty laundry stuffed into bags and left by the front door.

Mirai was even making a start on washing the pile of dirty dishes that had been stacked on the kitchenette's single counter.

"Wow. Until I saw it with my own eyes, I wasn't sure you actually knew how to use a dishtowel," joked Cara.

In response, Mirai tossed the damp towel at her. "Here. This needs to be washed, too. I assume you have clean ones somewhere?"

"I'll get one. And I'll finish the dishes, too. I don't expect you to clean my place up for me, Mir."

Mirai shrugged. "Why? You've cleaned mine more times than I can remember. That semester at Berkeley when you slept on the couch you insisted on tidying up every single day. Even now with the maid service my place isn't as clean as it was back then. And you can finish your dishes tomorrow. Rene's away with her boyfriend this weekend, so you should stay overnight and use her room."

"I have homework to do," pointed out Cara.

"It'll keep for one night. Besides, if you do your laundry at my place that'll save you time tomorrow. Stay at my place tonight, we'll go out to a yummy brunch in the morning, and then I'll drop you back here and you can study the rest of the day."

"Fine," agreed Cara reluctantly. "But only if you let me pay for dinner tonight. Or brunch tomorrow."

"Nope." Mirai shook her head. "Because I want really expensive sushi tonight, and brunch at Zazie tomorrow, where you couldn't even afford a Bloody Mary. And since I'm not willing to lower my standards to eat at someplace you *could* afford to take me, it's my treat for both meals. And I don't want to hear one single word of protest, okay?"

"Okay," replied Cara in a meek voice. "Thanks, Mir. I'll find some way of returning the favor one of these days."

"If you'd cashed that check from the two-timing bastard, you could have returned the favor by treating me to dinner in Las Vegas," muttered Mirai darkly. "Not to mention a massage and a cute new pair of shoes."

Cara laughed in spite of how depressed she'd been feeling. "He didn't two-time me," she insisted. "I've told you this. Say what you want about Dante – and God knows you've said plenty – but I know him well enough to say without the slightest doubt that he isn't the sort to cheat. And we've also discussed that damned check far too many times. I'm just sorry I ever mentioned the stupid thing to you. Even if I'd needed the money for some rare medical treatment I wouldn't have accepted that check. It's – it would have been blood money, Mir. Or a guilt offering. And I would have felt like a whore for taking it."

Mirai waved a hand in dismissal. "You worry about that stuff too much, Cara. Hey, it's not like the guy couldn't afford it. And so what if the only reason he offered it to you was because he felt guilty? He *should* feel guilty, damn it. He took advantage of you. Used you. And then dumped you when someone better came along. Uh, not better. That's not what I meant. Shit."

Cara patted her on the shoulder. "It's okay. I know what you meant. And frankly, Katie *is* better than I am. At least, she's much, much better looking. She's gorgeous, in fact. Frankly, I don't know what I was even thinking of going out with Dante after he'd been with someone like her. I mean, it's like settling for Andre after you've been drinking Cristal champagne on a regular basis."

Mirai gave her a none-too-playful smack on the upside of her head. "Would you stop it already?" she demanded. "I'm so sick of this pity party you've been hanging out at for the last month. And with the comparisons to Katie What's-Her-Face. In fact, that party is officially over with now. And that particular name is not to be mentioned in my presence again. Got it?"

"Yes, ma'am," answered Cara meekly.

After loading all of Cara's laundry into the trunk of Mirai's sleek Lexus sedan, they made the nerve-wracking drive to her place – nerve-wracking because Mirai was far from the best of drivers. She liked to joke that she was the stereotypical bad Asian driver, even though she was only half-Japanese. Cara had thus far restrained herself from telling Mirai that her horrific driving was no laughing matter, and merely made sure her seat belt was securely fastened and that she clutched the edge of her seat for dear life whenever she drove with her.

Once the first load of laundry had been started, Mirai ordered up dinner for them, pulling a bottle of wine out of the fridge while they waited for the food to be delivered. Cara curled up on the ultra-comfy white leather sectional sofa, a sofa that she'd slept on more than a few times since Mirai and Rene had bought the pricey piece of furniture. Or, more accurately, since their father had bought it for them, as he'd done everything else in this luxurious two-bedroom condo.

"Thanks, Mir. For everything. The wine, ordering in dinner, letting me do my laundry here rather than at the laundromat where you never know what weirdo, drunk, or homeless person is going to stagger through the doorway next."

Mirai nodded, and promptly refilled their wine glasses with the very expensive Chardonnay that her father had bought a case of during his visit last month. "No need to thank me. I'm just happy to see you emerge from your cave for once and looking halfway human. Please tell me you do not go to work looking as bad as you did earlier today. No offense, but you looked sort of scary."

Cara would have been tempted to give her BFF the finger, except for the fact that what she'd just said was all too true. "Of course not. Tough as it's been, I drag myself out of bed every day and make it to the office looking presentable. Though Angela's asked me several times if everything's okay."

"What did you tell her?" asked Mirai.

"Not the truth, of course. At least, not the real truth. She knows I was seeing someone named Danny, but thank God she's yet to put two and two together and figure out it was actually Dante. I just told her that we've stopped seeing each other, and that it didn't work out."

"And that you've fallen into a severe depression as a result," added Mirai. "Though by the time I drop you off at your place tomorrow, that will no longer be the case."

"Hmm." Cara regarded her friend skeptically. "And how are you planning to snap me out of my funk, huh? Let me guess. You're buying me a puppy? No, pets aren't allowed according to my lease. I've got it!

You're taking me to the circus. Oh, never mind. I forgot you have this deathly fear of clowns."

Mirai tossed a throw pillow at her. "Do not even mention those horrible creatures! And no, Smart Ass, my plan does not involve puppies, kittens, or anything else cute and cuddly. My idea for making you smile again is to help you make yourself over."

"Huh? You mean like makeup and hair and stuff? Mir, you know I can't afford any of those things, and I am *not* going to let you foot the bill. You do way too much for me already, like dinner tonight and this bottle of wine that you told me costs beaucoup bucks and brunch tomorrow at that place that has the nerve to charge eight dollars for a single slice of coffee cake. Do you have any idea how many coffee cakes I could make for eight bucks – *whole* cakes and not just a little slice. So you'd better forget.."

Mirai tossed a second pillow Cara's way, hitting her square in the forehead with this one. "My mistake in saying you were depressed. It sounds like you just drank five espressos instead. And if you could stop yapping for a minute, you'd let me explain."

Cara set the pillow aside. "Fine. As long as you stop throwing things at me. I feel like one of those bean bag toss boards."

Mirai shuddered. "Ugh! And that makes me think of clowns again. Once when I was around eight I went to a neighbor's birthday party and she had a bean bag toss board with a fucking clown painted on it. I had nightmares for a week. Anyway, back to what I was saying. Haven't you ever heard the phrase "looking good is the best revenge" Otherwise known as the Breakup Vendetta?"

Cara frowned, but her interest had nonetheless been piqued. "I guess I've heard the first part, not so sure about the second. But what does that have to do with me? I mean, as upset as I was when Dante ended things, it wasn't like he cheated on me, or was ever dishonest. Frankly, I'm surprised he dated me as long as he did, especially after seeing pictures of.."

Mirai held up a fist threateningly. "If you say her name one more time, I will not be responsible for my actions, okay? And maybe revenge or vendetta aren't exactly the right words to use under the circumstances. That doesn't mean you can't, uh, tone things up a little bit and get your hair cut. If for no other reason than to feel good about yourself, Cara."

They were briefly interrupted by the arrival of their food, but once they started eating the wide array of sushi Mirai had ordered, she resumed the conversation.

"Wouldn't it be awesome to have a little makeover, buy a few killer outfits, and then see Dante's reaction at the finished product?" prodded Mirai. "Come on, you've got to admit it's tempting as hell. No better feeling in the world than flaunting yourself in front of the guy who dumped you, and making sure he knows how stupid he was in letting you go."

Cara smiled wistfully. "It sounds awesome, no doubt about it. But sorry to sound like a broken record – where in the world do you think I can come up with the money for a makeover? My tuition went up this semester, and my rent's going up the first of the year."

"I thought Nick and Angela give you a nice bonus at the end of the year."

"They do, and I expect they will again this year. But I need that money to buy a new laptop," acknowledged Cara. "When Len fixed it for me last month, he warned it was just temporary and that I should start looking around for a replacement. I guess I could buy a used laptop and use some of the bonus to buy a new outfit or two and get my hair cut."

"Hmm. Except some new clothes and a hair cut are just part of it," mused Mirai. "You also need to get serious about those extra twenty pounds you keep bitching about but never do anything about actually losing. Diet and exercise, baby. Those need to be your two new favorite words."

Cara's chopsticks paused halfway to her lips, a piece of Lion King roll wedged in between them. "Well, I really can't afford to join a gym or buy a lot of healthy food like fruits and veggies."

"You don't have to join a gym," Mirai pointed out. "I've got a dozen different DVD sets of workouts – kickboxing, power yoga, boot camp, salsa dancing, some stuff you've never heard of. As you know, I've got a serious late night TV shopping addiction, so I'm a sucker for whatever new method comes out. We'll look through them after dinner and you can borrow whatever ones sound the best to you. And before you ask – no, I am not using any of them right now. I also get bored easily, as you also know. Right now I'm taking a Barre Method class."

"And exactly when am I supposed to fit in an exercise routine?" demanded Cara. "I do work fulltime and go to school, in case you've forgotten."

Mirai shrugged. "Get your ass out of bed an hour earlier in the morning. It'll suck but the results will be worth it. As for affording the food, I've got another idea about that."

Cara glared at her friend. "If you suggest I start growing my own fruits and vegetables in my landlady's backyard, I'm going to poke your eye out with this chopstick."

"Please." Mirai made a sound of disbelief. "As if I'd suggest something so, well – *rural*. No, I was going to point out that you do have another way to come up with the extra money. Re-directing it might be a more accurate term."

"I am not giving up my apartment and sleeping on your sofa for the next ten months," declared Cara. "So you can forget about my using rent money on shoes and makeup and better food."

"I wasn't going to suggest that," assured Mirai. "Though it goes without saying that the offer still stands. Tell me. How much do you think it costs you each year to fly roundtrip to Florida for Christmas? Not to mention your cab fare to and from the airport since your father's too much of a dick to pick you up. Oh, and for good measure let's add in the cost of the Christmas presents you buy for him and the wicked stepmother and the bratty half-siblings."

Cara set down her chopsticks, suddenly not hungry despite the fact that she'd only had a bowl of cereal all day. "Are you suggesting that I don't go home for Christmas this year?" she whispered. "That I use that money on myself instead?"

"That's *exactly* what I'm suggesting," confirmed Mirai. "Come on, Cara. You told me how horrible it was there last year, how unhappy you were. And once again you cut your trip short by two days because you hated being there so much. So why in the world do you want to voluntarily put yourself through all that bullshit again, waste all that money, when you could be spending it on a much worthier cause – yourself."

Cara's jaw dropped open in shock. "But – but I'd be all alone," she murmured. "At Christmas. You always spend the holidays in New York with your family, and I wouldn't have anywhere else to go. I – I don't want to be alone at Christmas, Mir. The rest of the year I don't mind so much, but not Christmas."

"Sweetie, I hate to break the bad news to you, but guess what?" replied Mirai snarkily. "You might be surrounded by a houseful of people down there in Florida, but you're still alone. And I don't want to make you feel bad, Cara, but can you honestly tell me that your father would really give a damn if you didn't fly down there?"

A tear began to track down her cheek as she sniffled. "No," she mumbled in a barely audible voice. "He – he'd probably be relieved, actually. If he even noticed I wasn't there, that is."

"Hey." Mirai rushed over to embrace Cara as she started to cry. "God, I'm sorry, *amiga*. I didn't mean to sound like a total bitch and make you sad. All I wanted was to have you think about yourself for once, instead of all these loser guys you've allowed to take advantage of you. Especially your father."

"I know." Cara picked up a paper napkin and blew her nose. "And you're right, Mir. He does take advantage of me, takes me for granted all the time. But missing Christmas – not giving the kids a little gift. I don't know if I'm ready for something that extreme."

Mirai returned to her seat and popped a huge piece of tempura shrimp in her mouth. "Tell me again what your dad and the wicked stepmother gave you for Christmas last year? Or your birthday this year."

Cara sighed, seeing all too clearly where her friend was headed with this line of questioning. "Nothing for my birthday. An email from my dad ten days after the fact but no gift or official card. As for Christmas – let's see. Oh, that's right. They gave me a set of bath gels.

The same exact set that someone gave Holly the year before. The one she bitched about because it had been bought at TJ Maxx, and the price tag hadn't been removed. And she didn't even have the sense to remove it when she re-gifted it to me last year."

"And how much did it cost?"

Cara's cheeks reddened in shame. "Around ten dollars," she admitted reluctantly.

"And how much did you spend on gifts for the four of them? Not to mention the gifts you send to the kids for their birthdays?"

"A lot more than ten bucks," replied Cara. "I get your point, Mir. My dad and Holly obviously don't give a shit about me, or wouldn't care whether I show up or not for the holidays. But to not spend Christmas with my father? He – he's all I have left," she whispered sadly.

Mirai shook her head. "That's where you're wrong, baby. Your father checked out of your life over four years ago. Now it's time for you to return the favor. And I realize it won't be easy, Cara, but it's like I said before – you need to kick all of the toxic guys you keep attracting in the ass. Starting with the worst one of them all."

"I know," acknowledged Cara wearily. "But I'm just not sure I'm strong enough."

"Of course you are," argued Mirai. "Cara, you're the strongest person I know. Now prove it, and tell your dad you aren't going to Florida this Christmas. Use the money you would have spent on airfare and gifts on yourself. You deserve it way more than he does."

Cara exhaled deeply. "You make it sound so easy. And I totally get what you're saying, understand the rationale. But accepting something and actually finding the courage to make it happen are two different things."

Mirai raised her wine glass in a little toast. "Well, if anyone has enough courage to do something like that it's you. Give me a call when you realize that for yourself."

CARA'S FINGER hovered over the speed dial button on her phone, wondering for the fifth time in as many minutes if she really had the nerve to make this call. Ever since Mirai had dropped her off an hour ago, she had been struggling with what the right thing to do really was. It was a certainty that the man she was thinking of calling wouldn't appreciate being contacted, but at the same time she desperately needed to get a few things cleared up. She had to know, needed to hear stark truths if need be, so that she could finally move on. So that she could find the courage to become stronger, and never again let herself be used or taken for granted by the men in her life.

"Here goes nothing," she muttered, pressing the call button. "Though there's only a fifty percent chance at best that he'll even answer."

The phone rang a total of five times, with Cara fully expecting it to go to voice mail as it so often did, when an impatient male voice finally answered.

"Cara. This really isn't a good time."

She sighed, also having anticipated this sort of greeting. "Hi, Dad. And sorry to bother you as usual, but this will only take a few minutes. And it's really important. Please."

Mark Bregante huffed in irritation. "It would be much easier for me if I could call you back. We have a houseful of people here right now for Hunter's birthday."

Hunter was Cara's little half-brother, and his third birthday was in a few days. Cara had already mailed him a present, one she had been ill able to afford, but it was important to her to try and maintain some semblance of a relationship with her half-siblings.

"Isn't it a little early for his party?" inquired Cara. "His birthday isn't until Friday."

Mark sighed, clearly not happy that she was still on the line. "Today's party is just for the family. We're having another, bigger party next Saturday for all of the kids. Look, I really need to get back, Cara. Holly wants me to get the barbeque going."

"Of course she does," muttered Cara under her breath. She thought back briefly to the small, simple birthday parties her mother had given her as a child, and was hard-pressed to recall even one time when Mark had been present, much less actually helping out.

It was that recollection, not to mention the remembrances of all the other times he had let her down or disappointed her or simply not been there for her, that strengthened Cara's resolve now.

"No, Dad," she told him firmly. "I need to ask you something right now. I won't keep you more than five minutes, I swear."

"It would be a lot better if I could just call you back," argued Mark. "What if I call you tonight after the kids are in bed and everyone's gone home?"

Cara had fallen for that particular trick too many times to count, and wasn't going to cave in this time. She knew from bitter experience that the promised call back would never materialize.

"That's the same thing you told me two weeks ago," she reminded him, uncaring for once that she wasn't bothering to disguise the snarkiness in her tone. "I'm still waiting for that call back. Just like I'm waiting for a reply to the email I sent ten days ago. Oh, and what about the text I sent you on Thursday just wanting a simple yes or no answer to see if Hunter's present had arrived?"

Mark was silent for several seconds before grumbling, "Sorry. It's been a busy couple of weeks. What exactly did you need, Cara?"

She wanted desperately to tell him *exactly* what she needed - financial assistance so that she could buy a new laptop and not have to struggle so much to make ends meet; his fatherly support and sympathy for the heartache she was still suffering after Dante had broken up with her; for him to answer her calls and emails on a more timely basis, and maybe even initiate contact between them every so often; for him to occasionally remember that he had another child, and to maybe just pretend that he gave a damn about her.

Instead, she merely asked him the question that had been weighing on her mind since Mirai had brought it up last night. "Dad, if - if I decided not to come out there for Christmas this year, would you - well, would that upset you?"

Mark sighed again. He seemed to do a lot of that, Cara realized, as though having to spare a lousy five minutes to speak to his daughter was an imposition of epic proportions.

"Cara," he replied irritably, "I really don't have time to talk about this sort of thing right now. I have people waiting for me, depending on me."

"What about me?" she cried. "Don't I get to depend on you anymore? Or would it make you happier if I just forgot I had a father. Just like you've obviously forgotten you have a third child."

Mark muttered something under his breath, and she just guessed it wasn't anything pleasant. "Jesus Christ, you're really turning into a little drama queen, aren't you?" he sneered. "Just like your mother."

Cara recoiled, her father's unkind words as painful as a slap across the face. "How dare you say something like that about Mom," she hissed. "After all the bullshit she took from you, how she supported you for years, looked the other way every time you broke her heart. But let's not go there right now, okay? Neither of us have anywhere near that much time. Just answer the question, Dad. About Christmas. How would you feel if I didn't make the trip to Florida this year?"

Mark blew out a harsh breath. "You're a grown woman, Cara, so you can do whatever you want."

"Yes or no answer, Dad," she insisted. "Would you be upset if we didn't spend Christmas together?"

"No," answered Mark bluntly. "No, it won't make any difference to me, so if you have other plans feel free. Actually, if you didn't come out this year that would solve a little problem that came up recently. Holly's aunt and uncle want to fly in from Houston for the holiday but nobody has room for them, so they were starting to look into motels. But if you aren't going to come we can just put them in the guest room you would have used. Holly will be thrilled."

Cara held the phone away from her ear, staring at it in disbelief, unwilling to admit that her own father had really said those callous, impersonal things to her. But, in a way, what he had just told her made the decision she was about to make that much easier.

"All right then. It's settled," she replied, feeling oddly calm. "I won't plan on coming to Florida for Christmas this year. Oh, and since I'm really strapped for cash between tuition and rent increases I'll have to skip sending out gifts this year, too. Tell Holly she can re-gift her crappy presents to someone else this year, maybe to her aunt from Houston."

"Cara," began Mark in a warning tone, but for once she ignored his obvious irritation.

"And since we're on a roll here, might as well keep going," she announced breezily. "You know, since you're such a busy guy these days, Dad, too busy to return my calls or even send a lousy one word reply to my texts, I've decided to put the ball in your court from here on out. After today I'm not going to call you. Or email you. Or text you. When you can squeeze out a few minutes from your busy schedule, or remember that Hunter and Bayleigh aren't your only kids, well - you've got my number. Oh, and if I don't answer my phone just leave a voice mail, and I'll get back to you. Eventually. You know, just like you do, Dad. You'd better get back to your party now."

She ended the call before her father could reply, taking several deep, fortifying breaths, as though she'd just sprinted a lap around the track. Cara watched her phone warily for a few minutes, half-expecting her father to call her back after she'd fired off such a bombshell just now. But, unsurprisingly, no call came, and it was with mingled relief and disappointment that she placed another call.

"Mir? It's me. Well, I've been thinking all day about what you proposed last night. You know, about the makeover and how looking good is the best revenge and stuff. And about how I could come up with some extra cash to make it happen. I just added up what I would save between not paying for airfare to Florida and cab rides to and from the airport plus Christmas presents, and I think I can scrounge up around seven hundred dollars. So I guess," Cara paused to take a deep breath before confirming, "I'm in."

19

Mid-October

DANTE CURSED beneath his breath as he waited impatiently for someone to answer Nick's office phone. He sure as hell didn't need this sort of aggravation right now, on top of what he'd already had to deal with today. This week in New York was supposed to have been something of a vacation, despite the finance conference that was his main reason in being here. But there had been several issues that had cropped up with clients and pending deals, and he'd spent far too much time thus far fielding phone calls, sending emails, and arguing long distance with Howie. And that didn't include the regular texts from his sister and brother-in-law and mother with updates on his new niece, and the almost constant influx of cute baby pictures.

The panicked phone call he'd just received a few minutes ago from Katie had been both ill-timed and aggravating as hell. He had an enormous limit on his credit card, since it was linked to the multi-million dollar brokerage account he had entrusted to Nick, and thus had zero idea why said card would now be blocked. Katie was waiting with ill-concealed impatience for a return call that would hopefully resolve this problem, clutching an armful of clothing she'd been in the process of buying at Barneys when the transaction had been denied.

Fortunately he had two other credit cards with him, but had no easy way to get one of those over to Katie right now. He'd tried to give the sales clerk one of those card numbers over the phone, but due to the sizeable amount of the transaction the store was requiring an in-person authorization. He'd urged Katie to stay put and be patient while he called Nick to unblock the card she was clutching in her hand at this moment. Patience, however, wasn't always one of her better traits, so he was desperate to get this issue resolved as quickly as possible.

Dante had fully expected Nick's humorless but efficient assistant Deepak to pick up the call, or perhaps one of his associates Tyler or Leah. What he had definitely not planned on, however, was to hear Cara's voice on the other end of the line.

"Nick Manning's office, this is Cara speaking. How can I help you?" she inquired, her voice polite but also sounding more than a little stressed out.

Dante hesitated, for this was the first time he'd had any contact whatsoever with Cara since their break-up, and he had zero idea what sort of reception he'd receive. "Uh, hi. It's, uh, me. Dante. How - how have you been?"

He was greeted with silence for long seconds, and he was half-afraid she'd hung up on him. But she finally answered, although her reply wasn't particularly cheerful.

"Fine, thank you," she said primly. "And yourself?"

It was if they were merely strangers now, instead of ex-lovers. And rather than Cara's usual bubbly chatter, he was being greeted with terse, stilted responses.

"I'm good. Officially an uncle now," he offered, trying desperately to get past this awkwardness. "My sister had her baby about three weeks ago. A little girl - Ariella. I've got something like a hundred pictures of her so far."

There was another awkward pause before Cara replied, again in that emotionless, almost hollow voice. "Congratulations. I'm sure your family must be very happy."

"Yeah." He cleared his throat before asking, "Is Nick around? Actually, Deepak would probably be better since this is an operational problem."

"Deepak is on vacation this week," Cara informed him coolly. "And Nick, Leah, and Tyler are all making a presentation to a potential client at their office. Angela is at an appointment, so I'm holding down the fort. Is there something I could help you with?"

Dante hesitated again, for the very last thing he wanted to do was ask for Cara's help to unblock the credit card that was currently in Katie's clutches. It would be, to say the least, something of a proverbial slap in the face.

"Um, I don't want to bother you with something like this, I'm sure you must be busy since you're the only one there. I probably just need to get a phone number from you so I can deal with it myself."

He paused, aware that for once he was the one who was babbling.

"What exactly is the problem?" asked Cara calmly. "And what sort of phone number do you need?"

"My credit card just got declined," he explained. "And I know there's plenty of cash available to cover any charges. The vendor isn't being especially helpful, so I – "

"Hold on a minute."

She put him on hold mid-sentence, leaving him to wonder whether he should wimp out and hang up before she could pick up again. But Cara was back on the line within moments, not giving him the opportunity to ponder what he should say next.

"Mr. Sabattini, I have Phil from our Card Services Unit on the line with us," announced Cara in her most professional sounding voice, even resorting to addressing him formally. "He's already identified the issue with your card, and just has a few brief questions for you."

Unlike Cara, Phil from Card Services was nearly gushing in his all-out efforts to be helpful. The Customer Service Representative had undoubtedly noticed the net worth of Dante's account, and was anxious to treat him like the VIP that he was.

"I'm so very sorry for the inconvenience this little problem has caused you, sir," offered Phil. "But in actuality the temporary block on your card was placed there for your protection. When our security systems notice a lot of card activity in a very short amount of time, in particular for the large amounts that have been charged, it puts out all sorts of red flags. That sort of credit card activity, especially when it's not customary for the card holder, is often a surefire sign of fraud."

Dante sighed irritably, well aware of what the CSR was patiently explaining to him. "Got it. In future I'll try to curtail the number of transactions at once. Or give you guys a call first to alert you. Right now, what can you do to get the block lifted?"

"I can take care of that for you right away, Mr. Sabattini," Phil replied soothingly. His voice was quickly beginning to irritate the hell out of Dante, and he almost wished he was dealing with the impersonal Cara instead.

Phil asked him a few questions to determine that this was really him - the same security questions he recalled now that he'd had to initially answer when setting up the account with Nick.

"All right, sir. Those all check out just fine. Now, one last quick thing and then we'll be able to unblock the card. I see that the unusual activity started about forty-eight hours ago. I'm going to need to run through all of those charges with you to make sure they're valid."

Dante's spine stiffened. "Is that absolutely necessary?" he snapped. "Can't I just give you a blanket approval or something like that?"

"I'm very sorry, Mr. Sabattini," apologized Phil profusely. "But that is our policy. It's for your protection, sir. And it will just take a minute or two."

"It *is* standard policy," offered Cara, the first time she'd spoken in several minutes. "Phil needs to do this for security reasons."

Dante cringed at the thought of Cara having to hear first hand the amount of money he'd already lavished on Katie, and the posh restaurants they had dined at thus far. He was just about to urge her to disconnect and get back to her work, assure her that he could easily handle it from here, but then Phil quickly launched into reciting the list of charges before he could protest.

"All right, Mr. Sabattini," chirped Phil. "Just let me know if any of these charges don't belong to you. They'll be in order from oldest to most recent, beginning with the first charge in New York two days ago. Here we go. Four hundred seventeen dollars at Tavern On The Green. One hundred and forty five dollars at Bar Sixty Five. Two thousand six hundred and sixty two dollars at Versace."

Phil admittedly read through each of the charges briskly, but Dante visibly cringed to hear each entry, shuddering to imagine poor Cara's reaction while listening to the same. He was a little shell shocked himself to realize just how much Katie had dropped this morning during her shopping spree. In just the space of four hours, she'd already hit up Bergdorf's, Bloomingdales, Saks, and was even now waiting at Barney's for that contested charge to go through. In all, between meals, clothes, accessories, and spa treatments, the total came to well over twenty grand - not counting the first class airline tickets, the limo ride from the airport, and the suite at the Waldorf Astoria. And their week in New York wasn't even at the halfway point.

In the past, Dante wouldn't have given a second thought to spending that sort of money in such a brief period of time. He'd worked damned hard for his success, and liked reaping the benefits, like pampering himself. But he was extremely, uncomfortably aware that Cara was still on the line, and was having to listen to all of this. And all he could picture at this moment was that tiny, miserable little hovel she called home, the bare bones wardrobe that she somehow made do with and had never once complained about, and her ancient, falling apart at the seams laptop. God, why did she have to be so damned stubborn, he thought wildly. Why couldn't she have swallowed that immense pride of hers for once and accepted that check he'd given her? The money could have helped her in so many ways, could have made her life so much better than it was.

'And it would have helped you from feeling so guilty right about now,' he admitted grudgingly. 'So you need to ask yourself and answer truthfully - did you try to give Cara that money to help her or yourself?'

Thankfully, the all-too-helpful Phil finished running through his list of transactions, and then cheerfully informed Dante that there should be no further issues with using his card but to call Card Services immediately if something came up. After apologizing profusely once again for the inconvenience, and thanking him for being one of their preferred clients, Phil finally ended the call - leaving an awkward, gaping silence between Cara and Dante.

He spoke first. "Uh, I'm real sorry you had to listen to all that. The list of charges, that is. I really don't think our buddy Phil needed to go through them in painstaking detail that way."

"No, it really is standard procedure," replied Cara flatly. "I've been through that a couple of times before with other clients."

"Yeah, but the other clients weren't - well, you know," he mumbled uneasily.

"Someone I used to fuck?" supplied Cara calmly. "And who just happens to be in New York right now letting their girlfriend rack up tens of thousands of dollars on their credit card? Is that what you meant to say?"

"Cara." He felt an overwhelming sense of sadness at her words, especially since he could have sworn she was fighting back tears, and wondered if he could possibly despise himself one iota more than he did at this moment. "Honey, I'm so sorry. The very last thing I wanted was for you to have to hear all that. But Phil started in before I could suggest you get off the line."

"It's no problem," said Cara crisply. "Just doing my job, helping out a client. It's what I do, after all. Is there something else I can assist you with?"

Dante made an impatient sound. "Really, Cara? Is this the way it's going to be between us from now on? What happened to being friends? I thought we said we would still do that."

"No," she corrected. "You said that, not me. I - I just don't think that's going to be possible. So I'm happy to help if you have a question about your account, or need something done, but otherwise no. We are not friends. We aren't anything. I'm just one of Nick's assistants as far as you're concerned, and you're one of our best clients."

He shook his head regretfully, even though she couldn't see him. "No, honey. Think what you like, but you're much more to me than that. I'm just sorry I hurt you so badly that I ruined our friendship in the process. You might not believe it, Cara, but I miss you. More than I can say."

CARA REPLACED the phone in its cradle slowly, then took several deep breaths as she struggled to keep herself from losing it completely. But as the hot tears began to trickle down her cheeks, she realized that it was too late for that. Grateful that the rest of the team was still out of the office, she dashed into Angela's office since her boss always kept a box of tissues handy. She grabbed a handful and made a futile attempt to stem the ever increasing flow of tears.

"Damn him," she whispered unsteadily. "Of all days, why did he have to pick today to call? And here I thought I was doing so well, feeling so much stronger since I basically told Dad to shove it. Instead, I'm just the same idiotic sap when it comes to men that I've always been."

Her sobs only increased after that, and she sank weakly into one of the guest chairs facing Angela's desk. She was weeping so intensely, in fact, that she barely felt the gentle touch on her shoulder.

"Hey. What on earth is the matter?" asked Angela urgently. "I know Nick couldn't have yelled at you since he isn't around. Not to mention the fact he'd have had to deal with me if he ever pulled a stunt like that."

Cara shook her head, mopping at her eyes in embarrassment to have been caught this way by her boss. "N-nno. It wasn't Nick. He - he's never really yelled at me. It's - I just - just talked to D-Danny out of the blue, and it took me by surprise."

"It upset you," added Angela gently, patting her on the back soothingly.

Cara had confided in her boss about the breakup with "Danny", but reluctantly so and only after Angela had pressed her as to why she was so down in the dumps. She had tried her best since then to put on a happy face, not wanting to have additional discussions on the matter.

Cara accepted the fresh handful of tissues Angela handed her and blew her nose loudly. "I'm so, so sorry," she sniffled. "I didn't mean to lose it here at the office. I know how unprofessional this is, and I promise it will never, ever happen again. Oh, God, and I've left the phones unattended and I know how annoyed Nick gets about that, so I'd better..."

"Stay right where you are," instructed Angela sternly. "I'll go forward the phones to voice mail and then you and I are going to have a little chat."

Cara wasn't sure she liked the implication behind her boss's words, but remained obediently in place regardless. A couple of minutes later Angela closed the door to her office, then took a seat in the other guest chair rather than behind her desk.

"Now," she began in a brisk, no-nonsense voice. "I recently developed something of a theory about this ex of yours, this Danny person. And I want you to be perfectly honest with me, Cara. Are Danny and Dante Sabattini one in the same person?"

Cara stared at Angela in disbelief. "What?" she wheezed in alarm. "Why - why would you even imagine something so far-fetched?"

"Because right around the time your Danny broke things off with you and you looked like the world had just ended," replied Angela calmly, "Dante rather coincidentally reconciled with his ex-girlfriend. And the said ex - a really, really annoying pain in the ass named Katie - always calls him Danny. I didn't put two and two together until we had dinner with the two of them last weekend, and it started me thinking. I wasn't going to say anything because – well, frankly, I'm not sure I really wanted to know the truth. But seeing how upset you are now, I had to ask."

Reluctantly, Cara nodded. "Yes. Danny and Dante are one in the same. But please, please don't say anything to Nick! Please, Angela? I know I screwed up big time, but I can't afford to lose my job right now on top of everything else."

Angela looked stricken. "Why on earth would you think for even a minute that you'd lose your job?"

"Because I dated a client," admitted Cara. "I knew it was against company policy, but I didn't care. I liked him too much, and we were really careful not to let anyone find out."

Angela shrugged. "I could care less about what this company says we can and can't do. You of all people should know how little attention I pay to stupid corporate policies. And I won't say anything to Nick, but not because I'm afraid he'd be angry at you. No, what would worry me is how many of Dante's bones Nick might break. If he knew you'd been seeing Dante - and worse, that he broke up with you to go back to that witch Katie - well, that could get real ugly. The sort of ugly that could end what's been a very close friendship between Nick and Dante. So you and I are going to keep this bit of news to ourselves, all right?"

Cara nodded anxiously. "Absolutely. Yes. In fact, the only other person who knows we were dating - well, besides Dante, of course - was Mirai."

"Good." Angela gave a regretful shake of her raven head. "What the hell is wrong with Dante, anyway? Not just for choosing that leech Katie over you, but for getting involved with you in the first place. He should have known better."

"I know," agreed Cara mournfully. "I'm not his type at all. Especially when you stack me up against Katie. She's so beautiful, and has a fantastic body. And knows exactly how to dress. Not to mention..."

Angela held up a hand, her signal that Cara was chattering too much. "Not to mention that she's a self-centered, manipulative bitch. And as smart as Dante is he's dumb as a rock where Katie's concerned. But when I said Dante should have known better than to get involved with you, I didn't mean because you weren't good enough for him. On the contrary, the horny bastard should consider himself damned lucky that you ever went out with him at all. No, what I was really trying to say is that you're just too young and sweet for a player like Dante."

Cara shrugged. "There's not that much of an age difference between us. No more than there is between you and Nick, for example."

"You've got a point," acknowledged Angela. "Except that I was never sweet and innocent like you are. I had to grow up fast, grow up tough, after the way things were for me at home. And when I got involved with Nick, I knew exactly what I was letting myself in for. I knew better than to fall in love with him."

"But you did anyway," reminded Cara.

Angela smiled. "Yeah. Stupid me. Though I suppose it all worked out eventually. But please tell me you weren't silly enough to make the same mistake I did - that you didn't fall in love with Dante."

Cara gulped. "I, um, wish I could tell you that. I really, really do. But since I hate lying, I won't do it."

Angela reached over and gave her a fierce hug, taking Cara by surprise because her boss was not by nature an affectionate person. "Silly girl," she chided. "So I understand now why you were so upset when I walked in a few minutes ago. Was that the first time you'd spoken to Dante since the breakup?"

"Yes. I'm pretty sure he's been avoiding me, why he insisted on having his monthly meeting with Nick outside of the office. And he didn't sound too thrilled when I picked up the phone, or to learn I was the only one here."

"Hmm. Why was he calling?" inquired Angela.

Cara hesitated before relating the whole story, including the part about Dante lavishing Katie with an extravagant trip to New York, and an even more extravagant shopping spree.

Angela was livid. "That fucker," she muttered darkly. "You know what. Forget about Nick breaking his jaw. I might just do it instead. Better yet, I'll ask Lauren to rough him up a little. Dante will never see her coming."

Cara shuddered. She'd met Angela's fierce, fearless best friend on several occasions, and had to agree that the tough as nails Lauren would have a good shot at landing a few blows on Dante.

"Thanks for the offer," replied Cara wearily, "but I'd really rather just try and put the whole thing behind me if it's all the same to you."

Angela patted her on the shoulder. "Oh, sweetie. If it were only that easy."

November

"Cara mia. *Time to wake up, you little sleepyhead. I've been watching you sleep for the last half hour, and I'm real close to jumping your bones. And since I'm not a real fan of necrophilia, I'd prefer you were awake while I'm fucking you.*"

"Mmm." *Cara made a little sound deep in her throat that was part purr of pleasure and part groan of protest at being woken from what had been a very sound sleep.*

The dark-haired, very naked, and very aroused man who was snuggled up behind her equally naked body chuckled at her reaction. "All right, have it your way then," he murmured in a low voice. "I'd rather have your full participation, but I want you too much to wait a minute longer."

But when one of his big hands cupped the heavy weight of her breast, his fingers tweaking the nipple, Cara gasped in reaction. And when the other hand slid between her legs and began to tease the damp flesh there, her eyes flew open wide.

Dante laughed huskily, his stubbled chin rubbing against her flushed cheek as he continued to spoon her. "Ah, there she is! Good morning to you,

Cara mia. And I can't think of a better way to start the day than sliding inside of this sweet, hot pussy."

"Ahhh." She was already breathless, already aroused, when he took hold of his fully erect cock and ran the broad head along the seam of her pussy.

Despite his very obvious arousal, he seemed in no particular hurry to complete his possession of her body. He took his time with her, sometimes thrusting his fingers with slow precision in and out of her vagina, other times rubbing his thumb over the hard nub of her clit, and still other times running his penis first against the cleft between her buttocks and then teasing the very wet creases of her inner labia.

She was so aroused by the time he finally began to feed his cock inside of her, one maddening inch at a time, that she came the moment he thrust all the way in. Her vaginal muscles clenched like a fist around his cock, causing him to growl in reaction. He sucked the skin on the side of her neck, hard enough that she knew it would leave a telltale mark, and began to increase the force and frequency of his thrusts.

"You're so fucking sexy," he rasped in her ear, both of his hands cupping her breasts. "So damned hot. I love these big tits, love the way your tight little pussy squeezes my cock like a vise. And I love y-"

Cara's eyes flew open at that precise moment, just before her dream got really, *really* good. Not, of course, that it hadn't been truly amazing up until now, but, gee whiz - did it really have to end *now*, just before the Dante of her dreams said the words she'd always wanted to hear from his gorgeous lips.

She dragged herself reluctantly to a sitting position, pulling her thighs up against her chest and resting her head on her knees. Her cheeks were flushed from sleep, as well as the vividly erotic dream she'd been woken from by the rude, insisting buzzing of her phone alarm. She knew without having to check first that she'd be wet, and that it would probably just take a few brief strokes of her fingers to make herself come. After all, this was far from the only stimulating dream she'd had about her former lover.

But she resisted, because she knew it just wouldn't be the same. Oh, there might be some brief, temporary pleasure, but any sort of orgasm she could provide for herself would be a total letdown after the true bliss she had known in Dante's arms. It was also why she had adamantly refused to even think about getting herself out there again - as Mirai had so crassly put it. Cara had dated a string of losers once before in her life, those months when she'd been so sad and lost and lonely at college, had settled for sex that was so spectacularly unspectacular that the recollection made her shudder in revulsion now. The fact of the matter was plain and simple - Dante had ruined her for other men, always and forever. Being with him for those few months had been a once in a lifetime experience, something that an ordinary girl like herself had simply lucked into, and would never be so fortunate to experience again. No, at some point, she'd have to settle for a nice but probably bland guy, one who would make her a good husband and be a great father to their kids. But the likelihood that he would ever come close to rocking her world the way Dante had was slim to none, and it made her feel very, very sad to accept that fact.

What also made her very, very sad at this moment was that it was still dark outside, freezing cold inside her apartment, and that it wasn't even four-thirty in the morning. She was mightily tempted to re-set her alarm for an hour from now, crawl back under the covers, and hope that somehow she might join her rudely interrupted dream in progress and get to the end this time.

Instead, she flung back the covers and hopped out of bed before she could lose her nerve, flicking on a lamp as she did so. She had set her workout clothes out the night before so that she wouldn't have to fumble around for them sleepily this morning, and therefore find one more lame excuse for skipping her morning exercise routine. Her teeth chattered from the chill of the room as she stripped off her pajamas, then donned her exercise gear in record time.

She'd also loaded up one of the DVD's that Mirai had loaned her into the fragile but still functioning laptop the previous evening, so that it was ready to go now. As she waited for the computer to power up, Cara did some stretches and kept her fingers crossed that the ancient laptop wouldn't freeze up halfway through the disc. She figured she only needed to deal with the temperamental old electronic device for a couple of more months, until she received her year end bonus from Angela and Nick and could finally afford to buy a new laptop. She'd already begun to do some research on the best model she could get for the money, and hoped to have plenty of cash leftover to save for next semester's tuition.

Cara yawned sleepily as the DVD finally booted up, and she reluctantly began the forty-five minute workout. After scanning Mirai's admittedly impressive collection of exercise videos, Cara had chosen the *Insanity Workout*, only to find from day one that it was very appropriately titled. For the first week or two of *attempting* the workouts, she'd felt alternately dizzy, out of breath, nauseous, and horribly out of shape. But slowly but surely her endurance and flexibility had improved, and she was able to get through the daily routines without stopping now.

It still wasn't any fun getting up so early on workdays in order to fit in a workout, especially now that it was so dark and cold in the mornings, but Cara forced herself to do just that. Weekends were better, of course, since she could sleep in later, as well as vary her exercise routines a little. Weather permitting, she'd been going for long walks and hikes in various places around the city - Golden Gate Park, Marina Green, the Presidio - and had recently begun incorporating a slow jog into part of the workout. Little by little, acknowledged Cara grudgingly, she was whipping herself into shape.

She was sweaty and out of breath by the end of this morning's workout, guzzling down a full glass of water to recover. Sugary, calorie-laden sports drinks weren't part of her diet plan, nor were they budget friendly, so she mostly stuck to water these days. There were a lot of different foods, in fact, that she'd brutally eliminated from her diet - or, more accurately, Mirai had ruthlessly crossed them off the list she'd compiled of allowable items.

Once Cara had placed that call to her BFF announcing that she was on board with this so-called makeover, Mirai had jumped into action immediately. Even though the two girls had just spent most of the weekend together, Mirai had headed over to Cara's place for what she'd deemed a farewell meal - though as it turned out Cara wouldn't be saying good-bye to her friend, but to nearly every single item of food and drink that she loved.

Cara had stared glumly at the list of "Acceptable and Unacceptable Foods" that Mirai had cheerily drawn up, with the latter the far longer of the two columns.

"No alcohol at all?" she'd asked wistfully. "Not even an occasional glass of red wine? I've heard that it actually has health benefits."

Mirai had given her a stern look. "It also has a hundred and twenty five calories, Cara. And since you'll only be consuming around thirteen hundred calories a day, do you really want to waste that many on a single glass? Especially since alcohol is basically empty calories, no nutritional value at all."

Cara had sighed in surrender. "Fine. No wine. No sugar. No pasta or bread or butter. In other words, no fun."

"Cheer up," Mirai had chirped. "It won't be that way forever. Once you drop the weight, you can have an occasional cheat meal. And speaking of the weight, might as well see what your starting point is."

Cara had squawked loudly but eventually gave in and stepped on the scale - though she'd insisted on stripping down to her underwear and weighing herself barefoot to eliminate every additional ounce. She hated weighing herself more than anything in the world, shuddered to see the dreaded number that popped up on the scale, and thought that she'd rather have a root canal, a bikini wax, or one of those horrifically painful Korean foot massages she'd seen demonstrated on TV rather than get on the scale.

But she'd been rather pleasantly surprised to see that the number on the scale was actually a few pounds lower than the last time she'd weighed herself, and realized that since the breakup with Dante her appetite had been waning. Plus, she hadn't been going out to dinner with him on Fridays, or cooking a big meal for them on Saturdays.

Nonetheless, even with the five pounds or so she'd managed to drop without even trying, she still had a long way to go until she achieved her goal. At Mirai's admonition, she didn't weigh herself every day, only a couple of times a week. And thus far, between the diet and exercise, she'd lost an additional seven pounds, enough that some of her old clothes from college and even high school were starting to fit reasonably well. But since most of those items were of the jeans and T-shirt variety, they weren't things she could wear to work, so her day to day wardrobe continued to be sparse.

Still, she was gradually beginning to feel a lot better about herself, had more energy, and the confidence that she'd be able to see this thing through to her goals. Cara didn't think she would ever be slim enough to be able to fit into Mirai's size two wardrobe, but honestly didn't think she would ever want to. All she really wanted was to look trim and toned and healthy, and feel more confident about her appearance. And if that meant dragging her ass out of bed at some ungodly hour of the morning so she could fit in a workout, well, in the end it would hopefully be worth it.

She took a quick shower, grimacing a bit when the water refused to heat up past the lukewarm stage. It took what seemed like forever to rinse all the shampoo out of her long, unmanageable hair, and Cara longed for the day when she had saved enough money to have it cut. She was still intent on having her out of control curls professionally straightened, and tried to imagine how she would look with long, sleek locks - much like Katie Carlisle's shiny blonde tresses.

"Stop it!" she scolded herself as she toweled off. "Remember, you are not supposed to be thinking about Dante or Katie or what expensive restaurant he's taking her to dinner at or how many new dresses he bought her. And you are especially not supposed to be comparing yourself to her. You and Katie are two completely different people, and while you might not ever be in her league, you're doing all the right things to feel better about yourself. So there!"

Cara wrapped her ratty old bathrobe around her, and pulled on a pair of threadbare slippers as she padded into the kitchenette area. She grimaced as she heated some water to make a bowl of oatmeal, one of the foods that Mirai had placed on the top of the list of approved items.

"It's super low calorie, very filling, and cheap," Mirai had declared. *"But don't start adding in stuff like brown sugar and raisins or you'll defeat the purpose."*

Cara had made a horrible face. "I hate oatmeal," she'd muttered. "Always have. It tastes like sticky paste. Blech."

Mirai had given her a playful swat on the ass. "You might hate it," she'd declared cheerfully, "but your butt will love you for eating it. Especially when said butt is several inches smaller after you lose all that weight."

Six weeks into her healthy eating plan, Cara still wasn't convinced about the oatmeal. Sprinkling cinnamon and Splenda over it helped some with the taste, but she didn't think she would ever really get used to the texture. Still, Mirai was right in that oatmeal was both filling and cheap as well as very low in calories, so Cara dutifully spooned it into her mouth in between sips of green tea.

She'd also cut way back on coffee, mostly because she liked to drink it with lots of cream and sugar, and also because it wasn't cheap. She would usually wait until she arrived at the office to get a cup since it was free there, but had grudgingly switched to using nonfat milk and Splenda in the brew.

She swallowed another spoonful of oatmeal, doing her best not to shudder. "What I don't do in the name of vanity," she commiserated out loud.

The rest of her daily menu wasn't much better - a scant handful of dry roasted almonds mid-morning; a bowl of vegetable soup and some carrot sticks for lunch; a piece of fruit in the afternoon. For dinner on the nights she had class, she microwaved a Lean Cuisine she kept in the mini-fridge in Angela's office, and then nibbled on a protein bar for dessert. On the other three nights of the week, she cooked something healthy - usually a small piece of chicken or fish and some steamed vegetables. And she allowed herself one tiny, delicious square of dark chocolate a day.

She quickly rinsed out her breakfast dishes before heading off to dress for work. Because her hair was so long and unmanageable - and also because her hair dryer had recently kicked the bucket - she had started pulling the heavy tresses back into a damp ponytail or braid on workdays. Beyond a flick of mascara and a swipe of lip gloss, Cara didn't bother with makeup.

She pulled on underwear, pleased to note that her bra felt a little looser. Impulsively, she dragged the scale out from beneath the sink and stepped on it, and was rewarded for her bravery by the discovery she'd dropped another pound this past week. That made her overall weight loss thirteen pounds, with less than ten to go until she reached her goal.

The waistband of a skirt that had always been snug was also much looser now, and she realized that she was going to need to move the button over a few inches. At some point she would need to buy new clothes, but she was determined to wait until she dropped those final pounds before rewarding herself in that way.

Just before shrugging into her coat and heading out the door, Cara gave herself one last critical look in the bathroom mirror. She looked - *good*, she realized in some surprise. And not just because of the weight loss that had put some definition in her cheekbones. Her skin looked healthier, more luminous, no doubt due to all the water she was drinking and the elimination of junk food from her diet.

But it wasn't just the physical changes that had made a difference. She appeared calmer, more mature, and somehow more serene. Each day that passed made the heartbreak she'd suffered after losing Dante a tiny bit more bearable. She was gradually starting to come to terms with the fact that he wasn't a part of her life any longer, and would never be again. She was focusing all of her attention these days on work, school, and taking care of herself, both physically and emotionally. She was also giving some serious thought to her future after she finished her degree next year, considering the potential jobs she might apply for, and even thinking about other cities she could move to and get a fresh start in.

Cara had feared that breaking off communication with her father would be too hard to deal with, and that sooner than later she would cave in and get in touch with him. So far, though, she had stuck to her guns and resisted the urge to call or text or email him, replaying that last conversation with him in her head anytime she was tempted to go back on her word. Mirai had been thrilled to learn she'd basically told Mark to go kiss off, and even happier that Cara wouldn't be going to Florida for Christmas and using the money on herself.

She wasn't going to lie and swear that Mark's neglect didn't hurt like hell. But if she was being honest with herself, the current situation wasn't really any different than it had been in years. She had always been the one to reach out to him, the one to cling desperately to their one-sided relationship. And perhaps not so surprisingly, she was actually happier now that she wasn't constantly trying to get her father to pay attention to her. After all, she theorized, if she didn't willingly put herself into situations where he could ignore her, then it shouldn't hurt so much when he continued to keep his distance.

There had been no attempt on her father's part to change her mind about traveling to Florida for Christmas, and it was now well past the time where she'd be able to book an affordable plane flight anyway. Thus far, Cara hadn't let herself think about Christmas, and the fact that she'd be alone for the first time in her life. First up was Thanksgiving, just over a week away, and she'd be spending it at Mirai and Rene's condo along with several of their friends. Cara knew she'd be doing most of the cooking, since the two sisters were terrible cooks - this despite Mirai's short-lived stint at the culinary academy. But Cara didn't mind in the least, relishing the opportunity to use the spacious, modern kitchen at the condo. It was also a small way to repay Mirai for all of her generosity and support.

It was still dark outside during her two block walk to the bus stop, since the sun wouldn't come up until seven o'clock or so at this time of the year. Cara was always watchful, always aware, whenever she had to walk to and from her apartment in the dark, whether early in the morning or late at night after returning from school. Fortunately, this formerly semi-rundown neighborhood was gradually being revitalized. There was such a shortage of affordable homes in San Francisco nowadays that prospective buyers were venturing into less popular areas just so they could own a place. In the two plus years she'd been living here, a number of homes had been sold to new owners, who in turn had worked hard to spruce their houses up.

Still, though, there remained any number of places that were on the shabby side and badly in need of some TLC. Not to mention the cars that drove by her as she walked briskly along, sometimes with occupants who would make lewd or suggestive comments directed her way. Cara always kept her cell phone in her pocket at the ready in case she needed to whip it out and call 911 in a hurry. Thus far it hadn't been necessary but she was determined to always remain on the alert. She'd even considered buying a canister of pepper spray, but had never been able to spare the money. Now with winter approaching, however, she was beginning to re-visit the idea.

She arrived into the office before Nick and Angela, but right around the same time as Deepak. They nodded to each other before jumping right into work. Leah and Tyler arrived minutes later, and by seven a.m. the phones were already ringing. Angela and Nick walked in shortly thereafter, his arm looped around her shoulders as though he was lending her assistance to walk.

Cara frowned, surging to her feet in concern. "Hey, are you okay?" she asked a pasty-faced Angela worriedly. "You don't look so good. I mean, you look like you don't feel well. You always look good, I didn't mean to imply.."

Nick held up a hand. "We get it," he assured Cara impatiently. "And to answer your question - no, this one is most certainly not well. She's been out of it for a few days, actually - tired, nauseated, dizzy. But do you think she'd actually listen to me for once and stay home? Nope. Stubborn as hell, as usual."

Angela glared irritably at her handsome, but domineering lover. "As I recall, I used to listen to everything you said. And do as you said, too. *Those* days are long over, Mr. Manning. And I've told you three times already that I'm fine now. It's just a bug I caught but I'm working through it."

Cara looked her boss over thoughtfully. "Hey, I'm not taking sides in your little spat here, but I do have to agree with Nick - you don't look at all well. Why don't you let me call an Uber for you so you can go home and rest? There isn't that much on the agenda for today, and I'm sure the rest of us can handle it."

"No." Angela shook her head stubbornly. "If there's one thing I hate, it's taking a nap or being idle during the day. I'll be fine, honestly. It's better if I keep busy."

Nick shook his head and shrugged. "Fine. Have it your way. But if this so-called bug of yours hasn't improved in a few days, I'm dragging your ass to the doctor for a check-up. Cara, do me a favor and keep an eye on her, hmm? Don't let her overdo it. And let me know if she looks ready to pass out again like she did earlier this morning, would you?"

"Absolutely," agreed Cara readily. "How about if I get you some coffee now, Angela?"

Angela shuddered. "For once, coffee sounds terrible. Must be a side effect of this bug. Do you mind getting me some tea instead?"

"Of course not. I'll head over to the lunchroom right now. Nick, can I get you a coffee?"

Nick smiled and gave her shoulder a little squeeze. "That would be great, kiddo. Thanks, Cara. You know, you're going to make someone a great wife and mother one of these days the way you always look out for everyone."

Cara gave him an impish grin in response. "Not if I become a super successful investment banker. Maybe I'd wind up married to my career instead."

Nick made a sound of disapproval. "Nah, you don't want to do that, kiddo. You'd run the risk of turning into Angela's old boss Barbara Lowenstein. Sorry to speak ill of the dead, but that woman - and I use the term loosely - was the biggest ballbreaker to ever walk this earth. You're way too much of a sweetheart to ever become like her."

Cara's cheeks flushed with pleasure at Nick's rare compliment, and she hurried off to get the promised cups of tea and coffee. As she did so, a sudden thought popped into her head, one she impulsively shared with Angela as she placed the mug of tea in front of her.

"You, uh, aren't pregnant, are you?" she asked her abnormally pale boss tentatively.

Angela shook her head firmly. "Impossible. My birth control method is nearly foolproof. I've used an implant for years, never failed me yet. And it's not due to be replaced for several more months. No, I've just got a good, old-fashioned bug. Pretty sure I caught it from my nephew when we were down visiting my family in Carmel last weekend. Giovanni was pretty sick as I recall."

Cara arched a brow in surprise. "Your nephew's name is really Giovanni? Is his father a native born Italian or something?"

Angela grinned. "No, just a pompous ass. He and my sister make a good pair. Nick says they both need a good slap on the inside of the head for sticking the poor kid with that name. But, hey, enough about my annoying family. I wanted to give you a heads up, Cara. Nick mentioned that Dante is coming into the office today for their monthly meeting and lunch. I'm just going to assume that you haven't spoken to him since that time he called last month?"

Cara's heart had started beating a little faster at the mention of Dante's name. "You'd be correct in that assumption. I have this sneaking suspicion that he's figured out what time my lunch hour is and always calls Nick then. There've been at least two or three times when I got back from lunch and overheard Deepak or Leah talking to him on the phone."

"Hmm. You're probably right. What a spineless jerk," scoffed Angela.

Cara shrugged. "It's really all for the best, if you want my opinion. I know it's been two months already, but I'm still not sure I'm ready to see him face to face. Stupid of me, I know."

"Not at all," assured Angela. "Hey, when Nick broke up with me I was so devastated that I actually quit my job so I wouldn't run the risk of seeing him every day. Gave up everything I'd built up and started from scratch, too. My old mentor Barbara really laid into me when she learned about that, told me to never do something so stupid again, and to remember that men always looked out for their own interests first."

"I guess so. I know my father was always that way with my mom," admitted Cara. "But I can't really say the same for Dante. I mean, he always treated me with respect when we were together, was always kind and considerate. But I'm still not sure I'm strong enough to see him just yet."

"I sort of figured that. Which is why I've got several errands for you to run today," announced Angela with a knowing little smile. "And they should conveniently keep you out of the office for the duration of Dante and Nick's meeting."

Cara walked around the side of Angela's desk to give her an impulsive little hug. "Thank you," she whispered. "I know this is just postponing the inevitable, that I can't keep doing this forever. But I don't think I'm quite ready yet to face him. Maybe next time I'll be strong enough."

Angela squeezed her hand reassuringly. "Hey, you're doing amazing, Cara. A thousand times better than I was after Nick broke things off. Then again, I was either drunk or hungover for the better part of a year so that's not saying much. And I already know you're way tougher than I was back then. So here's the list of things I have for you to do before and after your lunch hour. If my estimates are right, you should arrive back in the office about half an hour after their meeting wraps up."

Cara scanned the list of errands, which included dropping some documents off to one client, picking up papers from a different client, buying some office supplies, and a couple of personal tasks for Angela. Normally Angela wouldn't ask her to do those types of things, but Cara knew they were simply reasons to extend out the time she spent away from the office and didn't mind doing them in the least.

"Actually, why don't you text me when you've finished with those things, and I can let you know then if the coast is clear?" suggested Angela.

"Okay. And thanks again for understanding. I really appreciate it."

Angela nodded. "It's no problem." Her eyes narrowed speculatively as she studied Cara more closely. "Hey, you've lost some serious weight, haven't you? That skirt is practically falling off you."

Cara's cheeks pinkened in mingled embarrassment and pleasure. "Not quite," she demurred. "And I've still got a ways to go until I reach my goal. And, um, I've actually started jogging a little, only on the weekends though, since it's way too dark before I have to leave for work."

"You look great already," assured Angela. "And don't try to overdo it with the jogging. Build up your mileage a little at a time. Otherwise, you'll have shin splints or tight hamstrings or a whole host of other problems. But bravo for you, Cara. They say looking good is the best revenge."

Cara chuckled. "That's exactly what Mirai told me. After she finally dragged me out of bed and sort of shamed me into taking some pride in myself again."

"She's a smart girl, your friend." Angela took a tentative sip of the tea Cara had placed in front of her.

"You're sure that's all I can get you?" fussed Cara. "Have you had anything to eat this morning?"

Angela visibly shuddered. "God, no! Even the thought of a saltine cracker makes me want to retch. Maybe I will have an early day of it after all, go home after the market closes."

Cara eyed her boss skeptically, placing a hand across Angela's forehead. "You're positive you aren't pregnant? Because you don't feel the least bit feverish to me, and you don't seem to be having chills. So if it's just the nausea and fatigue, well - you can connect the dots as well as I can."

Angela shook her head fiercely, taking another sip of tea. "It's definitely just a tummy bug. Absolutely. There is zero, repeat zero, possibility that I could be pregnant."

21

"There's got to be a mistake. A big one. No, make that a huge one. What you're telling us is simply not possible."

Marilyn Kimball gave her patient a sympathetic look. "I'm afraid that it is, Angela. And I know exactly what you're going to say next – that you're using what's widely considered the most reliable, foolproof method of birth control on the market today. And that according to our mutual records, the implant isn't due to be replaced for another six months, which is very much within the normal time frame. But despite all of that, there is no denying the fact that you are definitely pregnant. I would estimate around six weeks at this point, but we'll need to do further tests and procedures to determine the exact stage."

"Before we even start discussing any of that," growled Nick, who was visibly struggling to remain calm, "why don't you tell us how the hell this could have happened?"

Doctor Kimball arched a brow at him, clearly annoyed by the arrogant attitude he'd been displaying since the beginning of this appointment. "The usual way, I would imagine, Mr. Manning," she replied sarcastically. "I assume your parents taught you about the birds and the bees quite a few years ago. Oh, my mistake. I expect you mean how could Angela fall pregnant while her implant was still supposed to be effective."

"Nick," admonished Angela, giving him a jab in the ribs when his eyes darkened angrily at her OB/GYN's coy response. "Behave, okay? Dr. Kimball, I have to admit I'm wondering the exact same thing."

Doctor Kimball nodded. "So am I, to be honest. And I would have to do some research, call the manufacturer to see if there have been other reports of the implants expiring early. It's certainly not unheard of, though. And before you leave today, we should plan on removing that implant. We wouldn't want it to have any adverse effects on the embryo."

"Embryo?" repeated Angela, sounding shell-shocked even to her own ears. "Oh. You mean the baby. Sorry, I'm really out of it at the moment."

"That makes two of us," muttered Nick beneath his breath. "To say the least."

Doctor Kimball ignored the glowering, noticeably tense Nick and focused her attention on her patient instead. "I realize that this is a shock to both of you, and that you're going to need some time to process the news. But sooner than later, we'll need to discuss your prenatal care, Angela. As well as schedule an ultrasound so we can determine exactly how far along you are."

Angela blinked, staring at her doctor numbly. "Um, that - that might not be, well, necessary. I mean, obviously Nick and I need to discuss this, given that it's so unexpected, but I'm not sure what we, well, plan to do about this."

"Of course." Doctor Kimball gave a brief, noncommittal nod. "Well, the two of you are certainly old enough to know what your options are in this situation. And whatever decision you make, it shouldn't be made lightly."

Angela's stomach was churning in agitation now, partly from the almost constant nausea she'd been experiencing lately, but mostly from nerves. "How - how long before we have to make a decision?" she asked in a small voice. "Before it's no longer safe to - well, you know."

Silently, Nick slid his hand over her tightly clenched ones, giving them a reassuring squeeze.

"You can safely terminate the pregnancy up through the sixteenth week, and beyond that under certain conditions," advised Doctor Kimball. "Though of course the earlier the better in terms of medical risks. So you have some time yet. And once again, the two of you should discuss this thoroughly, don't feel that you have to rush into a decision overnight. Think about it for several days, then call my office with your decision and we'll go from there. Now, unless you have any other questions, why don't we go ahead and remove that implant? I'll just call a nurse in to assist me. Nick, you're welcome to remain in the exam room during the procedure if you'd like."

Nick shook his head, surging to his intimidating height of six foot six. "I'll pass, thanks. Believe it or not, that sort of thing makes me a little squeamish. I'll be outside in the waiting room."

He bent to press a kiss to Angela's forehead before exiting the exam room, followed by the doctor as she went to summon one of the nurses. Angela was left alone in the stark white, sterile room filled with posters that depicted how to do a breast self-exam, illustrated common gynecological disorders, another about understanding menopause, and the last one that was a chart on prenatal development. She shuddered as her gaze fell on that one, and quickly looked away.

To say that she was in a state of shocked disbelief at this moment would be a gross understatement of fact. All of this had unfolded so rapidly over the course of the last twenty four hours that her head was spinning, and she felt overwhelmed by it all, despite the fact that Nick had been unwavering in his support thus far.

She hadn't felt well for close to two weeks now, being plagued with nausea, dizziness, and an overall feeling of lethargy. She'd convinced herself that all she was suffering from was the same tummy bug her nephew had picked up, even though he'd evidently felt much better within a day or two while hers continued to linger. Next, Angela had tried unsuccessfully to assure Nick that she was simply rundown and overtired, probably from overtraining for the mountainous marathon she'd competed in last month.

But when she'd spent the better part of yesterday morning heaving into the toilet, shuddered at the very thought of food, and fainted dead away, he'd promptly bundled her into the car and whisked her off to her internist's office where he had bullied his way into an appointment. The doctor had given her a brief exam, asked a few general questions, and then handed her a specimen cup so that she could provide a urine sample.

And when the sample had revealed that she was indeed pregnant, the doctor had drawn blood so that a more accurate lab test could be done, and also advised her to get in touch with her OB/GYN. Nick had hovered over her while she'd dialed that number, not making even the slightest attempt to give her privacy, or disguise the fact that he was blatantly eavesdropping.

Doctor Kimball had been able to squeeze her in this afternoon, by which time the positive results from the blood test had come back. A brief pelvic exam had further confirmed the accuracy of the diagnosis. Why Angela's previously foolproof method of birth control had suddenly failed still remained to be seen - just like the final outcome to this fiasco was anything but certain.

Nick had remained silent and brooding throughout, but then he often exhibited such behavior so she wasn't too surprised at his reaction thus far. And he'd been remarkably supportive in his own bossy way, giving her hand a reassuring squeeze or offering to bring her tea and saltine crackers or simply holding her close. But he had yet to offer up an opinion - something that was almost unheard of for him - and Angela truthfully had no idea of what was going on in that handsome but stubborn head of his right now. When she'd tentatively broached the subject after leaving the internist's yesterday, he had forestalled her and merely said they should wait until after today's appointment before jumping to any conclusions.

Now that her pregnancy had been confirmed by both blood, urine, and physical tests, however, the moment of reckoning had definitely arrived. Like it or not, she and Nick were going to have to talk about this whole mess rationally - something that wasn't always easy for the two of them - and come to the right decision.

She had never experienced an overwhelming desire to be a mother, probably because her own mother had done such a lackluster job in being a good role model. She'd liked spending time with her various nieces and nephews, and had even babysat them from time to time. And when her closest friends - Lauren and Julia, the McKinnon twins, whom she'd grown up with - had both given birth to twins earlier this year, Angela had felt the stirring of some very subtle maternal urgings. She was godmother to one of Lauren's little girls – Daisy - and made it a point to visit her and her twin Summer whenever she was down in the Carmel area. They were admittedly gorgeous babies, unsurprising since both Lauren and her hunky husband Ben were so attractive. The twins were also sweet-tempered, placid, and rarely if ever fussed - traits that Angela surmised they'd received from their laidback father rather than their confrontational mother.

But motherhood had changed Lauren, too, had smoothed out a lot of her rough edges, and brought out a softer, more mellow side of her that Angela would have never imagined existed. It made her wonder now if by some miracle she, too, had some hidden maternal instincts that she would have previously denied existed.

The nurse bustled cheerily into the exam room then, running a disinfectant swab over Angela's upper arm before injecting her with a numbing agent. It was on the tip of Angela's tongue to tell the nurse not to bother with the shot, since her entire body was basically numb right now. She barely felt the prick of the needle, just like she didn't even flinch when the doctor arrived a few minutes later to extract the tiny implant that had failed Angela so miserably.

"We'll save this in case the manufacturer wants to analyze it," explained Doctor Kimball as she dropped the device inside a specimen bag. "Your arm will probably feel a little sore for a day or so, but nothing major."

Angela nodded, too dazed by everything that had happened to think of a reply.

The doctor placed a light hand on Angela's shoulder, and when she spoke her voice was kind. "It's going to be okay," she assured. "Whatever you decide, you'll be fine either way. I've had any number of patients who've had to deal with an unexpected pregnancy on their own, with no partner and no financial means of supporting a baby. Now, I don't presume to know anything about the size of your bank account, but I'd guess raising a child wouldn't be a problem for you in that respect. As for the other, well, your partner isn't a warm and fuzzy one, is he? But he does seem to care about you a great deal, Angela, and I'm confident Nick will do the right thing by you. Give me a call when the two of you have made a decision and we'll figure out the next steps. Until then, get as much rest as possible, and read over that booklet I gave you, at least the part about dealing with the nausea."

Doctor Kimball exited the room then, leaving Angela to slowly pull on her clothes, and to ponder on one thing in particular that the doctor had just said - about Nick doing the right thing by her. Angela didn't doubt that fact, didn't believe for a minute that Nick would wash his hands of this whole mess and leave her to make all the decisions. This *was* Nick, after all, aka Mr. Control Freak, so there was no doubt whatsoever that he would definitely have some very strong opinions about the situation. And she could more or less guess what his solution was going to be.

If she had never envisioned herself as the motherly type, then there was no way in hell she could ever see Nick in the role of attentive father. He was gruff and temperamental, stubborn and arrogant, and had been used to doing things his way for most of his life. Living with him continued to be a learning experience - for both of them, if she was being totally fair - and try as she might, Angela simply couldn't envision how either of them would handle raising a baby. They had both come a long ways in their relationship, and in learning to trust not only each other but family members and friends as well, but the issues the two of them still had to deal with weren't the sort that just went away overnight. How in the world could they bring a child into such an unstable environment, at least without screwing the kid up big time?

Nick was silent as he drove out of the medical building's parking lot, and Angela was too tired to strike up a conversation right now. She didn't want to talk about the baby, about the decision they needed to make concerning this unexpected hand fate had dealt them. All she wanted right now was to change into her rattiest sweats, curl up in their oversized bed, and sleep for about eighteen hours.

But then it dawned on her that Nick wasn't headed to the home they shared high up in the hills of Sausalito. In fact, he was driving in the exact opposite direction of the Golden Gate Bridge that they would need to cross in order to reach their house.

"Where are we going?" she asked crossly. "It's too early for dinner, and I doubt I could eat a thing anyway."

He shot her a sideways glare. "You're going to have to start eating, Angel. It's morning sickness, after all, not afternoon and evening sickness. The doctor said she could prescribe something for the nausea, so take her up on it. And we're not going to a restaurant, at least not yet. Ah, here we are. And thank fuck there's actually a parking space for once."

Before she had a chance to protest, Nick was parking the Jaguar, inserting his credit card in the meter, and then tugging her out of the car.

Angela's heart started beating double time as she recognized the store he was propelling her into. "Nick, why in the world are we here of all places? The last thing I need right now is.."

"Is to argue with me," he finished commandingly. "Come on, Angel. We're expected."

The store he practically dragged her into was a very high end, very exclusive jewelers, and Nick had become one of their best customers since meeting Angela. Despite her protests that she really wasn't a jewelry person, he continued to surprise her on a regular basis with a new bracelet or pendant or a pair of earrings. He had brought her with him a few times, mostly to help him choose a gift for one of their mothers for some occasion, but also so that she could actually select something for herself for once without Nick arrogantly doing it for her.

They bypassed the usual display cases of necklaces and shockingly expensive watches, however, as Nick all but dragged her towards the back of the store to where a smiling salesman was waiting for them.

"You got what I wanted, Milo?" asked Nick gruffly.

The slender, meticulously groomed older man gave a brief nod. "Of course, Mr. Manning. I've had it set aside since you looked at it yesterday. Here you are, sir."

Angela watched the scene unfolding in front of her as though she was in some sort of bizarre dream sequence. Milo the jeweler placed a small, square box of dark gray velvet in Nick's outstretched palm before discreetly disappearing into a back room. Nick opened the box and withdrew whatever was inside before he turned and picked up her left hand.

"Don't say a word until I'm finished, okay?" he warned her. "And I'm going to tell you right now, Angel - I won't take no for an answer. I swear to Christ I would never in a billion years have envisioned myself doing something like this, but then I would never have been able to see myself as a prospective father, either. You and I both had fucked up childhoods, and I've rarely seen two people who have as many different issues as you and I do. God help this poor kid of ours, and let's hope we don't mess this whole parenting thing up big time. I know neither of us planned for this to happen – ever - but the fact of the matter is that's my baby growing inside of you, Angel. And there's no way in hell you're going to quote unquote terminate it. What you *are* going to do is marry me, and then somehow, someway help me figure out how to actually raise this kid. Got it? Oh, and I picked this one out yesterday after we first got the news. It's perfect for you, but I guess if you really don't like it we can look at some others."

She felt as though she was floating out in some other dimension as she watched Nick slide a ring onto the third finger of her left hand, and had just enough presence of mind remaining to feel grateful that the ring was both discreet and gorgeous – a platinum band encrusted with diamonds that framed the exquisite, square cut solitaire. It was, in fact, the perfect size and shape for her long, slender fingers, and to ask to look at anything else would have only been out of spite on her part.

"Nick." Her voice was hoarse, and she squeezed his hand for support. "You - God, Nick. You don't have to do this. Marry me, that is. I know how you feel about marriage, how you've always sworn it wasn't for you. And just because I'm pregnant doesn't mean you have to feel obligated to go that far."

He snorted. "Who says I feel obligated? Angel, you know me well enough by now to realize that no one makes me do something I don't want to do - even you, the only woman I've ever been in love with. I've made a lot of mistakes in my life, especially with you, and it's time for me to do the right thing for once. And forget all that bullshit about making an honest woman out of you or doing this out of obligation. This is just the right thing to do. Period. For you, for me, for our kid. For the family we're going to be. Okay?"

Tears were trickling down her cheeks, and she could only nod in agreement. "Okay."

Nick chuckled and enfolded her in his arms. "For maybe the first time since we got back together, you aren't being a pain in the ass about doing what I say. If this is what it takes to render you speechless, I should have asked you to marry me months ago."

She shook her head, wrapping her arms around his waist and burying her face against his shoulder. "Uh, uh. It wouldn't have been the right time. And I probably would have said no."

He kissed her on the cheek. "Yeah, most likely. But like it or not, Angel, you're going to have to do a lot of things I tell you from now on. Like eating more. And getting a lot of rest. And you'd better put those goddamn running shoes of yours away for a few months, because if you think I'm letting you compete in some insane trail race while you're pregnant, then guess again."

Angela laughed. "No trail races, I promise. But lots of pregnant women still do some running. We'll ask Doctor Kimball, okay? And I promise to follow whatever advice she gives."

"We'll see," grumbled Nick. "That OB/GYN of yours is kind of a smart-ass. I'm not sure I like her attitude."

She rolled her eyes. "Funny. I was just going to say she probably has the same opinion about you."

"Whatever. Look, let me round up Milo and pay for this ring, and then we'll go out to dinner to celebrate. And," he warned, waggling a finger, "you *will* eat. A lot. But alcohol is out until after the baby is born. Unless you decide to breastfeed, that is, because I understand that booze isn't good for the kid, which means you'll need to stay on the wagon that much longer."

"Fine." Angela sighed, then grinned at him mischievously. "Hey, at least with me being pregnant I'm sure to gain those last fifteen pounds you keep insisting I need to put on."

Nick arched a brow. "Fifteen? That's just for starters, Angel. You've got to put on a minimum of thirty. Oh, and one other thing."

She shook her head. "Why do I have the feeling this is going to be a very long pregnancy with you calling all the shots? What's the other thing?"

He scowled darkly. "I will tell you right here and now, Angel, that there is no fucking way we are calling this kid some sissy name like Giovanni. Or Donatella."

Angela caressed his cheek tenderly. "Agreed," she replied, laughing softly. "But we've got lots of time to think about baby names."

"You're right. Especially since we need to figure out how to break the news to your parents first. It ought to make for a hell of a Thanksgiving."

PREDICTABLY, even though Angela had requested that only her mother and father be present when she and Nick arrived, both of her sisters and brothers-in-law and at least a couple of their kids were assembled in the living room of her parents' house in Carmel when they walked inside. Nick merely shrugged as Angela fumed, murmuring under his breath that they might as well get this out of the way all at once.

All Angela had told her parents last evening was that she and Nick had some news to share with them upon their arrival the next afternoon. It was Wednesday, the day before Thanksgiving, a holiday that she somewhat reluctantly had agreed to spend with her family. The older of her two sisters - Marisa - was cooking dinner at her home again this year, though everyone knew that their mother Rita would really be the one in charge of the meal - just like she had always attempted to control everything that went on in the family.

'Thank God,' thought Angela as she and Nick joined the others in the living room, 'that we always insist on getting a hotel room whenever we come down here for a visit. And especially this time, when the sparks are sure to fly.'

She could almost predict how her mother was going to react to the dual shocks that were about to be delivered - a wedding in January, and a new grandchild next June - two life experiences no one in her family had ever expected Angela to actually have. Thankfully, she and Nick had briefly discussed the matter last night while packing for this short trip, and were in total agreement on how they wanted things to unfold.

And Nick, bless him, had volunteered to be the one to actually make the announcements, though they had hoped Angela's parents would get to hear the news before anyone else. It figured, though, thought Angela derisively, that Rita would ignore her wishes so blatantly.

'Story of my life,' she told herself as she took a seat. 'Literally and figuratively.'

Both of her brothers-in-law always gushed over Nick, in awe of his celebrity-like status as a retired NFL player, and wasted no time in asking his opinion about who was going to win the next Super Bowl.

Nick shrugged. "I haven't watched many games this season, to be honest. But from what I have seen Arizona is looking pretty good, and of course you can never count out New England. I wouldn't place a bet on any team right now, though."

Angela still didn't know how or where he found the patience to deal with all of her fawning male relatives during holidays and other family events they attended occasionally. She knew he did it for her, to try and smooth things over with the family she'd always had a contentious relationship with. She was alternately dreading and gleefully anticipating exactly how he planned to deliver the twin bombshells to everyone.

"Hey, enough about football, okay?" chided Nick. "Angela and I have something to tell all of you. Something important. Though I would have preferred to speak privately with Gino and Rita about it first."

Marisa glanced at her younger sister Deanna guiltily before telling Nick in a simpering voice, "I had no idea the two of you were going to be here tonight, Nick. We just stopped by to pick up the pies my mother baked for Thanksgiving dinner tomorrow."

"And Marco and I were just picking up the kids," Deanna chimed in. "My parents were watching them for a couple of hours while we ran some errands."

Nick looked neither convinced nor pacified by their hurried explanations. "Well, guess it's a moot point now, huh? So this is our news. Angela is having a baby, due around the first of June, we're not exactly sure yet. And we're getting married right after the holidays. January fourteenth, to be exact. And we've already started on the arrangements. The ceremony will be at three o'clock at the Swedenborgian Church in San Francisco, and the reception at the Gregson Hotel on Nob Hill. Small wedding, fewer than a hundred people, and Angela and I want to keep it simple. Actually, she wanted to elope but I talked her out of that idea, reminded her that Gino would have been devastated if he couldn't walk her down the aisle. That's all."

Angela had never been so tempted to burst into hysterical laughter as she was at this particular moment. She wasn't sure whose facial expression among those gathered in the living room was more comical - Nick, who looked like he needed a good stiff drink after all that; her father, who was grinning like a madman; her sisters, who had both turned white as a ghost; or her mother, whose mouth was hanging open in shock.

Her father Gino recovered first, hurrying over to envelop her in a fierce hug, his lips brushing her cheek. His voice was trembling just a little as he murmured in her ear, "I'm so happy for you, my little Angie. You've got a good man there, and he'll make sure you and your baby are taken care of."

Gino turned to Nick next, clapping him on the back before shaking his hand enthusiastically. "I would tell you to look after my little girl, to make her happy, but you've been doing a pretty good job of that for over a year now. I'm prouder than I can say to call you my son-in-law, Nick, and happy to officially welcome you to the family. And you're right - I would have been pretty ticked off if the two of you had eloped, so thank you for talking my Angie out of that crazy idea. Giving her away is something I've looked forward to for a long time."

Rita's reaction, however, was nowhere near as positive. She scowled darkly, first at Angela, then at Nick. "She's pregnant and you're still going to have a big wedding? And get married in a church? Don't you two have any sense at all? Next thing you know Angela will tell us that she's actually going to wear a white dress to be married in. *Vergognoso!*"

Gino waggled a finger in his wife's face. "Enough, Rita. Nothing about this is shameful. It's a happy day for our family, for our daughter, and I'm not going to let you spoil this for her."

"Gino's right," retorted Nick. "Angela can wear whatever damn color dress she wants to be married in. I don't give a rat's ass if it's white or pink or black for that matter. And I already told you we want to keep this small and simple, less than a hundred people. That's not exactly a big wedding by my calculations."

Rita sniffed, but backed down quickly when she realized she was outnumbered. "Between our family and close friends, that's well over a hundred people already," she declared, changing tactics. "And that's before we add in neighbors, Nick's family, and your friends. That's at least two hundred people, more like two fifty. There's no way you can plan a wedding that big in less than two months."

Nick shook his head. "That date is set, and you'll just need to accept it. And the guest list is going to be restricted to immediate family and a few friends and business associates. Angela and I don't want a big lavish wedding."

Rita was about to argue the matter further, until she saw the steely look in Nick's eyes. "Well, all for the better, I suppose," she sniped. "The fewer people the better, in fact. That way none of our friends have to see Angela waddle down the aisle with a big belly, and realize she had to get married."

Nick slammed his fist down on a side table, causing precious figurines and other collectibles to rattle precariously. "That's enough, Rita," he hissed. "You need to realize that this isn't about you, or your petty judgmental friends, or your gossipy family. This is strictly about Angela and me and our baby. As far as her *waddling* down the aisle, she'll only be about four months along by then and barely showing, especially since she's so tall and slim. And don't you dare *ever* imply that we had to get married. We might not have planned this pregnancy, but both of us are happy about it and want to do the right thing for our child. Just like you should want to do the right thing for your own daughter."

Rita was visibly shaken by Nick's outburst, and looked like she was going to start crying. Impulsively, Angela turned to her mother - the woman she'd been at odds with for so much of her life - and held open her arms.

"I know it's not ideal circumstances, Mom," she told her quietly, "but can't you be happy for me anyway? Please?"

Rita stared at her youngest child for long seconds before embracing her fiercely, even giving her a kiss on the cheek and tucking an errant lock of raven hair behind her ear. "Of course I can," she whispered. "And I am happy, Angela. It - well, this is all such a shock."

Angela nodded, smiling at her mother uncertainly. "For us, too. Nick is right. We definitely didn't plan this, but we're gradually getting used to the idea. And I hope you can come up to San Francisco one day next week to help me look for a wedding gown. I'm going to have to buy something off the rack since there's no time to get a custom dress made, but Julia's given me some ideas on that. You know what a fashionista she's always been."

Rita nodded. "Of course I'll go with you. I'd be honored."

"What about us?" whined Marisa. "Aren't we being invited along?"

"And of course we're going to be your bridesmaids," piped up Deanna. "You have to have your sisters in the wedding party."

Angela regarded her two much older sisters in disbelief. "You two aren't serious, are you? As I recall, Marisa, you refused to let me go along with you and Mom and your eight bridesmaids to try on wedding gowns because there wouldn't be enough room. And neither of you would agree to have me in your weddings because I was too old to be the flower girl and too young to be a bridesmaid."

Marisa's cheeks reddened. "Well, there wasn't enough room at the bridal salon," she replied defensively. "And you were just a little kid, what did you care about any of that stuff? As for the other, I let you hand out the favors at my wedding, while Deanna put you in charge of the guest book at hers."

Angela gave her sisters a not-so-nice smile. "Hey, that's a great idea! You can both have the same jobs at my wedding. As for bridesmaids, I'm having a grand total of one, and that's going to be Lauren. End of discussion."

Nick draped his arm around her shoulders. "We'll discuss some more details at Thanksgiving tomorrow. Right now, we need to go check into our hotel, and Angela needs to take a nap. She's had a rough go of it so far with the pregnancy, so it's important that she gets plenty of rest. And," he added in warning tone, "it's even more important that she isn't stressed out. So I'm telling all of you now to lay off of her, okay? We're doing this wedding our way. Don't make me regret talking her out of eloping."

He hustled her out of her parents' house less than five minutes later, bundling her into the car and taking off before her mother or one of her sisters could start discussing bridal showers or bachelorette parties or gift registries. Angela was drooping with exhaustion by then, worn out by the early stages of her pregnancy, but mostly from the stress of being around her difficult family. But that didn't stop her from reaching over to give Nick's hand a grateful squeeze.

"Thank you," she told him wearily. "I swear I don't know how I'd deal with that bunch if you weren't around."

He brought her hand to his lips briefly. "It actually went better than I thought it would," he admitted. "I knew your dad would be happy, but I figured your mother and sisters would put up more of a fuss."

Angela grinned. "That's because you scared them all shitless with that glare. Is that the same way you'd intimidate quarterbacks when you played football?"

Nick snorted. "Hell, no. I would just hit them as hard as I could. But I figured you wouldn't appreciate it very much if I tried something like that on one of your sisters."

She laughed. "If you had asked me that question when I was a teenager and hated the world, I might have told you to take them both out. Fortunately for them I'm older and wiser now. Besides, Marisa and Deanna would be way too easy of a target for you."

Nick rolled his eyes. "As out of shape as your sisters are, I think a toddler could take them out. Thank Christ you told them no go on the bridesmaid thing. They would have looked like Cinderella's ugly ass stepsisters walking down the aisle ahead of you."

Angela looked pensive all of sudden. "You don't think I'm going to look ridiculous wearing a wedding dress, do you? I mean, being pregnant and all."

He squeezed her hand. "No," he replied bluntly. "You're going to look gorgeous. Drop dead gorgeous. Like I told your mother, you'll be barely four months along by then, and not even showing yet. And I wouldn't give a shit if you did, Angel. Don't let your mother of all people make you feel ashamed, okay?"

"Okay." She heaved a tired sigh. "Jesus, what sort of a mother can I expect to be with her as an example? As ditzy as your mom is, I think she'd be a better role model."

Nick shuddered. "You'd be wrong. Let's face it - neither one of us exactly had an ideal childhood. That's why the two of us are going to do everything in our power to make sure our kid has just the opposite. And while I know we both have a helluva lot to learn about being parents, we've got at least one thing on our side."

Angela's eyes twinkled mischievously. "Enough money to hire a good nanny?"

He shook his head. "Not that. Though we might need to consider hiring one when you go back to work."

"Then what?" she asked curiously.

He pressed a kiss to her palm. "Love, Angel. Pure and simple. And a lot of it. We might end up sucking at changing diapers or knowing the best stroller to buy or shit like that. But the way you and I love each other, and the way we're going to love this kid – well, no one else could do it better."

22

One Week Before Christmas

"I GOT a few more RSVPs in today, Angela. We're only waiting to hear from about ten additional guests at this point. So far, though, we haven't received a single No response."

Angela sighed. "I was half-afraid you'd say that. And here Nick and I were so intent on keeping the attendance to a hundred people or less. What are we up to now?"

Cara checked the spreadsheet she'd been using to track responses for next month's wedding. "A hundred and twelve," she replied cheerfully. "So if all of the outstanding responses come back with a Yes, that would put the total attendance at a hundred twenty two. Not counting you and Nick, of course."

"I guess that's reasonable," acknowledged Angela. "When do we need to get the final count in at the hotel?"

"Right before New Year's. I already have it on my calendar. But hopefully we get the rest of the responses in before then so I can call them ahead of time. The wedding coordinator over at the Gregson has been so helpful that I'd like to get her the headcount as early as possible."

Angela smiled. "Speaking of being helpful, I honestly don't know how Nick and I would be able to pull this whole thing off without you, Cara. I know you've been working like a fiend to keep up with everything. Normally, I would have been able to ask Julia to help out since she loves this sort of thing, but having eight-month-old twins is keeping her pretty busy these days."

Cara waved a hand in dismissal. "It's not a problem, Angela, really. I'm more than happy to do what I can. And Mirai's been doing a lot of the work as well, since she doesn't return to school until after New Year's."

"Still, I know you're on break from school as well right now, and you should be kicking back and relaxing a little, not helping to plan my wedding. If only my mother and sisters weren't such pains in the ass, I'd have asked them to help. But knowing them, they would have insisted on doing everything their way, which is the total opposite of what Nick and I want."

"Simple but elegant," assured Cara. "That's how it's going to be. No frilly bows, no over the top floral arrangements, and not even a speck of pink anywhere to be found."

Angela grinned. "What would I do without you? I hope I never have to find out. Especially when I go on maternity leave next spring. It's a little early to be discussing all of this, and Nick and I have a ton of details to go over yet, but we're both hoping that you'll be willing to stay on with the team after you get your degree, maybe take over some of my accounts."

Cara stared at her boss in disbelief. "You're - you're not going to quit, are you? And, gosh, I'd love to talk to you and Nick about this, but why me? I mean, I'd have just assumed that Leah and Tyler would step in."

"No." Angela shook her head firmly. "Those two are going to kill each other one of these days, I swear. Either that, or Nick will do the job for them. They bicker constantly, and are so damned competitive with each other that it gives Nick a headache. He thinks it would be a lot better for the team, not to mention their marriage, if one of them went their own way professionally, or at least partnered up with a different broker. But that's confidential, as I'm sure you can imagine, and still to be discussed. Meanwhile, I have no intention of quitting my job after I've worked so hard at building up my accounts. But I am going to take an extended maternity leave, and might only work part-time for a year or so after that. Everything is still up in the air. Just think about what I said, hmm?"

"I will," assured Cara.

Angela returned to her own office after that, leaving Cara to attend to the dozen or so urgent matters awaiting her attention. It might have been the week before Christmas, when things were winding down a bit and clients heading off on holiday, but you wouldn't be able to tell based on how busy things still were here. Thank God she'd finished up the fall semester at school a week earlier, and now had nearly a month's break until school resumed in January. She was still on track to complete her degree by the end of next summer, and would be ecstatic when she no longer had to go to classes four nights a week or cram for exams on the weekends. And she'd be particularly thrilled when she no longer had to scrape together enough money to pay for tuition and books.

The weeks since Thanksgiving had been hectic ones for Cara - studying for semester finals, choosing her classes for the spring semester, working longer hours than ever. But she'd been so thrilled when Angela and Nick had announced that not only were they expecting a baby but getting married as well, that she hadn't dreamed of saying no when they had asked for her help in planning the wedding. And the extra work had helped to keep her mind off of things, particularly the stark realization that Christmas was exactly one week away, and that for the first time in her life she'd be spending the holiday alone.

Mirai had made an attempt to convince her to fly to New York and have the holidays with her family, but Cara had firmly refused. She had the money for the airfare, since she wasn't going to Florida or buying gifts for her father, but she was more determined than ever to use that money on herself. She was less than three pounds away from meeting her weight loss goal, and was already calculating how much it was going to cost to get her hair cut and straightened and to buy several new outfits, including the one she would wear to the wedding next month.

The wedding where she would be obliged to see Dante for the first time in over two months, since he had agreed to be Nick's best man. And Cara was hell-bent on looking her absolute best that day, to flaunt her new, trim figure, sleek new haircut, and some as yet-to-be-determined dress and shoes that would be both sexy and elegant.

Since she had offered to work during the two-week holiday period so that the rest of the team could take vacation, she had arranged instead to be out of the office several days before the wedding so that she could go shopping with Mirai and have her hair cut. Mirai was going to do her makeup and nails on the day of the wedding, and Cara knew from past results that her BFF would do an amazing job.

Cara was also thrilled that Mirai was going to return to school in January, to finish up the remaining units she needed to get her associate degree in fashion merchandising. Mirai had admitted with a sigh of resignation that it was finally time for her to grow up and get on with her life.

"I'm tired of watching everyone around me meeting their goals and actually doing something useful with their life," she'd admitted about a month ago. *"I mean, Rene's in medical school, you're going to finish your degree next year, and one of my half-brothers is a partner in one of the hottest new restaurants in Manhattan. Meanwhile, I sleep in until noon, workout, shop, eat, and watch way too much bad reality TV. I've gotta get a life, Cara. So I just signed up for the rest of the courses I need, and I'm counting on you to make sure I finish this thing."*

"I'll be the first one to give you a kick in the ass if you start slacking off," Cara had assured. *"Better yet, maybe we should make a little bet here. If you drop out of school, you have to take me to Las Vegas next year - a suite at Caesars Palace, champagne brunch, spa treatments, the works. So unless you want to max out your credit cards again, you'd better stick with it!"*

"I'll tell you what," Mirai had offered. *"When I finish up my degree next spring, you and I will go to Vegas anyway to celebrate. How's that?"*

"You've got a deal. And you can be sure that with a trip to Vegas on the line that I'm going to be pushing you like crazy to show up for classes every day," Cara had promised.

"That's what I'm counting on."

So it seemed that things were certainly looking up for several of the people closest to Cara. Her best friend was finally realizing that she needed to do something meaningful with her life, and it sounded like this time Mirai would actually follow through with her plans. Angela and Nick were getting married, something Cara would have bet would never have happened, and were also having a baby - another fact that she still couldn't quite believe. But, as her mother had been fond of telling her, time rarely if ever stood still, and change was something everyone had to accept as part of life. And while her own life had remained more or less stagnant for the past two years - save for the few magical months she had dated Dante - Cara knew that it would be her turn soon enough. Angela's somewhat casual mention a few minutes ago about helping out with accounts during her maternity leave was giving Cara serious cause for reflection now, and she was eager to have a much more detailed discussion with her bosses on the subject sooner than later.

The morning practically flew by, and before she knew it her clock read one-thirty in the afternoon. She'd completely forgotten to eat lunch, or her morning snack, and her tummy was rumbling in protest now. She rummaged through the desk drawer she had always kept snacks in and perused the contents. Before her diet had changed so drastically, that drawer - the one Angela had nicknamed the Sugar Rush Receptacle - Cara had kept unhealthy snacks like candy bars, packaged cookies, chips, and muffins. Now the contents included nuts, protein bars, apples, and kale chips.

She unwrapped a protein bar, figuring it could substitute for lunch today, and took a bite before washing it down with a sip of water. A major part of her job required constant multi-tasking, and Cara had become quite proficient at this in the two plus years she'd worked for

Angela. While she ate and drank, she fielded several phone calls from clients, entered data for a new customer account into her computer, prepared some documents to mail out, and printed out the various pie charts, graphs, and other statistical sheets Angela would need for the portfolio review she was conducting in a few minutes with a client.

Cara was so caught up in her work, in fact, that she didn't notice someone hovering in front of her desk until he spoke her name. And that achingly familiar voice made her freeze in place, as she realized in something of a panic that there was no possible way she could quickly hide beneath her desk.

"You can't keep avoiding me forever, you know," chided Dante teasingly. "Especially when I come bearing gifts."

She looked up at him then, and almost gulped as she met his dark, twinkling gaze. Cara realized with a sinking heart that the passage of time – more than three months by now – plus the vow she'd made to herself not to fall under any man's spell ever again didn't make a damned bit of difference at this moment. Dante still had the power to mesmerize her, to make her knees feel weak, and her heart to start beating double time. And it was with both joy and despair that she continued to stare at him, the former because she'd never stopped loving him for even a day, not even when missing him could cut like a knife. And the latter because she had naively believed herself stronger than all of that, had convinced herself that he didn't mean anything to her now, and that she had well and truly moved on with her life. All it took, apparently, was for him to say her name softly, and give her one of those panty-melting smiles, and every one of her good intentions went directly to hell.

"Um, hi," she mumbled as she nervously began to assemble the papers for Angela's client into a presentation folder. "And, um, I – I haven't been avoiding you."

"If you say so. It's just been sort of a coincidence that you haven't been in the office the last two or three times I've stopped by," commented Dante. "Almost as though you planned it that way."

Cara shook her head, unwilling to admit that she had, in fact, gone way, way out of her way to avoid running into him. "A coincidence is all it's been," she declared firmly. "I've been helping Angela with some of the wedding plans, so naturally that takes me out of the office more than usual."

"Okay." He shrugged carelessly. "Aside from that, how have you been, Cara? You look *different*, somehow. I can't quite put my finger on it, though."

She waved a hand dismissively. "Nothing's changed. Except that I've got my hair in a braid today. Haven't had time to get it cut lately, you know?"

"Hmm. No, that's not it. But I'll figure it out sooner than later. In the meanwhile, I wasn't joking earlier when I said I had gifts. Christmas presents, to be exact, for you and Deepak and the Bickersons."

"Who?" she asked in bewilderment.

Dante grinned mischievously. "The Bickersons was this old radio show about a couple who spent nearly all of their time arguing. Way before my time, of course, but my grandparents had records of some of the performances that I listened to from time to time. Leah and Tyler are like a modern day version of the Bickersons the way they go at each other all the time."

Cara gave a little shudder. "You've got that right. I'm surprised one of them hasn't stabbed the other in the back yet – literally as well as figuratively. And they're both at lunch right now, along with Deepak. I'm holding down the fort for a few more minutes until he gets back."

"Maybe I can just leave their gifts with you then?" he asked. "That is, if it isn't too much trouble. Just a small token from me to say thanks for all of the assistance you guys give me."

He was holding up a large paper shopping bag, and Cara could see that inside of it were four smaller parcels. She motioned at the guest chair next to her desk.

"Sure. You can leave it there and I'll make sure the others get theirs when they return," she told him.

"Okay." Dante placed the bag carefully on the chair. "Aren't you going to open yours? Or even take a peek?"

Cara looked at him derisively. "Don't have to. I can tell by the shape of the bags and boxes exactly what you got us – a bottle of wine and a box of candy. Which, by the way, is the same thing you gave us last year. Not, of course, that it wasn't appreciated. And, um, thanks for this year's, too."

She glanced away then, half-afraid she would start crying otherwise, and she had cried far too many tears over this man already. She'd known that she wouldn't be able to avoid seeing him forever, not as long as she worked in close proximity to Nick, but she hadn't believed it would be quite this difficult or heartbreaking. He was wearing one of her favorite suits today – a superbly tailored black pinstriped one that he'd teamed with a crisp white shirt and perfectly knotted silk tie. His thick, dark hair looked like it had been recently cut, and the subtle scent of his aftershave was every bit as intoxicating as it had always been. And drat him, he still had the ability to make her feel like a gawky, naïve adolescent, and she had to resist the urge not to squirm, uncomfortably aware that her panties were growing damp with arousal.

Dante's voice was gentle but held a touch of sadness as well. "Is this really the way it's going to be between us now?" he asked coaxingly. "I know things have been difficult – for both of us, I might add – but I had hoped that as time went by we could try to be friends again."

Cara kept her gaze downcast as she murmured in a low voice, "I don't know if that's ever going to be possible. Maybe someday, but right now – I just can't. I'm sorry."

He sighed. "No. You've got nothing to be sorry for, honey. I'm the one who made a huge mess of everything. But, hey, it's almost Christmas, so let's not hash over the bad stuff right now. You got any big plans for the holidays?"

She glanced up at him. "Nothing special. Just hanging out at home."

Dante looked relieved at this news. "Good. When do you leave for Florida then?"

Cara shook her head vehemently. "That's not my home," she all but hissed. "And I don't plan on going to Florida for a long, long time. If ever. I haven't spoken to my father in a couple of months."

He frowned. "Did you get into a fight or something?"

"Not exactly. I just decided I was tired of always being an afterthought for him, of always being the last priority in his life. So I told him that the ball was in his court now, that I wouldn't be getting in touch with him, and that he should call me when he had the time. Guess he's been super busy because he hasn't called yet."

Dante made a sound of disgust. "Asshole. I hate to say it, Cara, because I know he's the only family you have left, but you're probably better off without that sort of toxic relationship in your life."

"Yeah. I keep telling myself that. Unfortunately, it gets harder to believe it around the holidays."

"Wait a minute." Dante regarded her warily. "When you told me you were hanging out at home for Christmas, I thought you meant you were spending it with your father. But if you aren't going to Florida, where.."

"*My* home," she clarified. "My apartment. I know you don't think much of the place, but it's all I've got. And that's where I'll be on Christmas."

"Alone?" he asked, horror-stricken. "Jesus, Cara. You can't be alone on Christmas! Don't you have friends you can spend it with? What was your best friend's name again – Mira?"

"Mirai," corrected Cara. "And she'll be in New York for the holidays at her father's place. The few other close friends I have in the area all seem to be going away, too. And I'm fine with being alone on Christmas, Dante. In fact, I've already got my day planned out – sleeping late, reading, and eating a lot. And apparently drinking a great bottle of wine thanks to your gift. Believe me, that sounds a thousand times better than the last few Christmases I've spent with my dad and the evil stepmother."

But Dante was anything but convinced, practically wringing his hands in despair. "Cara. Jesus, I wish – I wish things were, well, *different*. I wish with all my heart that I could invite you to have Christmas with my family this year. You'd love it, and they would love to have you join us. But, well, it's complicated, as I'm sure you can imagine."

She shrugged, trying not to betray how much his words were affecting her. "I can imagine," she acknowledged. "It would be pretty awkward to have your current girlfriend and your former, uh, *date* there at the same time. Especially since no one in your family even knows who I am. But thanks for the thought."

He looked pensive for a few moments, then brightened as though a sudden thought had just occurred to him. "You must have friends back in Portland," he pointed out. "Have you kept in touch with any of them?"

"A few. Mostly my mother's best friend, Frannie. She checks up on me from time to time, even though she has three kids of her own. But I can't go to Portland for Christmas, Dante. Or anywhere for that matter. When I decided not to go to Florida, I volunteered to work through the holidays so that the others could spend time with their families. Leah and Tyler leave on Friday for southern California, and Deepak is taking next week off to go skiing with his brothers."

Dante shook his head in frustration. "Dammit!" he cursed softly. "I should never have – never mind. It's a moot point anyway. Have you told Angela about this – that you're going to be alone on Christmas?"

"Angela's got enough on her plate right now with being pregnant and planning a wedding," retorted Cara. "Besides, she's my boss and my friend, but not my mother. Nor is she responsible for me. Look, forget about it, okay? I'm sorry I even mentioned it. I'm a grown woman, Dante, and I've been looking after myself for a long time now. And by the way - *you* aren't responsible for me, either."

"Someone needs to be," he replied angrily. "It isn't right that you're alone like this, Cara. Especially during the holidays. I wish.."

"Cara. Do you have everything ready for the Raymond review? They'll be arriving in a few minutes and I'd like to go over all the charts first."

Cara and Dante's heads both swerved simultaneously to glance in the direction of Angela's voice – Cara's in silent gratitude and Dante's in visible annoyance. Angela looked anything but pleased to see Dante hovering over her assistant's desk, and glared at him disdainfully.

"Yes. Of course. I just finished putting everything inside a folder. Here."

Cara surged to her feet as she extended the folder towards her boss. Dante's eyes widened in surprise as they raked over her noticeably slimmer figure, but he remained silent as Angela continued to give him the evil eye.

"Nick's not around this afternoon, Dante," Angela informed him haughtily. "And Cara's got a packed schedule, so I'd appreciate it if you'd let her get back to work."

Dante chuckled before sauntering over to where Angela stood framed like an avenging angel in the doorway to her office. He gave her a quick, affectionate kiss on the cheek. "And here I thought impending motherhood would soften you up a little," he teased. "But you're still tough as nails, I see."

Angela scowled. "Seriously, Dante? I'm still suffering from morning sickness, Nick watches every morsel I put into my mouth to make sure it's nutritious, and he insists on accompanying me on all of my runs to make sure I don't overdo it. You're lucky I'm in *this* good of a mood right now. Why are you here anyway?"

"He, um, brought gifts, Angela," supplied Cara helpfully. "For me and Deepak and Leah and Tyler. Christmas gifts, that is."

Dante grinned at the stormy eyed Angela. "I'll be sending a gift for you and Nick to the house. It was a little too big to carry over here this afternoon. Just my way of saying thanks to your team for providing such exceptional customer service."

Cara met Angela's gaze briefly, reading the concern for her there. She gave a brief nod to indicate that she was doing okay with seeing her ex-lover again for the first time in three months, and that Angela didn't have to keep protecting her.

"It's what we do, after all," replied Angela briskly. "But thanks for your consideration, Dante. I'm sure everyone will appreciate your generosity. Cara, I'll be in the back conference room if you need me.

The receptionist knows to send the Raymonds directly there when they arrive. See you in an hour or so."

The moment Angela disappeared from view, Dante returned his attention to Cara, and she cringed at the fiery, almost angry expression on his face.

"Now I know why you look so different," he told her, his gaze once more roaming over her body. "How much weight have you lost? And what the hell compelled you to do something like that in the first place?"

Cara's small chin jutted forward defiantly. "I haven't lost *that* much weight, so you don't need to go ballistic on me," she scolded. "As for why I did it, that's really none of your business, is it? But if you must know, I did it to feel better about myself. I wasn't eating right, wasn't exercising enough, and now that I'm doing both I'm thrilled with the results."

She smoothed down the skirt of the black knit dress she was wearing today. It had been a gift from her mother the last Christmas they'd had together, not realizing at the time, of course, that Sharon would be dead by the spring. The dress was long-sleeved, with a narrow belt, the hem hitting a couple of inches above the knee. Cara had chosen to wear it today because it was so cold outside, and had been thrilled to see how well it fit after her nearly twenty pound weight loss. The last time she'd actually fit into the dress had been at Sharon's funeral more than four years ago.

Dante's mouth tightened disapprovingly. "Well, don't lose any more weight, okay? You're already too thin."

"Seriously?" she asked incredulously. "First, you don't get to tell me what to do. And second, I've seen pictures of your girlfriend online, and she's a whole lot thinner than I am. Do you try and control her the same way?"

He did *not* look pleased at the reference to Katie, and made a brusque gesture with his hand. "That's immaterial. And I'm not trying to tell you what to do, Cara. I'm just concerned about you is all. And losing so much weight in just a few months time isn't really healthy."

She shook her head. "I've been sensible about it. No crash dieting or anything stupid like that. And it really isn't as much weight as you might think. Being this short, carrying as little as an extra five pounds shows up pretty quickly."

"Fine." He shrugged in resignation. "I just wanted to make sure you weren't doing this to – well, because of me, I suppose."

Cara gaped at him in disbelief. "Omigod, you cannot be serious! And here I thought Nick was the one with the oversized male ego. But to answer your question – *no*. I did not set out to lose weight to impress you, Dante. Or make you regret breaking things off with me back in September. Or remind you of exactly what you could have had. I did this for *me*, dammit! Just for me. Not to impress you or my father or anyone else, male or female."

He stared at her for long seconds, as though unable to believe his previously sweet, docile Cara had so much fire in her. And then he nodded briefly, almost approvingly. "Good. Because as I'm sure you've realized by now, I'm not worth the effort, Cara. And believe me, honey, you don't ever have to remind me of what I gave up when I walked away from you. I'm all too aware."

They were both silent for what seemed like an endlessly long, extremely uncomfortable period of time, but what was likely just a minute or so. Both avoided eye contact with the other, the silence hanging heavy in the air.

Finally, Cara sat back down in her desk chair, mumbling awkwardly, "I, uh, have to get back to work now. Angela wasn't kidding when she told you I had a packed schedule today. I'll make sure everyone gets their gift. And thank you. For mine, that is."

"It's nothing," he replied in a hollow voice. "Just a thought is all. I wanted to do so much more for you, Cara. I wish you would have accepted that check, that you weren't so stubborn and proud."

"Well, I am," she declared fiercely. "Stubborn and proud and independent till the end. Unlike your girlfriend, I don't need a man to buy me expensive gifts. All I need is – never mind. Enjoy your holiday, Dante. Good bye."

The office phone buzzed then, and she snatched the receiver up on the first ring, giving silent thanks for the timely interruption. Cara glanced up at Dante as she answered the call, and the anguished look on his face nearly made her drop the phone and hurry over to give him a comforting hug. But before she could seriously consider doing just that, he whispered "Merry Christmas, Cara *mia*", then turned and headed out of the office as though the place was on fire.

———

THE KNOCK on her front door startled her, since the last thing she was expecting was a visitor, and especially not at ten o'clock on a Saturday morning. It had been raining off and on since last night, so Cara had elected to work out indoors this morning and was still wearing her exercise garb as she went to answer the door. She'd pushed herself extra hard this morning, determined to work off all the extra calories she had consumed at dinner last night.

Angela had been both alarmed and unhappy when she'd learned that Cara was going to be alone on Christmas, and not traveling to Florida as usual. She had initially tried to convince Cara to accompany her and Nick to her family's Christmas Day gathering down in Carmel, but had quickly abandoned the idea when Cara gently reminded her that she had to work the next day. Plus, Nick and Angela were flying to Mexico the day after Christmas to rendezvous with his mother, the famous actress Sheena Sumner, and vacationing there until New Year's Day.

As a compromise, Angela had insisted that she and Nick at least take Cara out to a nice dinner, which they had done last evening. They had brought her to the very private, very exclusive club Nick belonged to – the Biltmore – and Cara had been dazzled by both the elegant décor and the sumptuous food. They had driven her home afterwards, scoffing at her suggestion of taking a taxi or Uber, and hadn't bothered to hide their dismay at seeing how small and dismal her studio was.

"Hey," Nick had cautioned her, "make sure you put this deadbolt on every single time you're inside this rabbit hutch, okay? Jesus, I don't think I can stand up straight in here. This place makes the apartment Angela was living

in when I first met her look like a penthouse in comparison. I should have given you a bigger bonus, Cara."

Cara had given a firm shake of her head. *"No way. You've been more than generous to me, both of you. And I'll be out of this place in less than a year, I promise. I'll be able to afford something much better after I don't have tuition to pay."*

Nick had muttered something under his breath, but the only words Cara had been able to catch had been *"father"* and *"asshat".*

Nick had waggled a finger in warning as he and Angela left. *"And be damned careful walking through this neighborhood, okay? Do you have mace or pepper spray?"*

"No," she'd admitted reluctantly. *"I keep meaning to buy some, but I always get sidetracked."*

"Here." Angela withdrew a slim canister from her purse. *"I always carry some with me during my runs, and got into the habit of having one with me at all times. This is a spare. Considering that Nick and I live at the end of a private driveway, have a state of the art security system, and that he'd beat the living shit out of anyone who tried to attack me, I think you need this more than I do."*

They had both given her a quick hug good-bye, taking Cara by surprise since neither of them were overly affectionate, and wished her a Merry Christmas.

Cara glanced briefly at the canister of pepper spray that she'd left on the dining table, wondering if she should grab it before answering the door. But before she could, another knock sounded, this time accompanied by a voice calling out "Delivery".

She peered out the one small window her apartment boasted, and spied a Federal Express van double parked outside. Relieved, she opened the door and gasped in disbelief when she saw the number of boxes that the deliveryman had loaded onto his hand cart.

"You want me to bring these inside for you?" inquired the uniformed driver. "That's actually on the delivery instructions."

"Um, yeah. Sure. I mean, thank you," mumbled Cara, stepping aside so the driver could push his load a few feet inside the small room. She watched wide-eyed as he deftly lifted each box from the cart and stacked them neatly side by side. The entire process took less than ninety seconds, with the driver wishing her happy holidays as he wheeled the hand cart back to his van and drove off.

"What in the world could all of this be?" she asked out loud, taking a brief glance at the shipping labels. "More importantly, who sent it?"

As she rummaged through a drawer to find the scissors, Cara immediately eliminated Mirai from the list of potential gift givers. For one thing, her BFF had already decided that her Christmas gift to Cara was going to be a brand new outfit - complete with sexy undies - when the two of them went shopping after New Year's. And second, Mirai had once again maxed out her credit cards and was even now preparing to sweet talk her father into bailing her out one more time.

And there was no possible way that even one of these boxes was from her father, thought Cara wryly. She'd received a holiday card from him and Holly a few days ago, a photo card with the two of them and the kids with all of their names pre-printed. There had been no personal note, not even a signature, but Cara had frankly been surprised to receive even that much.

Nick and Angela had already given her the much-anticipated year-end bonus - an admittedly generous check that would finally allow her to replace the laptop that was definitely on its last legs. As she knelt to cut open the packaging tape on the first box, Cara wondered if perhaps the delivery driver had brought the boxes to the wrong door, and that all of this was meant for her landlady.

But the moment she extracted the contents from the first box, she knew that no mistake had been made. And she also knew without having to look at the enclosed card who had sent her all of this – Dante.

She ran a hand reverently over the top of the line Microsoft Surface Book. She'd read the reviews on this particular model while searching online for possible replacements to her aging laptop, but had immediately eliminated this one because it had been way, way out of her modest budget. She had never imagined she would ever own anything this nice, at least not until she'd been working for several years and was more financially stable.

The rest of the boxes revealed a veritable treasure trove of presents - an assortment of two dozen different DVDs, all of them recent movies and popular TV shows; a buttery soft cream cashmere bathrobe and matching slippers; an exquisite laptop case in dove gray leather; an enormous food hamper, packed in dry ice, that contained all manner of delicious things - an entire prime rib dinner including side dishes; imported cheeses, a charcuterie platter, and a fresh baguette; two bottles of wine, one each of red and white that she already knew were horrendously expensive; and enough sweets and desserts to feed the entire neighborhood – cookies, chocolate truffles, petit fours, a whole cheesecake. Cara shuddered a little to think about how many calories even a single slice of the latter must contain. There were also items for breakfast, and other snacks and delicacies.

Tears were already beginning to mist over her vision as she reached for the last box. She should have known that Dante wouldn't be able to handle the thought of her being alone at Christmas, but never in her wildest imagination had she envisioned him doing all of *this*. He'd chosen the gifts for her with care, too, making sure that they were things she needed and would like. And since there were no receipts of any kind, no tags, or packing slips, there was no way she'd be able to try and return anything. He had, she realized with a smile, anticipated her reaction all too well, and had carefully circumvented any possibility of her refusing the gifts.

As she opened the last box, she wasn't able to hold back the tears any longer, though they were happy, giddy tears as she gazed in amusement at the enormous stuffed toy. Cara drew it out carefully, unable to resist burying her face in the soft, plush fur. It was a dog of some sort, with huge floppy ears and a goofy grin, and it was nearly as big as she was. It was dressed for winter in a red wool hat, red and green plaid scarf, and matching vest. A card had been tied to the scarf, and she recognized the bold writing as Dante's.

"Hope this not so little guy keeps you company. Because nobody should be alone at Christmas. Happy Holidays, Cara mia."

Impulsively, before she lost her nerve, Cara sought out her phone, then scrolled through her modest list of contacts. It had never occurred to her to delete Dante's name from the list, mostly because she had contacted him so infrequently in the past. But she was so overcome with emotion right now, so deeply touched by his thoughtful gifts, that she had to let him know.

"Just finished opening all the beautiful gifts. A mere thank you couldn't begin to express how much they mean to me. And be prepared for a shock, because for once I'm not going to argue about accepting things from you. Or worry that I need to give you something in return. Thank you so much, and happy holidays to you and your family, too."

She began to unpack the food hamper, wondering how in the world she was going to fit all of the perishable items in her small refrigerator, when her phone pinged with an incoming text. It was from Dante, who hadn't waited more than a minute or two to respond to her message.

"I'm very happy to hear that you liked all the gifts, and even happier to know that you aren't threatening to take them back. As for giving me something in return, just knowing how much you like everything is all the gift I need. I'll be thinking of you on Christmas, and wishing like hell that you could be here with my family and me. Take care of yourself, honey."

Ever since making the decision not to fly to Florida for Christmas and set herself up for being alternately ignored and miserable, Cara had feared that she'd regret her choice after the reality of being completely alone set in. But as the day progressed quietly but serenely, she was pleasantly surprised to find that it was the best Christmas she'd had since the last one she'd spent with her mother.

She slept in late, worked out even though it was Christmas (because she knew she'd be going way off her diet all day), showered, and then ate a leisurely breakfast using some of the items from the food hamper Dante had sent over - freshly ground coffee, gourmet pancake mix and real maple syrup, fresh fruit, and a sinfully decadent caramel sticky bun. She spent a couple of hours transferring files and programs to her new laptop, then made herself a cup of cocoa and watched one of her new movies.

Mirai called at one point and they chatted for nearly an hour.

Angela called, too, as did Frannie, both of them wishing her a Merry Christmas, and none too subtly checking up on her.

And she was shocked when her father's phone number popped up in the caller ID, and answered the call a bit warily. The conversation was brief and somewhat stilted, with Mark rather reluctantly asking how she'd been and how she was spending the day. He had the good graces to sound guilty to realize she was alone, and mumbled something about "hopefully next year we can work something different out" before ending the call.

Surprisingly, Cara felt rather ambivalent after talking with her father - neither giddy with delight that he'd finally, albeit half-heartedly, called her, or upset because he had sounded so distant. She realized with an odd sense of relief that she simply didn't care all that much any longer, that she had finally arrived at a place where her father couldn't hurt her again.

The rest of the day passed by quickly, as she watched two more movies, ate part of the delicious prime rib dinner until she was too stuffed to move, and scrolled through photos on her new laptop for potential hairstyles.

But as surprisingly pleasant as this quiet day at home had proven to be, the very best part of the day was receiving a brief text from Dante just after dinner.

"Thinking of you just like I said I would, and hope that you're enjoying all of your gifts. Merry Christmas, Cara mia."

She was sorely tempted to call him, under the pretext of thanking him yet again for all of his fabulous gifts, but truthfully just to hear his voice. She imagined him with a roomful of family members, everyone laughing and eating and drinking and having a wonderful time together. And then she envisioned the beautiful Katie by his side, enjoying the holiday meal with all the others, everyone no doubt already considering her one of the family, and all of the pleasures she had enjoyed today were dimmed considerably.

In response, she simply texted back, *"Merry Christmas. Thanks again."*, before saying to hell with her diet for once and cutting off a generous slice of that cheesecake.

23

January

THE HAIRDRESSER HELD out a long lock of her hair and shook his head. "It would be a crime to straighten all of these beautiful natural curls," he clucked. "Now, your hair definitely needs a good cut and some definition, but I don't think straightening it is the right answer. That stick straight look wouldn't do a thing for you, sweetie."

"I've been trying to tell her that," Mirai interjected. "But she's been hell-bent on this Brazilian blowout thing for years now."

Ruben, who'd been cutting Mirai's hair for several years, grimaced. "That sort of treatment wouldn't last very long on your hair type, Cara," he cautioned. "At best, they last three months, maybe four. But your hair's so thick and curly it might not even be two months. And I'd hate to see you waste your money that way."

Cara hadn't expected this sort of resistance from Mirai's longtime hairdresser, and stubbornly stuck her chin out. "But my hair is so hard to manage this way," she pointed out. "And I'm terrible with a blow dryer, and don't have the time to style it every day. I figured if I straightened it all I'd have to do is wash it and let it dry naturally and it would look great."

Ruben, who was short, slim, and more than a little flamboyant in both his dress and mannerisms, continued to shake his head. "Frankly, with your hair type I can't even guarantee that the straightening treatment would work at all. And as far as the manageability is concerned, why don't you let me try and work a little magic on you, hmm? I'm getting a really fabulous idea here about what I'd like to do with this gorgeous mane, and I can guarantee you're going to love it."

"Let him try, Cara," urged Mirai. "There's a reason why Ruben is regarded as one of the top stylists in the city. Even my mom makes sure she stops in for an appointment with him whenever she's in town, and if he can please her he can make anyone happy. Trust me, okay?"

"She's right, sweetie," chimed in Ruben. "Tell you what. If you don't like the end result today, you come back to see me in a couple of days and I'll do the straightening treatment for free. Mirai's my witness, aren't you, girl?"

Mirai nodded emphatically, leaving Cara little choice but to sigh and nod in agreement. Ruben and Mirai high-fived each other triumphantly, and then Ruben got to work on what he termed "creating my masterpiece".

Cara still had serious doubts about the ultimate outcome, and half-wished she'd found her own salon instead of letting Mirai strong-arm her into coming here. But she obediently let Ruben shampoo and condition her hair with some admittedly divine smelling products, and then tried to keep an open mind as he began to cut and layer her hair. The one thought that continued to console her throughout the process was Ruben's promise to still straighten her hair if this cut didn't meet her expectations. And while that was cutting things a little close – no pun intended – she would still have a day to spare before the wedding on Saturday.

For the past couple of days, she and Mirai had been searching out the very best deals at all of the holiday clearance sales. Thanks to Dante's extremely generous gift, Cara had been able to use the money she'd earmarked for a new computer towards replenishing her wardrobe instead. Combined with the funds she'd saved by not traveling to Florida or buying gifts for her father and his family, she now had nearly a thousand dollars to spend on clothes, shoes, and lingerie, plus her haircut. And that didn't even take into consideration the dress and shoes Mirai had promised to buy her as a belated Christmas present.

But while that amount of money sounded like a small fortune to someone like her, who'd been scrimping and saving like a miser these past few years, a thousand dollars was a mere drop in the bucket to Mirai. Cara knew for a fact that her BFF could spend that amount on a single handbag or pair of shoes or, if she was lucky enough to hit a sale, maybe a skirt *and* a blouse. So when Mirai had tried to steer her into such high end stores as Neiman Marcus, Barneys, and Saks Fifth Avenue, Cara had balked and instead hit up more reasonably priced retailers like Macy's, H&M, and Marshall's. And while Mirai might have turned up her pert little nose upon entering some of the lower-end stores, she hadn't been able to deny the fact that Cara's limited funds had gone a much longer way there.

They had yet to find a dress and shoes for the wedding, however, and planned to continue their search once Cara's hair appointment was over. Thus far nothing had felt quite right to her, hadn't matched the mental image of herself that she'd formed. The problem, she realized as Ruben reached for the blow dryer, was that she wasn't exactly sure what sort of image she *wanted* to project at the wedding – svelte and sexy, dramatic and mysterious, soft and feminine, or none of the above. She had envisioned herself in all of those images with straight, sleek, and shiny tresses, however, and wondered just how different she was actually going to look when Ruben was finally finished.

But she had never in her wildest imaginations pictured herself looking quite like this – her formally untamable, overwhelming mane of curls tumbling in artless disarray over her shoulders and down her back. Ruben hadn't taken all that much length off, but he'd certainly added layers and definition to the style, with shorter strands around her face and forehead. He'd used some sort of finishing gloss on her hair, a spray-in product that brought out some very subtle red highlights she hadn't even realized were there.

The cut made her look older, more sophisticated, and definitely – well, *sexy*. And she realized immediately that this style was far more suitable to her bone structure and the shape of her head than the long, stick straight tresses she had initially requested.

"I love it."

Ruben beamed at her words, and impulsively pressed a kiss to her cheek. "Didn't I tell you, sweetie?" he replied triumphantly. "Ruben knows what he's doing. And you look amazing. No, amazing isn't the right word. She looks - "

"Stunning," inserted Mirai, touching Cara's glossy waves with reverence. "And drop dead gorgeous. Just wait until we find the right dress and shoes for you, Cara. And with the makeup job I'm going to do on you, everyone at that wedding is going to be staring at you all night. Especially that bastard who dumped you for his skinny blonde ex-girlfriend. You're going to look so amazing, in fact, that he'll beg you to take him back. But instead you're going to walk all over him in the stiletto heels you'll be wearing."

Cara rolled her eyes, exchanging a look with an amused Ruben. "She's watched way too many episodes of *Real Housewives*," she explained. "And I never agreed to stilettos. I'll fall flat on my face, or twist my ankle. Probably at the same time."

Ruben chuckled as he gave her hair a finishing comb through. "So you haven't found a dress yet for this wedding? Hmm, if I might make a suggestion? Look for deep, rich colors – maybe something in a jewel tone, like sapphire blue or topaz. Mirai, when you do her makeup make sure to do a bold brow, hmm? And red lips. Definitely red lips. She'll look like an Italian movie star, a real bombshell."

Mirai nodded. "Got it. And I was already thinking along those same lines."

Cara raised her hand. "Hey. Do I get a say in any of this?"

"No," Ruben and Mirai replied at the exact same time.

Cara sighed in resignation. "That's what I thought."

"SEE? Aren't you glad now that you let me have my way? Seriously, Cara, I'm really starting to think I should forget the fashion merchandising thing and go to cosmetology school instead. I have a real talent for this, don't you agree?"

Cara could only stare at herself in Mirai's bedroom mirror, reaching out a hand to touch the image reflected there to make sure this was really her. Mirai had done her makeup numerous times before this, of course, but she'd taken much greater pains today to make sure everything was perfect. And for once Cara hadn't protested that Mirai was using too heavy a hand with the blusher, or that she didn't like wearing eyeliner, or that the shade of lipstick made her mouth look too big – because the end result was positively stunning.

Mirai had followed Ruben's suggestions and given Cara both a bold eyebrow and ruby red lips. She had also made Cara's eyes look enormous with some subtle shadow, several coats of mascara, and discreet eyeliner. And Cara wasn't quite sure what products Mirai had used on her cheekbones, but they looked far more defined than usual. Of course, some of that was due to her recent twenty pound weight loss, which had helped to slim down her formerly plump cheeks.

"You're a genius, is what you are," enthused Cara, studying her face in the mirror in some disbelief. "And while you definitely have a talent for doing makeup and hair and nails, you should plan to stick with the fashion merchandising. *I* certainly wouldn't have chosen a dress like this for myself. It took someone with a real eye for fashion to know that this would end up being the perfect one for me."

After her hair appointment on Wednesday, she and Mirai had hit the stores yet again in search of the perfect dress for Cara to wear to the wedding. After striking out at a half dozen different large department stores, they had happened upon a small but charming boutique tucked away on a side street near Union Square. The place had specialized in petite sizes, and the moment Mirai had spied the emerald green gown she'd declared that this was definitely the one.

Cara hadn't been convinced at first, since green had never been her favorite color. Plus, she had been envisioning herself in something more overtly sexy than the sleeveless, tea-length dress with the semi-sheer lace panels covering the bodice – something shorter, tighter, more provocative, perhaps in black or red. But as soon as Mirai had zipped her into the gown, Cara had known instantly that it was perfect for her.

She'd been thrilled that she could actually fit comfortably into a size six now, but even more delighted by the way the gown flattered her newly slim but still curvy figure. The color had done amazing things for her dark hair and olive skin, and Cara had never felt prettier or more feminine in her life.

Mirai hadn't even glanced at the price tag when she'd paid for the dress, but admitted to Cara afterwards that it had cost far less than she had expected, especially since it had been marked down by forty percent from the original price.

Shoes had come next, and they'd snagged a pair of strappy gold evening sandals and a coordinating clutch bag at the Macy's storewide clearance. And while Cara was still definitely on the busty side, her bra size was also smaller now after the weight loss, necessitating the purchase of a new strapless bra and panty set in nude lace. She decided to forego stockings since her dress would reach nearly to the ankles, and had already agreed to borrow some jewelry from Mirai for the occasion.

"Okay," declared Mirai, setting aside her makeup brushes. "My work here is done. Time for you to get dressed. Kai's supposed to pick you up in less than half an hour so you'd better get a move on."

Kai was one of Mirai's half-brothers, the same one who co-owned a very successful restaurant in New York City. And when Mirai had seen him over the Christmas holidays, he'd casually mentioned a planned visit to San Francisco for the purpose of scouting out a location for a second restaurant. Determined that Cara arrive at Angela's wedding with a date – and not just any date, but a good-looking, well-dressed, and successful one – Mirai had talked Kai into being her BFF's escort.

Fortunately, Cara had met Kai on at least two prior occasions, and was at ease with the affable, charming man who was in his late twenties. Kai was the product of his father's second marriage to an Australian woman, and he had noticeable traces of an Australian accent when he spoke. He was also proudly bisexual, and currently living with an equally good-looking male model back in Manhattan.

Cara had resisted the idea of bringing a date at first, not wanting to feel like some pathetic wallflower who needed to get fixed up with her best friend's brother. But Mirai had insisted that she couldn't show up at the wedding alone, especially not with Dante's gorgeous actress girlfriend in attendance.

"Don't you want to rub all of this in his face?" Mirai had demanded. *"Remember the whole concept about how looking good is the best revenge? Well, you need to be holding on to some seriously hot man candy to complete the look. And even though Kai is my half-brother, there's no denying that the boy is droolworthy. Bringing him along as your plus one will definitely make that bastard Dante sit up and take notice."*

It had been pointless to argue with Mirai that she couldn't care less about Dante's reaction, either to the way she looked or to her bringing a date to Nick and Angela's wedding. For one thing, Mirai evidently *did* care – a lot – and second, she also knew that Cara was lying through her teeth with such half-hearted protests. And it might have made her seem petty and vindictive, but Cara found herself rather eagerly anticipating Dante's reaction to seeing her in just over an hour from now – looking better than she ever had in her life, and being escorted by a suave, sophisticated, and extremely attractive male.

If the gorgeous green gown had looked amazing when she'd tried it on in the boutique three days ago, it looked beyond mesmerizing now when it was part of the whole package – hair, makeup, shoes, and accessories. Mirai had loaned her a gold bangle bracelet and diamond studded gold hoop earrings, but not a necklace, insisting that it would be overkill with the dress's lace inserts.

"Stand still, would you?" demanded Mirai as she snapped half a dozen photos of Cara. "You might never look this good again, so we'd better make sure we document it."

Cara stuck her tongue out, then scowled when Mirai took a

picture of her in that pose. "Thanks a lot. Way to build up my confidence just before I have to face the music."

Mirai laughed merrily. "Oh, come on! You know I'm kidding. And speaking of facing the music, are you sure you've practiced walking in those shoes enough? Wouldn't want you toppling over when Kai twirls you around the dance floor. Did I mention that in addition to being too handsome for his own good, smart as hell, and successful, that my brother's a great dancer, too?"

"I don't recall hearing that part. But considering I haven't danced since my senior year recital, I'm not sure he'll be able to persuade me into humiliating myself," drawled Cara as she checked her clutch to make sure she hadn't forgotten anything.

"Oh, come on! You're a great dancer and you know it. And that's not exactly true about not having danced since high school. I seem to recall at least a couple of wild parties where you got up on a table to shake and shimmy," teased Mirai.

"Oh, God." Cara closed her eyes at the embarrassing memories Mirai had just evoked. "Okay, that *so* doesn't count! I was drunk and stupid and I like to think I've moved past that sort of behavior. Just in case, though, I'd better warn Kai to cut me off after two or three drinks."

"You'll be fine." Mirai gave her shoulder a squeeze. "And speaking of Kai, that's probably him now."

As Mirai let her half-brother into the apartment, Cara thought with a little sigh that it was really too bad he was currently in a relationship. Because Kai was without question one of the most attractive men she'd ever met. A quarter Polynesian, he was of above average height, lean-hipped, and with smooth golden skin. His dark gray suit and striped tie looked like they had been custom tailored to his slim frame, and if he took after his fashionista sister Cara was willing to bet his clothes had cost a small fortune. His black hair was cut in a trendy style, short on the sides and back and longer on top, and he sported a small diamond stud in one earlobe.

Kai was also incredibly charming, and his golden brown eyes twinkled merrily as they took in Cara's appearance. "You look so different than you did the last time we met," he marveled. "Not that you didn't look good then, of course, but now – well, you take my breath away. Almost makes me want to give my significant other the boot and switch teams again."

Cara laughed as he bent to kiss her cheek. "Oh, no! I can't see myself as the other woman under any circumstances. Though in this case, would I be the other man? I mean, how does that work when you, uh, play for both sides?"

Kai roared with laughter. "To be honest, I'm not sure what you'd call it," he admitted. "But as beautiful as you look, I'm pretty committed to Marcel right now so you don't have to worry about breaking us up."

Mirai did one final touch up to Cara's hair and lipstick, instructed her to take tons of pictures, and all but ordered her to have a good time.

"And Kai knows about the whole fiasco with Dante," Mirai whispered in her ear. "I told him to really lay it on thick whenever he's nearby. You know, holding your hand, body contact, whispering sweet nothings in your ear, that sort of thing. Make sure you flaunt yourself and your new man in front of the SOB whenever you get the chance."

Cara rolled her eyes. "Seriously, Mir? And I doubt that your brother would appreciate being referred to as my "new man"."

"Trust me," insisted Mirai. "Just follow Kai's lead, okay? And try to enjoy yourself, would you? Needless to say, I'll expect a full report when you return."

Since Rene was out of town for the weekend, Mirai had persuaded Cara to spend the night. Kai, who was far too fastidious to stay with his untidy half-sisters, was staying at the Ritz Carlton instead.

"I hope you don't mind that we're taking a taxi to the wedding," he apologized as he held the door open for her. "I've lived in New York so long, since my freshman year of college, that I use taxis and the subway exclusively to get around. I don't even have my drivers license."

"Of course I don't mind," assured Cara. "And I can't thank you enough for going with me to this wedding, Kai. I'm sure you have plenty of other things you'd rather be doing while you're in town."

"Nah." He waved a hand in dismissal. "I've already finished my business here, so the next day or so is just for enjoyment. And Marcel is kind of the jealous type, so he's relieved that I'm not going out clubbing or partying without him. A wedding is pretty tame in comparison."

They chatted companionably during the relatively brief taxi ride to the church where Nick and Angela were to be married. Kai was both witty and amusing, and their conversation helped keep Cara's mind off the fact that very soon now she was going to be seeing not only Dante – the man who'd broken her heart – but the woman he'd left her for as well.

Since they'd exchanged texts on Christmas Day, Dante had made it a point to contact her every other day or so, usually with just a quick text to wish her good morning or ask how her day was going. Cara had hesitated at first to respond, thinking guiltily that she really shouldn't be communicating with someone who was in a relationship, and especially since she still had such strong feelings for him. But the texts they exchanged were so harmless, so casual, and no different than something she'd send to a girlfriend, that she had continued to reply to him.

The quaint little church where the ceremony was being held was well over a hundred years old, and one of the most charming sites Cara had ever seen. The brick chapel was located in the exclusive Pacific Heights neighborhood of the city, and parking looked to be at a premium, so it was likely a good thing that Kai had chosen to take a taxi here.

"You ready?" asked Kai as he placed a hand at the small of her back.

Cara took a deep breath, trying not to think of who might already be inside the beautiful little church at this moment, and keeping her fingers crossed yet again that she wouldn't do something silly like trip over her own feet. "Ready as I'll ever be," she told him bravely. "Now, like my dance teacher used to say before one of our performances – it's showtime!"

"NOT GETTING cold feet are you, Nick? Because even though I wouldn't have a shot at taking you out myself, I think the matron of honor just might be able to kick your ass if you backed out of this now."

Nick shuddered at the mention of Angela's best friend and matron of honor. "I ever tell you about the time that bloodthirsty she-cat threw a switchblade at me? Barely missed, too. And as pissed off as Lauren was at me then, if I were to even think about not going through with this wedding – well, let's just say I don't think she'd miss this time."

Dante chuckled at the image of his imposingly large best friend at the mercy of a female who didn't look strong enough to fling a butter knife, much less a deadly weapon. "Yeah, she's a tough lady, that's for sure. And while Lauren is definitely a looker, she'd be way too much for me to handle."

Nick snorted. "You and ninety nine point nine percent of the male population of this world. Somehow Ben wound up being the one person in the world who could handle her. And you'd never guess it to meet him, since he's one of the quietest, nicest guys you'd ever meet. Go figure, huh?"

Dante patted the groom-to-be on the back. "Well, good to know that you aren't having second thoughts, regardless of the consequences. You and Angela belong together, you know. Always have. So I'm glad that you're doing the right thing by her, and for the baby. Though I won't believe you can actually change a diaper until I see it with my own two eyes."

"You and me both," grunted Nick. "But, hey, one thing at a time, man, okay? Let me get through this wedding first before I have to deal with fatherhood. Jesus, you do know I used to flat out refuse to attend *anyone's* wedding, don't you? And now here I am at my own. What the hell happened to me, Dan?"

"You grew the hell up, that's what. Oh, sorry. Guess I shouldn't be saying that inside a church, huh?" he asked sheepishly. "But it's true,

Nick. You and Angela were both pretty messed up people the first time you dated, and if you had asked me then if there was any chance at all you'd wind up marrying each other someday I would have laughed for a week. I think it took being apart for all that time to make you both wake up and realize the truth. And for both of you to get over your issues and learn how to actually have a relationship."

Nick peered in the mirror of the small waiting room he and Dante were utilizing until it was time for the ceremony to begin. "Speaking of relationships, how are things going with you and Katie?"

Dante paused before responding, choosing his next words a bit carefully since he knew that Nick wasn't Katie's biggest fan. "Okay," he replied casually. "She's still throwing hints right and left about moving in with me, but I'm not in any hurry to get that serious with her again. Especially since if I let her live with me, she'll lose whatever motivation she still has to find a real job or start school."

Despite all of their discussions on both matters, Katie had continued to procrastinate about enrolling in college or some sort of trade or vocational school, and had missed all of the spring semester sign-ups as a result. She was working at least, at a high-end designer clothing consignment store owned by a friend of her mother's, but kept insisting that it was only temporary until she found something more suitable. And just recently she'd moved in with a girlfriend here in San Francisco, though that situation also sounded short-term, only lasting until the friend's roommate returned from an extended work assignment in Europe.

And of course now that she was back living in the city full time, Katie expected to see him a lot more often than just weekends as they'd been doing since getting back together. Dante wasn't in any rush to change that state of affairs either, however, and they had had several near-arguments on the matter. Overall, Katie had become far clingier and more possessive than she had ever been previously, but instead of making him feel flattered by all of her attention, he just felt hemmed in.

She was also far needier than before, both in terms of financial and emotional support, and it seemed that her self-confidence – as well as her ego - had taken a severe blow when she'd been all but forced to give up the acting career she had loved so much. Nearly every time they went somewhere, she would fret over her appearance, and ask him repeatedly if she looked okay. She worried about gaining half a pound, and could spend as much as three hours getting ready.

And more recently, Katie had begun to flirt rather openly with other men whenever they were at a party or other event with a group. That type of behavior wasn't anything Dante hadn't dealt with before in their relationship, but oddly enough it didn't seem to bother him overmuch this time around. Before, it had driven him crazy to see her flirting with other men, and he'd been wild with jealousy if she so much as smiled at someone else. But perhaps because he had the upper hand in things now he found it didn't affect him nearly as much. If anything, Katie's often overt flirting was something of an embarrassment, particularly if she tried to use her wiles on one of his friends.

"Stick to your guns, man," Nick advised now. "It's my wedding day, so I'm not going to get into any sort of heavy discussions with you, but I'm damned glad to see that you're keeping a level head about things this time around. Make sure it's going to take this time before you move things to the next level."

Dante was saved from having to think up a suitable reply by the arrival of the minister announcing that it was time for them to go. He took his place by Nick's side at the front of the church, then turned to face the guests assembled in the wooden pews as everyone waited for the bride to walk up the aisle.

His gaze skimmed over the hundred or so people seated in the small, warmly lit chapel, recognizing Nick's flamboyantly dressed movie star mother, as well as several of his former NFL teammates. Angela's mother and sisters were easy enough to pick out, given Nick's less than flattering descriptions of them, as was the beautiful, shapely female seated several rows back who was the twin sister to Lauren, the matron of honor. Julia, too, was happily married, and was holding hands with her handsome husband Nathan.

Katie, who hadn't been especially pleased that she would have to sit alone during the ceremony, was nonetheless chatting animatedly now with Nick and Angela's boss Paul McReynolds - even though Mrs. McReynolds was seated on his other side and visibly displeased that he was basically ignoring her at this moment.

For once, Leah and Tyler weren't bickering with each other, though neither looked particularly happy, either. Deepak was here, too, with a pretty Indian girl that Dante was willing to bet he'd been set up with by one of his family members.

And then his gaze froze as it fell on the two other occupants of the row where Nick's support staff was seated. It was Cara and the debonair young man who was apparently her date, and she looked so unexpectedly gorgeous that she all but stole his breath away.

The green dress was the perfect color for her hair and skin, and from what he could see of it as she remained seated, the fabric clung to her newly svelte figure without being too tight or revealing. She'd cut her hair, though it was still luxuriously long, and the dark brown curls shone with health. She was wearing a tad too much makeup for his liking, but there was no denying that it made her big eyes look enormous, and her plush lips looked positively sinful glossed over in scarlet. She looked older, more mature, and far more sophisticated than he'd ever seen her. She looked, he realized with a little pang of regret, like a woman, instead of the sweet, guileless, and slightly ditzy girl she had always been until now.

Dante's fists clenched tightly as he watched Cara's male companion slide his arm around her shoulders, then murmured something that made her laugh softly. He guessed her date to be in his late twenties or very early thirties, and the young man looked as though he might have some Hawaiian or Filipino in his genetic makeup. Dante recognized the cut of the other man's suit as Dolce and Gabbana, his silk tie as Prada, and wondered where Cara had met someone as obviously wealthy as he appeared to be.

He was obliged to look away at that moment as the string quartet hired for the occasion began to play the processional music. All of the guests stood and looked towards the back of the chapel as first the matron of honor and then the bride walked up the aisle.

The matron of honor - the aforementioned Lauren - looked effortlessly beautiful in a simple gown of burgundy silk. It was difficult to believe that this was the same woman who'd hurled a switchblade at Nick, or who Dante had once seen dismount from the seat of a Ducati motorcycle.

But it was Angela who elicited a collective sigh of delight from the assembled guests as she glided along the aisle on her adoring father's arm. Her ivory bridal gown had long, sheer sleeves appliqued with lace, the same lace that adorned the V-necked bodice. The long tulle skirts of the dress skimmed over her still-narrow hips down to the tips of her white lace shoes. If one wasn't already aware of her condition, there would have been no possible way of knowing that she was almost four months pregnant, given how slim she still was, and the way the fabric of her gown hid any trace of a baby bump.

Dante had always considered Angela a beautiful woman, though he hadn't always liked the way Nick had compelled her to dress when they had first dated. Some of the outfits he'd chosen had made her look too old, and occasionally too flashy. Since the two of them had reunited about eighteen months ago, Dante had been pleased to see Angela asserting herself with Nick, no longer permitting him to boss her around or call all the shots in their relationship. Unlike, he realized guiltily, the way he'd always controlled things with Cara, how he had dictated when and where they would see each other. The words she'd flung at him last September about not being good enough to meet his family and friends still stung, but he had no idea how to ever convince her otherwise.

Today, in her bridal finery, Angela looked younger, softer, and exquisitely feminine, a look that wasn't always easy for a woman who was nearly six feet tall to pull off. And the expression on Nick's face as he beheld his bride was one of mingled joy and wonder, and he looked happier than Dante could ever recall seeing him.

Angela's father Gino was practically giddy with happiness as he gave his youngest daughter a lingering kiss on the cheek before placing her hand in Nick's. Dante knew that Angela's relationship with her family, particularly her mother, hadn't been an easy one. But at least it seemed far better than the distant, almost nonexistent one that Cara had with her father.

'Cara's probably closer to her half-senile old landlady than she is to that asshole of a father,' thought Dante grimly.

The ceremony began then, forcing his thoughts away from Cara, and focusing his attention instead on the bride and groom. Nick had insisted on keeping the ceremony as brief as possible, half-joking that the longer he remained inside a church the higher the chance that he'd burst into flames. But though the marriage rites were relatively short, the minister seemed unhurried, his voice clear and calm.

Dante did his part as the best man by handing Nick the wedding ring for Angela at the appropriate time, then joined in clapping with all the other guests when the minister pronounced them a married couple.

He and Lauren were obliged to remain behind after the ceremony for the dozens of pictures the photographer snapped. The photography session seemed to go on for nearly an hour, what with all of Angela's family members wanting to be included, and Dante had to stifle a grin as he observed how Nick's patience began to rapidly dwindle away.

Katie, it seemed, was even less patient as she remained seated in one of the wooden pews during the endless round of photos. Dante offered her up an apologetic smile every so often, but she was visibly displeased at having to wait, and probably even more so that she was being excluded. But since she wasn't a member of the bridal party, there was no logical reason for her to be included in this round of photos.

She was silent and moody during the drive to the Gregson Hotel on Nob Hill where the reception was being held, but for once Dante didn't try to cajole her out of whatever was bothering her. Frankly, he was getting a little fed up with her moods and demands and her ever escalating level of neediness. And where once upon a time he would have bent over backwards to make her happy and spoil her rotten - well, as the saying went, that was then and this was now.

The reception was in full swing by the time Dante and Katie

walked inside the elegantly appointed banquet room at the posh hotel. Nick was sparing no expense for this shindig, including an open bar with top shelf booze, so Dante wasted little time in ordering drinks for himself and Katie. She seemed happier now, but then she loved parties and being surrounded by lots of other people, so he wasn't all that surprised. She clung to his arm possessively as he introduced her around to Nick's former football teammates, said hello to several mutual friends, and inched ever closer to where Cara was standing, her date practically glued to her side as they chatted with the other members of Nick and Angela's office staff.

Dante didn't bother to disguise the scowl on his face as he continued to sneak sideways glances in Cara's direction. She looked happy, *really* happy, and beamed up at her date as he slipped an arm around her waist. Dante didn't care if it sounded like the biggest bunch of sour grapes known to mankind, but there was something about the guy standing hip to hip with Cara that rankled him. The guy was almost too handsome, too perfectly groomed, and if he hadn't seemed so enchanted by everything Cara was saying, Dante would have rather scathingly pegged him as gay.

"What do you keep looking at?" hissed Katie urgently, tugging at his arm. "You're being rude, Danny, hardly joining in the conversation."

"Sorry," he replied carelessly. "It's just that since I'm the best man I think we ought to make more of an effort to circulate. Let's go say hello to Nick's team from the office. They're right over here."

Katie grumbled a little at this, since they'd been conversing with one of Nick's biggest clients - a multi-billionaire magnate who apparently had numerous Hollywood connections. Dante was all too aware that Katie was still very, very interested in current goings-on in the entertainment world, was constantly reading updates online, poring through magazines, and keeping in touch with friends and associates in the business. And when he'd challenged her on this, reminding her about the numerous vows she had made that she was definitely, one hundred percent finished with that part of her life, she had made up one excuse or the other for her continued fascination with show business - none of which he truly believed. It gave him cause for concern that Katie didn't really mean what she'd assured him of countless times - that she had no further interest in pursuing an acting career, and would never even consider returning to Los Angeles under any circumstances.

And he wanted to shake her just a little when she barely acknowledged Tyler, Leah, and Deepak during their introductions. But it was when Katie got her first glimpse of Cara that the expression on her flawless face morphed from mere boredom into something more closely resembling a snarl.

Katie hated competition from another female, couldn't stand the thought that some other woman might be viewed as prettier or sexier. And while Katie looked undeniably beautiful tonight - in a short, close fitting dress of black lace that he privately considered a little too risqué for a wedding - she faded into the background standing next to Cara in that classy but still provocative emerald green dress.

"Hey, Cara," he greeted, striving with all his might to sound casual. He bent to brush a kiss on her cheek, just as he'd done to Leah as well as half a dozen other females here this evening.

But none of those other females had smelled as good as Cara did, nor had their skin felt as soft beneath his lips. And he hadn't been the least bit tempted to run a hand over their hair, or hook an arm around their waist and hug them close. And he definitely hadn't felt the urge to give the men standing by their side a good hard shove, and tell them to get lost.

"Dante." Cara gave him a brief nod of acknowledgment before taking a step backwards. She turned her face up to the man who was glued to her side, giving him a bright smile. "This is Kai Robinson, my, um, date for the evening. Kai, this is one of Nick's top clients - Dante Sabattini. And I'm sorry - I don't think we've met," she said to Katie, extending her hand. "I'm Cara Bregante, Angela's PA."

"Katie Carlisle," replied Katie, reluctantly taking Cara's proffered hand. "Dante's significant other."

As disinterested as Katie seemed to be in meeting Cara, it was just the opposite when she was introduced to Kai. Dante had to grudgingly admit that the other man was even more attractive up close, though a bit leaner than he had first assumed. Kai was also exceedingly personable, with an easy smile and twinkling eyes, and Dante was annoyed to realize that he and Cara matched up well.

After a few minutes of decidedly awkward conversation - with Katie doing her utmost to openly flirt with Kai - the call thankfully came to sit down for dinner.

Nick and Angela had nixed the idea of having a special table just for the bridal party, given that they each had just a single attendant, and instead were sitting with her parents, Nick's father and his current wife, and Nick's mother Sheena and her much younger boyfriend. Apparently it was to be the first time in two decades that his long-divorced parents would be in such close proximity to each other, and Nick was hoping that they would both mind their manners for the duration of the meal and be civil towards each other.

Katie's good mood was rapidly restored when she discovered they'd be sitting with another couple that they knew, as well as two of Nick's NFL teammates and their spouses. She turned on the charm that she could exude so easily when she wanted, laughing and smiling and regaling everyone at the table with stories of her Hollywood experiences.

Dante's mood, meanwhile, was anything but good at the moment, and getting worse with each passing minute. And his ill humor had little to do with the fact that Katie was blatantly flirting with the hunky retired football player seated to her right. Instead, he was becoming increasingly pissed off - and increasingly drunker - every time he looked across the banquet room and saw Cara.

Unlike him, *she* was having a wonderful time, chatting animatedly with the others at her table, and cozying up to the too-perfect-to-be-real Kai. Every time the bastard put his arm around Cara, or whispered something in her ear, Dante felt the urge to refill and then quickly drain his wine glass. It was either that, he thought grimly, or stalk over to their table and forcibly yank the two lovebirds apart.

Cara had a new boyfriend, he thought glumly. One who obviously cared for her, treated her like a queen, and made her happy. Unlike the way he'd treated her when they had been together. It was little wonder, Dante supposed angrily, that Cara had been more or less ignoring him all evening, not so much as glancing in his direction even once.

At some point, the wine wasn't enough to quell the burning anger he was struggling so hard to keep at bay, prompting him to make regular trips to the bar for a double shot of whiskey. By the time the dancing started, Dante was well on his way to being shit-faced, and protested when Katie dragged him out to the dance floor.

"God, how much have you had to drink tonight?" she hissed in a low voice as he clumsily stepped on her toe. "You reek of booze, Danny. And you look like you're going to keel over any minute. What's wrong with you anyway?"

He shrugged. "Nothing. Just having a good time at my best buddy's wedding is all."

"Well, you'd better stop enjoying yourself quite so much," admonished Katie. "That and have two or three cups of black coffee so you can sober up a little. There is zero chance you're driving me home in this condition."

"I'm not drunk," he insisted, his voice a little louder than he'd intended it to be. "And if it makes you feel better, I'll leave my car here at the hotel overnight and get us each a cab home."

"Or," she suggested sultrily, her arms clasping around his neck as she rubbed up against his crotch, "we could get a room here for the night. I haven't stayed at a Gregson hotel for years, but they've got a reputation for being the top luxury chain in the world."

"I'll think about it," he told her, trying not to make his reply sound like the brush-off that it actually was. If he was being really truthful, the hotel room would be a complete and total waste given his level of inebriation. Dante didn't think it was possible for him to get it up tonight, if his current physical state was any indication. Even with Katie rubbing her breasts and lower body against his in a very suggestive manner, he wasn't the least bit aroused, and he couldn't say for sure that all the booze he'd belted back was entirely to blame.

The band switched from the slow number they'd been playing to a much faster, up-tempo song. Dante groaned in protest when Katie insisted on dancing to this song, too, but shy of making a scene he wasn't left with much choice but to go through the motions and hope he didn't pass out there on the dance floor.

And then his foul mood *really* took a downturn when he spied Cara and Kai dancing together a short distance away. They moved together smoothly, as though their dance steps had been rehearsed, and were attracting a lot of attention from the other guests. Dante knew that she'd had some sort of dance training as a girl, had once flipped idly through a photo album in her apartment that featured pictures of her in a variety of costumes. But evidently her training had been a lot more intense than he had previously believed, given how practiced and professionally she was moving now.

Kai happened to catch his eye, and gave him a cheery little wave just before hooking an arm around Cara's waist from behind. Dante snarled as Cara began to deliberately grind her ass against Kai's crotch, both of them bending at the knee and dipping low as they dirty danced with great enthusiasm. He wondered wildly just how much of a scene it would cause if he rushed over there and slugged the sly little bastard in the gut.

Fortunately, the song ended at that precise moment, and he all but dragged Katie back to their table despite her protests. Feeling his head begin to spin, he followed her earlier suggestion and poured himself a cup of coffee from the carafe that had been left on each table. Katie glared at him before announcing that she was headed to the ladies room, but not before telling him to forget about the hotel room after all since he was obviously in no shape to take advantage of it.

'Good,' thought Dante sullenly. 'Saves me the trouble of telling her I wasn't about to get a room anyway.'

He drained his coffee, then poured a second cup, hoping that the jolt of caffeine would sober him up fast. If he made a drunken ass of himself at Nick's wedding, Nick would not only never forgive him but probably inflict some sort of bodily harm on him as well.

Dante watched as Katie re-entered the banquet room, only to take a seat at another table to chat up the billionaire client of Nick's she'd been flirting with earlier. She didn't even glance in Dante's direction, and seemed to have forgotten the fact that she was here with him tonight. Not that he blamed her entirely, though. Given his foul mood at seeing Cara fawning all over her new boyfriend, he certainly wasn't fit company for anyone right now.

And then it was Cara's turn to leave the room, ostensibly to visit the ladies room herself, and he wasted no time in following her out. Dante was relieved to find that the two hastily consumed cups of coffee had helped at least a little to sober him up, enough that he felt steadier on his feet. He remained a discreet distance behind Cara as she made her way to the restroom, being careful that she didn't notice him. He was pleased to discover an darkened alcove that separated the men's and women's bathrooms, and waited there none too patiently for her to reappear.

She gasped in stunned surprise when he stepped out from his hiding place, only to grasp her firmly by the upper arm and drag her back with him.

"Dante, you scared me half to death!" she protested. "What in the world are you doing out here anyway?"

He kept an iron grip on both of her arms, pushing her up against the far wall as he stared down into her enormous, still startled eyes. "I wanted to talk to you," he rasped. "To make sure that you're okay. That you know what you're doing with that - with Kai."

He almost spat the name out, the image of Cara dancing so blatantly, so erotically, with her escort this evening enraging him, bringing out a possessive side to him that he hadn't known existed where she was concerned.

"Seriously, Dante?" she sighed in what sounded like disgust. "What are you supposed to be - my big brother or something? If it makes you feel any better, I've known Kai off and on for several years now, and I trust him implicitly. He's been a good friend, and would never try anything that I didn't want him to do."

"A friend?" he asked incredulously. "Do you mean to tell me you dance that way with all of your so-called *friends*? Jesus, a few more minutes and the two of you would have really been giving everyone a show."

Cara's eyes darkened in anger. "We were just dancing, Dante. Not that anything I do is any of your business. And once again, you're not responsible for me, so why don't you just lay off?"

He made a low, feral sound deep in his throat as he pushed her closer against the wall, his own body now holding hers in place. "Well, maybe somebody should damned well be responsible for you," he muttered. "Because the way you're acting tonight makes me believe that you're too naïve to realize when a guy is putting the moves on you."

"Oh, for God's sake!" she cried, trying in vain to push him off of her. "Believe me, I know exactly what's going on with Kai, and he and I are just having some fun together, that's all."

"Yeah?" he demanded. "So is all of this for him then - the new hairstyle and the sexy makeup and losing all this weight? Did you do it so you could attract old Lover Boy Kai?"

"No!" Cara shook her head stubbornly. "I didn't do any of it for him."

Dante was quickly becoming aroused by his close proximity to the beautiful, sexy little thing he had pinned against the wall, his cock hardening rapidly as it nestled into the notch between her thighs. "So who did you do it for, Cara *mia?*" he murmured seductively, his hand caressing her bare arm. "For me? You knew I was going to be here tonight. Did you come here looking this way in the hope that you could turn me on? That I'd find you irresistible?"

She gasped in outrage, her lower body wiggling in protest as he continued to grind himself against her. "Are you out of your mind?" she squeaked. "I told you before, Dante - I did all of this for *me!* To make myself happy. To feel good about myself. I'll be damned if I'll ever be weak enough to let some man walk all over me again, to take advantage of me and use me. That was the old Cara, the weak, silly little fool. From now on, I'm going to be the new Cara. The one who won't hesitate to tell a guy to go fuck himself when he's being an asshole. And the one who's strong enough to say no when she doesn't want something. Or someone."

"Are you sure you don't want me?" he purred. "Because I can already tell your nipples are hard. Even without touching you."

"Ohhh!"

She moaned softly, her head falling back limply as he cupped one of her full breasts, his thumb brushing over the nipple that was indeed hard and pointed.

"I'm glad to see that you didn't lose too many inches here," he whispered, squeezing her breast roughly. "That would have been a crime, considering how spectacular these tits are."

"*Dante.*" Her voice was more like a whimper as he continued to fondle her breast.

His hand began to slowly work its way up under the full skirt of her dress, caressing her thigh as he hooked her leg around his waist. "Shh. I know, honey," he soothed. "I can already tell how wet you are, can smell the sweet scent of that pretty pussy. God, I've missed the taste of you, missed how tight you feel around my cock while I'm fucking you. Missed hearing the little moans you make when you come so hard."

He kissed her then, savagely, open-mouthed, and it was dirty and forbidden and goddamned erotic to hear her pant and groan beneath the pressure of his lips. As his tongue ravaged her mouth, he used two fingers to push aside the soaked crotch of her silk panties, then shoved those same fingers deep inside of her vagina. She climaxed instantly, her back arching gracefully off the wall as she continued to ride his hand.

Cara stared at him glassy-eyed, watching in stunned disbelief as he slowly withdrew his fingers from her body, only to bring them to his lips and carefully and deliberately lick off her juices from the tips.

"Mmm." He smacked his lips. "Tastes even better than I remember. Let's find a more private place to see if your pussy is still tight as a fist. Come on, Cara *mia.*"

But she pulled her wrist out of his grasp with surprising strength, giving him a little shove as she twisted away from his body. Hastily, she smoothed the skirt of her dress down, then patted her hair back into place frantically, looking around to make sure they hadn't been seen.

"I'm not going anywhere with you," she told him scornfully. "In case you've forgotten, your girlfriend is waiting back inside the banquet room for you. The girlfriend that you decided you were still so much in love with that I didn't matter any longer. So why don't you hurry on back to her now, hmm?"

"Cara," he began, wanting desperately to apologize, to explain, to beg her for a second chance, to tell her that – what? That Katie meant nothing to him, that things weren't the same with her any longer? Or that he'd suddenly realized he wanted Cara more, that he had feelings for her he hadn't realized until now?

But Cara held up a hand in protest, backing away from him in a near-panic before he could say anything. "You had your chance with me once, Dante," she told him angrily. "And you know what? I would have done anything you asked of me then, anything at all. But you shoved me aside when something better came along, let me down just like every other man in my life has done. So leave me the hell alone from now on, Dante," she cautioned. " No more texts, no more emails. And definitely no more of – of *this*!"

She gestured wildly at her body before turning on her heel and storming away, leaving him to gaze after her sorrowfully, regretfully, and hopelessly.

24

"How many texts does that make now?"

Cara glanced at her phone in annoyance before pushing it aside. "Four just today," she sighed wearily. "In total since the wedding? Frankly, I've lost count."

Mirai shook her head in exasperation. "Why in the world haven't you just blocked him, Cara? That would be a lot easier than just ignoring a constant stream of text messages."

"Because my phone is so outdated and crappy that it doesn't have the ability to block calls," admitted Cara. "And before you tell me that I really need a new phone, I'm already aware. Unfortunately, that's going to have to wait until I'm finished with school this summer. I shouldn't have spent so much money on new clothes, I guess."

"Of course you should have!" scolded Mirai. "I've known you for five years now, Cara, and I think you might have bought yourself three or four new things that entire time. You deserved to treat yourself for once. And God knows you didn't exactly go overboard on what you bought. You're a much better bargain hunter than I am, that's for sure."

Cara grinned. "That's because my idea of a bargain is spending ten bucks on a new blouse, while yours is paying two hundred for one.

But I guess I'm happy with finally having a few new outfits, and clothes that actually fit well for once."

One of those outfits was the pair of dark wash jeans and cute red and black polka dot knit top that she was wearing this afternoon. Her so-called bargain hunting skills had snagged her both pieces for less than twenty-five dollars combined.

But a new cell phone would cost a whole lot more than that, so she'd resigned herself to waiting patiently until tuition payments were no longer a monthly obligation. She'd thus far resisted pulling out a calendar and marking off the days until she was finally finished with school, but the temptation was growing stronger on a weekly basis.

"That is a cute outfit," Mirai acknowledged somewhat grudgingly. "And I guess if you really have the patience and the time, you can dig out some decent stuff at Marshall's." She checked her own phone, the newest, fully loaded model, of course, and surged to her feet. "Where did the time go anyway? Gotta run, girl, so I can get ready for my hot date tonight."

Cara arched a brow inquiringly. "Uh, it's barely two o'clock. What time is he picking you up, for God's sake?"

Mirai grinned. "Seven. But did I mention that this guy is really, really special? I'm going to try and bully my way into an appointment at the nail salon to get a mani-pedi. And considering how much business I give them, they'd better lay down the red carpet for me. Oh, and if there's time, I might buy that pair of shoes you and I were looking at after dinner last night."

"Mir, you do *not* need those shoes," scolded Cara. "Have you already forgotten that you promised your dad you wouldn't max out your credit cards again? Buying those shoes would break that promise in ten seconds."

"You're right." Mirai sighed in resignation. "What would I do without you, Cara? Between encouraging me to go back to school, being my conscience when I'm tempted to spend money on stuff I don't need, and fixing me brunch, you're the best girlfriend anyone could wish for. Even if I really, really wanted those shoes!"

Cara laughed and gave her friend an affectionate hug. "You'll thank me for it when you get your credit card statement in the mail," she teased. "And have fun on your date tonight. I'm sure you'll look amazing with or without the new shoes."

It had been a cold, rainy morning in San Francisco, so Mirai had convinced Cara to attend a barre method class with her on a guest pass, and Cara had returned the favor by whipping up brunch for both of them - a *healthy* brunch, much to Mirai's chagrin. Even though Cara had not only reached but surpassed her goal weight, she knew she couldn't just lapse back into her old eating habits, and was always mindful now of what she ate.

"I guess I don't need the shoes," grumbled Mirai. "Better to stay on Daddy's good side for awhile. Anyway, thanks for brunch and wish me good luck tonight."

"Have a great time, and be sure to tell me how it went. And - damn! There's my phone again. He really isn't getting the hint, is he?"

Ever since their disastrous encounter at Nick and Angela's wedding last week, Dante had been texting her several times a day, more or less begging for her forgiveness and offering up every excuse in the book for his inexcusable behavior - he'd had too much to drink, he'd been worried about her, he'd acted like an insensitive jerk. Thus far, there hadn't been a single excuse that Cara had necessarily disagreed with, but that didn't mean she was prepared to forgive him for the way he'd manhandled her. And the very thought that Dante, drunk or not, had arrogantly assumed that she'd willingly have sex with him in a public place - a place where his girlfriend and Cara's date were right in the next room, to boot - had enraged her. She was still so angry, in fact, that she refused to acknowledge even a single one of his texts.

"Tell him to go fuck off and leave you alone," advised Mirai. "Or threaten to tell his girlfriend about what happened. That should stop the constant texts. Really, Cara, it's getting kind of pathetic at this point, you know?"

"Yeah, I guess so. And I'm not going to say anything to his girlfriend, even if I knew how to get in touch with her. Dante wouldn't believe something like that anyway."

Mirai patted her on the shoulder consolingly. "You're too soft-hearted, that's your problem. Now if it was me on the other hand, I'd have emailed the bitch days ago with all of the details. Looking good might be the best revenge, but ratting the cheating bastard out to his girlfriend feels pretty awesome, too."

Cara's cheeks flushed in embarrassment. "He didn't cheat on Katie," she mumbled defensively. "I mean, not really. I guess it depends on exactly what one defines as cheating."

"From the little I know about this witch, she'd probably consider a handshake to be cheating," remarked Mirai drolly. "And based on what you told me, that bit of hanky panky between you and Dante went a whole lot farther than that. If she had any inkling whatsoever about what happened last week, blood would have been spilled by now. Especially since you cheated her out of catching Angela's bouquet."

Cara smiled triumphantly as she recalled that precise moment last week. At first, she hadn't even wanted to join the half dozen or so other single women gathered around to catch the bride's bouquet, but then a seriously buzzed Leah had all but shoved her out onto the floor. Katie, who was considerably taller than Cara, had actually got a hand on the bouquet, but at the last second it had tumbled into Cara's startled grasp. Angela had been thrilled, coming over to give her a hug, and whisper mischievously in her ear, "Thank God it was you! If Katie had caught it instead I would have been seriously pissed. Especially since I'd have had to take my picture with her."

The bouquet was taking up space in Cara's small refrigerator right now, the flowers still fresh. She was planning to return the bouquet as a keepsake to Angela on Monday, the day the newlyweds would be back in the office after a brief honeymoon trip to Maui.

"Yeah, she was pretty ticked off about that," agreed Cara with a wicked grin. "But I mean, come on. That's just a silly superstition after all. And I can guarantee you that Katie will be a married woman long before I will."

"Maybe. Maybe not," observed Mirai. "Anyway, you deprived the witch of her moment of glory, so that's worth something. Look, I've got to run. I'll call you tomorrow, okay?"

"You bet. Drive safely."

Mirai grimaced. "In this neighborhood I always do. And make sure my car alarm is set, too."

"It's not that bad, Mir," scolded Cara. "In fact, almost every house on this block looks a lot better than it did when I first moved here. And the new neighbors who've moved in have done a lot to fix their places up."

"If you say so. And you're right. This block isn't too bad. But watch it when you walk past the place on the corner two blocks from here. You know the house I mean, right? Where you make the turn for the bus stop? The guys who hang out there are mega creepy."

Cara couldn't suppress a little shudder. She knew exactly what house Mirai was referring to, one of the few remaining in this gradually gentrifying neighborhood that was still dilapidated and in serious need of renovating. The creepy guys seemed to have moved in within the last month or two, and had made leering comments to Cara a few times as she walked home from the bus stop. She'd ignored them, but had clutched the slim canister of pepper spray Angela had given her a little tighter.

"Yeah, I think they might have just moved in with one of their mothers or something. I mean, the place has always been rundown, but I never noticed either of those creeps until fairly recently. Let's hope they're only here temporarily."

"Well, just watch yourself around them," cautioned Mirai. "God, I'll be so glad when you finally move out of this place in the fall. We'll find you somewhere trendy to live. Like the Marina or maybe Mission Bay. Lots of new apartments going up there."

"We'll see," replied Cara diplomatically. "Let me finish school first before you start spending all my money. You've already told me I need a new phone and a new place to live. Next thing you're going to insist I buy a car."

Mirai grinned. "I wasn't going to say anything, but that should definitely be on your to-do list. Oh, and once you get your degree and become a big time stockbroker or investment banker, you'll need at least six to eight designer suits. You'll have to dress the part, Cara. The right shoes, too, and probably a great watch. Oh, and..."

"And time for you to get ready for your big date," interrupted Cara, practically shoving her friend out the door. "You'll never get an appointment at the nail salon if you don't leave now."

"Humph," sniffed Mirai disdainfully. "They wouldn't dare say no to me. Finding a parking space near the salon is another matter entirely though, so I'll head out now."

Cara was still smiling after her BFF drove off, thinking how Mirai could always put her in a good mood, no matter what other drama might be going on in her life. Mirai had certainly helped her survive these last few months after the breakup with Dante, cutting off communication with her father, and now this demoralizing incident at the wedding last week.

She'd been both furious and shaken to the core after the unexpected encounter with Dante at the reception, and had marched back to her table without a backwards glance. Kai had taken one look at her stormy expression, and merely poured her another glass of wine without asking a single question. He'd turned out to be the perfect date, the circumstances of his bisexuality and having a significant other notwithstanding. The only downside, it had seemed, from bringing him to the wedding with her was Dante's hair-trigger reaction at seeing them together.

Cara had fumed about his behavior off and on for the past week, and was no closer to forgiving him now than she had been six days ago - the day he'd sent the first of what would be dozens of texts apologizing profusely. There was no excuse for what he'd done, she thought angrily, none at all. Who the hell did he think he was anyway - dropping her like a hot potato so he could get back together with the girlfriend who'd kicked him to the curb, only to act like a jealous maniac the first time she showed up with a date of her own. He was like a spoiled little boy, Cara fumed, one who had cast aside a toy he was tired of only to throw a temper tantrum when another child dared to play with it. Well, she wasn't anyone's toy, anyone's property, and Dante Sabattini could go to hell for all she cared. She would never, ever, allow a man to manipulate or use her again, no matter how gorgeous or dreamy or fantastic in bed he might be. And especially not when said man already had a girlfriend.

She had just finished cleaning up the brunch dishes when her phone pinged with yet another incoming text. She was sorely tempted to just power the thing down, but instead found herself reading the latest message from Dante.

"Please just say you forgive me, Cara. I won't try and give you any more stupid excuses, except to say that my behavior was flat out inexcusable. I acted like a total ass last week, and I've been a mess ever since over what happened. So please, please say you forgive me, so that we can maybe find a way to get past this and be friends again. Please?"

Cara huffed impatiently, for she'd already read at least twenty such messages from him, and immediately deleted all of them. But she sensed that Dante wasn't going to just give this up so easily, so she sighed in resignation as she typed out a brief, terse reply.

"Fine. I forgive you. That doesn't mean I want to be friends with you, though. So go back to your girlfriend and leave me alone. Please."

She sent the message, then waited for him to respond. But when half an hour went by without an answer, Cara wasn't sure if she was relieved or devastated.

"I CAN ALWAYS TELL when something's bothering you, Dante. Your face has been an open book since you were old enough to walk. Even when you were three years old and insisted that you hadn't broken my favorite coffee mug I knew you were lying. So why don't we stop playing that particular game and talk about what's on your mind, hmm?"

Dante gave his mother a rueful smile. "And I never could fool you. Or get you to believe my wild stories. Dad, yes. Occasionally I could pull the wool over his eyes. Even Nonna would give me the benefit of the doubt once in awhile. But you? Nah. I think sneaking into a bank vault would be easier than slipping anything past you, Mom."

Jeannie Sabattini patted her oldest child on the back. "At least I taught you something in thirty-three years. So, tell your mother what's on your mind. You look like you've lost your best friend, your job, and your entire collection of cars all at the same time. And as depressed as you'd be if any of those things happened, you seem even sadder right now."

"Yeah." Dante exhaled sharply. "Though I don't think sad and depressed are exactly the right words to explain what I'm going through. I just - I think I made a huge mistake, Mom, and I'm not sure I can fix it."

Jeannie took a sip of her coffee, having brewed a fresh pot when Dante had unexpectedly walked in unannounced fifteen minutes ago. She hadn't expected to see him until tomorrow during his usual Sunday visit. The fact that he was here on a Saturday afternoon, and not getting ready for a date this evening, had made her suspect right off the bat that something was bothering him.

"Is this mistake you made getting back together with Katie?" she asked quietly. "Because forgive me for saying so, but you just haven't seemed all that happy since you started seeing her again."

"I know." Dante took a long drink of his own coffee, choosing his next words carefully. "And I don't think it's so much a matter of making a mistake reconciling with Katie as it was breaking things off with the girl I was seeing for awhile last summer. I'm pretty sure I blew it big time with her, Mom. And I only made things worse when I saw her at Nick's wedding last weekend."

Jeannie's surprise was evident on her pretty, still-youthful face. Save for a few wrinkles on her forehead, and the laugh lines around her eyes that she refused to refer to as crow's feet, she certainly didn't look old enough to be a grandmother or have four grown children. She was trim and fit, and vain enough to cover up the occasional gray strands that appeared in her chestnut hair. Otherwise, though, she rarely fussed with her appearance, and Dante had never met a female who was as comfortable in her own skin as his mother had always been.

"Okay," she replied slowly. "I'm not sure where you should start with that little bombshell. Obviously, this is the first I'm hearing about a girl you dated last summer. I assume I'm not the only one you kept that bit of information from?"

He didn't even try to mask the guilt in his voice. "You'd be correct in that assumption," he admitted. "I didn't tell anyone I was seeing her, not the family or any of my friends."

"Not even Nick?" inquired Jeannie. "I thought he was supposed to be your best friend."

Dante shuddered. "I especially didn't tell Nick about this girl. And that's because she works for him. Well, technically for Angela, but all of that is tied in together these days. And Nick probably would have wrung my neck if he'd ever suspected I was dating her."

"Why?" asked Jeannie curiously. "Conflict of interest or something like that?"

"Nah. Nick doesn't give a crap about that sort of thing. But, well, he's sort of protective of this girl, looks out for her in a way. She's, uh, sort of on the youngish side, and he sees himself in the big brother role occasionally. The sort of big brother who'd do physical harm to anyone who messed with his little sister."

Jeannie shook her head in dismay. "How young is youngish, exactly?"

Dante forced himself not to cower a little in fear when he spied the reproachful look on his mother's face. "She's, ah, twenty-two. In fact, the first time I took her out last April it was to celebrate her birthday. I felt sorry for her because she doesn't have any close family, and instead of doing something fun on her birthday she was going to night school. So I invited her out to dinner. It was supposed to be a casual thing, just the one time, and just between friends. But, well, one thing led to another, and we sort of wound up dating for a few months."

"Hmm." Jeannie regarded him over the rim of her coffee mug. "I'm guessing that dating really means sleeping with her. And I can understand why you didn't tell me about her, Dante." Her eyes narrowed dangerously. "Because if you'd told me you were dating a girl barely out of her teens who happened to be more than a decade younger than you are, *I* would have wrung your neck and saved Nick the trouble. What were you thinking of, honey?"

"I never meant for things to go that far," he replied defensively. "At first, it was because I was lonely and still hurting after Katie broke things off, and being with Cara made me happy. And it made her happy, too. She has nothing, Mom. Nothing and nobody, and I guess I just convinced myself that I was making her life a little better for awhile. We kept things casual, low-key. And I didn't tell you or anyone because I wanted it to remain that way. You know how this family gets when they learn you're dating someone."

Jeannie grinned in spite of her irritation. "They'd want to know when the wedding was going to be, and what you're going to name your kids. Your Nonna would start buying sheets and towels for the girl's hope chest. So, yes. I understand why you didn't mention anything, or bring her home to meet everyone. But none of that is a good enough reason for why you got involved with this girl - Cara's her name? - in the first place. She doesn't sound like your usual type, Dante. And what's all this about her not having any family?"

Briefly, he filled his mother in on the basics about Cara - losing her mother while still in high school, then watching helplessly as her worthless father got remarried to his pregnant girlfriend, sold the house, and moved to Florida all within a few months time. Jeannie scowled darkly when she learned that Cara's father had abruptly cut her off financially with little to no warning, and that she'd been taking care of herself for the past three years.

She gave his hand a comforting squeeze. "I can understand a little bit now why you felt compelled to help this girl," she acknowledged. "After all, you took on the role of protector and man of the house at a very young age. And you've been looking out for me and your siblings ever since. Not to mention a host of other family members, including your grandmother - even though she'd never in a million years admit she needed anyone to look out for her."

"I guess that's part of it," he agreed. "But another part was just because we had a good time together. Cara's young and sweet and funny, and she just made me feel good about myself again. She's also mature and independent as hell, and probably the most stubborn woman I've ever met. She'd insist on cooking me dinner once a week as her way of paying me back for taking her out. And don't you dare tell her this, but Cara's scampi and risotto put Nonna's to shame."

Jeannie winced. "You're right. That will remain our little secret. So should I assume that your Cara is Italian?"

"Half. On her father's side. And unfortunately, she hasn't been *my* Cara since I was stupid enough to end things with her back in September," he lamented.

Jeannie regarded her son thoughtfully. "Coincidentally, the exact same time you started seeing Katie again if my dates are right," she mused. "So if I'm putting all the pieces of this puzzle together correctly, this means that you broke up with Cara soon after Katie breezed back into town. And I'm going to assume you did that because you thought you were still in love with Katie. You know, Gia told me right after Brandon's wedding that she had an awful feeling Katie would try to sink her hooks into you again, but I told her she was imagining things. Guess I was wrong, hmm?"

"Yeah." Dante exhaled tiredly. "I'd sworn up and down that I was finished with Katie, that when she broke my heart I would never be so stupid as to trust her again. But talking to her at Brandon's wedding, she seemed different - more vulnerable, like what she went through in L.A. really humbled her. And the more we talked over the next few weeks, the more I realized that I'd never completely gotten over her. She was still the one that got away, the one that I truly believed was going to be my one and only. I kept remembering how happy I'd felt during that year we were together, and I guess I wanted to try and recapture that feeling again."

"Except it hasn't exactly worked out that way, has it?" guessed Jeannie.

He shook his head. "Not at all. And I keep thinking about why not, about what's different this time around, why I just don't feel the same connection between us that I did before."

"And have you figured that out yet?" inquired his mother.

"I think so. And there are several reasons actually. First, I'm not sure I'll ever really be able to forgive Katie for breaking up with me for the sake of her career. I mean, I've tried like hell to get past that, to not let it have a negative impact on our relationship. But it's been a few months now since we've been back together, and I can't quite forget about it, can't let it go," admitted Dante.

Jeannie shrugged. "That's understandable, honey. You were head over heels in love with Katie, were all set to pop the question. And for her to come out and admit that she was choosing her acting career over you - well, I'm not sure anyone could really forgive and forget that sort of thing. I know I couldn't. And most people I know wouldn't have even given her a second chance. At least you've done that much, though God knows why."

Dante gave his mother a sheepish look. "I was more or less convinced that she'd changed," he confessed. "I mean, I'd watched a few episodes of that sitcom she was on, and let's just say her acting skills leave a lot to be desired. So when I met her at the wedding and she seemed so sweet and contrite, I figured there was no possible way she could be acting, that she had to be sincere."

"And has she been? The few times you've brought her to the family doings she was polite but a little distant, the same way she was in the past, so it's hard for me to tell how things really are between you."

He hesitated before telling his mother the next part. After all, he could barely admit the truth to himself, much less voice it aloud to another person. But to continue living in denial wasn't being fair to either himself or Katie.

"Things have been - different," he acknowledged. "Katie is different. Or maybe she was always that way and I was just too dazzled by her to know any better. But I notice things about her now, that she's manipulative and needy and throws a fit when she doesn't get her own way. And even though she's been insisting for months now that she's finished with the whole acting scene, she keeps very close tabs on what's going on there, and stays in touch with her former agent. Plus, all of that talk about finally starting college, getting a degree, having a real career - well, so far that's all it's been - talk. She's only working part time, spends money faster than she makes it, and still relies on her parents for financial support, though she's mentioned that they keep threatening to cut her off. And in spite of how much she insists that her acting career is a thing of the past, I'm not convinced she's entirely given up on the idea."

"Hmm. My guess would be not. She hasn't moved in with you, has she?"

"No, but not for lack of trying," replied Dante dryly. "I think she brings up the subject at least every two or three days. And doesn't understand why I'm not ready to make that sort of commitment just yet, why things are so much different than they were the last time between us."

Jeannie looked uncertain, as though what she had to say next was something she knew he wouldn't like. "Honey, have you considered the fact that Katie might be - well, using you I suppose is the most polite way I can phrase it. After all, if her acting career has dried up, if she doesn't have any other realistic job prospects, and her parents are getting fed up with giving her money, it's only natural that she'd find some other means to support herself. And I don't want to hurt your feelings, Dante, but is it at all possible that the main reason Katie reached out to you was because you have money? She's well aware that not only are you filthy rich, but the most generous person I've ever known. And if all of her other prospects have turned into dead ends, becoming Mrs. Dante Sabattini wouldn't be such a terrible fate for her. Or any woman."

He clenched his fists tightly, not wanting to admit to his mother that he had in fact considered everything she'd just suggested on multiple occasions. But he hadn't allowed himself to believe or even suspect that was Katie's real motivation. Hearing his own mother - the person who'd always taken his part, who'd always supported and encouraged him for his entire life - make those same suggestions, however, gave him cause to reconsider now.

"It's more than possible, Mom," he acknowledged reluctantly. "In fact, it's probably all too true. Which makes me feel like the biggest, most naïve dumbass in the universe."

"You don't know that for sure," consoled Jeannie, taking one of his hands in hers and giving it a squeeze. "I'm positive that Katie has feelings for you, that she cares for you, Dante. Unfortunately, I think she's the sort of person who will always love herself more, will always put herself before anyone else - even the man she might end up marrying someday. And you're too good of a man, honey, to settle for someone who doesn't love you the way you deserved to be loved. You need the love of a good woman, the kind of woman who will love you more than her own life. The kind who'd take a bullet for you. The kind," she added with a grin, "who'd impress you enough with her cooking that you'd have the guts to compare it to your grandmother's."

Dante chuckled. "And you want to know something else about that, Mom? Cara doesn't even have a real stove in her apartment, just a cooktop and a microwave and a crockpot. But somehow she'd throw together these incredible meals, some of the best food I've ever had. Though once again, don't you dare repeat that to Nonna."

Jeannie made the sign of the cross. "Not on my life," she promised. "Even after knowing her for almost forty years, Valentina still scares the crap out of me most of the time. Can I ask you something, honey?"

"You know you can always ask me anything," he assured his mother. "Especially since I'm a terrible liar. And did I mention that I've never once been able to get anything past you?"

"You did. So answer me truthfully, Dante. Is one of the reasons things haven't been so great with Katie this time around because you care more about this other girl than you're willing to admit? And what exactly happened between the two of you at Nick's wedding anyway?"

He gave a slight shudder at the recollection of what a pig he'd been last weekend, and made a silent vow that he would *never* tell his mother the real truth. "I said some things to her I had no right to say, acted like a jealous control freak when I saw her there with another guy. She got mad – rightly so - and told me to get lost. I've been texting her all week trying to apologize, and she finally answered me just before I arrived here, saying that she forgives me but that I need to leave her alone."

"And that's upsetting you," observed Jeannie.

"Yeah." He blew out a frustrated breath. "I guess you could say that. But I understand her reaction, given what a jerk I've been to her. I should never have gotten involved with her in the first place, Mom. Cara's too nice, too sweet, for someone like me. All she ever wanted was to be with me, to enjoy the time we spent together. And she never asked me for a single thing. In fact, she tore up the check I gave her right in front of my face and washed the pieces down the drain."

"You gave her a check?" asked Jeannie, frowning. "For what?"

He resisted the urge to squirm, much as he had at the age of sixteen when his mother had found an empty six-pack of beer in the backseat of his car. "Just to - well, help her out a little. I told you already that she's got no one, that her dad is a total loser and never helps her out. I felt guilty, breaking things off with her when she had no one else to depend on. And I thought that it would be a nice gesture to offer her some cash to help with her tuition and other expenses."

"Jesus." Jeannie shook her head in disbelief. "Exactly how much cash are we talking about here?"

Dante gulped. "Twenty five grand. But she refused to even consider taking the money."

"Of course she did. Because she's a good girl, a nice girl. And I know your heart was in the right place, Dante, but I'm afraid you only insulted her by offering to write her a big fat check. *Stupido.*" She gave him a smack on the side of his head.

"Ow." He rubbed his temple. "Hey, I get it. That probably wasn't the best idea I've ever had in my life. But my intentions were good."

"I'm sure they were," agreed Jeannie. "That doesn't mean you should have followed through on them. Let me ask you a question, honey. If you were to present Katie with a check for twenty five thousand dollars right now, what do you think she'd do with it?"

He gave a bitter little laugh. "Deposit it before the ink could dry.

And then proceed to spend every penny as fast as she could. You've made your point, Mom. But I already knew that Katie and Cara are as different as day and night. There's never been any doubt in my mind about that."

"No. But what you do need to decide is what's right for you at this time in your life. The night or the day."

The sun was beginning to set on what had been a gloomy, rainy day as Dante gazed out of the kitchen window. "I don't know what's right anymore, Mom. Can't you just tell me what to do?"

Jeannie stood, picking up their empty coffee mugs, and pressed a kiss to the top of his head. "No, honey. I can't. After all, you aren't five years old anymore, are you? But I can tell you this, which is something I've told you and your siblings since you were old enough to know better. When in doubt, go where your heart leads you. Unfortunately, you're the one who's going to have to figure out where that is."

"Oh, my, God. You did *not* just say what I thought you did. I mean, is this some sort of sick joke, Danny? April Fool's Day isn't for another two and a half months. And this isn't the least bit funny, not even a little."

Dante regarded the outraged, visibly upset woman who sat across the table from him with a sort of tranquil, almost detached sense of calm. "I didn't mean it to be funny, Katie," he drawled. "And I also meant what I said a hundred percent. This isn't working out between us, it was a huge mistake to get back together, and this time it's really and truly over. In other words, I'm breaking up with you."

Katie made a sound that was part gasp, part squeal, a sound that was loud enough to make Dante thankful he'd requested a table in the very back of the restaurant. Normally, it wasn't like Katie to make a scene, but then again men normally didn't break up with a woman as beautiful and supremely confident of herself as she was.

"*You* are breaking up with *me?*" she shrieked incredulously, her voice loud enough now that it carried to several nearby tables, judging from the curious looks they suddenly began receiving. "How dare you! How - how could you! No one has ever broken up with me before, ever! You should be grateful I ever went out with you in the first place, or that I agreed to take you back."

He stared at her in shock. "Uh, pardon me, Katie, but I believe you've got that last part all wrong. *I* was the one who agreed to give our relationship a second chance, and only after you called and texted me a dozen times a day apologizing for what you'd done, and telling me what a terrible, terrible mistake you'd made. As for being grateful - you know what? At one point in time I probably was grateful that you'd noticed me, had agreed to go out with me. I was crazy about you, Katie, would have given you everything I owned. But when you chose your career over me, I think it broke something inside of me. And I thought I could get past it, thought I could eventually forgive and forget what you'd done. But I've tried, really tried, and I find I can't forget it. Especially since I'm no longer convinced you're sincere about giving up hopes of an acting career."

Her beautiful face was a myriad of emotions right about now - surprise, anger, irritation, panic, dismay. Almost desperately, she grabbed hold of his hand, squeezing it so tightly that he winced. In a flash, she modulated her tone, changed her tactics, as she gazed at him imploringly.

"Danny, you can't leave me," she pleaded prettily. "Think of all we've meant to each other, all the wonderful times we've had together. And I swear that I'm totally and completely over the whole acting thing. I promised you that when we first got back together, and I would never dream of going back on my word."

"Really?" he drawled lazily. With a lightning fast move he grabbed her cell phone where she'd left it sitting by her place setting. For as long as he'd known Katie, she had always kept her phone close at hand, just in case her agent called with a job for her. And when he had recently inquired why she still felt compelled to do that, given that her acting career was supposedly over, she had just laughed dismissively and called it force of habit.

"Give me that phone, Danny!" she shrieked, her normally soft, sweet voice sounding shrill as a fishwife's right about now. "What the hell do you think you're doing now?"

"Confirming what I've suspected all along," he replied as he casually continued to scroll through her text messages. "That you've never had any intention of giving up hope that you could return to acting one day, provided the right thing came along. Why else would you be texting your old agent on a weekly basis? And don't bullshit me by claiming it was just to keep in touch. Keeping in touch usually doesn't involve messages like this one - "Hey, Doug. Just wanted to say hi and see if you've got any news for me. Sorry to be a pest but I really think that I'd be perfect for that new summer replacement show we discussed. I could fly down to L.A. on half a day's notice to audition. Keeping my fingers crossed." That message sure sounds like you're still keeping your options open."

Katie glared at him sullenly. "It was a pointless message anyway. Doug didn't even reply to me."

"Ah, but never fear," he replied in a falsely cheery voice. "Because even though good old Doug is ignoring you, it looks like you've set your sights quite a bit higher than your former agent. And didn't waste much time, either. I mean, considering that you just met Nick's client at the wedding last weekend, the two of you seem awfully cozy already, given the number of texts you've exchanged."

Katie slammed her fist down on the table, causing the dishes and glasses to rattle precariously, and attracting still more attention from the nearby tables. "Give me that phone, Danny!" she hissed. "You have no right to go through my private messages. No right at all. How dare you!"

He shrugged, blithely unconcerned as he chose a message at random. "Here's the most recent text from your new friend Archer Wayne - "I must tell you again how wonderful it was to meet you at Nick's wedding last Saturday. I enjoyed our chat very much. And I'm looking forward to seeing you for lunch again next week. I'll be making several calls on your behalf before then to some producers and casting agents I know well, and I'm certain they'll find something suitable for you." Tell me, Katie, what is the very charming Mr. Wayne expecting in return for these calls he's making on your behalf? Men like Archer - mega-rich, mega-powerful, mega-arrogant - they'll want something in return for any favors they hand out. And my guess is that he'll expect *you* in return."

Katie wrinkled her perfect nose in reaction. "That's disgusting, Danny," she retorted, though she sounded anything but convincing. "My God, Archer is nearly as old as my father! And he's just being nice. And supportive, which is more than I can say about you! Now, can you please stop invading my privacy and give me my phone back?"

"Fine." He slid it back across the table to her. "Frankly, seeing those messages wasn't all that shocking to me anyway. I knew almost from the beginning that you hadn't really let go of the idea of resuming your acting career. It was why you procrastinated for so long about starting college. And why you haven't gotten serious about finding a permanent job."

"Is that why you're breaking up with me?" she asked in disbelief. "Because I haven't found a damned job?"

"No." He took out his wallet and extracted enough cash to pay for their dinner and leave a generous tip. "I'm breaking up with you because I realized I'm not in love with you any longer. And that I made what might have been the biggest mistake of my life in giving you another chance. Because in doing so I lost the person I was actually in love with."

Katie was shocked speechless by his rather blunt announcement, and could only watch numbly as he got to his feet.

"I'll order a car for you from Uber on my way out," he told her. "It should probably be here in less than five minutes. Take care of yourself, Katie. Who knows? Maybe meeting Archer last week was a stroke of good luck for you. I hope it all works out for you."

And for the second time in the past eleven months, Dante found himself walking out on the woman he'd always sworn had been the one for him. Only this time he knew the truth - that the one he was really meant to be with was Cara. And that he was going to have to do some serious groveling before she'd even agree to talk to him.

25

Cara picked up her pace as she neared the end of the block where she would turn for the bus stop, partly because it was chilly outside this early in the morning, but mostly because she dreaded walking past the infamous corner house that Mirai had warned her about. Just yesterday, in fact, when she'd made her usual Sunday trip to the laundromat, the two creeps who lived in the house had harassed her, calling out lewd, suggestive comments, and even following her a short distance as she'd walked briskly to the bus stop. Unfortunately, there was no other route she could take to the bus stop, at least not one that wouldn't take her several blocks out of the way, so she resolved to not only remain extra aware of her surroundings but to keep her little canister of pepper spray in her coat pocket at all times.

She hated this time of the year, not only because the weather tended to be cold and rainy, but because it was still dark outside when she left for work and darker still when she arrived home late at night from her classes. Most days were so busy at the office that she often didn't go outside for more than a few minutes, if at all, so her exposure to daylight was greatly reduced. Winter was the most depressing time of the year for her as a result, giving her cause to worry at times that she was suffering from Seasonal Affective Disorder.

Classes would be starting up again a week from today, an event that alternately dismayed and thrilled her - the former because it meant the resumption of late nights, weekends spent studying and writing papers, and not having a minute to herself; the latter because this would be the second to the last semester before she completed her studies and earned her degree. *And* the last few months where she would have to scrape together enough money to pay for the ever increasing costs of tuition, books, and fees. And then it would finally be time to start contemplating her future - where she would end up working and living, whether she would elect to remain in the San Francisco area, or perhaps move elsewhere in the country where the cost of living was cheaper.

Nick and Angela had been far too busy preparing for their wedding, and then heading out on their honeymoon, to have discussed the future with her just yet. But Cara would go into such a discussion with an open mind, knowing that she truly enjoyed working with both of them, and that if the terms were right she would probably welcome the opportunity to stay right where she was. Both husband and wife were equally brilliant in terms of their financial acumen, and she knew she could learn a great deal by becoming an official part of their team. Working for them would also allow her to remain in San Francisco, a place she'd gradually come to regard as her home, and where her best friend resided.

But remaining at Morton Sterling would also mean having to encounter Dante at least once a month, perhaps even more frequently if she began to work more closely with Nick and his clients. And that was definitely something she'd have to come to terms with at some point, and find a way to treat him in a professional manner without the past getting in the way.

There had been no further texts or other communication from him since Saturday afternoon when she'd finally replied to him, and Cara still wasn't sure how she felt about his continued silence. She wondered if perhaps she'd been too hard on him, but then she recalled how humiliated she had felt after he'd shoved her up against a wall, kissing and groping her like she was some sort of horny slut, and thought angrily that she'd been *too* easy on him.

But now that the constant barrage of texts had finally stopped, it felt like - well, the end. And while she should have been both happy and relieved, all she felt was sad.

"Hey, baby, whatcha doing out this early? You need a ride somewhere? Cause we can do that. Hot babe like you shouldn't have to take the bus everywhere, not when she's got two guys like me and Joey who'd like nothing better than to show her a good time."

Cara was startled out of her reverie when a car pulled up alongside of her. She was still half a block away from the dreaded corner house, and had planned to cross the street just prior to reaching it. But it seemed like the two creeps - Joey and his unnamed friend - were either heading out very early or arriving home very, very late, and it was her very, very bad luck to have been walking by at the same time their junky, lowrider car was cruising by.

She tried ignoring them, as she'd been doing these past few weeks, continuing to walk at a brisk pace and look anywhere but at them. But then Joey jumped out of the car and directly into her path, and his much larger frame wouldn't allow her to pass.

"Excuse me, I need to get to work," she mumbled, still refusing to meet his gaze. "I'll miss the bus if you don't let me by."

Joey reached out and grasped her by the arm, startling her, and his leering, menacing face was mere inches from hers. "My friend Ricky just told you, babe - we'll give you a ride anywhere you want. And maybe in return you can give us a little ride, hmm? Come on, get in the car."

"No." Desperately Cara tried to yank her arm out of Joey's strong grasp, but only managed to wrench her shoulder in the process, causing her to yelp in pain. "Please leave me alone. I just want to get to the bus stop."

Ricky had double parked the car by now, and joined the two of them on the sidewalk. "Too bad. Cause we're in the mood for some fun. And we've had our eye on you for awhile now. You're just the sort we like - long hair, nice ass, big tits. And Joey and I can show you a real good time, baby. Ever had two guys at once before - one fucking your cunt and the other up your ass?"

Joey reached out and squeezed one of her breasts through her coat, and Cara was so revolted she instinctively kicked him in the shins. She was wearing the new pair of boots she'd bought for herself, the ones with pointy toes, and Joey yelped in pain as the point connected with his lower leg.

"Fucking bitch!" he yelled, as he slammed a fist into her ribs, quickly followed by a vicious blow to her cheekbone.

Cara screamed, doubling over from the pain in her ribs and face, and struggled to remain upright. She felt two pairs of hands now grabbing at her, pulling at her coat and her purse. Desperately she fought to keep hold of her purse, which only earned her another blow to the ribs, this one administered by Ricky's heavy black work boot. The pain was so intense that this time she did drop to her knees, scraping them on the sidewalk as she fell. One of the thugs succeeded in jerking her purse away, and wasted no time in rifling through it.

"Shit!" cursed Joey. "What a piece of crap phone this is, not worth a damn. And can you believe this cunt only has a fucking ten dollar bill in her wallet and no credit cards? What a fucking waste!"

"Guess she'll have to make it up to us in some other way," jeered Ricky, as he began to pull Cara to her feet.

She had trouble drawing in a breath due to the pain in her ribs, and she was willing to bet at least a couple of them were broken. Fighting off the overwhelming dizziness and her desperate fear, she shoved her hand into her coat pocket and pulled out the slim canister of pepper spray. Praying that she was using it correctly, she depressed the nozzle directly in front of her tormentor's face.

From Ricky's screeching and cursing, Cara guessed that she'd hit her target, and took off running, not bothering to look back. But she hadn't gone more than a few steps before a hard body tackled her from behind, slamming her to the ground. The pain from her cracked ribs was so horrific that she passed out just as her head smacked against the sidewalk.

DANTE NODDED at the receptionist as he exited the elevator. "Hey, Anna, how's it going this morning?"

Anna gave him a little wave, preoccupied as she was with answering calls and signing for a delivery from UPS. She knew from his frequent visits to Morton Sterling that it wasn't necessary to call ahead and announce his arrival to Nick and his team, even for an impromptu visit like this one.

And Anna didn't need to know that for once Dante wasn't here to see Nick. Instead, he was hell-bent on seeing a very different employee - one who hadn't answered any of the dozen different texts and emails he'd sent to her so far today.

After breaking things off with Katie last evening, he'd been sorely tempted to drive directly to Cara's and demand that she hear him out. But considering how emotionally exhausted he was after the ordeal with his ex, he'd decided instead to get a decent night's sleep before pleading his case before Cara. God knew he hadn't slept well since Nick's wedding, and he wanted all his wits about him when he pulled out all the stops to try and coax Cara into taking him back.

He'd done as his mother had so wisely advised him, and followed his heart when it came time to make this momentous decision. Dante was both proud and stubborn, and admitting to himself that he'd made a huge mistake in going back to Katie hadn't been an easy task. But he was also man enough to own up to his mistakes and do the right thing when the situation called for it. And after a sleepless night of soul-searching, he'd known exactly what to do next.

He'd left Healdsburg right after lunch with his family yesterday afternoon, calling Katie on the way to ask if she was free for dinner. She'd accepted at once, sounding positively delighted with the idea, little knowing what his purpose was in extending the invitation. His next call had been to the restaurant, an establishment he'd patronized many times before and where he knew the maître d' very well. Snagging both a reservation and the secluded table had been the easiest thing about this whole ordeal.

And of course Katie's ego hadn't allowed her to just let it go without a parting shot or two. Before he'd even reached home, she had sent a barrage of texts, emails, and voice mails, each one more virulent than the next, and all of them filled with insults, recriminations, and half-threats. He'd calmly deleted them all before deftly blocking her number.

He'd had a decent night's sleep, though he had been awake before dawn this morning, mentally rehearsing what exactly he was going to say to Cara - provided, that is, she would even permit him to speak to her. He knew that she was also an early riser, and thus didn't waste any time in texting her first thing. But when she stubbornly didn't respond after so many messages, Dante decided to take the bull by the horns and confront her in person. Ideally, that particular confrontation should have taken place at her apartment after work, but he wasn't sure if she had already resumed her night classes. And since there was no way this conversation was going to wait until ten o'clock tonight, he'd headed over to Nick's office like a man with a purpose - a description that fit him to a tee right about now.

But when he arrived at Cara's desk, he frowned to find her absent. Not only that but her computer was still off, and her desk neat as a pin. Adding further to the confusion, it appeared that both Nick's and Angela's offices were dark, even though he was positive they were due back at work today after their Hawaiian honeymoon.

"Oh, Dante. I - I'm sorry, I didn't realize you had an appointment with Nick today. It's just been such an awful, awful morning! Like a nightmare, really."

He glanced up as Leah appeared by his side, looking both stricken and ever so slightly crazed, and was quick to reassure her. "Hey, take it easy, Leah. Nick doesn't know I was stopping by, it was sort of an impulse. But what's going on here? You look pretty upset."

Leah nodded, and he realized now that she'd been crying earlier. "Oh, God, it's terrible, just terrible, Dante! Poor little thing. Angela was so upset when she got the call, she just ran out of here like the place was on fire. Nick almost didn't catch up with her."

Dante's pulse rate ratcheted up in alarm. "Is something wrong with the baby? Is Angela having a miscarriage or something?"

"No, no," reassured Leah. "Nothing like that. Angela's fine. Well, except for being all upset about Cara, of course. We all are. I just wish one of them would call with an update."

"Whoa." Dante held up a hand. "Slow down there a second, Leah. What about Cara? Did something happen to *Cara*?"

Leah's eyes filled with tears again, and she sniffled loudly. "She - she was mugged or attacked, nobody's exactly sure what, on her way to work this morning. Her friend called Angela from the hospital to tell her. I swear that Nick and Angela had barely walked through the door, hadn't even taken off their coats, when the call came in. Angela didn't know all that much, just that Cara was in the ER, but she promised she'd call with more information. We're still waiting to hear, but I don't want to bother her. Oh, God, poor Cara!"

Dante's heart was racing so fast by now that it was a wonder he could even speak. "Jesus Christ." He ran a hand through his carefully styled hair, not giving a damn what he looked like at the moment. "Do you know what hospital she's at, Leah?"

"What?" Leah was weeping softly, and obviously distracted. "Oh, uh, she's at General. San Francisco General. Why do you ask?"

He gave her a reassuring pat on the shoulder. "I'm going to head over there right away. I'll track down Angela and Nick and find out what's going on."

Leah looked greatly relieved at his announcement. "Oh, thanks, Dante! That's good of you to offer. But can you really spare the time? I mean, I can just try calling Angela to get an update."

Dante didn't bother telling her that nothing and no one could have prevented him from dashing over to the hospital right now to find out what had happened to Cara - the woman he'd likely been in love with for months, but had been too blind to see what was right in front of his eyes until just recently. "I wouldn't have it any other way," he told Leah. "Cara's important to all of us. Look, I'll make sure someone calls you as soon as possible, okay? Take care of yourself."

During his mad dash to the elevator, down to the lobby, and then summoning a taxi, he toyed with the idea of calling Nick to get more information on Cara's condition, then thought better of the idea. Nick would start asking questions, like why Dante was so interested in Cara, and especially why he felt the need to rush over to the hospital to check on her. Dante was going to have some serious explaining to do, but for now the only thing on his mind was getting to Cara as quickly as possible, and finding out what her exact condition was.

'Jesus, please let her be all right,' he prayed silently. He recalled a dozen different prayers he'd learned during his many years at Catholic school, and prayed every one of them during what seemed like an interminably long taxi ride to the hospital. He tried to remain calm, telling himself that getting mugged could mean a lot of things, some more serious than others. And he would have hoped that Leah would have been more specific if something truly horrific had happened to Cara - like being shot or stabbed.

'Don't go there, just don't,' he scolded himself. 'Don't jump to conclusions until you see what's happening for yourself. And, fuck it, why did I have to get the slowest fucking taxi driver in this city? I'm pretty sure I could walk there faster at the rate we're going.'

When the driver finally pulled up outside of the hospital entrance, Dante all but shoved the fare in his hand, not waiting for change, and jogged inside. He made three wrong turns before he found the ER, and once inside the area found it to be total and utter chaos. Fortunately, it was hard to miss someone as tall as Nick, so Dante was able to locate him and Angela fairly quickly.

The newly married couple glanced up in surprise as he approached, though he could swear the look on Angela's face told him she knew exactly why he was here. But he was far too worried about Cara to wonder if and when she'd confided in her boss about her past relationship with him.

"How is she? I went by the office and Leah told me what had happened," he explained in a rush. "But she didn't have any details so I headed over here to get the most updated information. What the hell happened?"

Nick's scowl was terrifying to behold. "Two punks accosted her on the way to her bus stop this morning. Tried to rob her, I guess, but aside from her phone being all busted up her friend didn't think they actually took anything. One of the neighbors heard some commotion, called 911, and an ambulance and the cops arrived less than a minute later. The punks ran off, but they live in the neighborhood, so I'm guessing they'll get picked up sooner than later. Unless I find them first, that is."

"Stop it." Angela held up a hand in protest. "Nick, stop talking like that, please? It's not helping Cara. Or me, for that matter."

"Sorry, Angel." Nick slid an arm around her shoulders and pressed a kiss to her temple. "I'm just so fucking furious right now that I really, really need to hit something. Like those two fuckers who did this to her. Or her total loser of a father who hasn't even bothered to return any of my messages. What a fucking loser that asshole is, huh?"

The woman who'd been sitting on the other side of Angela suddenly vacated her chair, and Dante immediately slid into it. He placed a hand on Angela's forearm, calling her attention his way.

"How is she?" he asked urgently. "What exactly is wrong with her? Jesus, they didn't - you know - "

"Rape her?" finished Angela in hushed tones. She shook her head. "No, it doesn't appear that way. But she does have a concussion, bruises and scrapes all over, and they think two or three cracked ribs. She's having some x-rays done right now so they can determine that. They'll probably be admitting her after that."

"Christ." Dante ran a hand over his face, forcing himself to take several deep, calming breaths. He now knew exactly how Nick felt, because his own fists were practically itching with the need to punch someone, to inflict serious bodily harm on the punks responsible for what had happened to Cara - his sweet, vulnerable little Cara, who'd never hurt anyone in her life. She'd suffered through far too much for someone so young, and this morning's vicious attack was beyond reprehensible.

"Leah mumbled something about a friend of Cara's calling you?" prodded Dante.

Angela nodded. Her hands were trembling a little, even clasped tightly in her lap, until Nick took them between his own to still their shaking. "Yes, her best friend from college. Mirai. She was listed as Cara's emergency contact on her insurance, and dashed right over here the minute she got the call. Nick and I had barely walked into the office when Mirai got ahold of me, and we came right over. But she's left now, said something about it being her first day of classes, and that Cara would be furious if she missed attending. She'll be back later today."

"Okay." Dante exhaled sharply. "And what's this about her asshat father not having called back? What the fuck is wrong with that SOB anyway?"

Nick frowned, his dark brows furrowing together. "How do you know so much about Cara's father?" he asked sharply. "And tell us again exactly why you felt the need to rush over here? I mean, I guess it's nice of you to be so concerned about one of our employees, but a phone call would have probably sufficed."

Dante hesitated, not sure if he really wanted to further provoke a pissed-off Nick right now. But before he could think up a believable response, Angela saved him the trouble - even while she opened up a giant can of worms in the process.

"He's here because he and Cara were seeing each other for a while last summer," she stated bluntly. "And I'm guessing he feels guilty about breaking up with her so he could get back together with Katie. Does that about sum it up, Dante?"

Angela was glaring at him now, but he'd rather face a dozen angry Angelas than a seriously enraged Nick. And there was zero question that his best friend was good and mad at this moment - at the punks who'd attacked Cara, at her useless father, and now at Dante. Unfortunately for him, he was the only one within striking range at this exact moment.

"You fucker," hissed Nick, starting to rise to his feet. "I cannot fucking believe you had the balls to mess around with that - that little girl. She's a kid, Dan, just a kid! And I lost count years ago of how many women you've had. What the hell were you thinking of?"

His voice had become louder and more forceful with each word that rumbled from his chest, and several other people in the waiting room began to turn and regard him with concern.

Angela tugged urgently at his suit jacket. "Sit down!" she demanded. "Right now. I'm going to tell both of you this just once, so listen up. You two are *not* going to get into this right now, understand? The waiting room of an ER is not where you get to hash all of this out. So knock it off, and let's focus on the real reason we're all here - Cara."

Nick took his seat reluctantly, though the expression on his face was nothing short of murderous. Both men glared at each other for several minutes, with Angela unfortunately being stuck in the middle and thrust into the unwilling role of peacemaker.

Dante was the one to break the uncomfortable silence first, grudgingly admitting to himself that he owed Nick and Angela an explanation. "I never meant for things to go that far between us," he muttered. "I was just going to take her out to dinner the one time, because it was her birthday, and I was trying to do something nice for her. That was going to be it. But, well..."

Nick rolled his eyes. "But old Casanova here couldn't resist laying on the charm and getting another notch in his bedpost."

"No." Dante shook his head emphatically. "It was never like that with Cara, not at all. Hey, I'm not a complete bastard, Nick. Not like you were. I mean, before you met Angela, at least," he amended hastily.

Angela gave him a tight smile. "It's okay. I already knew what an asshole he was. Fortunately, that's all different now or I would never have agreed to marry him, baby or no baby."

Nick cuffed her playfully on the chin. "What can I say, Angel. I'm a changed man thanks to you, that's the honest truth. But at least I did the right thing by you eventually - which is more than I can say for Dante."

Dante winced at the accusatory tone of his best friend's voice. "You're right. I was a first class jerk. But without getting into all the private details of our relationship, I will tell you that Cara knew exactly what to expect between us. She'd be the first one to tell you that I never lied to her, never led her on. And when things ended between us, I tried to be as sensitive about it as possible, even though I know it hurt her a lot."

Nick scoffed. "Well, of course it did, asshole. She's just a kid, a babe in the woods compared to your other women. Compared to Katie. Speaking of which, how do you have the balls to be here pretending to care about Cara when you're still involved with another woman?"

"I'm not," assured Dante. "Involved with Katie, that is. As of last night officially. Things haven't been the same between us since we got back together, and I've been seeing a whole different side of her this time around. Or I guess I just never wanted to notice it before since I was so blinded by her."

Nick and Angela exchanged a look before he grinned at Dante. "What you really meant to say was that you were too dumb to notice it last time around," corrected Nick. "See, if you had gone to Stanford like Angela and I did, you would have had a real education and been smarter about stuff like that."

"Hah, hah." Dante wasn't about to debate the merits of their respective colleges, given that it would be two against one. "Book smarts don't always equate to good old-fashioned common sense. Or listening to the advice your mother always gave you."

Angela snorted. "Maybe *your* mother gave you good advice. Nick and I can't say the same for ours. But why break up with Katie now? Did you two have a fight or something?"

"No. At least not until I told her it was over between us. Then she didn't hold anything back, let loose with a string of insults that made my ears burn. I'm guessing Nick hasn't heard some of the stuff she was flinging at me, even after spending all those years in NFL locker rooms. As for the timing of it all - I guess you could say the catalyst was seeing Cara at your wedding cozying up to her date. It sort of brought out the caveman in me, made me realize that I had real feelings for her. So I'm going to try and make it right between us now. If she'll even agree to hear what I have to say that is. She's pretty pissed off at me for some things I said to her at your wedding," admitted Dante reluctantly.

"Hmm," remarked Angela thoughtfully. "You know, I'm not even going to ask what you did to make her mad. But since Cara's the nicest person I've ever known, it must have been something pretty rotten."

Nick didn't seem particularly happy even after Dante's humble confession. "Listen up, buddy, and mark my words," he warned, waggling a finger at Dante. "If you break that little girl's heart again, I will make you regret you were ever born. Got it? I'm still so pissed about the fact that you got involved with her in the first place, and then made the bonehead move of the century by leaving her for that airhead Katie. So you'd better fucking make it right between the two of you again, or you'll have to answer to me. And speaking of answering to me, what the *hell* is wrong with that loser father of hers? What sort of man gets a phone call - six of them, to be exact - saying that his daughter was mugged and taken to the ER and doesn't immediately call back?"

Dante was about to offer up his own unfavorable opinion of Mark Bregante when a slim African-American woman dressed in hospital scrubs walked over to where the three of them were sitting.

"You're here for Cara Bregante, right?" she inquired of Angela. "I think the nurse said you work with Cara."

Angela nodded. "Yes, she works for my husband and me. Do you have an update on her condition?"

The woman, whose name badge read Rachel Selby M.D. - and who looked far too young to be an actual doctor in Dante's opinion - nodded. "She's being transferred to a patient room now, and we'll be keeping her at least overnight. The CT scan we did of her head shows a definite concussion, but as long as she gets plenty of rest that should resolve itself over the next few days. We also did X-rays which determined she has two cracked ribs. Unfortunately, aside from wrapping them and giving her regular doses of pain medication, those will have to heal on their own. Aside from that, she's got a number of bruises and scrapes, and I'm sure it will take her some time to get over the trauma of the attack. She's been in and out of consciousness, though most of that is because she's sleepy from the pain meds. But she was able to give a statement to the police officers earlier and seemed pretty lucid. Even recalled that she was able to zap one of the jerks who did this to her with pepper spray. Physically, she'll be fine after some rest and just letting everything heal up."

"Can we see her now?" asked Angela, already getting to her feet.

Doctor Selby glanced at the two men who flanked Angela, then back at her. "Not all of you at once," she cautioned. "One, maybe two at a time, and then just for a few minutes each. She really needs to rest right now, that's going to be the best thing for her. And don't let her talk much, as even that can make the pain in her ribs worse. She's in Room 424, but wait about ten more minutes before heading up there to make sure she's all settled in. I'll be in to check on her during afternoon rounds, and we'll determine tomorrow morning if she's ready to be discharged. Does she have anyone living at home with her? Between the concussion and the ribs, she won't be able to stay on her own for at least a week."

"She lives alone but she can stay with - " began Angela.

"With me," interrupted Dante. "She can stay at my place. I can arrange to work from home for as long as I need to and look after her."

Angela looked dubious at this impulsive announcement. "Dante, honestly, I'm not sure that's the best idea. Nick and I have plenty of room, and she might feel more at ease with us."

Dante shook his head firmly. "The two of you just got back from your honeymoon yesterday, and the last thing you need now is a houseguest. Besides, you need to take care of yourself, Angela, and that baby. Cara's going to stay with me."

The doctor shrugged. "Look, I'll leave the three of you to figure out the details. Or let's have Cara decide what she wants to do. So long as she's not alone, then it's really up to her where she winds up. I've got to dash off now to see another patient, but one of the nurses can call me if something comes up."

She hurried off then, leaving Dante to face a scowling Nick and an anything but convinced Angela.

"What makes you think that she'd *want* to stay with you if she's that pissed off?" asked Angela calmly.

Dante sighed. "Guess I'll have to convince her otherwise, huh? But if she'd rather stay with you, I won't fight her on it. So now that that decision's been made, how do we determine who gets to see her first?"

Nick and Angela exchanged a look, and he merely shrugged, silently leaving the decision up to her. She sighed, throwing up her hands in surrender.

"I'm too tired to argue with you, Dante. You can go in and see her first. But if she doesn't want to see you, or you start upsetting her, forget about Nick kicking your ass, because it will be *my* foot doing the job," she threatened.

Dante squeezed her hand. "If she really doesn't want to see me, I promise I'll leave immediately," he assured her gently. "Let's head on up, shall we?"

Despite Doctor Selby's assurances that Cara would be all right after resting up and recovering for a few days, Dante felt like he'd just taken a blow to the gut when he saw her for the first time. She looked so tiny and fragile in the stark white hospital bed, an IV tube in her arm, and hooked up to a monitor of some sort. Her face was ghostly pale, save for the bruises that had already begun to darken her jaw and cheekbone. Small bandages covered the scrapes on her forehead and left forearm, and he guessed angrily that there were more scrapes and bruises hidden beneath the hospital gown she wore and the blankets that covered her body. The rage he felt at seeing her this way - bruised, bandaged, helpless - made him want to kick a hole into the wall, or throw the first heavy object he could find through a window. But he knew that violence and anger weren't going to help Cara at this moment, so he took a few deep, calming breaths before murmuring, "Hi."

Cara blinked sleepily, raising one eyelid to peer up at him as he stood by the side of her bed. Even as doped up as she so obviously was, though, she seemed startled to see him.

"Dante." Her voice was barely audible, not much more than a

hoarse whisper. "What – did - did Angela call you? Is that why you're here?"

"No." He pulled the guest chair up to the side of the bed, getting as close to her as he possibly could. Careful not to interfere with the various tubes and wires, he placed a hand gently on her shoulder. "Leah was the one who told me you were here. I went by the office this morning, determined to see you since you weren't replying to my texts. I had something important to tell you, really important, and when you weren't answering me, I realized it was going to have to be face to face. I figured you were still mad at me, and that's why you weren't answering my messages. But this - Jesus, Cara. This is the very last thing I expected."

She nodded, her eyes closing tiredly. "Yeah, me, too. So much of it is still fuzzy to me right now. And - and it hurts to talk, to breathe. My ribs…"

Dante caressed her cheek tenderly. "Yeah, a couple of them are busted up, I'm afraid. And coming from someone who's had their fair share of injuries from all those years of playing soccer, I can unfortunately tell you that it's going to hurt like a bitch for a few weeks. Which is one of the reasons you need to take it easy and let someone look after you. Why you're going to come stay at my place and let me be that someone."

"What?" she asked incredulously, her head lifting up off the pillow in surprise. "Oh, ow!"

He grimaced as she clutched her ribcage. "Hey, take it easy, honey. Shh, just lay back and rest, okay? Guess I shouldn't have sprung that on you without warning. But your doctor said you can't be alone for the next week or so between the concussion and those ribs. And since I absolutely refuse to ever use that futon of yours again, you're staying with me. In a very large, very comfortable king sized bed that doesn't have to be folded out every night."

Cara gazed up at him in bewilderment. "Um, I know I'm spaced out big time on meds right now, but aren't you forgetting something here? Namely, your girlfriend? Remember her?"

Dante took her hand in his, the one that didn't have an IV needle inserted in it. "Wish I could forget her, actually," he admitted. "And I really, really wish I hadn't let myself believe that she had changed, or that things would just go back to the way they'd been between us before she broke up with me. Speaking of break-ups, Katie and I are officially over as of last night. Done. *Finito*. For good this time."

She gave his hand a tiny squeeze. "I'm sorry. Actually, I'm really not, but I'm sorry if you feel badly about it."

He guffawed. "That's one of the things I love the most about you, Cara *mia*. You're always honest, always say what's on your mind, and never pretend. And I'm handling it just fine, thanks."

Despite her drowsiness, her eyes widened in shock. "Did - did you - what did you just say? That first part, I mean."

Dante bent forward to press a little kiss to the tip of her nose, just about the only place on her beautiful face that wasn't bruised or scraped to some degree. "Oh, you mean the part about how I love you? Oops, guess I sort of sprung that one on you, too, didn't I? Yeah, it's true. I'm crazy about you, Cara, and I think I have been from the start. And if I hadn't been so stubborn, and so messed up over what had happened with Katie, I would have realized it a long time ago. And I don't expect you to forgive me that easily, or agree to give me another chance, but I swear to you, Cara, that if you do I'll do everything in my power to make it all up to you. And the very first thing I'm going to do - well, once you're all recovered and up for the ride - is to take you to meet my mother. I told her about you, you know."

Tears were glistening on her eyelashes, and he brushed them away with his thumb. "You did?" she asked in disbelief. "When?"

"Saturday. And you know what? I should have asked my mom's advice a long time ago, should have brought you to meet her last summer. Because she would have told me the same thing then that she told me two days ago - when in doubt, follow my heart. And when I finally did, it told me what I think I knew all along - that I should have picked you, Cara. That you were the one who made me truly happy, the one I belonged with. So if you could possibly find a way to forgive me even a little, I promise to make everything up to you."

Cara gave a brief shake of her head, wincing as even that tiny movement caused her pain. "You already have," she whispered. "The moment you told me you loved me nothing else mattered. I love you, Dante. I have from the very beginning, even though I wasn't supposed to."

He pressed a soft kiss to her lips, then grinned as she promptly fell back asleep.

"SO WHAT YOU'RE telling me is that you'd rather take your trophy wife on some little getaway to celebrate her birthday instead of flying out here to see your daughter who was viciously attacked earlier today? Wow, you know, when Cara told me about you, Mark, I thought maybe she might have been exaggerating a little. After talking to you for five minutes, though, I see it was just the opposite - she couldn't begin to describe what a total waste of space you really are."

On the other end of the line Mark Bregante sputtered and stammered angrily. "Now listen here, Dante - whoever the hell you are. You don't know shit about my life, or about my relationship with Cara. So don't start passing judgment about things you don't understand."

"Oh, I understand plenty, Mark," replied Dante testily. "I understand that you more or less abandoned your daughter so you could play happy family with your new wife and kids. I understand that you cut Cara off without a cent or any warning, and used the money that you promised your first wife - on her fucking *deathbed* - would be spent on Cara's college education on your spoiled, selfish wife instead. And I *totally* understand that you sure as hell don't deserve a daughter like Cara. Now all I have to do is figure out a way to break it to her gently that her own father doesn't care enough about her to fly out and see for himself how she's doing after getting punched and kicked and traumatized. Then again, she might not be all that surprised."

There was silence on the other end for long seconds, before Mark spoke again, his voice sullen. "It's just not that easy," he argued. "Holly and I made these plans months ago, and she'd be devastated if we had to cancel or postpone them. Not to mention the airfare and hotel are non-refundable, and I just can't afford to lose that sort of money."

"Tell you what," offered Dante. "I'm a rich guy. Why don't you tell me how much your little vacation is costing you and I'll wire the money to your bank account? And on top of that I'll pay for you to fly out here to San Francisco to see Cara, put you up in a hotel for a few days, the works."

"Why the hell would you be willing to do all that?" asked Mark in disbelief. "You don't even know me, haven't even spoken to me until just now."

"Because it would mean a lot to Cara to have her father here by her side right now," answered Dante. "And making your daughter happy is my number one priority right now. So do we have a deal?"

There was another long pause before Mark told him, "I can't. I'm sorry, I don't expect you to understand, and you can think the worst of me, though it sounds like you already do. But I love my wife and making her happy is *my* top priority. And even if I re-scheduled this vacation for next week or next month, Holly wouldn't understand. She - well, I'm afraid she's always been jealous about Cara. And if I chose Cara over her, there'd be hell to pay from here until eternity. Look, I'll call Cara tonight, I swear it. I'll explain things to her, maybe arrange to fly out there next month sometime."

"No, you won't," Dante told him sternly. "First of all, her cell phone was damaged when she was attacked, and isn't functional any longer. And second, I'm not going to permit you to upset her when she's already in such bad shape. You've apparently made your choice, Mark, and now there's going to be hell to pay for you in a very different way. Because my advice to Cara is going to be to forget she even has a father. She has me now, and I'm more than happy to take care of her, something you've been a complete failure at."

He disconnected the call then, so enraged that he didn't dare remain on the line a second longer for fear that he'd say something *really* vile to Cara's father.

"Here's your phone," he told Nick, holding it at arm's distance.

"Better take it from me quick, otherwise I'm liable to hurl it against that wall right over there."

Nick somewhat gingerly removed his very expensive phone from Dante's outstretched palm. "That bad, huh?"

"Worse. Can you even believe someone as nice as Cara has such a total dickwad for a father? Wait until I tell you what he said."

When Mark had finally returned one of Nick's multiple messages, Dante had demanded to speak to him instead, figuring that he had a better chance of keeping his temper under check than the fiery Nick. But that was before he'd realized just how small of a man Mark Bregante really was.

Nick shook his head as he listened to the details of Dante's conversation with Cara's father. "Unbelievable. You know, as much of a tool as my own dad was, even he would have flown out on the next plane to see me if I had wound up in the hospital. And when Angela had that accident a year and a half ago, her parents and her sisters drove up to see her. Admittedly, her father was the only one of the bunch who was actually worried about her, but be grateful for small favors, I guess."

Angela walked over to them then, looking elated and exhausted at the same time. "You guys won't believe this one," she said, giving her head a little shake. "I just got off the phone with the police officer in charge of Cara's case, who told me they've already apprehended the thugs who attacked her. And you will not believe where they caught up with the idiots."

"Don't tell me," drawled Nick. "They were stupid enough to go back to where they were living, even though the neighbor who called 911 had already told the police what house it was."

"Stupider than that," corrected Angela. "Dumb and Dumber walked into the ER at this very hospital a little while ago so the one that Cara pepper sprayed could get treatment. Apparently she got him real good, and none of the home remedies they tried were working. Of course the ER staff was on the lookout for anyone coming in who'd been sprayed, so they called the police right away. Dumb and

Dumber are officially in custody as we speak, being booked at the county jail."

"Good news," replied Dante. "Real good news. Now, you two should head home. At least Angela should. You need to take care of yourself, especially since Cara won't be able to come in for at least a week, maybe longer."

"No." She shook her head stubbornly. "We've both got way too much work to get caught up on right now. I'll be all right, just need some food and coffee. But if you don't mind, Dante, we probably should get back to the office now."

"I don't mind at all," he told her. "My schedule is clear for the day, and I've already told Howie I'll be mostly working at home this week. I'll stay here with Cara, maybe duck out and get some lunch for a few minutes when her friend returns. Otherwise, I plan to be here until they boot me out."

Angela gave him a brief but fierce little hug. "Maybe I won't have to kick your ass after all," she joked. "You know, as awful as Cara looked when I went in to see her, she was also happier than she's been in months. Maybe you do deserve her."

"I'm going to do my damndest to convince everyone of that," he assured her. "Look, I'll call you later to update you on her condition, okay? You just make sure to take care of yourself and that baby."

Nick slid an arm around his wife's still-slender waist. "She will," he said arrogantly. "Be sure to call us, Dan. And take good care of Cara for us."

Dante waited until they were out of sight before extracting his own phone from inside his suit jacket. He scrolled through the list of contacts until he found the one he was searching for, an old high school buddy that he admittedly hadn't kept in very close contact with as of late. But he knew that Carlos wouldn't mind, and moreover that his old friend would be more than happy to accommodate his request.

"Carlos? Hey, que pasa, man? Yeah, I know. Go ahead and chew my ass out. Yeah, I know it's been over a year since I called you last. Tell you what, let's make sure to get together for dinner soon so I can introduce you to my new girlfriend. No, not the sexy blonde, that ended up being a big mistake. But listen, I've got a little favor to ask you, buddy."

Carlos had worked for the San Francisco Sheriff's Department for a decade now, and was fairly high up in the rankings from Dante's recollection. And while Carlos didn't work directly at the county jail, he definitely knew people who did, people who wouldn't hesitate to help him out.

Briefly, Dante told his friend about what had happened to Cara, and that the two thugs who'd mugged her had just been taken into custody.

"Which in a way is kind of a shame, because my friend Nick and I - yeah, the football player - would have liked to get our hands on the little punks first. I don't suppose you could maybe ask some of the officers there at the jail to, uh, make life something of a living hell for those thugs, could you? Ah, now that's what I like to hear, Carlos. You're a good buddy, you know? And dinner will be on me for sure, you pick whatever place you like. All right, it's a deal. I'll call you in about a week. Thanks."

Dante was grinning from ear to ear as he ended the call. Under normal circumstances, he wasn't one to condone violence. But every time the image of a bruised and battered Cara came to mind, he had to fight off the urge to hit something. And while what he'd told Carlos was true - that it would have been so much more satisfying to dole out the punishment to those muggers with his own two fists - at least he would have the satisfaction of knowing that they'd be pushed around mightily by the guards at the jail.

Whether it was telling off her loser father, or making sure the creeps who'd attacked her got what was coming to them, Dante vowed that he would do whatever it took from here on end to look after Cara. And to make sure no one ever had the chance to hurt her again.

"Hey. What exactly are you doing? You're not supposed to be exerting yourself. And by my set of rules, cooking dinner is definitely exerting yourself."

Cara wrinkled her nose as Dante all but stormed inside his kitchen. "Honestly? All I'm doing is heating up the soup you brought home from Whole Foods yesterday. And slicing the bread."

He sniffed the air suspiciously. "I smell something besides vegetable soup and sourdough bread."

She flicked her fingers in the direction of the microwave. "That would be the fully cooked rotisserie chicken you also brought home being warmed up. But if you think it's too physically demanding for me, I'll let you carve it when it's done."

Dante gave her a playful swat on the butt. "Smart-ass. If your sassy mouth is anything to go by, then you're feeling a whole lot better."

Cara laughed and looped her arms around his necking, standing on her bare tiptoes to reach his mouth and plant a smacking kiss on his lips. "I *am* feeling better. I've been trying to tell you that for the last two days, but you still insist on treating me like an invalid. Oh, and by the way, I'm going back to work on Monday *and* starting my classes that night. And short of tying me up there's no way you're going to keep me from doing either of those things."

He gave her a lecherous grin. "Hmm, I'll have to give that one some thought. I mean, given that you're still recuperating from those cracked ribs, I guess some light bondage wouldn't be very considerate of me, would it? But seriously, Cara, if you're intent on going back to work and school in two more days, it's going to have to be on *my* terms, not yours. Otherwise, sore ribs or not I'll find a way to restrain you. Okay?"

She sighed dramatically, turning the gas burner down to low as the soup began to bubble up. "What are these so-called terms of yours exactly?"

"First off," he began, holding up his index finger, "starting Monday morning I drive you to and from the office, *and* to and from your classes. That is not negotiable, Cara. In fact, you might as well turn in your bus pass because you aren't going to be using it again. Until you get your driver's license renewed, I'll either drive you where you need to go or you'll use Uber or Lyft. That is also non-negotiable. Following me so far?"

Cara scowled, not really sure she was liking this bossy, dominant side of him. "Yes. Not liking what I hear, but I'm listening at least. Go on."

"Next, you're going to move in here with me permanently. As in bag and baggage. Except of course for that crappy futon, which I never, ever want to lay eyes on again. Maybe some homeless person will take it off your hands. When is your lease up at that little box you just think is an apartment?" he asked.

She held up a hand in protest. "Hey, do I get any say in any of this? Did you even ask my opinion about whether I wanted to live with you full time?"

Dante smirked. "Come on, Cara. Can you seriously admit that you don't like it here a whole lot better? And look, I even have a real stove you can cook on."

She gave him a shove, wincing when her still-sore ribs protested with the effort. "That's not fair," she whined. "And don't think I haven't noticed that you've been deliberately tempting me all week, pointing out how nice this place is, how much space there is, how much safer it is, blah, blah, blah."

He placed his hands on her shoulders, gazing down at her mischievously. "Ah, but you forgot to mention the biggest attraction about moving in here - me. Waking up next to me, showering together, taking turns fixing breakfast for each other. After work we'd have a quick dinner before you went to class. And then comes the best part of the day."

Cara had felt her resolve weakening with each deliberately seductive word that had come out of his sinfully handsome mouth. He was very intentionally wooing her right now, doing his utmost to persuade her into agreeing to his suggestion. "And what would that be?"

Dante cupped her cheeks between his palms, holding her head still as he kissed her, his tongue making slow, sensual sweeps through her mouth. She was gasping for breath by the time he finally lifted his head, his forefinger brushing over her swollen lips.

"The time of the day when I'd undress you very, very slowly," he murmured huskily, his hand sliding down her arm until it cupped her breast. His thumb rubbed the already erect nipple through her ribbed sweater. "Next I'd spread you out on my bed - correction, *our* bed - and take my time with you. Mmm, I'd touch and kiss and adore you from head to toe and then back up again. I'd worship this beautiful little body of yours all over, every single inch. And then I'd make you come two or three times for starters, with my fingers and my tongue, just to get you ready for me. Because then I'd want to fuck you for a really long time, until you fell asleep from exhaustion. But I'd be considerate and let you sleep for a little while, only to wake you up in the middle of the night because I'd want you again."

Her breathing had turned positively shallow by then, an action made that much more difficult by her cracked ribs, and she thought for a few seconds that she might just pass out from lack of oxygen. Her cheeks were flushed - correction, her whole *body* felt hot, every pulse point racing madly. The sexy, knowing smile on Dante's devilishly handsome face made her knees grow weak, and she absentmindedly clutched the granite counter just behind her for support.

"You really do play dirty, don't you?" she said accusingly, but it was a half-hearted accusation at best. "And it's not very nice of you to get me all hot and bothered when you know we can't do anything about it for a few more days."

"I could take care of you, honey," he murmured, sliding his hand down over her belly until he was cupping her between the thighs. "Of course, you'd need to keep very, very still so that you didn't make the pain in your ribs any worse, and I'm not sure you're capable of that. And since the last thing I'd want to do is cause you even a second of pain, guess we'll have to wait on this a little while longer."

He grinned evilly as he removed his hand and stepped away, then yelped as she snapped a dishtowel at him, connecting with his upper thigh.

"You're going to pay for that, mister," she threatened. "Starting with tonight."

Dante's grin widened. "Oh, yeah? What sort of revenge are you plotting?"

Cara smiled serenely just as the microwave pinged. "Well, you can start with cutting up the chicken as we've already discussed. And then after dinner you can do the dishes."

He smirked as he took the chicken out of the microwave. "Hate to break the news, honey, but I was planning on doing that anyway."

She patted him on the butt as she passed by on her way to the dining area. "Oh, that's just for starters. You'll have to wait until I'm all healed up before I exact the next phase of my revenge. Let's just say I might be tempted to leave you, uh, hanging. After all, turnabout is fair play, isn't it?"

Dante glowered at her in mock-severity. "Lucky for you that you're still indisposed. Otherwise I'd be showing you just how *unfairly* I can play."

Cara blew him a saucy kiss. "Raincheck?"

He winked at her in return. "That goes without saying. Now, let me get to work here, hmm? And no, you are not lifting another finger this evening. Keep your cute little ass where it is and let me pamper you, okay?"

"You've been pampering me for days now, Dante," she reminded him. "A girl could get used to this real quick."

Pampering didn't begin to describe the way he'd been taking care of her these past six days. She could also include words like coddling, spoiling, indulging, and fussing, and that still wouldn't go far enough.

It had begun on Tuesday morning when she'd been declared well enough to be discharged from the hospital. Unbeknownst to her, Dante had taken care of the bill, paying it off in full, as well as paying for her prescription pain medication. And even though he owned a dozen luxury vehicles, he'd hired a town car to pick them up from the hospital and take them to his condo, so that he could tend to her during the relatively short drive.

From the outside, his condo building had looked older, less modern, than most of the others in the immediate neighborhood. But as he'd wheeled her inside the high-ceilinged, marble floored lobby - Dante had insisted on renting a wheelchair even though she'd protested that she would rather walk - Cara had realized that the building had oodles of charm and character, something more modern structures seemed to lack.

His penthouse was spacious and open, with floor to ceiling windows that let in natural light even in the middle of January. And while there were many modern touches - like the huge kitchen that boasted every appliance and gadget a cook could ever dream of, and the bathroom with its huge tiled shower and heated floors that was bigger than her entire apartment - Dante's condo also had gorgeous crown molding, original hardwood floors of polished oak, and a window seat in the master bedroom that Cara knew could quickly become her favorite spot in the whole place.

He'd taken care in decorating the rooms, too, and she knew without having to ask that he had chosen most of the furniture and other items himself, instead of hiring a professional to do it for him. There were framed photographs of his family on nearly every surface, and Cara felt instantly at home in these elegant but comfortable environs.

Dante had been true to his word, too, about working from home, making use of the office he'd set up at the condo to call clients, send emails, and even participate in meetings via Skype. He'd tucked her into his enormous king-sized bed, where she could watch TV or read the dozens of e-books he had already loaded onto the brand new tablet computer he'd surprised her with - a "welcome home" gift, he had called it.

And somehow, in between spending the better part of the day at the hospital on Monday, and picking her up the next morning, Dante had found time to do quite a bit of shopping – buying all sorts of pre-prepared foods and snacks, an assortment of toiletries that she might need, and several sets of loungewear and lingerie. And when Mirai had popped in after school to visit with her for awhile, Dante had headed over to Cara's apartment to pick up her laptop and some other clothes and things she needed.

Mirai, of course, had been completely bowled over by the size and elegance of his condo, insisting to Cara that the place had to be worth well over five million, given its prime location. During Dante's absence, Mirai had poked around a little, oohing and ahhing over the high quality of nearly everything in the place - from the latest model flat screen TV, to the contents of his wine refrigerator, to the plush towels in each of the three bathrooms.

"He's loaded," she'd told Cara rather matter-of-factly. "I mean, really loaded. Probably way more than even my father. You landed yourself a big fish, girl."

Cara had fidgeted a little on the sectional sofa where she'd insisted on moving after lunch. "I don't care about how much money he has, Mir," she'd replied quietly. "If he was as poor as I was, and we had to live in my little apartment and take the bus everywhere, I'd still be as much in love with him."

Mirai had grinned. "Well, duh. That's because he's also a hottie. Like a scorching hot, triple digit hottie. And not only is he gorgeous and hunky, but he's nice, too. Sure seems like he's going way out of his way to make everything up to you."

"Hmm." Cara had regarded her BFF dubiously. "What happened to the part about telling him to go fuck himself? As I recall, you advised me to do just that about three times a day after he broke up with me."

"All is forgiven now," Mirai had said cheerfully. "I mean, you just cannot stay mad at a guy who buys you an entire black and white cake from Whole Foods, now can you? How did he know this was my favorite?"

"He didn't," Cara had retorted, watching as Mirai shoved a whole forkful of cake into her mouth. "I'm pretty sure he bought it for me. Luckily it's a big cake, and there's no way I can eat the whole thing."

"Hey, I was starving," Mirai had protested. "I rushed over here the minute my classes were over with so I could check up on you, and didn't stop for lunch first."

"I'm joking, Mir," she'd assured. "Besides, these pain meds I'm taking tend to make me a little queasy, so I'm not eating much right now. And you've done so much for me that even if I gave you a dozen black and white cakes it wouldn't even begin to repay you. So eat up."

"Really?" Mirai had brightened. "Were those fresh crab cakes I saw in the fridge? And a container of those Thai noodles I love?"

Cara had laughed, still wondering how her thin as a rail friend could possibly pack away so much food without also packing on the pounds. "Help yourself. Though one usually has the entree before the dessert."

Mirai had forked off another bite of cake. "No worries. I'm pretty sure I also saw a peach cobbler in there somewhere."

Over the last day or so, Cara had begun to wean herself off the strong prescription pain meds, not liking the way they made her so sleepy as well as nauseous, and was now using an over the counter product instead. The resulting dizziness from the concussion had more or less gone away, and while the pain in her ribs continued to throb pretty much consistently, it was a duller, more manageable ache now. She was taking fewer naps, and forcing herself to move around the condo at regular intervals, trying to get her strength back. It would probably be a few weeks yet before she could resume her normal exercise routine, but she was determined to remain as mobile as possible until then.

And while Dante watched her like a hawk to make sure she didn't overdo, he hadn't stopped her from exploring around the condo at her leisure. She had looked through every cupboard and drawer in his huge, well-equipped kitchen, and was already planning out what she would cook for him once she had recuperated a bit more. The kitchen was every aspiring chef's dream, and she wondered if he had bought all of the gadgets and tools himself.

He shook his head at the question. "Not everything, no. I made the mistake of taking my grandmother with me to the kitchen supply store when I first moved into this place, and she filled the basket with stuff I didn't even know existed. I doubt I've used even a third of the things we bought. So feel free to experiment to your heart's content, honey. Maybe you'll know what to do with a mandoline or a pair of herb scissors. And I swear I have no idea why anyone would ever need an apple slicer. What's wrong with just using a knife?"

She giggled at the look of disgust on his face. "I promise I'll actually get use out of all those things. That is, if you'll ever allow me to lift anything heavier than a soup spoon. And since I'm not taking those prescription painkillers any longer, don't you think I could have a glass of wine?"

"Hmm. I guess so. Just half, though. Those meds could still be in your system, and you know how sick they made you the first few days."

He snagged a wine glass for her, the ones Mirai had blithely declared cost at least a hundred bucks apiece, and poured a careful measure of pinot noir inside. Cara took a deep, appreciative sniff of the wine before sipping it slowly.

"Mmm. That's delicious. But you're right, I'd better stick to half a glass. After all, not only are you feeding me all of this incredible food, but I haven't been able to exercise for almost a week. All that weight I worked so hard to lose is going to creep back on awfully fast at this rate," she lamented.

"Good," retorted Dante. "You're too thin right now. And maybe you were right about dropping a few pounds, but you went way overboard, Cara. We need to fatten you up a little."

"No." She shook her head stubbornly. "You have no idea how hard

I worked to take those pounds off, Dante. And while I don't intend to lose any more, I'd also like to maintain my current weight. I'm nowhere near being skinny, you know. And my ass is still too big."

He waggled a finger at her. "Your ass is perfect," he corrected. "Just like the rest of you. So while I won't bug you to put weight on, I'd also be ticked off if you lost anymore. After all, the last thing you'll want to happen when you meet my grandmother next weekend is for her to call you *la ragazza magra.*"

Cara's brow knitted together in confusion. "Sorry, my high school Italian is a little rusty. Which I'd better brush up on fast if I'm going to meet your grandmother, by the way. What does that mean - *la ragazza magra?*"

Dante grinned. "The skinny girl. And in my family, that isn't considered a compliment. So you'd better eat up, honey."

"I DON'T THINK I've ever been so terrified in my life, Dante. Even getting mugged two weeks ago wasn't as scary as this."

Dante reached across the gearshift to give Cara's thigh a reassuring squeeze. "Relax, would you? My grandmother might come off as a little intimidating, but she's not scary. Well, unless she's angry, of course, and then you'd better find a good hiding place until she calms down. But there's no reason in the world you have to feel nervous about meeting her, honey. Nonna is going to love you, just like my mom and my sister did when they met you last night."

He'd intentionally driven them up to Healdsburg last night – a Friday - after work, even though the traffic had been hellacious and the weather unsettled. There was no way he wanted Cara to have to meet all of his family at once, and thought it would be easier on her to at least spend some time with his mother, sister, and brother-in-law first. Jeannie had offered to fix a simple dinner, and invited Talia, Tony, and baby Ariella to join them.

Jeannie had taken one look at Cara before breaking into a wide grin, and wasting no time in giving her an exuberant welcome hug. The two women had taken to each other right away, and Cara had scored immediate points by asking how she could help with the dinner. She'd also found the time somehow between work and classes to bake a French apple pie to bring along for dessert.

Cara hadn't hesitated for even a minute to jump right into the conversation at the dinner table, and before the salad plates had been cleared away, Dante knew she'd already won his mother and sister over. By the time coffee and dessert had been served, it felt like Cara had been one of the family for years already, instead of just a few hours.

And she'd been nearly delirious with happiness as they'd made their way to the bedroom Dante always used when he visited, her pretty face wreathed in smiles.

"Your mom is so sweet," Cara had gushed as they got ready for bed. "And hilarious, too. You should have seen the look on your face when I was holding Ariella, and your mom asked if we'd picked out baby names yet. I thought you were going to bust a vein or something!"

Dante had shook his head in disgust. "Yeah, my mother can be a real comedienne at times. But that crack about the baby names is something of a private joke."

"I figured that. But she was so nice to me, Dante. Your sister and brother-in-law, too. I guess if the rest of your family is the same way, it won't be so bad tomorrow, right?"

Tomorrow - Saturday - was his Aunt Dolores' sixty-fifth birthday, and a big party was being held at the family restaurant to celebrate. He'd hesitated initially at throwing Cara to the wolves - figuratively, of course - given that there would be at least a hundred people in attendance between family and friends. But she'd quickly dismissed his doubts, assuring him that she wouldn't mind in the least.

"The more the merrier!" she'd declared cheerily. "Well, except for your grandmother, maybe. I have this awful feeling that she's going to hate me, Dante."

*"She is **not** going to hate you," he had insisted. "Stop thinking that, okay? Now, I'm not guaranteeing that she's going to take to you immediately like my mom did - Nonna isn't exactly known for being warm and fuzzy - but everything will be fine. Trust me, okay?"*

"Okay."

She'd snuggled up against him then, and the feel of her soft, curvy little body had aroused him instantly. Despite Cara's assurances that she was feeling much better, and that she barely noticed the pain in her ribs any longer, Dante had been wary of any attempts as yet to make love to her. But his ability to resist her had been wearing perilously thin, and when her small hand slid down over his stomach to begin stroking his cock persuasively, he was a total goner.

Cara had gasped as he divested himself of his gray cotton briefs, then just as swiftly yanked her little sleepshirt off over her head. His hands had taken quick possession of her full breasts, groaning aloud at the feel of their heavy weight in his palms. He hadn't been able to resist running his tongue over each erect nipple, then sucking one areola into his mouth before moving on to the other.

Her hands had tangled in his hair, pulling him closer against her as their legs quickly became intertwined. He'd been so hard that his balls ached, his cock practically begging for release, and he hadn't especially cared at that point how or where the orgasm he needed so badly would be achieved. The choices were Cara's hand, mouth, tits, or pussy, and he'd impulsively decided on the latter.

"You'll need to be on top," he'd rasped, rolling onto his back and then pulling her astride him. "I know you keep insisting that your ribs feel better, but I'm still afraid of hurting you if I'm on top."

Cara had bent low over his prone body, her breasts crushed against his chest as she'd kissed him. "You could never, ever hurt me," she'd murmured. "But we'll do it your way. Otherwise, I'm afraid you'd feel like you had to hold back."

He'd gritted his teeth, his hands clutching the bedsheets as she had slowly guided the tip of his throbbing penis inside of her, then even more slowly lowered herself until he was buried to the balls.

His hands had gripped her hips fiercely, holding her in place as she would have otherwise began to ride him. "Stay still for a minute or two, okay?" he'd choked out. "You feel so fucking tight and hot around my dick that I'm afraid I'll come within about thirty seconds if you move just yet. Just - let me get control of myself."

She'd complied with his hoarsely uttered request, remaining perfectly still while he took several deep breaths, willing his heart to stop racing. He gazed up at her, studying her nude body for the first time since he'd brought her to live with him last week. Oh, he'd seen her naked, or partially so, during the times he had helped her to dress and undress, or assisted her out of the shower. But he'd grimaced each time he had spied the ugly bruises along her ribcage, as well as the other various scrapes and bruises she sported, and he'd quickly looked away, too overcome with anger at what she'd suffered to see any more.

But now, when she had mostly healed, and the bruising was nearly gone, he looked his fill. She was slimmer, of course, since the last time he'd seen her nude body - her breasts a bit less full, her torso leaner, her belly far flatter. But she was every bit as soft and tempting and womanly as ever, and he couldn't resist running his hands along her firm thighs, or sliding them back to squeeze her taut buttocks. She'd whimpered impatiently beneath his touch, wanting, needing him as much as he craved her.

His hands at her hips guided her then, coaxing her to ride him with the rhythm he showed her, slowly at first and then becoming faster and faster until he was fucking her frantically, thrusting his cock as deep inside of that sweet, snug pussy as hard as he could. As tight as she felt in this position, she took all of him, took every deep thrust, every powerful rock of his hips, every rasp of his thumb over her clit. She braced her hands on his thighs when she came, the inner walls of her vagina squeezing his cock like a fist with the orgasmic contractions. And seeing the pleasure wash over her face, watching as her eyes closed in reaction and her breathing become uneven, was all he needed to climax, spilling himself inside of her almost violently.

Cara had collapsed weakly onto his chest after that, her lips pressed against his shoulder as he'd soothingly rubbed little circles over her back.

"I didn't use a condom," he had mumbled. "First time in my life I forgot. Shit."

"It's okay," she'd assured him sleepily. "My period just ended three days ago, so we should be safe. Unless, of course, you really do want to pick out baby names."

He'd given her a playful smack on the buttocks. "Smartass," he'd chided. "And the answer to that question is no. At least, it's no for right now. I do want kids one of these days, though. You?"

Cara had nodded. "Of course. But again, not right now. So I should probably get myself back on some sort of birth control real soon. I used to take the pill, but it made me gain weight and bloat up so I stopped a couple of years ago."

"We'll figure something out," he'd agreed. "And it would be nice not to have to use condoms for once in my life. It felt pretty fucking amazing to ride you bareback just now."

She had bit down gently on one of his nipples. "And here I thought I was the one riding you."

Dante had chuckled. "Figure of speech, Cara mia. But it did feel fantastic, so if you're willing to take care of the birth control from now on, I'll happily toss my supply of Trojans in the trash."

"It's a deal."

She had yawned sleepily then, and even though he could have happily slid back inside her tight little body and lingered there awhile, he'd acknowledged that she was still in recovery mode from her injuries. He had tucked a long strand of her hair behind her ear, and kissed her forehead.

"Get some sleep now, honey," he'd told her.

"Are you sure?" she had asked in concern, her hand pressing against his chest. "You, um, don't feel like you've, ah, had enough." She'd given his semi-erect cock a little nudge with her knee.

Dante had stifled a groan, but had been determined to do the gentlemanly thing. "I never have enough when it comes to you," he'd replied softly. "But I can wait until the morning. After all, given what a jerk I was to you about never spending the night, we've also never had wake-up sex."

"Are you positive that's safe?" she'd fretted. "And I'm not referring to the birth control thing. I just want to make sure that - well, that your mom won't be able to hear us, uh, waking up that way."

He'd laughed in response. "No, she won't hear us. For one thing, her room is on the opposite end of this floor. And second, when I convinced her to let me have this house remodeled a few years ago, one of the first things I did was to have all the insulation replaced. This room is practically soundproof now."

"Okay." Cara had given another huge yawn, satisfied with his answer. "Good night, then. I love you."

"I love you, too, Cara mia. Rest up, okay? We have a busy day tomorrow."

She'd nodded, closing her eyes, and was silent for long seconds. But just when he figured she had fallen asleep, she murmured, "Just so we're clear. If you ever break up with me again, I'm claiming custody of your family."

Laughter had rumbled in his chest. "We're clear. But nothing to worry about, because I've got no plans to ever let you go again. Not when I came so close to losing you."

She'd fallen asleep instantly after that, a smile on her face, and he hadn't been able to resist hugging her tight, as though afraid she might slip away during the night. It hadn't been the first time Dante had shuddered at the realization of exactly how close he'd come to losing her, of how much worse things could have turned out if an alert neighbor hadn't called 911 so promptly and caused the muggers to run off.

But she was here with him now, he'd acknowledged with relief, and safe and warm in his arms - a place where she would fall asleep every night from here on end if he had his way.

"You're positive I look okay?" fretted Cara as he pulled into the parking lot of the restaurant. "That this dress was the right choice?"

"Yes." He parked the car, then reached over and gave her a quick kiss. "To both questions. And my mother and brother told you the exact same thing, so believe it, okay? You look beautiful, Cara. And I can't wait to show you off to the rest of my family. Let's go in now, okay?"

Dante had suspected that Cara would have any number of doubts and insecurities about meeting all of his family today, so he'd gone out and bought her several new outfits for this weekend - including the simple but stunning midnight blue wrap-front dress she was wearing now. She had protested mightily, of course, when she'd discovered the half dozen shopping bags he had brought home for her, the ones that had contained not just dresses but skirts, jeans, trousers, blouses, sweaters, shoes, lingerie, and the black cashmere overcoat she was currently belting around her waist. But after a good-natured argument, Cara had finally relented and thanked him profusely for all of the beautiful things. Dante hadn't dared break the news to her just yet that these few bags were merely the tip of the iceberg of all the things he planned to buy her.

As he helped her remove the coat once inside the restaurant, he gave her one more lookover and smiled in satisfaction. Cara had fretted that this dress was too low-cut, or made her look too old, or, worse - made her butt look too big. He'd assured her multiple times that the dress was perfect for the occasion - not too dressy nor too casual, and that it shrieked class. What he hadn't told her - quite intentionally - was that the silky fabric also molded itself to her lush breasts, and emphasized her small waist. The rich blue color was a good one for her, lending her youthful complexion a healthy glow, and complimenting the rich fall of her lustrous, dark hair. There was no disguising the fact that she was young - probably *too* young for him, most of his family would whisper - but Cara also looked every bit like a woman. A woman that he was exceptionally proud to usher inside the big, noisy banquet room where more than fifty people had already gathered.

Dante snagged both of them a glass of red wine from a waiter whom he'd known for twenty years, then touched his glass to hers.

"Here goes nothing," he told her with a wink. "Too late to back out of this now, honey. The horde is already descending on us."

For the next twenty minutes or so, he introduced Cara to every aunt, uncle, cousin, in-law, family friend, and neighbor who approached, making sure that she didn't look overwhelmed or close to tears as a result. But then he realized that he shouldn't have worried for even a minute, because Cara was quite obviously having the time of her life. She was by nature a friendly, outgoing person, so it was no surprise when she wound up charming everyone she met.

But there was still one person - one very, very important person - that Cara had yet to be presented to, though Dante knew his grandmother had for certain been keeping an extremely close eye on her grandson's new girlfriend. He took Cara by the hand, pulling her along in his wake as one of his aunts would have kept chatting with her for the next hour if he had allowed it.

"Come on. It'll be time soon to sit down for the meal, and I'm guessing Nonna is getting awfully impatient to meet you. Ah, there she is, in her usual spot, of course. Just like a queen. Which, by the way, she tends to act like most of the time. Not a queen exactly, but there's not a single person in this room who doesn't know she rules this family."

Cara gulped, looking helplessly at her empty wine glass. "Do I have time to chug-a-lug another glass?" she whispered. "One wasn't nearly enough to prepare me for this."

Dante shook his head, grinning as he placed a hand at the small of her back. "It's going to be fine," he whispered. "I promise."

He steered a hesitant Cara over to where Valentina Sabattini was holding court - seated in a high-backed chair in a spot where she could easily view all of the goings-on in the banquet room. She was as flawlessly groomed as ever, despite her advanced years - her snowy white hair impeccably coiffed, her makeup and nails perfect, with gold jewelry sparkling at her ears, throat, and wrists. She was even wearing purple - the color of royalty - though Dante supposed the wool dress was really more of a plum shade.

And her sharp, observant eyes were fixed directly on him at the moment as he made his way to greet her - or, more accurately, on the young, slightly terrified woman he was half-guiding, half-pushing forward.

"Hello, Nonna," he told her warmly, bending down to kiss her proffered cheek. "You look beautiful as always. And I have someone I'd like you to meet." He gave Cara a little nudge and she slowly took a couple of steps forward. "Nonna, this is Cara Bregante. Cara, meet my grandmother, the owner of this restaurant and the head of the family - Valentina Sabattini."

Valentina, who'd been unsmiling up until now, perked up a bit when she heard Cara's last name. "Bregante?" she repeated. "*È lei italiana?*"

Dante nodded. "*Sì.* Cara is half-Italian, Nonna."

Valentina looked at Cara expectantly, no doubt well aware that she was scaring the bejesus out of her, then extended her beringed hand.

Cara, to her credit, gave his grandmother her biggest and brightest smile before taking Valentina's hand in her own.

"It's a pleasure to meet you, *Signora* Sabattini. Thank you so much for having me here today. Dante has told me many times about what wonderful food you serve, so I'm looking forward to trying it."

Cara's words were clear and steady - and had been delivered in perfectly pronounced Italian. He recalled some mention she'd made recently of having studied the language in high school, and lamenting that she would really need to brush up on her skills prior to meeting his family. Somehow, she'd found time to do a good deal of brushing up over the past few days.

Valentina did something that she seldom did nowadays - smile. And not just any smile, mind you, but one that rivaled Cara's in size and brilliance. The old woman was obviously delighted, evidenced by the way she clutched Cara's hand tightly. In Italian, she told Cara that the pleasure was all hers to meet her grandson's new friend, and that she guaranteed Cara would have the best meal of her life today.

Cara nodded in agreement, seeming to understand everything Valentina had just said. But then his grandmother turned to him, speaking in such rapid-fire Italian that even he had to focus to understand. He merely grinned at her in return, then nodded and pressed another small kiss to her cheek.

It was time then to sit down for what was to be a late lunch/early dinner, so he guided Cara to where their assigned seats were. She tugged anxiously at his coat sleeve as they walked over to their table.

"What exactly did your grandmother just tell you?" she whispered urgently. "I got about ten words out of the whole dialog, none of which made any sense to me."

Dante slipped an arm about her waist, giving her an affectionate little squeeze. "What she said," he told her with a wink, "was that I had finally brought home a girl she could approve of. And that if I ever dared to let you out of my sight, she would personally find both her heaviest cast iron skillet *and* her biggest carving knife and use both of them on me until I came to my senses."

Cara cupped his cheek tenderly. "Well, guess you'd better listen to your Nonna then, hadn't you?" she teased. "After all, she seems like a very wise woman to give you that sort of advice."

He gave her a quick kiss, ignoring the interested stares they were bound to be receiving from his nosy family members. "The best advice she ever gave me," he agreed. "Oh, and before I forget. She also wants to know what your favorite colors are. You know, so that she can start buying sheets and towels for your hope chest."

EPILOGUE

One Year Later – St. Lucia

"HERE YOU GO. One very cold drink for one very hot babe. Cheers."

Cara grinned as she clinked the glass containing a delicious frozen melon margarita against Dante's. "Cheers. Mmm, this really hits the spot. Thanks."

"My pleasure." He leaned across his padded lounger to plant a kiss on her mouth, his lips cool from the cocktail. "Especially since I told the bartender to add an extra shot of tequila to yours. I like how you get a little wild and crazy when you're tipsy. One of these days I'll convince you to dance on a tabletop for me."

She groaned, covering her face with her hands. "I swear I am going to kill Mirai for telling you that. Some best friend she turned out to be."

Dante laughed. "You know you don't mean that. And you also miss her like hell right now. How much longer is that internship of hers?"

"Until the end of July. Though she's taking a week off in April and flying back to San Francisco to visit. And as much as I miss her, working in New York for a year is good for her. And she's enjoying the extra time with her father."

Mirai had finished her certification program in fashion merchandising, and with the help of Angela's friend Julia had landed an internship working at Bergdorf Goodman in Manhattan. Julia's aunt was the head buyer at the exclusive department store, and had arranged for Mirai to work under one of her assistants. And while Cara had been missing her BFF like crazy, she knew that the opportunity had been too good to pass up. Besides, she reasoned, she'd been so busy herself that she barely had a minute to spare nowadays.

She had been living with Dante full time for over a year now, having happily given up her lease on the tiny apartment, and moved in with him bag and baggage - sans the detested futon, of course. True to his word, he'd driven her everywhere, at least until he had bullied her into renewing her lapsed drivers license. For her twenty-third birthday last April, one of the many gifts he'd given her had been the keys to a brand new car of her very own - a fire engine red, fully loaded Lexus LC.

"Because red is your best color," he'd told her as she had stared at the luxury vehicle in speechless surprise. "And seeing you behind the wheel of this car will always remind me of how you looked the night of our first date - wearing that red dress and making me realize I was really seeing you for the first time."

Somewhat to Cara's dismay, she'd had to quickly get used to receiving such extravagant gifts from her very generous boyfriend. Dante had blithely ignored her protests about buying her a whole new wardrobe, and simply dragged her along with him on an extended shopping spree. He set up an account for her at the beauty salon where Ruben worked, and insisted that she make appointments whenever she liked to get her hair and nails done, have a massage, or any other treatments she desired. She now had a membership at the gym he and Nick worked out at, though she mostly attended classes - spin, barre method, boot camp - rather than lifting the sort of heavy weights the two men preferred.

Dante had also given her carte blanche to spend whatever she wanted at the grocery store, and that at least was one perk she took full advantage of. Cara adored cooking in the condo's fully stocked kitchen, and having an unlimited food budget had allowed her to create some incredible dishes. They also ate out a few times a week, especially when work had been extra hectic. At first, he had made it a point to take her to only the trendiest, most exclusive restaurants in the city, until she'd admitted that she didn't always like the pretentious dishes they tended to serve in such places. Instead, she preferred some of the cozier neighborhood establishments he'd brought her to when they had first dated.

She had finally finished school last August, a milestone that had been celebrated in grand fashion with a big party Dante had thrown for her up at the family restaurant in Healdsburg. It had easily been one of the happiest days of her life, eating and drinking and laughing with all of his family members and friends who'd come out to commemorate the occasion. Mirai had flown in just for the weekend, declaring that there was no possible way she would have missed such a momentous event. Angela and Nick had been there, too, along with their infant son Dylan. And Cara hadn't been able to hold back the tears when her mother's best friend Frannie had shown up, a closely guarded surprise that Dante had organized.

The only person who hadn't shown up, or sent his congratulations, had been her father - largely because Cara hadn't bothered to remind him that she'd received her degree. Contact with Mark, in fact, was nearly nonexistent these days, limited to a handful of brief, stilted phone calls or an occasional email a few times a year.

But her father's lack of interest in her no longer bothered Cara. It was something she'd worked hard to get past, but she could now honestly say that she didn't care one way or the other. She no longer needed or wanted her father's support or attention, and certainly not his approval. Dante more than provided her with all of those things and more, and in a much deeper and more meaningful way than her egocentric father ever could.

Dante had very quickly become everything to her - her lover, protector, confidante, friend. After struggling to take care of and support herself for so long, it had been a blessed relief to now have someone who was so eager to look out for her. At the same time, though, he was all too well aware of her need for independence, and was careful not to cross the fine line between support and domination - at least, most of the time, she thought wryly. Dante was also extremely protective, something she teasingly attributed to his Italian blood and *machismo*, but she had to secretly admit that she did love it when he would go all caveman on her at times.

And Cara enjoyed teasing him every so often that what she loved most about him was his family, while he would joke that they liked her more than they liked him. But she knew how much it pleased him that she loved spending time with his family, how she adored every single dinner and party and holiday they were invited to. Jeannie had quickly become like a second mother to her, and fussed over Cara as though she were her own child. Dante's roguish younger brother Rafe flirted with Cara outrageously, even though she'd told him impishly that she really preferred older men. And while his tough as nails little sister Gia hadn't been won over quite so easily, by now she adored Cara as much as the rest of the family did.

Cara swapped recipes with his aunts, had helped plan a baby shower for one of his many cousins, attended a bachelorette party for yet another cousin, and organized a birthday dinner for Jeannie. She'd overheard numerous speculations among his family members about when and if Dante was going to pop the question to her anytime soon, though the only one bold enough to actually voice that inquiry aloud had been Valentina.

Cara usually just blushed and looked at her feet when Dante's grandmother asked when he was going to make an honest woman of her, while Dante would gently chide Valentina to mind her own business, and remind her that there was plenty of time for all that. But the gift that Valentina had presented to Cara last month for Christmas had been a none-too-subtle push in that direction - a set of sheets and a linen tablecloth - for her hope chest, the elderly woman had instructed. Cara still wasn't quite sure if this hope chest was supposed to be an actual piece of furniture, or was simply a term someone had dreamed up long ago.

It had been the happiest, merriest Christmas she'd had since the last one spent with her mother. And even when Sharon had been alive, their simple, quiet holiday celebrations had been nothing like a Sabattini one. This past Christmas had been filled with laughter and presents and more food and drink than Cara had ever seen at one time. She'd been almost delirious with happiness, and that had been without all of the beautiful gifts Dante had lavished on her.

The one gift he hadn't given her, though, had been the much-hinted-about engagement ring that nearly every member of his family had been expecting to see gracing the third finger of her left hand on Christmas Day. Cara had scolded herself for feeling even the tiniest bit of disappointment that Dante hadn't in fact popped the question by now, reminding herself that she was completely, utterly content with their current situation. The boyfriend whom she was insanely in love with was not merely gorgeous, filthy rich, and an insatiable but generous lover, but he was also kind, protective, funny, and a gentleman. They complemented each other in every way, rarely argued (and usually only when he was acting a little too domineering), and Cara had never before felt so cherished and adored. Expecting anything more at this point in their relationship would just be greedy on her part.

And really, she argued with herself now as she sipped the icy cold, deliciously fruity cocktail, she certainly didn't have time to deal with stuff like planning a wedding, even if Dante had proposed. Nick was a demanding boss, expecting nothing short of perfection, and Cara often worked exhaustingly long hours. She'd made the decision - with Dante's blessing, even though he'd teased her about feeling hurt that she didn't want to come work for him - to remain part of Nick and Angela's team at Morton Sterling. Even before her college graduation, she'd begun assuming more responsibilities and working more closely with clients.

And when Angela had started her maternity leave two weeks before her due date, Cara had moved into her boss' office for the next few months. Baby Dylan had been born in June, and despite their initial misgivings, Nick and Angela were proving to be competent, dedicated, and rather obsessive parents. Nick in particular had shocked everyone who knew him with his devotion to his son, and Dante had nearly choked the first time he'd observed his arrogant, controlling best friend actually changing a diaper.

Angela, in fact, had just returned to work on a part-time basis a couple of weeks ago, reluctantly leaving six-month old Dylan in the hands of a very competent nanny. The new mother had confided to Cara that Nick had been rather ruthless when it had come time to hiring a nanny, grilling each applicant as though they were applying for a job with the CIA instead of looking after a baby. He'd rejected the first ten applicants, before they had finally agreed on one, though Angela had also mentioned that Nick was watching the newly hired nanny like a hawk.

Leah had left the team to work with another top broker in the office, eliminating the tension and bickering that had always occurred between her and Tyler. Cara worked alongside of him these days, and he'd confessed that his marriage was much stronger now that he and Leah weren't constantly together. The PA whom Cara had trained to take over her duties - a recent Stanford graduate who was the younger sister of one of Angela's former collegiate volleyball teammates - completed their team.

Because work had been so demanding these last few months for both of them, Cara and Dante hadn't been able to take a real vacation since last spring, save for a few long weekends when he'd taken her to places like Palm Springs, Las Vegas, and Vancouver. But now that Angela was back to work for a few hours each day, Cara had finally stopped feeling guilty about taking a whole week off.

She and Dante had arrived on the Caribbean island of St. Lucia just yesterday, and her jaw had dropped at her first sight of the luxury resort they would be staying at for the next week. She'd thought that the Jade Mountain Resort had to be the most beautiful place on the face of the earth, with not one but two beaches and a coral reef just offshore of the property. Their open-air suite had its own private infinity pool, and was equipped with every amenity one could desire, with the exception of a TV. The on-site restaurant provided three delicious meals a day, and there were a variety of activities offered - hiking and biking trails, a fitness center, yoga classes, tennis, scuba diving, and a host of others. But what Cara was most looking forward to was simply relaxing on the beach, or alongside their private pool as they were right now.

"Mmm, a girl could get used to this sort of thing," she purred, stretching luxuriously on her own padded lounger. "Private pool, luxury suite, even a butler to bring us drinks at the push of a button. And the weather is perfect, not too hot or humid, and with just the right amount of breeze."

Dante grinned, lowering his sunglasses to ogle her cleavage. "Not to mention a perfect woman. You look fantastic in that bikini, honey. Did I tell you that red's definitely your color?"

Cara glanced down at the bright scarlet bathing suit that barely covered her body. "At least once a week, I think. And this bikini had better look good, considering how much you paid for it. Geez, two hundred dollars is highway robbery for these little bits of fabric. Do you realize how far I used to be able to stretch that much money?"

His grin faded to a scowl. "Don't remind me, okay? Every time I think about how hard you had to work, how many little things you went without, it pisses me off. That father of yours - he never deserved a daughter like you, Cara, and I hope one of these days he wakes up and realizes how badly he treated you."

"Shh." She placed a finger over his lips. "And you shouldn't remind *me* about my father. Look, all of that's in the past now, so we should let it stay there. Especially this week, when we're here in paradise."

"Agreed." Dante took her hand in his, pressing a kiss to the palm. "You're already getting a tan," he observed, running a finger along the low-cut neckline of the bikini top. "Too bad you won't sunbathe naked like I suggested. That way you wouldn't have tan lines."

"I don't think so," replied Cara primly. "There's no way you're going to convince me that those kayakers out there can't see us up here. Besides, what's the point of paying two hundred bucks for a bikini if I don't wear it? And this is just one of the five you bought me for this trip, along with all of the other clothes and stuff. Did I tell *you* that you really went overboard with the gift giving at Christmas?"

"Ah, that reminds me." He set his nearly empty drink down on the glass-topped table that separated their loungers, before swinging his legs over the side. "Be right back."

Cara felt far too lazy to look back and see where he was going, content to merely lay against the plush cushion of the lounger and let the warm Caribbean sun wash over her face and body. She hadn't realized until now how much she'd needed this break, how hard she'd been pushing herself at the office these past few months. It was going to be hell to go back in a week's time, especially since it was the dead of winter in San Francisco, with a near-record amount of rainfall already.

'Why are you even thinking about leaving when you've just arrived,' she scolded herself. 'And especially with all of these incredible views. Like this one, for example.'

Dante returned to his lounger, a mysterious grin on his handsome face. He was so gorgeous, she thought with a sigh, more so than ever clad in just a pair of light blue cotton swim trunks that showed off his tanned, buff body to perfection. He hadn't shaved today, and he looked more dark and dangerous than normal with the stubble that covered his cheeks and chin. Cara licked her lips as her gaze traveled down his taut abs to where she knew he'd already be semi-aroused.

"Tsk, tsk," he scolded, wagging a finger at her. "None of *those* looks right now, okay? You know, we did just get out of bed less than three hours ago. And since I'm so much older than you are, I need some time to rest up and recover in between."

Cara snorted in derision. "Oh, yeah, you're *so* old. In fact, I didn't want to mention it, but I'm pretty sure I saw a few gray hairs on your head last night. As far as resting up, give me a break. All I'd have to do is drop my top and you'd be good to go for at least an hour."

Dante grinned, swinging his legs around the side of the lounger so that he was sitting up facing her. "Tell you what. You drop that top and I'll start my stopwatch."

But as she teasingly began to untie the strings around her neck, he stilled her hand, causing her to quirk a brow. "Changed your mind already?" she teased.

"Just putting that idea - a really, really good idea, by the way - on hold for a few minutes. There's something I want to ask you, Cara *mia*. Something I've been wanting to ask you for awhile now. And I'm well aware that my nosy ass family was very, very disappointed that I didn't ask you this in time for Christmas last month. But that was very intentional on my part. I love my family to pieces, but there are certain times when they just need to butt out. I knew we'd be making this trip here, and I wanted it to be just the two of us when I asked you this very important question."

Cara's heartrate had begun to accelerate the moment he'd told her he had something to ask her. 'Oh, God, oh, God,' she thought wildly. 'Do *not* jump to conclusions, Cara, do not *dare*. Because for all you know what he has to ask you has absolutely nothing to do with what you think it does, and you're going to feel like a fool for even imagining it. So don't...'

Dante withdrew a small black velvet box from the pocket of his swim trunks, then flipped open the lid to reveal a dainty but dazzling little ring inside. It looked, she thought with a gulp, as though it would be the perfect size and shape for someone with hands as small as hers.

"Cara." Dante's voice was hoarse, maybe even a little unsteady as he took hold of her left hand. "Cara *mia* - my darling. Would you marry me? Please? Because if you don't say yes, my grandmother will never let me hear the end of it. Not to mention the fact that it would break my heart. And I know you're too sweet and kind and wonderful to even think of doing something that cruel. So, will you be my wife, Cara? Spend the rest of your life with me? Well, me and my nosy family, that is."

She placed her free hand over her heart, as though she could still its frantic beating that way. "Yes," was all she whispered, but it was all the answer he needed. Tears were falling from her lashes as she flung herself at him, the two of them tumbling onto his lounger as their lips met in a long, searching kiss that told him everything else she wasn't able to put into words just yet.

He slid the beautiful little ring onto her engagement finger, nodding in satisfaction when it proved a perfect fit. "I had to guess about the size since you never wear rings," he explained. "We can bring it back to the jewelers if it needs any adjusting."

Cara shook her head, studying the stunning, square cut diamond solitaire on its slender platinum band. "It's perfect just like it is. And I love it, Dante. I love *you.*"

They cuddled together on the lounger for a time, content to simply bask in the tropical sunlight and marvel at what had just happened.

Cara broke the peaceful silence first. "Shouldn't we call your mother and tell her the good news? I'm guessing it would take just the one phone call, and your entire family would know within ten minutes."

"It wouldn't even take that long," he retorted. "But to answer your first question, the answer is no. The minute my family and our friends know we're engaged they'll start hounding us about wedding plans, bridal showers, registries, all that stuff."

She grinned. "Thanks to your grandmother's Christmas gift to me, we already have a head start on the registry."

Dante gave a little eye roll. "Yeah, don't remind me. Besides, I'd rather tell my mom and Nonna in person. So we can keep this news to ourselves for the rest of the week, and enjoy the last few days of sanity we'll have for a very long time. We can also talk a little bit about the sort of wedding we want to have, since I guarantee you everyone else will be all too happy to share their opinions of how it should be."

Cara nodded. "I know exactly where I'd like to be married. I mean, if it's okay with you, that is. The first time you brought me there I thought about what a wonderful place it would be for a wedding."

He smiled at her tenderly. "I'm guessing it wasn't Pasquale's. Or Tommy's," referring to the pizza joint and the sports bar he'd brought her to on some of their earlier dates.

She wrinkled her nose. "Uh, your guess would be right. And you know exactly what place I'm referring to, Dante. You even told me once yourself what a perfect location it would make for a wedding."

"The winery next to the family restaurant," he confirmed. "And I couldn't agree with you more, honey. But are you sure that's okay with you? It isn't the fanciest location. If you'd rather get married at a big hotel like Angela and Nick did, that would be fine with me."

Cara shook her head. "No. I couldn't think of a more perfect spot to be married - outdoors among all those gorgeous oak trees, with that old stone farmhouse in the background, all of your family and our friends around us. And Labor Day weekend, I think. If we can make all of the arrangements by then, of course."

Dante snorted. "This is my family's place we're talking about, honey. And if my family gets involved with the planning - which they will, like it or not - we could have all of the arrangements made by Valentine's Day if we really wanted to. Which, by the way, is not such a bad idea. You could wear a red dress if we got married then."

She socked him on the arm, a bit too hard to be considered playful. "I am *not* wearing red at my own wedding," she insisted.

He rubbed his sore arm. "I was just kidding. Besides, one of my top two fantasies of all time is seeing you walk down the aisle towards me wearing a beautiful white gown."

"Really? What's the second one?"

Dante gave her an unholy grin as he deftly untied her bikini top, baring her breasts to his eager gaze. "Watching you sunbathe naked."

The End

Dear Readers,

This does, in fact, mark the end - not just of this particular book, but of the entire Inevitable series. I can hardly believe that it's been nearly four whole years since the release of Serendipity, my very first book and the first in this series.

I've loved creating these characters, and making them come to life. To me, they often feel like real people, like longtime friends, rather than just characters in a book I've imagined. I know that for some readers the stories have seemed too long, too detailed, at times, but it was vital for me that in creating these characters I was able to truly make them seem alive. And doing that required perhaps far more details that some readers are used to seeing in a book nowadays, but I've never been one to compromise my standards or what I believe is crucial to a story.

I'll be embarking on a brand new trilogy next, each book a standalone but connected to the other two, and will have more news on this over the next few months.

And for those of us who just can't get enough of the characters we've come to know (and hopefully love!) in the Inevitable books, I do have some exciting news to share! I'll be releasing a holiday-themed anthology featuring each of the couples from the series. The anthology will be a free read, available to my newsletter subscribers, so if you aren't already on the list, please head over to my website and sign up. I'll also be posting more information on the anthology and how to sign up for the newsletter on my Facebook page.

I cannot express how much I appreciate all of the kind words of support and encouragement I've received from readers, reviewers, and bloggers over the past four years. It has been your support that's kept me going over the years, especially during times when I received a negative review, or didn't get invited to an author event, or simply hit a writing slump. I hope to continue creating these amazing, vital characters and their stories to share with all of you for a long time to come.

Please be sure to keep in touch! I try to be as responsive as possible with answering emails, messages, etc., and love to interact with readers, bloggers, and other authors.

Happy reading!

Janet

ABOUT THE AUTHOR

Email – janetnissenson@gmail.com
Website/Blog - http://www.janetnissenson.com
Facebook - https://www.facebook.com/janetnissensonauthor
Twitter - https://www.twitter.com/JNissenson
Goodreads - https://www.goodreads.com/janetnissenson
Pinterest - http://www.pinterest.com/janetnissenson/
Instagram - https://www.instagram.com/janetlnissenson/

ALSO BY JANET NISSENSON

Made in the USA
Columbia, SC
25 March 2018